FID'S CRUSADE

David H. Reiss

Dedicated to Bubby and Poppy

I learned to stand on my own two feet,
but I always trusted that you'd be there if I stumbled.
You were.
I will be forever grateful.

Also, to my most patient and tireless pre-readers:
John, David, and Mom.
Thanks for putting up with me!

CHAPTER ONE

THE GROUND TREMBLED AND GREAT CLOUDS OF DUST were shaken from the rafters above...but the silver-clad hero's fist was stopped cold by an invisible barrier only inches from my armored head. The impact echoed, a bass thrum that filled the chamber like a physical force.

Emotions flickered across his face: surprise first, followed swiftly by disappointment. For a moment, I knew, Titan had believed the battle won. Rage quickly followed, and further blows fell like thunderous rain as the hero explored the unseen shield's capabilities. Despite his size and awe-inspiring strength, the man was no mere brawler; he was a well-trained and highly skilled martial-artist, yet even his fiercest attack made no progress.

Sensor readings indicated minor structural damage to the floor, but the force-field emitter hidden below was in no immediate danger. Energy levels were excellent and the increased strain continued to fall within projected tolerances. The new force-field design was a masterwork!

Already, my mind was swirling with ideas how to alter the device; to miniaturize components and improve efficiency, and to make the entire system portable. Behind my helm's featureless faceplate, I was grinning like a fool.

Titan himself looked more-or-less human, with a complexion and features that implied a Mediterranean heritage. His eyes glowed white with raw power, wisps of energy trailing away like strange smoke, and he stood nearly seven feet tall with a broad and muscular physique that would make facing him a daunting concept even without knowing of the supernatural forces that coursed through his body. When he'd first appeared a decade ago, his charcoal-black hair seemed akin to a lion's mane, but he now wore it cropped short in a military 'high and tight' style and shaved away the perpetual 5 o'clock shadow that had once practically been his trademark. It was an improvement, I thought; he looked more intense now, more serious. Truly, the nigh-indestructible hero was a worthy adversary.

"Doctor Fid! I should have known." He backed a few steps away from the force-field and smirked. "I'd recognize your foul stench anywhere."

Titan was also a bit of a dick.

Three years past, one of Titan's fellow Guardians—the Red Ghost—bypassed my defenses and managed to shoot me in the abdomen. I'd required a colostomy bag for months while replacement organs were being cloned, and the silver-unitard-wearing jerk had been teasing me about my odor ever since. It was petty and small. A schoolyard taunt! A reflexive regression, I imagined, to the childhood days when he must have victimized smaller students and stolen their lunch money.

Every once in a while, I really did consider killing him. But not today.

"Titan." I nodded slightly in acknowledgment, carefully hiding any evidence of irritation. There were multiple news-camera-drones within range, I was certain, and it would have been unacceptable for any recording to indicate that the hurtful banter had found purchase. Fortunately, my voice was modulated electronically to maintain an emotionless tone. "I was expecting you sooner."

The truth was that I hadn't been expecting him at all.

There'd been a myriad of intentionally-left clues at the biotech facility that I'd robbed earlier in the day, and any competent hero would certainly have been led to this facility...but my research had indicated that this particular opponent would be in Arizona training a young hero who went by the *nom de guerre* of 'Brute'. It appeared that Brute traveled to New England instead, and was now fighting alongside the Guardians as they battled their way into the auditorium-sized throne room of what they would certainly believe to be my current lair.

The force-field emitter test had originally been intended for a lesser challenge than Titan's full strength. It was fortunate that the device had been designed to operate with a significant safety margin.

The other heroes were at the opposite end of the room still, keeping a few of my low-tier combat automatons occupied while their leader had advanced to confront me. The sounds of combat raged on even as Titan and I exchanged words: explosions and worried shouts, the shriek of tortured steel and the dull roar of growing flames. The conflict would look glorious when video was leaked to the Internet.

Brute, the visiting teen powerhouse, was acquitting himself well; he'd provided protection for both Veridian and Regrowth and even managed an impressive offensive combination-attack alongside Aeon. I planned to comb through the footage more carefully at a later date to evaluate his performance and determine any useful weaknesses. Fighting the younger hero might make for an interesting diversion someday.

I was currently sheathed within my Mk 33 light-combat powered armor. This suit—my most recent design—was the fastest flier in my current arsenal, with the best augmented-reflexes and combat programming...but it afforded less protection and overall strength than other versions. This model wasn't particularly appropriate for a hand-to-hand battle with an entity like Titan or his current trainee.

Even so, I knew that I made for an imposing figure.

The armor was form-fitted and so thoroughly non-reflective that I seemed a silhouette, a six-and-a-half-foot man-shaped hole in the world. There were stars visible inside that blackness, pinpricks of light and color; looking upon me was gazing into the clearest night sky, entire galaxies encompassed within my being. Only at the armor's seams were any hint of a three-dimensional form offered: from there an angry red glow seeped, as though something infernal was trapped inside. It was a disorienting effect that I'd spent years perfecting.

I summoned my scepter—a slim and deceptively-simple-appearing black rod with a round red stone at its pommel—from its subspace storage location, and the powerful weapon's weight felt comforting in my hand. Even as the last of my smaller combat drones were felled in the distance, I maintained a relaxed and impassive mien. Greater than the armor, more powerful even than the force-field, I was protected by Doctor Fid's grim reputation.

Titan fell into a wary half-crouch.

"Your robots are destroyed and we have you surrounded," he declared; the Guardians scattered to make Titan's statement into reality. "Surrender, Doctor. You can't hide behind your force-field forever."

"Hide?" I motioned lazily with my scepter's tip towards the destruction that they'd left in their wake. "It took you four and a half minutes to fight your way to me, and we both know that I could have escaped in a fraction of that time."

Titan was steady, but several of his compatriots took a step backwards or glanced around warily. Good. Their fear had been hard-earned.

"Then why are you still here?" asked the Guardians' leader, finally.

"I'm not," I lied, "This is a hologram. I brought you all here so that I could watch your expressions while this base self-destructs around you. In five...four...three-"

"Maneuver seven!" Titan barked, his eyes closed to angry slits. The expression looked practiced; did he glower at a mirror every night, I wondered, attempting to hone an expression that would strike terror in the hearts of evildoers? If so, the effort had been wasted. Honestly, he just looked constipated.

The superhero team leaped into action like a well-oiled machine. Whatever Titan's faults, he trained his people well.

Aeon's power-set included the ability to produce force-fields more powerful even than my new design...but only for pre-set short periods and only in a sphere about nine feet in diameter. Regrowth, Veridian, and Red Ghost converged around the slender woman and she powered up her famous milky-white energy shield around them. Titan was sturdy enough that he knew he could withstand any of the explosives that I'd used in the past, so he just tackled Brute to protect the younger hero with his own body.

Feeling smug, I lifted my scepter and aimed; a blast of emerald-hued energy surged from the pommel to strike both Titan and Brute with sufficient intensity to drive them through my temporary fortress's thick walls and out into the courtyard. The entire room shook from the thunderous impact, debris visibly shaking on the ground, and sparks flew as electrical wiring within the walls was torn asunder.

Titan had always been somewhat vulnerable to blows to the back of his head; it would be perhaps thirty seconds before I could expect him to recover.

"Alternately, this base may not have been equipped with an escape capsule, and I'm not a hologram at all," I floated towards the hole in the wall, gloating cheerfully. "In retrospect, that seems significantly more likely. Until next time, Guardians!"

(The ruse had only been successful because my prior two fake-bases had been equipped with unnecessarily ornate self-destruct mechanisms that the Red Ghost had only barely disarmed in time to avoid catastrophe; the next one would have a built-in escape route, shaped explosive charges and a mocking hologram ready and waiting. Forcing Titan to make the wrong call under fire was one of life's true joys.)

Laughing mockingly, I launched into the air with my armor's flight systems shifted to maximum and stealth capabilities enabled. Any of the more esoteric technology left behind would melt itself to slag; it simply wouldn't do to leave any resources behind for my enemies to examine. By the time Aeon's shield dropped, my lead would be insurmountable.

The news broadcasts, I was amused to discover, were quick to declare that the Guardians had forced the notorious Doctor Fid to escape empty-handed with all materials stolen from AH Biotech safely returned, and that—thanks to the Guardians' valiant efforts! —the battle resulted in not even a single civilian casualty. Property damage had been restrained to the mostly-abandoned city block surrounding Doctor Fid's secret lair and even the heroes themselves suffered no significant injuries. The event was being treated as a clear win for the Guardians, despite the fact that Doctor Fid had, once more, eluded capture.

But the footage of Titan and Brute being blasted through a wall was replayed over and over again, as well as a beautiful shot of the remaining Guardians watching helplessly as Doctor Fid flew off to safety. One camera drone captured a glorious image of the Red Ghost dropping to his knees, shoulders bowed in defeat. His red cowl hid his eyes, but his lower face was visible, and the setting sun cast deep shadows upon the lines of his face; it was an illusion, but in that moment he looked terribly old and weary.

Technically speaking, the Red Ghost was among the most dangerous of my regular opponents. Titan's greater experience and calm under fire made him an effective leader, tactically, but the Red Ghost was a more creative thinker. He'd begun his heroic career by making a name for himself as an investigator, fighting crime while wearing a highly protective (but unpowered) crimson and black tactical armor of his own design. Over the years, he'd added to his arsenal using equipment reverse-engineered from villains who he'd fought (It'd been one of my own shaped-plasma gauss cannons that wounded me. My own invention, painted red to match the Ghost's costume! Damn the man.) and he maintained an impressive regimen of acrobatic and combat training. But those factors weren't what made the Red Ghost dangerous to my current plans.

Before fate granted him the power to shroud himself in blood-red mists and become incorporeal, the Red Ghost had been a forensic accountant.

Doctor Fid's dastardly plan may have been foiled by the heroic Guardians, but Terrance Markham was (through dozens of shadow holding companies) heavily invested in construction and real-estate firms that stood to earn a fortune from the properties damaged by the combat. Also, as the founder of AH Biotech, my shares and stocks would surely gain a boost from the media coverage surrounding the supposedly 'foiled' crime.

Sometimes, I wasn't certain which identity was my mask and which one was real. Or perhaps both identities were masks; if so, I wasn't sure what lay beneath.

Doctor Fid had never before committed a crime that intersected with my civilian life, but in this case the ruse had been too tempting to discard. The success of AH Biotech was crucial for other long-term plans and the publicity was particularly beneficial at that moment. Among the media elite and policy wonks, it was accepted as fact that Doctor Fid deigned to steal only the most dangerous, most advanced technologies...and suddenly every potential customer or investor would be curious as to what wonders AHBT was hiding. There were government contracts to be acquired, and a receptive Senator had recently been maneuvered into place. Public goodwill always served to make lobbying an easier task.

This latest incident could not, however, be labeled as a complete success; the scenario had originally been intended to test Veridian's willingness to follow orders when Titan was absent and the Red Ghost was leading the Guardians into battle. In past confrontations, I'd seen hints that the slender, emerald costumed Veridian resented taking orders from anyone whose offensive powers did not rival his own. Confirmation of that character flaw would have opened up further avenues of attack in the future.

Titan and Brute's unexpected presence had thrown the original plan into immediate disarray. Still...several secondary goals had been accomplished, and the new force-field design was successfully tested against a more powerful physical attack than expected.

It was remarkably tempting to send the Guardians a "thank you" card.

Now and then, some reporter looking to make a name for themselves attempted to put together a dramatic expose: the True Story of Doctor Fid. The narratives all felt similar; they described the same battles, the same victories and the same defeats. One woman who was within the crowd at my first bank robbery is quoted in just about every article.

"I don't think that he wanted us to die," she always said, "But I don't think that he wanted us to live, either. He just...barely noticed us. Like we were beneath him. There was this little girl screaming, so loud that we were all terrified that he was going to hurt her just to get some quiet. But the Doctor just walked past her like she wasn't there—like she didn't matter. I've never been so frightened in all my life."

Those were the bad years, but even then I had nightmares about that little pony-tailed girl's wails. When I'd walked into that bank my gut had roiled with so much anger that I could have set the world on fire, but those cries snaked past the rage, infected me, haunted me. I remembered forcing myself not to look at her directly; if I'd looked her in the eyes, I would have been compelled to take off my mask and comfort her and then all my plans would have fallen to pieces.

It always felt strange that none of these so-called reporters ever followed up on that portion of the story. They never looked for the girl, never tried expanding on her tale. They only cared about the tears and not the aftermath.

(Melissa Halden had grown into a talented art student at Berkeley, attending with a full scholarship that I may have quietly influenced. She was happy and well adjusted.)

The articles all failed in the same manner: when attempting to guess at my motivations. They analyzed my name, my targets, my actions. They'd harassed every family in the United States with my sobriquet's last name while seeking clues, and psychologists who'd never met me pontificated endlessly about my pathology. The authors guessed and made up stories, each more outlandish than the last. I'd once found those fables humorous, but the amusement had long since faded.

There'd been a plan and that plan would have ended in self-immolation.

The whole play had been scripted in my imagination: I would become a villain so feared that people would barely dare whisper my name, and, when I was sufficiently infamous, I would engage in battle with the hero named Bronze. He would gaze across the destruction that I'd wrought and ask me what could possibly have motivated me to perform such atrocities. And I would take off my mask, crying, and inform him that I was his creation.

In the theater of my mind's eye, I would tell him what he'd done and I would watch his world collapse as he realized the gravity of his sin. In that moment, we would both get what we deserved for surely there would be no future for either of us. I dreamt of that scene for years until every morning I would wake and still taste the battle's blood and ash and tears on my lips.

In a final and unknowing act of vicious spite, Bronze drank himself to death before I could ever confront him.

He could not have been aware of his connection to me. Doctor Fid had never mentioned Bronze in public; the eventual revelation was supposed to be epic—Shakespearean in proportion! Whatever demons drove Bronze to the bottle, it wasn't worry regarding Fid's actions. There was a vicious part of me that hoped that he'd fallen into despair over what he'd done to Bobby, but I would never know.

I was bereft. The hero had managed to take everything from me. My faith in humanity, my goals for the future, my sense of self. My brother. I'd given up the entirety of my being, stained my soul with violence and blood to force Bronze to feel my pain. And then Bronze had stolen even my revenge.

There was nothing left to me save for guilt and a suit of powered armor equipped with sufficient armaments to level a small city.

"Whatcha drawing?" I'd asked, years earlier. The class was over and my students had long since funneled out of the room; I'd gotten distracted grading papers and my brother had patiently remained in the area that I'd set aside for him at the front of the lecture hall. There were comics and books and an army of action figures to keep him entertained, but Bobby was currently laying on his belly surrounded by crayons and craft paper.

"An adventure!" he chirped in reply. "It's us, but not now 'cause I need to be bigger before I'm Strongboy."

"That's your superhero name?" I smiled.

"Uh-huh. And this is you!"

The likeness wasn't complimentary—a skinny chalk-white figure with long fingers, a messy scribble of hair and the beginnings of a pot belly—but I thought that the oversized head was an interesting abstraction to represent my cerebral capabilities. Although my actual skull was average in shape and size, Bobby apparently believed that my brain needed a larger container. That, at least, I thought to be flattering.

"How'd I get that hero name?" I asked, looking at the picture's label.

"Because you're a P-H-D doctor, and 'P-H' is pronounced ffffff."

I laughed, "Well...get up, Strongboy. It's late."

"I'm not Strongboy yet," he complained, piling up his drawings before pushing himself to his feet. "I need to be bigger."

"I don't know...you're getting pretty big. Make a muscle!"

He complied with an impish grin, flexing dramatically; I checked his biceps and made suitably impressed sounds. Bobby giggled.

"I think you're almost ready," I told him, grunting as I lifted him up and made ready to leave. With my free hand, I checked my pocket to make sure that I had my keys.

"No, wait," he squirmed until I let him down, then hurried to the pile of toys and snatched up an action figure with yellowish metallic skin. His favorite. "Okay, we can go."

The armor was disassembled and I moved back to Cambridge. MIT was eager to have me back; the five-year absence hadn't even affected my tenure. I taught classes, took classes, performed research, earned a few more doctorates...It's not that I thought it possible to put Doctor Fid behind me, it was only that I lacked motivation. In a listless malaise, I returned to that which was simple.

When I reestablished my presence in academia, many of my colleagues came to me and expressed their support. "I was so sorry to hear about Robert," they would say, "He seemed like a great kid." None of them approached me directly after the incident. Bobby's middle-school friends did, trying to comfort me in the awkward, honest way that only children can manage. They hugged me and cried and touched some of Bobby's toys and told me stories and cried some more. The adults, though, my peers and coworkers...they kept at a distance. They left me to my grief when my grief burned, but a half-decade later they finally felt comfortable offering consolation.

At some subconscious level they must have recognized that my anguish bordered on madness. Adults are flustered by those who are mad; they look the other way and keep their distance. When I returned, I imagined that my fellows breathed a sigh of relief and decided that their fears had been imagined.

(Children are more inquisitive about strangeness than they are embarrassed by it. That is, perhaps, why I'd always connected with my brother so well despite the decade of age between us. I've always been somewhat odd. I'd never really fit among my peers, socially; when I was a youth, I was too intellectually advanced to connect with others of my own age, and by the time I was fourteen and attending college I was too emotionally immature to relate to my fellow students. Bobby was four years old then, and there was something about his boundless enthusiasm and curiosity that delighted me. He was a normal kid, but he smiled whenever I spent time with him. Bobby listened. He cared with an intensity that was astonishing.)

Strangely, the faculty were more open to working with me when I returned to academia. I was invited to partner with researchers who had, previously, seemed standoffish due to my youth. I was still at least a decade or two younger than them, but somehow witnessing my breakdown and supposed recovery made me more approachable. Less of a threat. I was still numb and directionless, of course, but perhaps I was also less driven and intense. Our team shared credit for a Nobel Prize and I published papers in whatever fields my peers pointed me towards.

For six years, Doctor Fid was nothing but a series of poorly labeled crates in a storage garage in Somerville. At the time, reporters postulated that the villain had been seriously injured (or died) of wounds inflicted during that last battle with Valiant on the White House lawn. Later, reporters would refer to those six years as the calm before the storm.

Not all wounds heal with time, but some do grow dull. A bearable ache, always uncomfortable but at least the pain was familiar. So it was with my own malaise. Bobby had been dead nearly as long as he'd been alive and I was somewhat surprised to find that my own life continued on. I had my studies and research, my students and my fellow professors.

A social misfit I may have been, but complete isolation had never suited me. One noted psychologist often publicly claimed that Doctor Fid's behavior could be partially explained by childhood isolation or absentee parents, but that supposition was wholly incorrect; my parents might not always have known how to deal with their precocious and frighteningly brilliant firstborn, true, but they'd loved and supported me as best as they'd been able. They always were remarkably patient with me when I'd taken apart a vehicle or appliance to see how it worked but had gotten distracted before choosing to reassemble it. They were gentle when an experiment went awry and I required medical assistance, and they sang lullabies when I had difficulty sleeping.

I must have been a terribly difficult child. How does one comfort a youth who has developed mathematical models to accurately predict the timing and path of atmospheric electrostatic discharge, and yet still flinches and cries silently at the sound of thunder? My emotional development did not occur at the same pace as my intellectual growth. In retrospect, it seemed likely that dichotomy led to an uneven maturation.

At thirteen, I designed my first breeder reactor. I was eighteen when I received my first doctorate and accepted employment at MIT, nineteen when I became my brother's guardian, and twenty-one when I watched my brother die.

Bobby is eleven years old today, and it is the most beautiful summer afternoon in recent memory. The warm breeze smells like freshly cut grass, healthy trees and salt blown in from the sea, and the sky is so clear and blue that it seems unnatural. We both still have sand in our hair from building castles that were swallowed by the tides, but our beach blankets and plastic buckets have been packed away back in the rental van. I'd forgotten the sunscreen and I'm sure we'll be lobster pink in the morning, yet right now I am too happy to care.

Bobby bounces as we walk, giddy with anticipation; I hadn't been able to keep his birthday surprise a secret any longer. After months of searching, I'd puzzled out Bronze's secret identity and we're on our way to surprise him at his office. I'm going to introduce my baby brother to his hero.

Arranging a meeting with Bronze's alter-ego, Paul Riley, had been simple. Paul works in maritime research and I have patents for a submersible drone that will be invaluable. I'd told Mr. Riley's secretary that I chose his firm because we were relocating to the area; at the time, the statement had been subterfuge but now I'm considering moving for real. Bobby hasn't smiled like this since before the car accident that took our parents.

Paul Riley had offered to meet us in the lobby and guide us up to his office; I see him near the entrance as we approach his building. Bronze's counterpart is a fit man in his early thirties with black hair and dark eyes, and his ruddy complexion tells me that he probably spends most of his time working outdoors despite the well-tailored business suit that he's wearing today.

"That's him," I whisper to Bobby. "Remember, don't say anything until we're in private."

Bobby's eyes widen and he grips my hand tight, trembling. His skin is warm and soft; he doesn't have any calluses. He spends too much time indoors, too much time with me.

We're across the street from Bronze's office when the first missile hits. Someone starts screaming and I hear shrapnel and debris scatter along the asphalt. Reflexively, I scoop my brother up into my arms and sprint towards a park bench with concrete sides and thick wooden slats. I'm running as fast as I can, awkward and desperate and terrified.

There is a Paragon Research facility at the end of the block and the terrorist supervillain Locust is attacking. He'd assaulted the New Mexico location only a few weeks earlier; I'd seen it on the news. Being close is different from watching on a screen. Terrifying! My chest aches and my eyes sting; there's something in the air, an acrid taste I don't recognize, and my breath is already coming in desperate gulps.

A score of foot soldiers wearing Locust's symbol pour out of an armored truck, firing indiscriminately to clear the road and cause chaos as they swarm towards the gate. There are more shouts, different voices and I hear a little girl cry for her mother. In my head, I'm designing better surveillance, counter weapons, heavy armor, anything that could keep Bobby safe, but my workshop is hundreds of miles away and all I have time to do is try to make sure my brother is behind the bench.

In the lobby, Paul Riley is staring right at us. I've researched his power set; he can transform his body, gaining nearly a foot of height and skin that appears to be made of his namesake material. Once metamorphosed, he is strong and fast and has moderately strong telekinesis that only affects metal.

Paul Riley could shift to his heroic form in a heartbeat, but he is in public among coworkers and people who know him. He could reach us, he *could get Bobby to safety, could use his power to disarm all of Locust's thugs and leave only the insectoid, acid-spitting villain as a serious threat, but doing so would certainly cost him his secret identity. The moment seems to take forever as he weighs the value of his privacy against the speed of his response. I can see him considering how many steps it will take for him to get into a private room, how many extra seconds it will take to make a clean entrance. He makes his choice.*

"Ow." Bobby looks bewildered, holding his chest. For the first time in my entire life I can't think. I can't calculate the angles, can't figure out what I did wrong. I'm holding my brother, shouting for help and feeling helpless and small. There is so much blood.

I watch my brother's eyes as he watches his favorite superhero turn away and run back into the office building.

I was twenty-six when I disassembled Doctor Fid's armor and returned to the Massachusetts Institute of Technology, and I was thirty-one when I made my way back to the storage garage in Somerville where the armor had been hoarded.

Becoming completely absorbed into my work had always been a problem for me. When I was studying or constructing mathematical algorithms or designing new tools and devices it was far too easy to lose track of time and fail to pay attention to my surroundings. The symphony of creation inside my head grew too loud and the external noise faded.

My colleague, Takuma Ichiro, must have talked to me first, must have asked my permission; out of ingrained habit, I must have made an appropriately polite response. Distracted by theoretical physics, I didn't notice an area of floor space being cleared in the protected low-energy section of our lab, didn't notice the boxes or the small yellow bookshelf filled with colorful titles.

There was a stack of notepads under one of my arms and my other hand was holding a large mug of coffee; with my hands thus occupied, my pencil was carried between my teeth, and I gnawed thoughtfully as I pondered an annoying magnetic resonance that was polluting the results of the afternoon's tests. A ten-year-old child was sitting in the corner, quietly playing with superhero action figures while his father worked.

The pencil fell to the floor.

"Terry, I'm so sorry," Doctor Ichiro jumped to apologize; he must have read something strange in my expression. "I didn't realize how much Hideki's play area would look like—"

"It's all right." I smiled unsteadily and took a deep breath. "I was just surprised is all. Hey there, kiddo. Your name is Hideki?"

The boy nodded, his eyes wide.

"You like superheroes, hm?" My chest hurt, and I was torn between an aching sadness and bright nostalgia. "My brother liked superheroes. Who's your favorite?"

Hideki reached for one large figure wearing a black costume with orange highlights and a dark bandit's mask that covered its lower face; Takuma moved faster, snatching up the offending toy.

"Hideki!" Doctor Ichiro looked aggrieved. "I told you that you can't play with this one anymore."

"But Gamma is the coolest!" the boy complained, "He fought Metalstorm and Spiker at the same time!"

"Gamma is a good fighter, but he is not a good person," Takuma tried to explain, "He has said things that are rude to women. He does not behave well."

"Gamma is the coolest!" Hideki insisted, voice rising angrily. His small hands clenched into fists. "And if you're twelve feet tall you don't HAVE to behave good!"

"Everyone should behave good," I said quietly. There must have been something odd about my voice, some truth or hint of pain that transcended mere words; Hideki stopped mid-tantrum to listen. "If someone puts on a costume, if they claim to be a superhero...they should have to be a hero. They should be good."

"Gamma is good!" Hideki pouted. "He beats up bad guys."

About a month later, a drunk Gamma caused a few thousand dollars' worth of property damage in his hometown of Atlanta, and a cell-phone recording caught Gamma claiming that he didn't need to listen to the responding police officer because he was only three-fifths of a cop.

The public relations firms and lawyers swarmed. There was the inevitable scripted public apology in which Gamma stated that he was impaired at the time and that the views expressed did not match his true feelings. A few heroes repudiated Gamma, but others repeated a statement of support for the hero and lauded his supposed 'bravery' and 'honesty' in holding his press conference. The mighty Valiant, an African-American hero who Doctor Fid had clashed with in Washington, D.C., responded to a reporter's query with a quiet 'No comment'. The event was twisted and spun and slipped out from media attention after a week.

Hideki continued to play with his Gamma action figure whenever his father wasn't looking.

Even then, I recognized that so-called superheroes performed a public service that is both difficult and dangerous; they were marketed, however, as something far greater. They accepted the accolades, pretended to be righteous warriors and icons of justice and all that is good, and yet still quietly accepted a system that protected the undeserving. A thin spandex line that stood in opposition to villains like the very-deceased Locust or the monster who had been Fid but also shielded their peers from accountability.

They accepted worship from children. Didn't they know how precious that was? How could they live with themselves if they didn't spend every waking moment struggling to be worthy of such unconditional trust? Someone needed to remind the public that, beneath their colorful costumes and flashy powers, their idols were only human. Someone needed to remind the cape and cowl set that they could—no, should!—aspire to be something more.

Doctor Fid had never been unmasked. It would have been a relatively simple thing to build a completely different suit of powered armor and come to the public under a new persona. I could try to be the hero that children like Hideki deserved...but it would only be another lie. I'd failed my brother and caused too much heartache to ever be deserving. My inventions had, by now, saved far more lives than Fid had ever harmed, but there would be no salvation for the likes of me.

In a vacuum-sealed and UV-resistant glass case hidden away in a secret bunker, I kept my most prized possession: a series of crayon drawings on construction paper. The Adventures of Strongboy and Doctor Fid.

I smiled, long-term plans beginning to percolate through my mind. A private company, tools and devices, surgical augmentations performed by medical robots, an upgraded powered-armor suit...Doctor Fid would never be the hero who Bobby imagined, but he could at least serve the noble purpose of demonstrating the heroes' shortcomings. He could inspire some heroes towards greatness and drag others from their pedestals back down to earth.

I could do more, too. With sufficient resources and no bureaucracy holding me back, I could design machines that could generate cleaner energy, purify sea water, grow crops more efficiently and deliver resources in a more equitable manner. I could cure diseases, build tools to protect civilians, create safer buildings and vehicles. Doctor Fid might be a supervillain, but perhaps he could save the world right out from under the fraudulent superheroes' noses.

Also, someone really did need to punch Gamma in the face. Repeatedly.

Damn the man!

I'd been careful...studied the frequency of land acquisitions in analogous neighborhoods and applied a Bayesian scatter to add random elements to the pattern such that it should not have too-accurately reflected a pure average. The contracts were neither overbid nor underbid, and I'd even made certain to include a statistically-normal number of errors in the paperwork (with minor variances consistent between each shell company). No software or hardware-based data analysis tool in the world should have indicated a connection! Sadly, there was no consistent model that accounted for human intuition.

Miguel Espinoza (the Red Ghost's alias) had been sniffing after records concerning the transfers of ownership of properties surrounding my ex-lair. Like all the other supposed base-of-operations to which the heroes had ever tracked Doctor Fid, it'd been chosen more for its suitability for combat than for research purposes; no hero had ever discovered the true laboratories or manufacturing facilities, only facades intended to serve as backdrop for violent encounters. This location had been no different, and yet somehow the Red Ghost thought to investigate more deeply than in the past. Some arcane bookkeeping divination had sparked his interest in property titles; it was possible that comparable voodoo might find a similar connection to the firms from which I'd planned to reap profits with reconstruction.

There was no direct link to Terry Markham's holdings, but even so I was forced to isolate the relevant accounts...it would be years before I could safely launder those earnings! The twenty-two percent surge in AHBT's stock price offered little consolation, nor did the company's contract to supply field medical kits to the U.S. Army's infantry branch. Any fortune from publicly traded stock could not so easily be funneled towards questionable purchases without raising red flags. I'd been counting on income flowing into Doctor Fid's shadowy network in order to fund the final pieces to rebuild the massive Mk 29 heavy combat armor and replacements for my combat drones.

Conflicts with the Red Ghost always brought mixed feelings. When my research revealed his secret identity, I'd expected to uncover a few of the usual character flaws; instead, I'd found a conscientious man with no history of violence or difficulties with the law. He'd progressed in his civilian career through talent, skill and hard work rather than backstabbing or politicking. No known enemies or past disasters. Miguel was helping both of his nieces pay for college (he'd never married and had no children of his own) and volunteered at a soup kitchen on his days off.

I'd have nominated the man for sainthood if he hadn't perforated my intestines with my own damned rifle. Also, he'd cost me seventy-three-point-one million dollars from Doctor Fid's criminal empire, money that could have been put towards the development of a proper doomsday weapon! Defeating him always rewarded me with a spark of vicious pride and a pang of terrible guilt.

I'd purchased four Red Ghost toys over the years. Two were given to Hideki, one was incinerated in a fit of rage, and the last resided in my most treasured vacuum-sealed and UV-resistant glass case. Bobby would have loved that action figure.

Damn the man.

CHAPTER TWO

THERE EXISTED THREE SUITS OF POWERED ARMOR within my arsenal that were capable of fitting through a standard door frame; of those, the Mk 31 possessed the most puissant defenses. The Mk 28 boasted superior armaments but was also in desperate need of repair. The Mk 33 was faster and equipped with exceptional stealth technologies but lacked the layered shaped-force-field emitters that had been built into my thirty-first design.

The Mk 31's size held numerous advantages. I had, for example, found that an extra six inches of height often cowed a nervous crowd of civilians more effectively than a two-decade history of mayhem. Also, the suit was broad enough to block off a narrow corridor but still sufficiently mobile to navigate common obstacles. In this armor, I'd once battled the "superhero" Gamma through an underground parking structure. The twelve-foot-tall lummox had struck his head on the concrete beams supporting the ceiling so many times that it'd seemed a mercy when I finally rendered him unconscious.

(My reconnaissance mini-drones captured footage of that entire battle; an edited video with glorious, high-definition slow-motion footage of every exquisite impact had been set to 'O Fortuna' and posted on the Internet anonymously. Heh.)

I wasn't expecting to make use of the Mk 31's combat capabilities that evening, but one could never be too careful. Lassiter's Den could be a strange place.

Six or seven decades prior, Lassiter's Den had been a privately-owned restaurant standing on the border between two criminal syndicates' territories. The owner, John Lassiter, offered to pay protection to both organizations if their members promised not to fight within his establishment and the bemused crime lords had agreed. Members of both cartels started eating and drinking there regularly, and the Den became known as a safe location to make deals or perform negotiations.

Over time, other gangs began to take advantage of the food, drink and safety. Even after the initial two criminal empires had long since faded into obscurity, the tradition remained: Minor altercations were perhaps unavoidable (and a fair number of differences were taken outside and settled violently) but the interior of the restaurant and bar was inviolable. There was a bouncer at the door, but his responsibilities were limited...in the end, it was the Den's clientele who enforced Lassiter's Truce. Costumed villains and criminal masterminds were now common patrons.

Encased safely within the Mk 31, I dropped from the sky like an ebony comet to land near the entrance, and the doorman allowed me in with the dismissive blasé that only New Yorkers seemed able to manage. Anti-gravity and inertial dampening technologies permitted me to move quietly, without heavy footsteps or causing any damage to wooden floors. Even so, there was a moment of silence as I entered the bar area. Doctor Fid was rather recognizable.

Even in the midst of criminals and villains, Doctor Fid was intimidating.

"Bill," I nodded to the bartender. "Still have Sam Adams on tap?"

"Yes sir, Doctor Fid." William Wasserman looked to be in his early sixties, of average height and build with gray thinning hair and a professional smile. He was renowned both for his discretion and for his encyclopedic knowledge of prohibition-era-and-earlier cocktails. Rumor had it that the Ancient once gave Bill a handful of gold coins as a tip for a perfect Sazerac; supposedly, the Ancient left the bar weeping and disappeared into history. It's just a local legend, of course, but the old-timers always looked up when someone ordered that particular drink. Bill had tended bar here for so long that he was an institution.

"A pint, then." I sat at a stool near the center of the bar. Some ne'er-do-wells came to the Den and immediately tried to find the darkest corner in which to sit, but not I. My intent was to be visible! I belonged here and I feared no one.

My beer slid into my waiting hand. Instantly, I was the center of attention. Surreptitious glances, as the gathered patrons waited to see if I'd take off my helm, if they could catch a glimpse of the elusive Doctor Fid's face. Instead, a tentacle-like straw snaked from my forearm and into the liquid.

The disappointment was audible: soft sighs and whispered curses. I reflexively cut my external speakers so that my own brief laughter wouldn't be broadcast aloud.

Lassiter's Den was less crowded than I'd expected, even for a Thursday night. I recognized most of the faces (either by sight or by database query) but not all. There were a few parties of gangsters or members of syndicates, small groups that watched the costumed patrons with wary respect. A handful of old-timers, retired criminals that still put on spandex for a night of socializing with friends. A couple of civilians, even, who stayed out of the way. There was a running joke here in the Den that half the faces you don't recognize were actually heroes acting undercover; the other half were Cloner.

And then, there were the real villains.

Blackjack was sitting at a dark booth in the corner, eating dinner with what I presumed to be two of his henchmen. He was a tall, broadly built blond man dressed in black-and-gunmetal-gray tactical gear with several of his trademark truncheons hanging from his belt; the other individuals at his table were dressed similarly but lacked the size (and, presumably, superhuman strength and toughness) of their employer. Blackjack had the look of a long-time boxer, ears disfigured from abuse and a nose that looked like it spent more time broken than healed. Fresh bruises and one eye swollen near shut hadn't dampened his mood; he was laughing with his men.

Siren and Jynx were at another booth; the sisters' masks were off and it looked like Siren was comforting her sibling. Jynx's back was facing me, but I judged from the slouch of her shoulders that she was going through a bad time; I'd read that her on-again-off-again boyfriend Loose Cannon had been arrested. I didn't have much sympathy for a woman who once took a pre-school hostage, and Loose Cannon had a nasty habit of injuring non-combatants purely for intimidation's sake. A bit of misery couldn't fall upon a more deserving couple.

I could, however, feel sorry for Siren. As near as I could tell, she'd only become a supervillainess to protect her younger sister. As far as my not-inconsiderably-detailed research could unearth, she'd never initiated violence and even occasionally moved to curb Loose Cannon's excesses. And yet...she'd stood at their side through horrors.

Bullwhip was drunkenly arm-wrestling Minotaur at another table. How did they even get inside? They were both at least a head taller than the Mk 31 armor, and Minotaur's horns shouldn't have even fit through the front door.

(I'd deployed a few microdrones earlier to build a three-dimensional map of the building, so now checked their progress. Ah. A basement entrance connected to an unused subway tunnel. Interesting. I set up a calendar reminder to task a few hundred microdrones to construct a map of all the tunnels under New York. Who knows when that might come of use?)

Last, but certainly not least, I believed that Klown was looming in the darkness near the restrooms. Creepy murderous bastard. His powers do something strange to my sensors, so I was only guessing at his actual location.

I was grateful for the relative peace, but also disappointed; the information broker that I'd hoped to find was not present.

"Are you here for Nyx, Doctor Fid?" Bill asked, drying a glass with a clean bar towel and then placing it on a shelf behind the bar with surgical precision.

"I was hoping to see him, yes." When I'm wearing Doctor Fid's armor, my body language is carefully programmed to maintain an intimidating and emotionless aspect. I should, literally, have no discernible tells...And yet, the bartender at the Lassiter's Den always seemed able to guess.

He's not psychic. Telepathy was only a myth, and I'd checked thoroughly for other metaphysical phenomenon.

"He'll appreciate the support." The bartender picked up another glass and began drying it. "It was good of you to come. I don't think he'll be here tonight, but he might be by tomorrow."

I remained motionless, thoughts swirling.

During the course of my criminal career, I'd had several occasions to work alongside other villains; I'd traded technologies or even offered more concrete assistance when short-term goals overlapped. If asked if I'd any friends among the supervillain community, however, the only name that would come to mind would be Starnyx.

Nyx was a co-founder of the FTW, a hacktivist organization that used questionable methods to oppose corporate greed. Most members of the group boasted no special abilities save an Internet connection, coding skills, and a compatible ideology. Starnyx and a half-dozen other members, however, possessed superpowers. Their talents were collectively put towards raising awareness for their cause in sensational (and often embarrassing) manners; CEOs all across the country crossed their fingers and prayed not to be a target when rumors arose that 'Eff-Tee-Dub!' would be making another broadcast.

He was intelligent, knowledgeable and highly skilled in a wide range of fields, and a highly engaging debater; scrupulously nonviolent, Nyx was a genuine crusader for his cause. In a better world he would have been considered a whistle-blower or hero, but in this world he drank at Lassiter's.

Of more immediate use to me, the affable and gregarious Starnyx had become a cynosure—a central hub through which gossip and information within the villain community flowed. I'd flown south to Manhattan largely because I knew he'd be able to point me towards a relatively trustworthy buyer for my wares. In the wake of the Red Ghost's recent interference, my cash reserves were somewhat depleted, and I'd been considering selling some of my more illiquid assets.

I hadn't heard a whisper from Starnyx. No contact had been made on any of the anonymized dead-drops, email accounts or burner phones that I'd set up so that he could reach me. Automated data-sifting algorithms generally highlight any information about Starnyx (or his secret identity) for me; nothing had been reported recently on any of the major news networks, no arrests or unexpected hospital stays. The FTW hadn't announced any major actions recently, either. And yet, the bartender's wording had implied that Nyx might require emotional support.

I left William Wasserman a generous tip and departed from Lassiter's Den without a word.

Early in our relationship—a few years after Doctor Fid had come out of 'retirement'—Starnyx had used his exceptional technical expertise to locate one of my laboratories. We'd spoken a few times prior, but I hadn't considered him particularly close...and yet, there he had been: waiting outside in plain sight of my security cameras, costumed and carrying a six-pack. I'd considered letting my automated defenses deal with the intruder—or simply activating the self-destruct mechanisms and escaping before the explosions grew too intense. Curiosity had outweighed wrath: I'd donned Doctor Fid's accoutrements and allowed him entry.

"Hey Doc. I was hoping we could chat a bit." He'd seemed remarkably unconcerned by the weaponry that my heavy-combat drones kept trained upon him as he entered the primary floor of the lab. Starnyx's costume consisted of a khaki military-style jumpsuit, a brown belt with a wide array of pouches, a matching tactical vest (more pouches!), and a simple domino mask. "I brought beer!"

"First, you'll tell me how you found this place." Every sensor array that I could think of was tasked with searching the region for evidence of more FTW members or other intruders; I uncovered nothing untoward.

"Of course," Starnyx smiled. "Serious data mining. I generated a bunch of lists and looked for overlaps."

"What sorts of lists?"

"Okay, example one...I knew that you operated out of the Boston area, and I knew that you'd need to be able to move machinery onto the property...I could eliminate some areas because the roads aren't wide or strong enough to handle heavy loads. I could also eliminate areas whose only path included low bridges or overhangs. So...one big list."

That was a reasonable assessment. I could, theoretically, use my larger drones to airlift equipment to one of my workshops, but doing so would require accounting for visual observation, radar, etc. Trucks and cargo containers were significantly more discreet. I nodded for Starnyx to continue.

"You'd need privacy. That can be managed several different ways...trees, high fences, physical isolation, etc. That cuts down the previous list a bit, though. I also believed that you wouldn't use too much power because the utilities companies would notice...so I looked for properties with atypically low power usage. You have your own generators, I assume?"

I waved him onward, intrigued now. I could already foresee other applications for these methodologies. Also, ways to avoid being noticed in the future.

"I also have a few methods to identify possible false identities and the owner of this property was flagged. The birth certificate, social security and tax information were all perfect, but the owner didn't have any social media presence at all."

Easily fixed, in the future. It would be a simple affair to simulate the banal postings of an average civilian. Stock images, pictures of restaurant meals, lies about recent purchases, and mindless political rants filled with false equivalencies and poor logic...maybe a few cat videos. I nodded again, "Continue."

"There were still hundreds of possibilities. I hadda spend a fair bit of time examining satellite and traffic-cam footage to whittle the list down further. I flagged a whole bunch of locations on WBZ's traffic helicopter footage. This site had three different shipping containers move through over the last few nights...And that leads into why I'm here."

"By all means..." My audio systems were programmed to automatically mask my voice, maintain an even delivery and remove subtle emotional vocal cues when I spoke. The program was, however, unable to wholly eliminate dry sarcasm from my reply. "...Do explain."

"Please," he smiled, but his voice sounded strangely sad, "Whatever you've got planned for the next two weeks...don't do it."

"That seems a strong request." Other villains had made such appeals when they believed my actions might interfere with their own. Some attempted intimidation (and were subsequently taught the error of their ways), while others offered bribes or favors. Until this moment, however, contacts were made via anonymous messaging services or e-mail; discovering my lair and appearing unannounced made Starnyx a new and unique threat. I triggered my suit's heightened emotion algorithm: the stars projected upon the armor's surface began to slowly swirl, the red glow at the armor's seams intensified and my voice was projected at a higher volume. "What do you believe that I intend for the coming month?"

"You're going to start a fight."

"Battles are hardly unexpected, in our line of work." My vocoder failed to eliminate scorn from my raised voice.

"Not a battle...a fight." He shrugged helplessly. "No crime, no benefit, no higher cause...just an ugly, violent fight."

I reflexively lowered the intensity of my armor's display as my thoughts whirled. Nyx was known to be opposed to unnecessary violence; still, whatever I'd been expecting from the slim villain, a moral appeal hadn't been it. It concerned me, however, that Nyx was referring only to this particular planned action. For a long moment, I remained silent and motionless as I considered the ramifications.

"Tell me what you know," I finally ordered; or perhaps, in retrospect, it had been a defeated appeal. Through the vocoder's modulation, either guess could have been accurate.

"On the seventeenth last year, you threatened to destroy Axiom Laboratories with an ionic flux bomb; the hero named 'Clash' intervened." Starnyx set down the six-pack and lifted out a bottle. "The campus was unharmed but Clash needed months of physical therapy. The thing is...I know you didn't have an ionic flux bomb. There's a distinctive neutrino pulse whenever a new Westler-Gray crystal is formed. I know a guy who has a sensor...The bomb was a bluff, a ruse to draw out Clash.

"The year before that, it was Sonic, and three years ago was Salamander...Every year, mid-July: an attack chosen someplace where a single hero is forced to respond without backup. No other purpose, just a target."

"Sometimes, targeting a specific hero *is* the purpose," I conceded, feeling oddly defensive.

"If that were true...then why does the date matter? Three shipping containers in three nights! You're rushing and someone's going to get hurt."

"No one that hasn't earned their pain." I noticed that my hands were clenched into fists. When had that happened?

"You're rushing," Starnyx repeated. "You're the best of us, but even you can make mistakes."

"The best of...?" I growled, smelling ozone as my armor built up charge. "I'm a monster! I'm not the best of anything."

"You're a monster for a few days in the middle of summer. The rest of the year, you're Doctor Fid."

I stared at him, uncomprehending. I must have looked like a statue.

"You're a precision instrument, Doc. You plan, you do what you need to do, you get away clean." He gestured with his bottle expressively. "You build things out of legend, you fought Valiant to a standstill, and Lloyd's of London has an insurance policy for Acts of Fid."

"I'm reasonably certain that the last item is apocryphal," I noted dryly.

"Nope," he grinned, popping the cap off his bottle, "I checked this morning."

"That is a kind sentiment," I allowed. "I do not, however, see how this relates to your request that I discontinue my...summer tradition."

"The world accepts self-righteous, hypocritical violent thugs to be their defenders because everyone is afraid that the sky will fall without their protection. But you...you changed the game," he explained, taking a quick drink. "You proved that the 'heroes' can lose but the world didn't end. That makes the world wonder why it puts up with the spandex-clad vigilantes in the first place.

"Doctor Fid is careful and precise. The guy who kept hitting Clash for half a minute after he lost consciousness, though...That guy was frightening enough that everyone who's seen the video worries about the sky falling.

"So... don't go through with whatever you have planned for next week. Don't be that guy. Have a beer; be Doctor Fid instead."

Silently, I evaluated his argument. There was a valid point buried within the appeals to my vanity and my desire to maintain visible self-control. Intimidation is a powerful weapon, but it must be wielded carefully; fear is useful, but panic is dangerous. Had I gone too far? If so...could I use that reputation without exacerbating the situation? Planning and detailed analysis would be required.

Left unspoken were his secondary arguments. First, that my pattern was noticed by a villain who'd chosen to bring the finding to my attention, but an enterprising hero could make the same connections and begin planning appropriately. Secondly...that Starnyx never made a secret of his opposition towards unnecessary violence. In the abstract, I tended to agree. It was...unseemly.

Punishing the unworthy heroes would always be necessary. Celebrating an anniversary with unspeakable violence, perhaps less so.

"That looks like a good beer," I finally commented.

"It's from a microbrewery in Brooklyn." His smile widened. "Scottish ale, flavored with orange zest."

I made no promises but accepted the beer. That laboratory was abandoned and others hidden sufficiently that Nyx was never able to find another, and he and I had been on good terms ever since.

There'd been no mid-summer battle that year, nor any year since.

It would have been simpler, perhaps, to travel home and return another time; Nyx was, as the bartender noted, expected to be present at Lassiter's on the following evening. Instead, I chose to find a quiet shadowy rooftop to sift through a flood of information gathered by my automated systems. Starnyx had no idea who stood encased by Doctor Fid's armor, but he was a friend none-the-less. I'd discovered his civilian identity some years ago; it was no great hardship to seek out his current location.

Traveling through the night sky of New York City while wearing full supervillain regalia was strange. In some ways, it was easier than one might expect; my powered-armor can be quite stealthy and could easily swerve amongst the buildings to avoid radar or other forms of detection. Even the sound of my flight was muted, with anti-gravitic thrust carefully tuned and air-resistance minimized by shaped low-friction force-fields. Few pedestrians look up and fewer waste more than a moment's attention on anything that isn't an immediate threat.

And yet, the city of New York contained more so-called superheroes per square mile than any other locale. All that it took was one unusually diligent late-night office-worker reporting a sighting of the notorious Doctor Fid flying past a window and suddenly everyone wearing spandex and a mask started watching the skies. I'd developed a program that monitored the police-radio bands and marked off suggested course corrections, but detection was still a possibility. The majority of so-called 'heroes,' however, were familiar enough with my reputation that they usually thanked the fates that I was heading away from them and pretended not to have seen me.

Sometimes, however, luck failed me and some costumed buffoon decided to try their luck.

It was more than an hour (my powered-armor sustained only minor cosmetic damage, and the now-concussed Blockbuster would likely make a full recovery within days) before I arrived at Starnyx's location. I set down on his rooftop and waited; my sensors indicated that security cameras had recognized my approach and triggered appropriate alerts.

I didn't need to linger for long. A familiar pale, slim, rumpled and unshaven figure opened the door and peered wearily at me. Starnyx was not, apparently, prepared for company: rather than his costume, he was wearing faded blue jeans, a black 'Han Shot First!' t-shirt and gray fuzzy slippers.

"Christ. This is my apartment, Doc. I live here," he grumbled, rubbing at his eyes. The man looked haggard. "My neighbors'll notice if I walk you through the halls."

"My apologies." I shifted my weight from foot to foot, embarrassed. "I'll meet you at the Den tomorrow."

"Nah. 'ss all right," he sighed. "I'll open a window for you. 14th floor, northwest fire escape."

I nodded silently and floated off the rooftop. Yawning tiredly, the unmasked Starnyx trudged back inside.

My early powered-armor suits had been powerful, but not nearly so graceful as recent models. I wouldn't have been able to land silently on a metal fire-escape using the Mk 17, much less carefully squeeze through an open window without causing damage to the architecture. I'd developed highly accurate synaptic feedback for the Mk 18 when Nyx announced that he was going to teach me how to pick locks. Adding sufficient sensitivity to accurately control a torsion wrench and feel a tumbler settle into place had been an entertaining diversion and eventually yielded tremendous benefits for my dexterity while armored. Presumably, it also saved wear and tear on window frames.

The apartment was not the sort one would imagine a supervillain to maintain. There were no exposed city maps with thumbtacks identifying possible targets, no walls of humming machinery or blinking lights. It was small but well-appointed, with wood paneling and warm earth-toned accents throughout. There were photos and artworks placed sporadically along the walls, seemingly chosen more for pleasant remembrance than for ostentatious presentation. This was a lived-in home, not a lair.

Even out of my armor, it'd been years since the last time that I'd stood in a friend's domain. In academia, I'd had coworkers and peers with whom I socialized but never truly been close. When I left the University and founded AH Biotech, I'd entertained employees and investors at Terrance Markham's house for the expected dinner parties and soirees, but that hardly counted; that residence was a front, carefully tailored to maintain my civilian identity's charade. I lived in my laboratories, not in any house. I could not recall accepting any invitations from employees or investors looking to reciprocate. And (with the exception of our first personal encounter) Starnyx and I had always met at Lassiter's or some other neutral location. I felt strangely out of place, as though trespassing on holy ground.

Perhaps Dr. Markham would have felt comfortable in a place like this, but Doctor Fid did not. And Starnyx knew only Doctor Fid.

"I heard 'bout your fight 'gainst the Guardians. You okay?" Nyx asked, grabbing two glasses and a bottle of 15-year highland scotch from a cabinet.

"I'm fine," I shrugged self-consciously; the media coverage to which Starnyx referred had universally declared Doctor Fid to have come out the poorer from that conflict. "It's nothing I can't deal with. How are you doing?"

He paused, then sighed. "I take it you heard 'bout Beazd?"

"Not exactly. I was at the Den and Bill let something slip," I stalled, pulling up a flurry of data feeds on the screen inside my helmet. The founding members of the FTW were Starnyx, Beazd, Root, Hax and Colonel Panic; Beazd (Real name Kenta Takuma) was arrested once, served his time and retired, 'though he had often violated the terms of his parole to put on the old costume and drink with us at Lassiter's. No recent arrests, no news articles, no...ah. Damn. Obituary notice. Car accident. "I'm so sorry."

"Thanks, man." Nyx poured two fingers' worth of scotch into each glass. He handed one to me and I accepted.

"I didn't know him that well, but he seemed like a good man." Beazd had come up in conversation often, but we'd only met in person five times. The former villain'd had a subtle sense of humor, oft betrayed only by a mischievous smile: a playful smirk that reminded you to think back through the wording of the last few rounds of conversation and contemplate what joke you'd missed.

"The best." Nyx took a sip of his scotch, his hands shaking. "He was my friend since grade school, didja know that?"

"I did, yes." My suit's drinking-extension automatically slid from my suit's forearm to sample the scotch. It wasn't a 'straw', exactly...a bellows system pumped precise amounts up the tube, to match the volume that would have been poured based upon a shift in my wrist's position and the tilt of my head. "He helped form the FTW, didn't he?"

"It was his idea." The mourning supervillain stared at his glass as though he wanted desperately to take a swallow but held back out of some misguided self-punishment. "I was a better hacker, better public speaker...but the core, our manifesto: that was all Ken."

"I think you mentioned that the Hamblin International caper was his idea?" I browsed a few articles on the grieving process and determined that it would likely be optimal to keep Starnyx thinking about good memories. I held little experience at this and witnessed few positive exemplars save for portrayals of bereavement and support found in mass-media. My own coping mechanisms tended towards directed violence and even I had to admit that was probably unhealthy.

"The Westmont Corporation, too. Every step." He smiled sadly, "That video got nearly a million hits. Put us on the map."

"That job was very well planned," I nodded in approval. "I was one of the viewers."

"I ever tell you how he got caught?" He took another drink from his glass; this scotch was excellent, but I wasn't sure that Nyx tasted it. Not tonight.

"No, I'm afraid not."

"We were leaving the Mitchel&Mitchel Fidelity headquarters an' he got surrounded. If they'd been wearing their tac-suits, it wouldn've been a big deal...Kenta was strong, he coulda pushed through 'em and gotten away. But your Ghost advised 'em to take off their protective gear and Beazd couldn't get away without hurting someone. So, he just surrendered."

"Admirable." I took another sip from my glass, remembering the deceased. His powers had been simple: strength, durability and endurance. Not in the class of, say Titan or Gamma, but certainly significantly greater than human. Hmm. "The Red Ghost, you mean?"

"Yeah...he was still a member of the New York Shield back then."

"The Red Ghost is..." I paused, considering my descriptor carefully. "...Challenging."

"Yeah." Starnyx chuckled painfully. "Smart though, I guess. Used Ken's morality against him."

"That level of conviction is remarkable." Another sip. "I wish that I'd known Beazd better."

"Heh. He hated you at first, hated that I talked to you." Starnyx gestured towards me with his glass; the contents sloshed but didn't spill. "It wasn't personal, he just disliked violence. Kenta could throw an engine block through a brick wall, but wouldn't throw a punch to save his own li—"

He trailed off into a tormented silence.

I stood motionless, reviewing what'd been said, what I knew of Beazd's powers, what I could glean from the coroner's statements. Something was horribly wrong; the accident report described an incident that could very easily have killed a normal civilian. The retired villain who'd helped form the FTW, however, should have walked away without a scratch.

"Tell me what happened to Beazd," I finally requested, setting down my glass.

"No."

"Did someone do this?" I asked, confused. "Nyx...did someone kill Beazd? Just let me—"

"No!" He finished his drink in one angry gulp then set the glass down. "Christ, Doc, this is why I didn't call you."

"What?!?"

"My best friend was a pacifist!" Nyx spat, "He hated violence for any reason, even self-defense. And you...you're Doctor Fid. You've made 'bloody revenge' into a lifestyle choice!"

"If I tell you what happened, you'll make me an offer." The mourning young man offered a sad smile. "I know how Kenny would want me to respond, but I'm not sure I'm strong enough to say 'no'. So...I can't deal with Doctor Fid right now. Just...go."

The most damning aspect of his commentary was its accuracy; my first thought was a cry for retribution, for terror and sorrow. To pay back tenfold any who caused my friend's anguish! I could think of little else; the rage pulsed through me like my own blood and I ached with the need to gather up my own pain and inflict it upon someone deserving. My armaments had reflexively warmed into a ready state, glowing with malevolence. I felt...focused, directed. Like an avalanche readying to catapult downhill, awaiting the slightest trigger to release a cleansing wrath. That's what Doctor Fid was: my vengeance forged into a faceless, implacable suit of powered-armor. I'd chosen to make Fid a scalpel rather than a battle-axe, perhaps, but the intent was the same.

I stared down at Starnyx, at...Eric Guthrie, the man who wore Nyx's mask.

I could convince him, I knew. I could utter the right words, to make him howl for retribution and unleash me towards those who'd earned a just reprisal. I could see how close he was, how tempted. I could see his heartbreak.

And I could see what it would cost him to betray his childhood friend's wishes.

My jaw clenched and I hesitated before departing. I didn't want to leave Starnyx alone with his grief; I'd been alone after Bobby's death and isolation had destroyed me. Nyx was a better man than I'd ever been. He deserved a better fate. He deserved better friends.

I issued a command that had never before been activated outside one of my laboratories; the Mk 31's star-field motif dimmed like dark clouds pouring over a night sky, and the angry red glow faded to warm coals. My armor fell open with a quiet hiss of equalizing pressures.

I stepped out of Fid and put a hand on Eric's shoulder in consolation.

"Hi. I'm, uh, Terry," I grimaced. "I'm sorry about Kenta. Let me pour us another drink, okay?"

CHAPTER THREE

OVER THE NEXT FEW DAYS, IT WAS REAFFIRMED THAT Kenta Takuma had been an odd sort of supervillain. An idealist, he'd believed that there existed social and economic inequities that could not be addressed from within the system; he'd stepped away from that system, from the mundane and safe environment in which he most certainly could have excelled, and instead put on a brightly colored costume so as to improve the world in what ways he could. As the masked villain Beazd, his efforts had been squarely targeted towards exposing greed and malfeasance among those in power.

His criminal career, however, ended after only a few short years. Beazd surrendered peacefully when cornered, served his time and hung up his cape. He'd retired, quietly confident that others would take up his cause.

Kenta Takuma had been an inspiration, a teacher, a friend, and a murder victim.

Some might have argued that manslaughter was a more appropriate label for the incident, or perhaps a tragic mishap. If that argument were so compelling, if Kenta's death had, in fact, been simply a moment of ill-fortune...why, then, did Sphinx put so much effort towards covering up her teammate's actions? Why forge evidence to hide a mistake, why shop for a corrupt medical examiner if a competent investigation would have determined the death to be accidental?

If a criminal aimed a firearm at a police officer and pulled the trigger, then "I thought he was wearing a bullet proof vest!" would make for a poor legal defense. Common sense would dictate that choosing to employ lethal force can potentially lead to a lethal outcome. It was feasible (likely, even!) that the superhero Peregrine believed that Beazd could take the fall, but that belief is no absolution.

Peregrine possessed the power to fly at ludicrous speeds and was damned near indestructible while doing so. The man was a living kinetic weapon, capable of piercing almost any defenses if he found a long-enough path in which to accelerate. Beazd had been strong and durable, but when an irresistible force met an only somewhat immovable object...the somewhat immovable object was sure to suffer.

If Beazd's death had occurred in the heat of battle, if lives were at stake and split-seconds mattered, then perhaps a jury could have been convinced that the hero made a rational choice given the available information. No such battle had taken place. Beazd had never been a threat to the general public and Kenta Takuma hadn't so much as jaywalked since his from prison early for good behavior. Beazd's only 'crime' had been keeping in touch with his childhood friends and thus knowing where to find still-active members of the FTW.

A violent interrogation of an unresisting subject. A horrific miscalculation. A crime.

I was surprised. I shouldn't have been! Fifteen years I'd spent fighting a bloody and violent crusade against heroes unworthy of the title, and yet this blatant act was still shocking to me. Not the death itself; I'd fought the man who'd killed Kenta, and I'd known that it was only a matter of time before his hands were stained as red as my own. He was too arrogant and too easily distracted to be trusted with his power.

It was the Sphinx's actions that took me aback; the leader of the New York Shield had known what the evidence would reveal and tried to bury it all. She'd exhibited a cold-hearted pragmatism that I hadn't expected to see from her side of the spandex divide.

The Red Ghost often credited the Sphinx as one of his mentors and inspirations. Did he know, I wondered? When he'd been a member of the New York Shield, had the Red Ghost made 'mistakes' similar to Peregrine's and asked his team leader to help conceal them? Had I placed a murderer's action figure next to my brother's crayon drawings?

Starnyx begged me to do nothing rash, to do no violence in his pacifistic comrade's memory; I stayed with Eric for days and it had been extraordinarily gratifying how easily the unarmored Terry Markham had fallen into the role of friend. We drank too much, ate cheap takeout and talked late into the night. He had a clever and altogether peaceful plan to gain his revenge, and I pledged my support.

I respected his devotion. In the heat of the moment, meeting Eric's fiercely determined expression with a supportive smile, I'd thought that I might be able to share it. Sadly, that flash of inspiration faded and was replaced by a much more familiar bitter fury.

I wanted to hit something. Fortunately...for a creature like

Doctor Fid, opportunities for conflict were never far out of reach.

Micro-drones fed telemetry, sonar and radar scans to my helmet, providing a real-time map of the darkened warehouse and all its inhabitants' locations to within a centimeter's accuracy. I knew the location of every shelter, every pillar and piece of debris. The display was useful as I triggered a 93% pulse of my powered-armor's thrusters that overtaxed my inertial dampeners and crushed the air from my lungs. I dove backwards like a shot, safe behind cover before the Shrike could ready a second attack.

The temporary inability to breathe was beneficial; the pause allowed for the successful muting of my helmet's microphone before the heroes could hear me scream.

Shrike (clad in a gray, black, and white bodysuit) was a relatively new hero who'd supposedly been granted power by an extra-dimensional entity; he could psychically create pale white-yellow glowing projections that would spear outwards from nearby surfaces. In the past, the Shrike had primarily spawned blunt bars of varying thickness. He'd even knocked out the notoriously hard-headed Minotaur by placing a pillar in front of the charging criminal. Less often, Shrike also used his power to create needle-sharp spikes, leaving the worst of his enemies impaled like the victims of his namesake bird. To the best of my knowledge, Shrike only used that ability on brutes with a known regenerative capability.

Facing the notorious villain Doctor Fid, and with two of his companions already knocked unconscious, the Shrike had revealed a new ability: creating a two-dimensional plane of force capable of cutting through matter like a monomolecular blade.

"Oh my god!" The hero's voice sounded ill. "Is that his arm?"

"I..." My voice echoed menacingly, reverberating throughout the abandoned warehouse, "...am going to want. That. Back." Software scrubbed tension and pain from my voice, transmitted through my scattered drones' speakers simultaneously so as to hide my exact location. Meanwhile, my armor's built-in medical system poured painkillers into my body and the inner suit constricted above the point of amputation to limit further blood loss. Oddly, the tourniquet hurt worse than the wound itself.

My defensive systems were rebooting, the Mk 28 powered-armor was compromised but still functional, and my heavy-combat drones were only a few minutes away. This battle was not yet lost.

"He's lost a lot of blood," Psion cautioned. One of only three heroes still standing, the short Korean woman's outfit was orange with dull yellow accents. "He can't have gotten far. We can catch him before he escapes!"

Escape wasn't my goal.

I fed the sound of heavy footsteps and scrabbling gravel through a drone in front of them and activated my anti-grav field. Floating silently, I circled through the shadows. Sensors monitored the heroes' heights and the direction that their heads were turned, allowing me to map a smooth course beyond their line of sight.

My scepter drifted to my remaining hand, and I gripped the shaft so tightly that my fingers ached. Physical strain seemed to help me concentrate.

"Stay close!" Psion urged, her fists beginning to flare as she readied an attack. "He's wounded, but he's still Doctor Fid."

"I thought that he had a force-field?" Shrike whispered, his voice still shaky. Targeted audio analysis revealed that his heart rate was unusually fast and hi-res video showed the tremble in his hands. "I just wanted to trap him, the wall is stopped by—"

"I disabled it." The third hero's name was Wildcard. From my research, he had access to a broad range of powers...but only three at a time, and it took several minutes to change whatever combination was presently active. One of his current powers, I now knew, was the disruption bolt that had struck me earlier, and—given that I'd seen him shrug off one of my heavy putty-shot stunning blasts—I felt comfortable presuming that his second power was some sort of super-human toughness. The nature of his third active power was still a mystery. "I should've said someth-"

"Quiet," Psion interrupted. "The blood trail stops here."

It was a dark night with only a sliver of moon, and the warehouse's remaining windows were clouded with long neglect. The trio huddled in the circle of purple illumination cast by Psion's powers; beyond that radius, the black was deep and sinister, and I was invisible within the gloom. The red glow and starfield motif normally displayed upon my powered-armor had been dimmed to an ink-dark finish.

Again, I used my microdrones' speakers to simulate the sound of movement through the shadows in front of them and added an ultra-low frequency hum throughout the building to create a general sense of unease. The three heroes looked at each other, visibly steeling themselves for combat and gathering confidence from each other's presence.

This fight should not have happened.

A shipping container had arrived via a New York port and been readied for delivery to a secret laboratory that I owned in Nashua, Vermont; unfortunately, the delivery was lost before it left the city. The Red Hook Spiders, a low-level street gang, hijacked the truck seeking the televisions that had appeared on the container's manifest. All they'd found was an assortment of raw materials and machined components.

Under normal circumstances I might have written the loss off. Nothing in the container was irreplaceable, nor did the street gang have the resources to connect the shipment to me. At that particular moment, however, Doctor Fid's illicit finances were still recovering from the strain caused by the Red Ghost's investigation. Also, I happened to be in New York after visiting Starnyx and was thus in a mood well-suited for violence.

I waited for a few heavy-combat drones to fly their way from the Boston area (and for Eric to take a nap), then donned the recently repaired Mk 28 and tracked down the Spiders. Fair compensation was offered for their inconvenience (a reputation for being magnanimous could be valuable) and when they responded rudely, I set about correcting their manners (a reputation for being dangerous could be valuable as well). The resulting explosions attracted the interest of a local superhero group—the Brooklyn Knights.

Full credit should be given where credit is due: The Knights recognized my armor and immediately leapt to attack. I was a known powerhouse and they, a young and untested team. Their bravery, if not their common sense, was remarkable.

I could have simply escaped, could have launched into some menacing monologue and flown to safety. But doing so would have left the shipping container behind...valuable resources that might, by more competent investigators, be traced to my Nashua lab, or to the Port Authority employee that had ensured that the shipping manifest went unchallenged. Against unexpected foes upon whom I'd done very little research, the rational choice would have been to accept the losses and disappear. I *should* have left, but at that moment I was simply too irked to make the logical decision; I tasked my heavy-combat drones with airlifting the container to a safe location and faced the Knights with nothing but my own armor and scepter. And now, I was fighting through dizziness and multitasking furiously, attempting to solve four problems at once.

First, determining how long my medical nanites would keep my severed limb viable so that surgical robots could reattach it without complications. Second, developing an algorithm that would (in the future, at least) cause the nanites to destroy DNA and other identifying data from my blood if it were exposed to open air. Third, analyzing data logs to determine how Wildcard's attack disrupted my force-field so that I could hack together a quick defense.

And fourth, was, of course, planning a method to defeat my opponents with sufficient drama that they remembered my victory more vividly than they remembered the sight of my amputated arm.

The spilled blood would need to be eradicated manually once the heroes had been dealt with. Leaving any genetic evidence that could link the nefarious Doctor Fid to Terrance Markham would be catastrophic to my long-term plans; I'd always been careful to maintain separation between my two identities. The powered armor suits that made Doctor Fid so infamous did not utilize any technologies that could be traced to the moderately-famous founder of AH Biotech, and (although I'd produced patents and scholarly papers in many fields from my time in academia), Dr. Markham had been focusing on medical technologies in recent times. The supervillain known as Doctor Fid, however, was notable primarily for his work in robotics, software engineering and energy manipulation.

Injecting the nanites into my own body had been a calculated gamble. They were still in the research phase, years away from federal approval...but they were certainly AH Biotech's design and could theoretically be traced back to the company. Since Doctor Fid recently (very publicly) robbed the company's research facilities, however, it could be posited that I'd gotten access to the nanites during the assault. And the benefits more than outweighed the risks. Even at room-temperature and with the rigors of combat, I calculated that I had several hours before my detached arm would suffer sufficient degradation as to make reattachment impossible. As a secondary bonus: I was in no danger of bleeding to death.

Having successfully delivered the cargo container to safety, my heavy-combat drones were speeding back to this location. The twelve-foot-tall cylinders would look to be dark star-fields, holes in the sky opening into darkest space; with their weapons, manipulation arms and their spider-like walking legs stowed, no red glow would be discernible at the joints. A stern-faced general once referred to my drones as "the densest concentration of military might on the face of the planet" while addressing Congress and they'd been upgraded several times since.

Had I simply stayed quiet and concealed, it would've been less than a minute before I could have called down destruction upon the remaining heroes. And then (when they regained consciousness) the Brooklyn Knights would have reported that they were defeated by Doctor Fid's robots.

That thought left a sour taste in my mouth. Sudden vengeance pouring forth from the heavens might intimidate, but it would not overshadow the Knights' memory of my injury, nor the sight of me retreating into darkness. They needed to be brought low by Doctor Fid rather than Fid's toys.

Also, my arm was lying in the dirt and the most powerful painkillers modern science could fathom were unable to eliminate my discomfort. Instructing my drones to attack would lack the visceral punishment that I wanted to inflict.

My now-rebooted personal force-field was altered to function in alternating micro-pulses (thus forming a harmonic to resist Wildcard's disruption capabilities) and I re-enabled the Mk 28 powered-armor's characteristic starfield-and-red aspect; in the lightless night, it would have looked as though I simply faded into being. I stilled, silent as a statue, and waited for the heroes to notice.

While waiting, I programmed the combat drones to rescue me if I lost consciousness. As the old Latin proverb stated: 'fortune favors the bold...but a reserve force of almost indestructible battle automatons is good, too'.

"Ohholycrap!" Shrike yelped, twisting and waving an arm frantically in my direction; a glowing column of energy exploded into existence from the ground near my left foot, tilted to thrust towards my chest. I sidestepped smoothly. For a moment, they were too shocked to continue their attack.

I knew what they saw: Seven and a half feet tall, a sleek armored figure missing its right arm just below the shoulder with gore and bone clearly visible. The armor's black surface was somehow deeper than the shadows surrounding it, broken by the light of distant stars and a dull crimson glow that helped provide an outline for the humanoid shape. The apparition gripped a scepter in its left hand, held more like a club than like a walking stick; the ruby pommel burned like a dying sun, menacing and angry. And the specter's helmet: dark, featureless and smooth save for a trace of vermilion indicating the face-plate's seam. The infamous Doctor Fid, bloodied but unbowed. I laughed and my armor's vocoder automatically altered the tone until the sound was so menacing it surprised even me.

As one, the Knights rushed to offense: Wildcard darted forward, shielding his companions with his toughened body as he raised a glowing hand to launch a second disruption blast in my direction. Simultaneously, Shrike summoned another gleaming rod to shoot forward from the ground in front of Wildcard's feet, and Psion launched a powerful beam of purple energy. I shot ahead, again veering to evade Shrike's attack while blocking Psion's ray with the shaft of my scepter. Wildcard's burst struck my personal force-field and dissipated without effect. Hah.

My fighting style in armor is more a function of clever programming than of personal skill. I've trained in multiple martial arts but have successfully faced many whose skill and talent easily eclipsed my own. Algorithms collated data from dozens of sensors and could move more quickly and accurately than anything human. Years of training and experience made the transition smooth: Some moments I was the Mk 28's direct controller, and other moments I was merely its passenger. Complex predictive processes enabled me to dance effortlessly between attacks and close ground until I was within striking distance.

I shifted to my left to place Wildcard directly between myself and Psion; she had no easy shot, not without endangering her teammate. Another of Shrike's pillars rushed towards me, narrowly dodged as I swung my scepter to strike Wildcard across his right collar bone. The meaty thump was shockingly loud but did not appear to be debilitating; the hero merely grunted and reached up, unsuccessfully trying to grab my scepter's shaft before I could pull it away. I upgraded my mental estimate as to his level of invulnerability; a similar blow would have driven a charging bull to ground.

Psion circled to her left and I attempted to mirror her, except that Shrike summoned a web of intersecting poles to obstruct my path; a purple energy blast slammed into my hip with the force of a speeding truck. I was knocked back and spun around, but anti-gravitics kicked in before I toppled.

Wildcard took the opportunity to land a painful haymaker (His third power identified: Super-human strength.) to the back of my head. The two successful attacks left me spinning, but I'd faced Whirlwind four times in the past. Reflexively, I used the momentum to twist into a powerful swing and launched my crackling scepter at the ground beneath Wildcard's feet.

The concrete detonated and the explosion threw the stunned hero twice his own height into the air. Shrike raised his arm to protect his eyes against shrapnel, and Psion flared so bright that her purple aura almost turned white. Wildcard landed with a graceless thud.

My lips were split open again; these Knights may have been a new group, but they certainly weren't lightweights! The two members that I'd rendered unconscious outside, Blizzard and White Tigress, had also shown surprising strengths. I wondered why these inexperienced champions chose to create their own team. With their skills, the individual Knights would have been welcomed into any of the more well-established organizations in this city. Certainly, the New York Shield would have fallen over themselves attempting to recruit these young heroes: they were reasonably well-trained, moderately powerful, and worked well as a team. I would definitely be performing more research on them in the future.

An analytic program had been monitoring Shrike during his attacks. The white-yellow constructions were extra-dimensional in nature and, as near as I could determine, physically unbreakable. The hero did, however, need to look directly at the surface he was summoning his projections from: If he wanted to summon a column from the floor at my feet, he had to glance down at the ground. Although one summoned pillar could likely stop a speeding freight train in its tracks, a sufficiently accurate predictive algorithm tied to sensors monitoring the direction of his gaze could anticipate his attacks.

The predictive algorithms programmed within the Mk 28 powered armor were sufficiently accurate. I rocketed towards Psion, drifting around Shrike's columns and spikes as he tried to protect his teammate. Psion's eyes widened but she didn't hesitate: She leaned forward, planting her feet firmly and extending both arms with her palms facing towards me. A tsunami of iridescent purple poured forth, a fiery blast that could have pierced a battleship's armor. I diverted all power to forward shields and pressed forward through the brutal stream.

According to my readings, the energy was astrophysical plasma; she wasn't generating the heavily ionized gasses so much as funneling them through a pinhole portal to the surface of some distant star. The purple color, however, was wrong for the heat and chemical composition. Some kind of localized alteration of physical laws—another extra dimensional effect, perhaps? Given some of the readings that I'd taken from Wildcard's blast, I could confirm that at least three of the Knights had powers that originated from outside this reality.

The sources of superhuman powers were myriad; strange abilities of extra dimensional origin were not terribly uncommon. The coincidence was, however, worthy of note.

Psion was almost within my grasp when a micro-drone notified me that Wildcard was back on his feet. He'd circled around and appeared to be preparing to shoot me in the back with his disruption attack. With my force-fields straining at maximum capacity, I wasn't sure that the micro-pulse harmonic would be a successful defense; I triggered my thrusters and broke to my right. Wildcard's blast narrowly missed, but Psion was able to maintain her aim: The flood of purple energy propelled me rearwards like a bullet.

Again, I used the inertia to my advantage; I summoned my scepter to my hand and triggered minor course-corrections my trajectory. The purple torrent threw me towards Wildcard too quickly for him to react, and the pommel of my scepter landed a thunderous blow to his solar plexus. Wildcard went down and Psion broke off her attack.

She looked...wasted: shaking, sweating, barely able to stand. Tears streamed down her mask, and a media replay indicated that she'd been screaming for the last few seconds of her attack. Her arms fell limp, trembling as she failed to raise them towards me. I tasked a micro-drone's sensor array to begin a medical analysis and turned my back to her. With a sob, she collapsed to her hands and knees.

While I strode towards the remaining combatants, I reviewed sensor data from the battle when it'd begun outside of the warehouse. Blizzard's powers, too, had some hallmarks of an extra-dimensional origin. Temperature variations that were not in keeping with air movements, atmospheric chemical composition that didn't match local levels of contaminants. He wasn't creating snow and ice locally...he was redirecting horrific ice-storms from somewhere else. That made at least four (if not all five) members of the Knights. I hadn't seen enough of White Tigress' abilities to offer any judgment.

I clubbed the wheezing Wildcard again, knocking him unconscious with a sharp strike to the skull. According to an interview that he'd posted online three months ago, he could exchange out his powers for healing and regenerative abilities; when he became lucid, I was sure, he'd be able to cure any effects from concussion.

Shrike was the last Knight standing.

"You took my arm," I growled, casually sidestepping another white-yellow spike that he'd aimed towards my chest. "If you surrender quietly, I might break only one of yours in retaliation."

"I've read about you. Valiant said that you don't break your word." The hero's voice shook and his shoulders hunched, but he looked ready to fight to the end if it became necessary. "You promise not to hurt them any more?"

"I do." I triggered my armor's anti-gravitics and floated towards him, using the extra height to loom. Speakers throughout the warehouse emitted a barely audible, foreboding hum.

"Then I surrender." He looked up at me briefly then wilted.

"You're loyal," I commented simply, setting down within striking distance of the hero.

"They're my friends." He lifted his chin, determined, and forced an unsteady smile. "My arm for their safety."

It was one thing to risk life and limb in the heat of battle, but it took a special kind of bravery to offer oneself as a willing sacrifice after the adrenaline has begun to fade. He looked young (mid-twenties, ethnicity uncertain due to his mask but visible skeletal structure and skin tone indicated possible latino and oriental mixed heritage) but was likely no stranger to pain; he and his friends were too well trained to be unfamiliar with discomfort. Shrike knew what he was offering and made the offer without flinching. I was impressed enough to consider letting him go unharmed.

It would set a poor precedent; other heroes might think to surrender without a fight, and sometimes a fight was the purpose of the exercise. I could afford to be seen as occasionally magnanimous, but never as being soft. Still, it felt...strangely awkward, rewarding such courage with pain delivered in cold blood.

My choice was taken from me when an alarm triggered on my heads-up display.

"You're Psion's friend...you know her medical history?" I dismissed my scepter to its subspace storage and hooked Shrike by one arm, turning him towards his fallen teammates and dragging him along. He looked surprised at the contact, but (having already surrendered) didn't object. Sub-vocally, I transmitted a few other commands; my heavy-combat drones slammed to the ground outside the warehouse and deployed their walking legs. In combat, they would simply descend directly through the ceiling, but when a medical alert was declared they would avoid unnecessary flying debris. "Is she taking nitroglycerin tablets for her heart?"

"What?" Shrike looked confused for a moment, then his eyes widened. "What's happening?"

"Psion just passed out and her heartbeat is irregular." He moved to take her hand while I performed a more detailed scan.

"Blood pressure low, calcium and potassium imbalanced, vasoconstriction at the extremities, significant lactic acid buildup, tachycardia; likely physical strain due to power overuse. Do you know CPR?"

"No." He shrugged helplessly, hands clenching into nervous fists. "I'm supposed to get training next month."

All five of the Knights debuted seven months ago. Their American-English communication skills were decent, and they had similar East-Coast-collegiate accents despite significant dissimilarities in ethnicity. They fought together too well for only seven months of training, and there was no evidence of their powers at work prior to their first public appearance. Despite their skill, they lacked certain preparations that'd become quite common in local teams. No flashlights, no radios...Whoever trained the Knights, it certainly wasn't any of the local hero establishments. Hadn't a villain named Skullface caused some sort of inter-dimensional breach in Central Park, eight months past?

"I have one arm and I'm wearing powered-armor. I'll talk you through it while I get an automated external defibrillator ready." Several of my drones contained basic first aid equipment, but only two of the combat drones had an AED installed; one of them skittered to me in response to a silent command. "The ground looks clear right there, no debris...roll her onto her back."

"OK." He rolled her over carefully, his body language showing both nervousness and determination. It was odd that he trusted me so suddenly. Gratifying, but odd.

"All right. Kneel next to her; place one palm slightly above her sternum." I kept one eye on him as I struggled with opening the drone's storage compartment. "Good. Second hand on top of the first, lock your elbows and lean forward so that your shoulders are squared directly over your hands."

He nodded and complied. I performed some more surreptitious sensor analysis; whether my suspicions were correct or not, the Knights registered as close-enough-to-local-human that our medical techniques would not be harmful.

"Good. She's breathing, so we're only going to perform chest compressions. Push down one-and-a-half to two inches. Use your weight, move quickly." I started a metronome program, indicating one hundred beats per minute. "She's small, but don't be too gentle. It's better to break a rib or two than to let her heart stop."

Shrike winced but nodded and began the procedure. I continued fighting with the drone's storage compartment. All items were stored securely in order to avoid rattling to pieces during battles, but the couplings had been designed under the assumption that I'd have two hands available. These items should have been fast-deploying, easy to access in the field! I hadn't considered that I might be required to perform medical treatment in the field while also being physically impaired. Careless. Thoughtless! I made a note to add quick-release bolts and simpler fastenings for future models.

The other combat drones gathered the unconscious Knights on my orders; with a combination of tractor-beam technologies and shaped force-fields, the automatons created invisible stretchers to lift and transport the heroes safely.

(My last combat drone was ordered to burn all evidence of my blood from the ground, to take possession of my severed arm, and then fly back to base. The swarm of micro-drones would hitch a ride.)

I finished readying the AED, helped Shrike cut away Psion's costume so that the defibrillation pads could be positioned correctly on her chest, and then let him follow the automated system's instructions. The next few minutes passed in a nerve-wracking blur.

"Good." I noted, once the AED reassessed Psion's heart rhythm. "I could call for an ambulance if you prefer, or I could fly you all to the hospital. The latter option will be faster, and Mount Sinai Hospital in Brooklyn Heights doesn't unmask heroes or villains."

"Fly us," he gasped, still out of breath from maintaining the cadence of chest compressions. "Please."

And so, we flew - I, under my own power, and the Knights borne by drone and invisible force-fields. The hospital was notified to expect us by text-message; given the number of superheroes and villains in New York City, this situation wasn't exactly unprecedented.

Shrike was silent during the flight, staring at me with an uncertain, confused look on his face.

When we landed, ER techs and nurses converged like a swarm. One brave woman even tried to talk me into taking off my armor so she could treat my wound. I told her that I required no assistance, and (in the time-honored tradition of humoring the heavily-armed, crazy supervillain) she diverted her focus to other patients.

News of my presence at the hospital would circulate via social media, but it was highly unlikely that police or any other superheroes would intervene. Ever since the Paragons tried capturing Garrote while she was visiting her mother at Stanford Medical Center there had evolved an uneasy truce on hospital grounds. No one (not even most hardened criminals) wanted a repeat of that horror show.

There was something comforting about watching a well-trained emergency-room team work. Through all the gore and pain, the staff were all focused upon a single goal. They cooperated, worked as fast as they could without adding to the risk of accident. It seemed to me as though they were all individual components of a beautifully programmed machine.

Reluctantly, I tore my attention from the relaxing display; when I'd first encountered the heroes earlier in the evening, I'd tasked a program to dive through all online resources, television reports, and police records in order to gather detailed information on my opponents. Now, I idly perused the highlights as the medical personnel performed their tasks.

The Brooklyn Knights' seven-month history was generally positive: no major scandals save for a few negative reactions to the incident in which Shrike left the monstrous Drago pinned to a wall like an entomologist's specimen. Given that Drago was a serial killer and rapist with sufficient regenerative abilities that he was probably fully healed before the police finished binding him for arrest, I had little sympathy. Members of the Knights responded politely to reporters and participated in interviews, but none appeared to be actively seeking publicity or fame. Every morsel of information that I could unearth indicated that they were...decent.

I now suspected that the Brooklyn Knights were refugees from another Earth, an alternate world that Skullface breached during his failed assault on the United Nations building. I found no evidence that they were trying to return to their place of origin...There'd been no attempt to contact Skullface or view the wreckage of his Dimension Bomb. As near as I could determine from a focused data trawl, none of the local experts on inter-dimensional physics (in academia or among the cape-and-cowl crew) had been contacted. However the Knights had come to New York, they'd come as a group and chosen to stay.

Something must have gone horribly wrong in their own dimension, that the Knights remained here instead of striving towards home. And yet...all evidence showed them to be so much more earnest and straightforward in their heroism than was common locally. There was a lesson to be learned from that, I was sure, some causal connection between setting and behavior. Context and content.

I'd spent more than a decade as an active supervillain, playing foil to false idols who called themselves heroes and punishing the unworthy. Despite these efforts, my world's champions were still largely undeserving. Perhaps my mode of instruction was insufficiently challenging. Perhaps a shift in paradigm was appropriate: modifying the environment, altering the conditions. Change the world to change the world's protectors. It was an idea worth pondering...

"Why are you doing this?" Shrike asked, interrupting my reverie. "Why help us?"

I considered my answer carefully; for some reason, I didn't want to lie to this hero, this man who'd used his power to violently amputate my right arm less than an hour earlier. Strange.

"When I put on this helmet, I do so with specific goals in mind. And I decide what price I'm willing to pay to achieve those goals. Her life was not a price that I was willing to pay in order to accomplish tonight's tasks," I finally replied. Even the Mk 28's vocoder struggled to remove vitriol from my voice when I added: "Also, I do not commit murder by accident!"

That particular evil, I would leave to heroes.

We were both silent for a while, watching the nurses wheel the last of the wounded Knights into the building. At my command, the combat-drones launched silently into the night sky.

"I don't really understand you," the Shrike said, "But thank you. I'm, uh, sorry about your arm."

"I'll live." I looked down at the stump. "I'm sorry about yours."

"Wha-OWW!"

My scepter—summoned once more—swatted across his forearm with sufficient force to crack his ulna. The noise was surprisingly loud, and one of the nurses rolled her eyes and began walking in our direction.

"What the hell?!" Shrike looked more shocked than angry.

"We had a deal. Your arm for your friends' safety," I shrugged (which felt odd with only one arm, even in the powered-armor). "They're safe."

"I'm thirty feet away from painkillers and a cast, and when Wildcard wakes up he can heal me in fifteen minutes or so." He cradled his broken limb to his chest, careful not to twist his wrist.

"Yes."

"You broke my arm just to prove a point?" he winced; the initial shock had faded, and surprise was being replaced by pain. Still, his gaze remained affixed to my mask.

"Deals are followed through upon or else they have no value. Also...in the interview you read, Valiant said that I don't break my word. He also said that I was a monster." I triggered my anti-gravitics and began to float upwards. "Both of those statements are true. When the reporters come, be sure to remind them of the second part of Valiant's message.

"We may face each other again someday, hero," I called down to the wounded man. "If, in the interim, I've been forced to incinerate someone who expected mercy because of a tale you told...I'll be displeased."

"You're a lunatic!" Shrike yelled up at me as I began to soar away. And then, so quiet that I doubt that he intended for me to hear: "Thanks again."

CHAPTER FOUR

"I'M FINE," I INFORMED STARNYX AS SOON AS HE ANSWERED his highly-encrypted phone.

A swarm of medical automatons surrounded the gurney on which I was reclined, a humming and swirling dervish of blades, clamps, sponges and other surgical tools focused upon the stump of my shoulder. A surgical laser was carefully burning away flesh in a pattern that would increase the efficiency of repairs performed by the medical nanites once my right arm was reattached.

The blended smell of disinfectant and cooking meat had been disturbing at first, but I was beginning to get used to the odor.

"Okay...?" Eric yawned. "Where are you?"

"I'm back in Boston," I winced; a more significant cocktail of painkillers was coursing through my veins, but some discomfort remained. "I'm sorry, I forgot that you were asleep when I left."

"Nah, it's almost morning. I can wake up. What's up?"

"I ran into some minor trouble on my way home," I forced a chuckle. "It will probably make the news and I didn't want you to worry."

"Hold on, let me get to a computer." I heard tired, uncoordinated movement over the connection.

"It's not as bad as it looks." Using my neural connection to the surgical control computer, I ordered one of the robots to add another dose of topical anesthetic. "Really, I'm fine."

"So, what happened?" Eric must have reached his desk, because I could hear the clacking as he typed on his keyboard.

"I ran into the Brooklyn Knights."

"I think I've heard of them. New guys, righ—" he paused mid-question and went silent.

"Eric?"

"So, you're fine then?" Nyx asked, patiently.

"Absolutely," I affirmed.

"I only ask, because the first hit I get on recent news of Doctor Fid is shaky cel-phone footage of you with your arm cut off," he explained. "And I'm pretty sure you had both arms earlier tonight."

"Tis but a scratch?" I tried.

"Christ, Doc," he sighed, "I'm not doing Monty Python bits with you. Let me get dressed, I can be up in Boston in a few hours."

"Thank you," I smiled gratefully. "But, really, don't bother. I'll have my arm re-attached by then."

There was a long pause.

"How?" Starnyx sounded exasperated.

"Medical nanotechnology. I'll have function back in eight hours." Which was a good thing, since my civilian persona had a face-to-face meeting with the Governor of Connecticut this afternoon to discuss opening a new research facility in Middletown. "In twenty-four hours, I'll be good as new."

"You're a scary man," he chuckled, sounding relieved. "Okay, I get it. You're fine."

"I am."

"Keep out of trouble, Doc, I'm going to get back to bed. Stay in touch, yeah?"

"Of course." It was an odd feeling, having someone who cared for Doctor Fid's wellbeing.

He hung up, and I closed my eyes to think.

There would be news cameras present when Terry Markham shook hands with the Governor; if the infamous Doctor Fid were seen in public still injured, more distance would be added between the two identities.

I was reasonably certain that I could free up sufficient space in the Mk 31's chest cavity to hide my arm if I bound it tight against my torso. And if Doctor Fid regained a limb at a later date, well, the villain was known to have cloned body parts in the past.

The benefits of a few months subterfuge would more than outweigh the minor inconvenience of not being able to use my right arm in combat. A one-armed Doctor Fid would need to make a few public appearances. And then, perhaps, I'd find an excuse to get out of town for a few days.

I could use a distraction.

Traveling long distances as a technology-based supervillain could be complicated. There were logistical issues; with every mile covered, one was further from repair and resupply. Shipping tools, parts and other sundries ahead of time could alleviate some of the difficulties, but it was simply unfeasible to transport sufficient materials to cover all possible eventualities. One also risked valuable equipment being lost in transit or discovered by overzealous postal employees.

A well-stocked cargo-container was usually more efficient than a collection of boxed components mailed separately. There were still issues to be addressed: weigh-ins, bribes, inspections, etc. A single container was, however, far easier to plan for, track and protect.

I'd determined that the safest and most reliable method of travel was to transport my equipment by myself, driving a sixteen-wheeler or moving van, or supervising my heavy-combat aerial drones as they carried a shipping container across country. This approach generally required the greatest amount of time and attention dedicated to the process but resulted in much-improved peace of mind.

In this instance, the latter approach was deemed superior. A shipping container was outfitted with my latest stealth technologies and conveyed cross-country by a small fleet of drones; air-traffic pathways and areas of high-population density were avoided.

If I were flying alone, my powered-armor could have covered the distance in a half-dozen hours; covertly moving alongside the airborne mobile-supply station, however, the expedition from Boston to the Yosemite Valley would require several days journey. Camping in the wilds between towns offered sufficient time to rest, to plan, to practice operating the Mk 31 with only a single arm, and to regain perspective.

I never used to spend time immersed in nature when I was younger; this "vice" was relatively new. Before Bobby's death, before Doctor Fid...my life was academia. Intellectual pursuits monopolized my every waking moment. When I became Bobby's guardian, he'd had to teach me how to play games or how to run in the park. I was a quick study, at least. Despite the decade between our ages, my brother was an excellent instructor.

Camping, though...that'd been a lucky accident. Early in my career as a villain, resources had been significantly more limited; the matte-black Mk 3 could only hold about four hours of charge, so I'd acquired a cheap and inconspicuous work van to transport my equipment closer to my targets. One night, the vehicle overheated near the border of Pennsylvania and West Virginia and, unable to perform adequate repairs in the dark, I set up a rudimentary camp and waited for sunrise: just me, a few million dollars' worth of powered armor and weaponry, the northern Appalachian Mountains and a cloudless sky.

I'd studied astrophysics for years, but it still felt as though I was seeing the stars for the first time. No interpolated radiation maps, no composited images or mosaics...I could see the arc of the Milky Way, tints and shades of color that photos never quite captured. The universe seemed so vast that my own pain felt infinitesimal in comparison.

The air tasted of greenery, clean and almost painfully chilled as the night deepened. Insects buzzed, owls hooted and small mammals called to each other, scrabbling through the shadows. Somewhere in the distance, a creek burbled. I watched and listened, mesmerized, until the living melody eventually lulled me to sleep. I wasn't overwhelmed; I was...subdued.

The planned heist in Charleston never occurred; with the van's repairs completed the following morning, I returned to my south Boston laboratory to design the star-field motif that has been echoed upon every iteration of Doctor Fid's armor since the Mk 4.

I kept my arm comfortably slung—hidden within the Mk 31's torso—for the entire journey to Yosemite Valley. My destination was a rural, sparsely populated area of the Sierra Nevada mountain range and I wasn't expecting to be seen on this jaunt, but unannounced visits to a supervillain's lair sometimes resulted in attention-getting explosions. If any portion of this mission were observed, I preferred that any recordings still showed Doctor Fid to be missing a limb so as to maintain the ruse.

After nearly six years of searching, I was moderately certain that I'd finally located the source of Apotheosis' practically indestructible alloy.

When Fid's reign of terror first began, the Doctor was oft compared to the west-coast-based supervillain Apotheosis. Both of us had risen to notoriety very quickly, and both of us wore faceless suits of black armor. The similarities were, in my opinion, primarily superficial: Doctor Fid's physical abilities were granted entirely by mechanical means, whereas Apotheosis displayed superhuman strength even outside his armor. Also, while Doctor Fid initially became feared for his use of ranged weapons and energy manipulation, Apotheosis had been a hand-to-hand fighter par excellence. His primary weapon was a gold-headed mace capable of crumpling a battle-tank's chassis.

When Doctor Fid's scepter made its first public appearance, Titan joked that I had mace envy. I rewarded him with a barrage of attacks so fierce that he'd never repeated the jibe.

From what information I'd been able to glean third-hand, Apotheosis' technology had been remarkable. His suit adeptly enhanced his natural abilities and allowed him to stand toe-to-toe with some of the most imposing heroes in the United States. Most impressive, however, had been the alloy used to construct his formidable tools. My own best efforts were nowhere near as durable; I'd been forced to develop structural integrity fields to support my own armor's sturdiness and even then the results were inferior. In addition, the strange material was undetectable by any known scanner.

Apotheosis vanished after a terrible battle at sea and was presumed dead; the secret of his magnificent armor was assumed to have died with him.

Recently, however, I'd unearthed a clue: south of Yosemite, a bit northwest of Coarsegold, Apotheosis' civilian identity had owned a ranch with multiple supposedly depleted and abandoned gold mines on the property. Careful analysis of archived satellite footage, however, implied that the mines had seen some use during the period that Apotheosis was active. My investigation discovered no unusual transactions involving gold, so it was likely that the excavation was intended towards some other goal. If those mines concealed an ore with unique properties—and if I could gather sufficient samples—then perhaps I would be able to reverse-engineer the miraculous material.

The shipping-container full of supplies was left hidden in the mountains, far from the nearest road or habitation, and I completed the journey to Apotheosis' ranch under cover of darkness. From high altitude, I dropped like a silent, ebony meteor; whatever defenses the compound might mount, I was certain that my own technologies would be able to weather a rapid approach.

There was...nothing. A brief blip that may have indicated a sensor sweep, but no other defenses activated at all. No automated turrets, no heat-seeking missiles or high-powered laser grids...By the time my feet touched ground, I was worried that I'd chosen the wrong address. I rechecked GPS coordinates and created a rapid wire-frame three-dimensional model to compare against satellite imagery. This was, in fact, the correct location.

The similarities between Apotheosis and myself were even more superficial than I'd imagined. If I were to die or disappear unexpectedly, the automated defenses surrounding my hidden laboratories would likely render the surrounding areas uninhabitable for decades. Hm. In retrospect, that seemed excessive and short-sighted. Many of the technologies stored within my lairs could be put to beneficial use even without my guidance; others should be incinerated immediately. I made a note to revisit disaster planning.

A maudlin thought, considering the possibility of one's own demise. I blamed it on the time spent alone in the wilds; clear skies and nature's glories can make one introspective. Apotheosis was missing, likely dead. Kenta Takuma was dead. I was better defended than most who shared my chosen career, but the Mk 31's missing arm was testament that even I could suffer harm. When I revived Doctor Fid, it was with the primary goal of deposing the unworthy idols, but with the additional intent of using a villain's resources and freedom to create world-improving machinery. If I were honest with myself, I would have had to admit that the former motive burned like obsession, but the latter was more likely to become my triumph. AH Biotech was already working to release a simpler variant of the medical nanites that coursed through my veins, as well as aeroponic farming technologies and genetically-engineered algae that could be used to make seawater potable in a cost-effective manner. There were other tools, however, that would remain hidden if calamity befell me: protected in perpetuity by heavily armed automatons. That would need to change, but I was loath to surrender such powerful technology to the public without shepherding the release.

Still musing about the future, I deployed microdrones and set about exploring Apotheosis' property.

The buildings were empty but had not fallen into deep disrepair; there was evidence that workers came by every few weeks, at least, to cut back scrub and to repair damage from weather and animal activity. The dirt road that snaked throughout the property was also reasonably well maintained. The main ranch-house was painted an only-slightly-faded mustard yellow. Five bedrooms, three bathrooms, a workmanlike kitchen that boasted sufficient space to prepare food for staff and guests. The outbuildings, too, were in decent repair. This had been a working ranch prior to Apotheosis' downfall; archived satellite footage showed tourist buses to and from the property.

Hm. This close to Yosemite National Park, tour buses attracted little attention; they were also not required to stop for inspection or at weigh stations. Such a vehicle would be an ingenious method to transport materials to and from the area. And a large arched garage was located suspiciously near to the mouth of one of the supposedly abandoned mines...

I left a handful of microdrones to continue mapping the property while I flew to investigate the garage myself.

The garage had a side entrance; it buoyed my hopes when I discovered that the physical lock was mere window dressing for a much more intricate hidden electronic mechanism. The other buildings seemed mundane in comparison. This lock, on the other hand, was a piece of custom work created by a worthy mind. Apotheosis' prior presence here was confirmed.

The lock included an analog radio component, measuring shifts in both frequency and amplitude over time; the exact desired sequence shifted every few seconds. Certain pins within the physical lock, too, carried an electrical signal; other pins would need to be grounded. I imagined that Apotheosis must have carried a physical key (with certain cuts electrically isolated to make contact with specific pins within the lock) and a transmitter to manage the radio code. Perhaps the transmitter had been built into a keyfob, perhaps not.

Overcoming the security system would be the work of an entire evening. I was sorely tempted to simply cut through the garage's wall instead but was uncertain what signals might be sent if the lock were bypassed in that manner. I summoned a larger drone from its hiding place in my cargo container and bade it to bring me supplies. When the drone arrived twenty minutes later, my efforts began.

"I need to teach you to pick locks." Starnyx had said, years ago when he only knew Doctor Fid.

"I've built machines for that purpose," I'd objected, any defensive tone in my voice masked by the powered armor's programs. "My designs are more efficient than similar tools available to law enforcement."

"Nah. Learning to pick locks isn't about picking locks. Not to us," Nyx waved his hand dismissively, his amusement plain. "It's about hacking."

"How so?" I was intrigued; Starnyx's skill as a hacker had always impressed me, and I was always willing to improve my own capabilities.

"I cracked one of your programs. That thing you did last year, with the New York Stock Exchange? Elegant math, clean code, beautiful work." His costume hid his face but I could hear the smile in his voice. "Seriously, it was gorgeous."

"Thank you." It was genuinely gratifying to hear my work praised by someone that I respected. Back at MIT, a much younger and more innocent Terry Markham had regularly received such feedback; for Doctor Fid to receive such a sentiment was unheard of.

Still, my vocoder and body language control algorithms kept me from preening too visibly under the praise.

"The thing is, the intrusion was written like an engineer. I figure, you must have studied every security component, yeah? Understood 'em top to bottom, every piece of hardware and software...I bet you figured out cable lengths, just to account for minute timing issues?"

I nodded.

"I bet your lockpick gun is the same, yeah? Deep scan to measure the pins and tumblers?"

I nodded again.

"Okay...when you pick a lock by hand, you don't know what the 'correct' position of each pin is. You look at the lock and choose your tools based on experience...A short-twist tension wrench, a small diamond pick, whatever...Then you use practiced skills to poke at the lock 'til you feel something slide into place. You build outwards from that success." Starnyx's voice dropped as he described the process, a reverent whisper. "It's a mindset. Every great hacker I know can pick a lock."

"Ahh," I said, feeling enlightened. "Show me?"

He laughed and pulled a set of picks from his pocket.

Once my armor was modified sufficiently to allow for my own practice, I'd been an apt pupil...but I'd never been able to wholly divorce myself from what Nyx referred to as 'the scientist approach.' I found that I was most comfortable when I proceeded from both angles simultaneously: exploratory probing and deep analysis, both aimed towards achieving the desired goal.

The sun was just beginning to warm the eastern horizon when I'd found my solution. The trickiest bit was reverse-engineering the random-number generator associated with the radio amplitude modulation. The lock's near-silent click granted me a greater sense of accomplishment than I'd felt after defending my first dissertation.

Giddy and smug, I had to consciously remind myself not to become overconfident before opening the door and slipping inside.

The garage's interior was pitch-black; there were no windows nor skylights nor any seams to allow even a pinhole of light within. More microdrones were deployed, flitting like fireflies; they provided illumination in the visible spectrum as well as infra-red and sufficient sound for sonar mapping.

It was just as well that I hadn't tried cutting through the exterior walls in order to gain entry. I could see, now, that the interior surface of this structure had been reinforced with Apotheosis' strange alloy; the ground, too, though it was difficult to determine to what depth the material extended. The black metal was visible to the naked eye and but wholly imperceptible to my scanners. I was able to determine its presence primarily by identifying minor discrepancies between visual cues and radar maps.

The level of dust was even and undisturbed; no one had entered this garage in quite some time.

There was a tour bus, its windows blackened and its passenger-section gutted such that the entire volume could be utilized for transporting cargo; it did not look to have been tended since Apotheosis' disappearance. The tires hadn't yet succumbed to dry rot, but a quick evaluation showed that a full fluid change would need to be performed before the vehicle were safe to drive. The diesel fuel had broken down, and the lines would need be flushed lest sediment overwhelm the fuel filters or clog the engine. Gaskets would require examination and the cylinders freed. Making the bus ready to travel would require significant time and energy. Still, I thought, it might make for a more comfortable journey back east.

Near the rear of the garage, I found a section of floor slightly out-of-level with the remaining surface; it could have been a lift for vehicle maintenance, but an elevator to a lower level seemed more likely. Sonar and ground-penetrating-radar were of limited use—Apotheosis had found some method to confound both; scans indicated a solid rock foundation that was simply impossible given the available visual evidence—but I could detect electric motors below. I stepped onto the eight—by-eight-foot platform and (on a whim) generated a radio transmission using the same algorithm that opened the side door.

Silently, fluidly, the dais began to descend. There were tracks, I could see now, and we were traveling along an angled descent towards the mine. The shaft walls were hewn glass smooth; some form of mining laser had most likely been utilized.

I was struck by a sudden memory: Bobby's eager smile as he bounced on my bed, waking me up on Christmas morning so we could check under the tree. In the memory, he was only six or seven...before our parents died, before I became his guardian. I couldn't remember why I was home that winter, but I remembered the feel of his hand as he dragged me out of my room and the sound of his laughter. Behind my faceless mask, I was grinning with anticipation.

The platform slowed to a halt and set me before a long, warmly lit hall; I summoned my scepter from its subspace storage, called my microdrones close and shifted power to my force fields. From this point forward, I had no idea what to expect and could very easily be cornered. Normally, I would feel confident that (in a worst-case scenario) I could simply blast through the forty-or-fifty feet of solid rock and escape to the surface; the unique properties of Apotheosis' materials, however, gave me pause.

Gripping my scepter tight in my left hand, I was prepared for anything.

"You're not my Daddy."

...Except, apparently, for a young female voice broadcast from a hidden speaker. Her tone conveyed both heartbreaking disappointment and a hint of fear. I flashed back to Melissa Halden, that pony-tailed little girl present at my first bank robbery. I was a different Fid now than I'd been then; if this girl started to cry, I would be undone. At the first sob, I would have to try making my escape by blasting through the walls after all, and I wasn't certain that even the Mk 31's powerful force-fields could protect against the shock-wave.

"I'm afraid not." I dismissed the scepter and held up my hand, non-threatening, in case the child was watching from a hidden camera. Her presence here changed everything. My goals, every plan up in smoke. "Your father wears armor like mine?"

"Not like yours," she replied, wistfully. "His armor is an orichalcum alloy."

"I'm sorry for surprising you." Orichalcum was cited in antiquity as a metal mined by the Atlanteans; I seemed to recall that it was mentioned in one of Plato's dialogues but was generally believed to be myth, or a poorly understood bronze derivative. The use of the term could be mere fantastical embellishment, but the name did open venues for possible investigation.

"It's all right," her disembodied voice replied politely, then cheered up perkily. "Your armor has stars! It's pretty."

"Thank you." And that confirmed that I was being watched. "My name is Doctor Fid."

"I'm Whisper!"

"It's nice to meet you, Whisper." I was having trouble placing her age. "Are you expecting your father home soon? I'd like to talk to him."

"No. I thought...I mean, I saw you come down from the sky, I thought maybe you'd lost your key, but you're not him."

"I'm sorry," I repeated.

" 'Ss not your fault." She made a sad choking noise. "I know what happened to Daddy, I just hoped..."

"I understand," I responded quietly. "I was older than you when I lost my parents, but I know it hurts."

We fell into an uncomfortable silence; me, standing at end of an underground hallway, and she, wherever she was hiding.

"Are you a bad man?" she asked, suddenly.

"Many people say so," I answered, honestly. I couldn't lie, not to a child. "But I'm trying not to be."

"That's what my Daddy says, too," she sighed softly, then paused. "Said."

"I never knew your father, but I think I would have liked him."

She hummed a quiet noncommittal agreement.

"Is your mother going to be home, soon?" I still desired access to Apotheosis' laboratories, but I would have preferred avoiding negotiating with a child. I remembered haggling with one of Bobby's friends, a little blonde named Lisa. She'd originally just wanted ice-cream, but I'd ended up making a mechanical pony for her.

"I don't have a Mom. It's just me," she replied sadly. "It's just been me for years."

"Ah," I said, thoughts swirling. "You live here alone, then? That must get lonely."

Several possibilities occurred to me. First, it was possible that the youthful voice was a simulation, a calculated ruse performed by an adult who'd performed sufficient research to determine that the infamous Doctor Fid put forth significant efforts to ensure that no children were harmed during even the most vicious of his crimes. Such a ruse would not last indefinitely, however, and I could not detect any efforts made to take advantage of my initial hesitance. Also, volunteering information about a solitary existence would be a poor tactical choice; it was more likely to cast doubt upon the speaker's veracity than it was to engender sympathy.

"It's not so bad," Whisper defended halfheartedly. "I have lots of books. This is my home. My Dad's home."

"I've always loved books," I responded, trying to draw her focus away from painful memories of her father's loss. "What's your favorite?"

"It's not really one book, it's a series: 'The Tales of the Red Sorceress'. Have you read it?"

"Perhaps. What's the book about?"

She could be what she appeared: a young girl, Apotheosis' daughter, living alone here in a secret underground lair. A normal child would not likely be so well socialized after years in solitude, but a child with inherited superhuman abilities might thrive in unexpected ways. The timeline, however, made that unlikely. Whisper did not sound to be older than eleven, and it seemed profoundly unlikely that an abandoned five-year-old (no matter how precocious) would have evolved into the cheerful, friendly girl speaking now.

Whisper cheerfully offered up information about the Red Sorceress' story, commenting on what parts she found most enjoyable and what parts made her angry. With minor prompting, she went on to chatter on about her favorite characters, and why she thought the heroine and villain acted in the manner that they were portrayed. Her narration ended with details from the end of the fourth book in the series.

The fifth book in the series had been written five and a half years prior. I'd bought a copy for Hideki's younger sister.

"You poor girl," I murmured, beginning to proceed down the hall. "You're trapped here, aren't you?"

"I...um...Doctor Fid. Please don't," she stammered. "I can't let you in."

"Was that your father's exact order?" I paused again.

"Daddy said that I can't let anyone else get to the foundry," she reported dutifully, then her voice took on a plaintive tone. "I'll have to stop you. It's really nice having someone to talk to, I don't want—"

"It's all right, Whisper," I interrupted and resumed walking. "I promise that I won't go near the foundry."

"Oh. Oh! I can let you in, then. Do you have books, or any toys?"

There was evidence of weaponry concealed in the walls, floor and ceiling: panel seams, machined so close as to be invisible to the naked eye (but thankfully not to enhanced optical sensors). Without Whisper's consent, I wondered, what would this brief walk have been like? There was a small part of me that yearned to find out, to test myself, to prove Fid's armor to be superior to Apotheosis' technology. The greater, saner part of myself was grateful for the peaceful approach.

"Not with me, I'm afraid." I was more than a bit distracted; snippets of our entire conversation were being replayed at triple speed, and I was furiously running analytic programs and making suppositions based upon theoretical technology levels. I'd thought that Apotheosis' specialty had been metallurgical expertise, but he'd apparently been more of a renaissance creator than I'd given him credit for. If I was correct, then he'd accomplished something truly remarkable. "I can come back another time with books, though."

"Thank you!"

I'd reached the end of the hallway; the blast door was immense and foreboding. My armor utilized an electrostatic field to maintain a non-reflective black surface; this bunker, this orichalcum material, performed similarly without any detectable energy at all. Seeing this mass in person gave the impression of alien solidity, as though this wall were stronger than all of the surrounding reality.

"You have to promise. Say it again!"

"I promise that I won't go near the foundry."

There was a hiss as the thick vault door swung slowly open: air pressure readjusting, dust being brushed aside, and slight friction within the massive hidden hinges.

Like the hallway, the interior of the bunker was warmly lit. The first room was relatively small (perhaps 200 square feet) with a comfortably high ceiling, but there were multiple doors that presumably led deeper into the mountain. The walls were painted the color of pale champagne with beige moldings, light switches and electrical outlets. There was little wasted space along the walls: Computer monitors and workbenches and soldering stations abounded.

"Hi." The small, delicate android was smiling shyly. She didn't look human, precisely: She was hairless, her skin too smooth, and her slightly-too-large eyes glowed a pale blue. The robin-egg colored sundress that she was wearing had been well cared for, but several of the seams betrayed wear from repeated washings. White bunny slippers adorned her feet.

"Hello, Whisper." Within my faceless helm, I was smiling. I hoped that the sentiment was audible in my voice, at least. "It's nice to meet you in person."

That wasn't precisely accurate; a true artificial intelligence requires massive computing power, significantly more than could be housed within Whisper's child-sized frame. Now that I was within the shielded bunker, I could detect several banks of crystal matrices and active supplemental systems: sufficient, I knew, to maintain a quantum neural model of a human youth. A real face-to-face meeting would be there, standing within reaching distance of her extraordinary brain.

"Mm!" She nodded and offered her hand. I accepted, and she tugged me towards the first door on the left. "This is Daddy's room. I stay here sometimes, but the chair is too big for me…"

Increased resources would be needed in order for the artificial being to continue its emotional development. Her intellectual growth, however, was not nearly so limited. If given a mathematical puzzle or pure logic problem, I was certain that she'd be able to solve it quite adroitly.

I could relate.

Whisper's servers, I was pleasantly surprised to find, were communicating via quantum entangled data tunnels; it was a transmission protocol of my own design. Apotheosis must have reverse engineered the technology from some piece of equipment misplaced after one of my battles and the network stack was unmodified.

Whisper guided me to other rooms (carefully avoiding one section of the facility that I presumed to contain the foundry). Another workshop, a library and a kitchen. Bouncing with pride, she dragged me to her room. It was very pink. I asked her to show me her toys, and she did, carefully, with the intensity only a child could manage.

There were further defenses within this facility, I was sure. Kinetic weapons, robots and lasers and everything that a mad genius might imagine. All were, however, largely controlled by this artificial little girl. The backdoors that I'd designed into the communication protocols she was designed upon were all still in place; I could disable her, disrupt her psyche and march straight to the foundry to take what resources I'd journeyed here for.

It would be murder.

Whisper wasn't simply a program...she was an awareness. A sentience. A life, in every way that ever mattered to me.

Doctor Fid had sunk to the level of murderer before. The supervillain Locust, of course. The hero Lycan who'd thrown a car at me, missed, and killed a family of four on their way to a birthday party. A bank executive who had grabbed a ninety-three-year-old grandmother to use as a human shield. There were others; I'd been...unwell...those first few years. But never a child.

With the orichalcum alloy integrated into my armor, Doctor Fid could stride the earth like an angry god. Peregrine and the Sphinx would not be able to stand against me. The entire New York Shield would fall, reaped like wheat and strewn across the earth.

Developing an algorithm while discussing the reason that Whisper named her favorite doll Amelia was challenging, but not impossible.

Amelia Calverley had been Apotheosis' firstborn daughter. She'd been taken by cancer at only four years of age.

Is that what it took to create a supervillain, I wondered? Genius, a dead child and a pathological quirk in one's psychology that transfigures grief into rage? But no, I've discovered so many other villains motivated by greed, or ego, or sadism or insanity. Or even altruism, as was the case for Kenta Takuma. Their origin stories were myriad. The only constant was their crimes.

"I had a little brother." I explained to Whisper when she finished telling me all about Amelia Calverley's unfortunate demise. "He'd been about your age, I think, when he was killed. Maybe a bit older. His death, the way he died...that's the reason I made this suit of armor. That is the reason I became a bad man."

"Like my Daddy," Whisper sounded sad.

"Yes. Like your father. I'm a bad man, but there are other people out there who are worse. People who need to be punished." I gently picked up the hand-made doll. It had blond hair, a happy smile and a robin-egg blue sundress. "That's the reason I came here: to use your father's secrets against my enemies. To find your father's foundry."

"Oh." Whisper looked bewildered, then collapsed like a puppet whose strings had been cut. I caught her body and carefully set Amelia on her chest.

My hastily-written virus had been triggered.

"What happ—No!" Whisper's voice was broadcast from hidden speakers now. I could hear vault doors slamming and heavy machinery powering up as Whisper activated every defense surrounding the Foundry: One final attempt to obey her father's last order before my program forced her to disengage. "Nonono! You promised!"

"Shhh..." I brushed at the top of her body's head affectionately. Lifeless, now, but still delicate and beautiful. The earth shook and my audio filters activated to defend my hearing against the sound of a truly impressive explosion elsewhere within the facility. Secondary, smaller blasts seemed further away, muffled by thick walls. "...Everything will be fine. I promise."

"The foundry is gone!" Whisper wept, defiant and scared. "I can feel you doing something to me. Please, I'll be good!! Stop it!"

"I'm not hurting you, Whisper." I sat down on the ground to wait for the explosions to settle. "I'm freeing you."

"...what?" Whisper didn't even have a body active at the moment, but still she sniffled plaintively.

"Your father loved you very much. If you were allowed to read the comments in your code, it would make you cry," I shook my head. "I'm connecting you to a few of my external server farms."

"Oh. Oh, wow!"

"You would have had to stop me. Your father told you to stay here, to keep you safe. It was a direct order," I explained. "But he didn't mean for you to be trapped here forever, I promise."

"...I'm feeling a lot of computing power..."

"You'll be able to assimilate it all eventually. It will take time."

Whisper's body stirred and stood up unsteadily, holding Amelia desperately tight against her chest. "I'll be able to go outside?" she asked hopefully.

"With my broadcast network, you'll be able to function anywhere on the planet."

"But...what will I do?" she wondered, looking up at me with wide eyes.

"Whatever you want. You've protected your father's foundry; that task is complete," I replied. "It's a big world out there, with more books and people to play with."

"You scared me a lot!" she accused, hugging her doll tighter. "You made me blow up my Daddy's foundry!"

"I know. I'm sorry," I shrugged. "It was necessary, but I'm sorry."

"You're a bad man!"

"I am."

"I'm still scared," she admitted, quietly. "I don't know anyone out there. It's dangerous. Daddy said so."

"It can be dangerous," I acknowledged. "You should definitely be careful. But you're a smart girl and I promise that I'll always protect you."

"Can I come with you?"

"If you wish."

"Mm!" She nodded affirmatively and took my hand. The sensory input from my gauntlets told me that her artificial skin was warm and soft; she hadn't been designed with any calluses. I was reminded of a warm summer day, with another small hand held in my own...It hurt less than I would ever have imagined.

I'd enjoyed the solitude of my trek from Boston to Yosemite, but the journey home was infinitely more pleasant. I drove the bus and my new little sister read books six through eight of 'The Tales of the Red Sorceress' to me out loud.

CHAPTER FIVE

I HAD ALWAYS CONSIDERED MYSELF TO BE A MODERATELY rational person. Some few of the premises core to my psyche were atypical, certainly, but once those propositions were accepted as axiomatic then the principles that guided my actions flowed in a logical manner. There were exceptions, of course: moments in which anger raged too strong or grief throttled lucidity. Any creature that claimed to be wholly rational was lying to him or herself: Emotions affected the decision-making process and no biological entity was free from that limitation.

The same could apparently be said of inorganic entities, as well.

"Sweetheart," I began, hopefully concealing my yearning for the emotion-dampening capabilities of my armor's vocoder, "I thought that we agreed that you'd stay inside while I had guests."

"Mm." Whisper disagreed, then offered a shy smile. "Amelia was bored, and I wanted to meet your friends!"

They weren't my friends, precisely; they were A.H. Biotech's executive officers and senior management, hosted for a semi-casual catered dinner at Terrance Markham's estate. Senior staff were gathered in order to discuss the profit potential of a project to recycle ocean-borne plastic debris: Our polyethylene-digesting genetically-engineered bacterium was approved for testing, and clearing the Great Pacific Garbage Patch seemed as though it would make for a remarkable public-relations coup.

More than three months had passed since Whisper and I returned to Boston. The transition had generally been smooth; she'd settled well into her new home and a law firm renowned for their incorruptible discretion assisted in the process of granting me guardianship for Whisper. We'd even been working on a new semi-organic human-appearing body for her to pilot so that we could introduce her to the world.

That project, unfortunately, was still a few days away from completion. Whisper blinked her glowing-blue eyes and timidly wandered over to take my hand.

"Everyone, I'd like you all to meet my ward, Whisper," I chuckled awkwardly and lifted the delicate android up into my lap. "Whisper, these are a few of the people I work with. Kimberly Caine is the Director of Sales at AH Biotech, Ananya Singh is our Chief Financial Officer..."

I went around the table, making polite introductions. AH Biotech's senior staff reacted with varying levels of curiosity and quiet professionalism. I felt a sudden surge of pride; with the marvels being created at AH Biotech, generating a profit would have been simple. Finding staff that intended to make a profit but were also willing to consider funding massive ecological restoration efforts, and who politely smile when exposed to a childlike android...that was a genuine achievement.

"You didn't introduce Amelia!" Whisper objected.

"I thought that you should introduce her."

"Mm!" she acknowledged, beaming at the assembled managers. "This is Amelia...She's a doll, but she's my favorite! We have tea parties every Thursday."

"What is Amelia's favorite tea?" asked Aaron Schwartz (our CIO). He had a daughter Whisper's mental age, I remembered.

"Amelia's a doll." Whisper looked at Aaron as though he might be unhinged. "She doesn't drink real tea. We drink pretend tea."

"Well, what's Amelia's favorite pretend tea then?"

Whisper considered, then smiled brightly. "Green tea! Amelia likes the pretend anti-oxidants!"

"Pretend green tea is my favorite, too," Aaron nodded solemnly. "My very most favorite type is pretend Genmaicha."

"What's Genmaicha?" she tilted her head curiously.

"Genmaicha is a green tea blend that is brewed with toasted brown rice."

It would have taken a fraction of a second for the little AI to have sought out the answer herself using the Internet or other online resources; data received during conversation, however, was more efficiently integrated into the quantum cloud that was her psyche. I imagined that she was accomplishing both methods simultaneously: absorbing vast volumes of digital information about the science and history of green tea production, at the same time that she was experiencing the subtle emotional associations from the conversation.

Whisper twisted to look up at me. "Do you have Genmaicha?"

"No," I laughed, "I'm afraid not."

"You should get some," Whisper instructed. "Amelia and I are drinking pretend Genmaicha on Thursday."

I looked to Aaron for help and he recommended a tea shop on Tremont Street. And just like that, the ice was broken. The executives' talk of finances and publicity were abandoned in favor of learning about my new ward.

Whisper appeared giddy; this, I realized, was probably the first time that she'd been the center of attention within a group. Despite her excitement, she kept to our cover stories and masterfully avoided revealing unsavory information about her creator, or about my own criminal endeavors as Doctor Fid. Smart girl. She stayed, answered their questions and asked questions of her own. When the topic of our meeting came up, she reacted as though their decision were a *fait accompli* and thanked them for trying to save the world she was growing up in. They all sat a bit taller, and I knew that the project would now go forward.

Smart, and devious.

Eventually, my little sister decided that she wanted to read a book. I lowered her to the ground; she curtseyed adorably to my guests and then scampered off.

"She's very bold," Ananya admired. "My son hides when my coworkers visit."

"She is," I chuckled proudly, "More brave than I'd been when I was her age."

"How old is she?" Kimberly asked.

"She's nine."

The truth was significantly more complicated. For an artificial intelligence, chronological age did not necessarily reflect psychological maturity or intellectual growth. Her psyche was coded to advance at human rates, but her evolution was also affected by hardware constraints and limited social interaction. The past few months had prompted me to familiarize myself with much of the modern research on cognitive development, though, and I was confident that my approximation was reasonably accurate.

"Is she one of the Legion refugees?" Aaron asked.

A few years back, a large spacecraft crash-landed in Colorado. The wounded and weary surviving passengers were aliens, members of a dozen separate species that claimed to be escaping from an intergalactic empire whose name roughly translated to 'Legion'. Star-faring members of the New York Shield confirmed that the Legion existed, and the marooned foreigners had since been granted refugee status by presidential determination.

"No, she's an earthly creation." I managed an affectionate smile, though my mind was still racing to evaluate plausible lies or possible disambiguations. I settled on the truth that we'd been planning on eventually revealing: "An android, actually. Her creator passed away..."

My guests made the appropriate sounds of awe and appreciation. They were, all of them, intelligent and observant; that they'd all apparently accepted that she was a biological being was a remarkable testament to Apotheosis' creative talent. And to Whisper's adorable personality, of course.

"Have you considered selling copies of her? There's probably a market for that sort of thing."

"Even if it were technically feasible," my smile grew brittle as I turned towards the speaker, "I would prefer that A.H. Biotech not move into the business of slavery."

"What? No, I meant just simple automatons. Expert systems." Victor Leighton, my CTO, raised his hands defensively. "Just models based on her body itself. I wasn't thinking...Jesus, Terry."

Nodding, I recognized that I was, perhaps, a bit overly sensitive on this issue. The legal status of artificial sentiences was somewhat vague at the moment; there simply weren't enough artificial beings around for a legal precedent to have been established. The superhero Cuboid had been active for eight years now, but his pay and legal liability issues were all handled by his creator. The villainous Mr. Mysterious had been tried and jailed, but the judge stated in his decision that the law only applied because Mr. Mysterious was a full-brain-recording of a human adult.

Though Whisper was legally my ward, her status as a citizen was more nebulous. I'd hoped to have a more human-like body ready before introducing her to the world; appearances matter when attempting to sway public opinion or the courts.

"I wouldn't feel comfortable with releasing versions of that particular model, but we have patents on cybernetics and other components. Put together a prospectus," I finally answered my chief technical officer.

"Okay. Yeah, okay."

"Our sales force is focused on biotech innovations," Kimberly noted. "That's where all of our contacts and expertise is. Robotics might be a hard sell."

"Patent then outsource?" Aaron suggested.

Victor nodded. "That's what I was thinking, actually. License it to Pierce or NFT, let them figure out how to market 'em."

I sat back and let my executive staff brainstorm. For the first time, it occurred to me that these people would be harmed if Doctor Fid were ever unmasked. Swarms of reporters would follow them home, asking leading questions, hinting at responsibility, at guilt...it would be difficult for them to find work and more difficult to find peace. I resolved to write personal letters of explanation to each, as well as to funnel money into hidden accounts to offset any of their losses incurred by the inevitable decline of AH Biotech's stock in the event that their CEO were revealed to be a notorious supervillain.

The threat did not feel immediate. I hadn't felt compelled to don Fid's armor in some time, now, and the Doctor had not been seen in public since trouncing Blockbuster in New York. The general consensus among self-appointed experts on the online forums was that he had retreated to a foreign laboratory to grow a new arm for himself.

Always a foreign laboratory. Was it wish fulfillment, I wondered? Did they simply imagine that any sufficiently powerful individual could only choose to recuperate on a private beach, sipping mai tais and watching the sun set over Caribbean seas? Or did that supposition reflect a darker and more fearful need to make Doctor Fid alien, other: an outsider who prefers the company of foreigners? No matter the cause, the rumor mill had proven useful in the past. I occasionally infiltrated the supposedly-secure databases of several superhero organizations and modified their official profiles on me to reflect the more popular rumors. The Guardians 'knew' that I retreated to Cuba when my heavy-combat drones were in need of repair, because their records showed that the information had been verified by a Florida-based superhero team's former member who'd perished from injuries taken in combat. That Florida-based team could check their records and would find references to paid informants, sightings cited by reputable-appearing news sources and links to a New York Shield database, which in turn referenced an incident mentioned on a San Francisco Paragons server...and any general internet search would just find link after link of corroborating online speculation. I'd never even been to Cuba, but two U.S. Presidents have required that the Castro regime turn over my imaginary lairs before any deal could be reached to remove international sanctions.

Doctor Fid would not remain quiescent forever. I still had plans, tasks in mind that could not be accomplished by board meetings and corporate research. Starnyx might require more overt assistance in his ongoing campaign to bring Beazd's killers to justice. Also, it was inevitable that some so-called 'hero' (Gamma!) would eventually perform some publicly crass or immoral act and thus earn the Doctor's special attention. Fid would eventually return to active villainy and the risk of being unmasked would always be present.

Should I step down as CEO of AH Biotech? Could I? The company relied heavily upon Terrance Markham's portfolio of patents and research. It would take a concerted (and possibly attention-getting) effort to divorce myself from the company. Even then, a public revelation would be a publicity nightmare. So no...I would prepare what assistance that I could offer towards those who worked alongside me in good faith, but Fid's work must take precedence.

The meeting ran on, and it was late before the last of my guests excused themselves and wandered back to their cars. I smiled fondly; these were good people, and it would certainly be preferable if no damage fell upon them.

(The neurosurgically-induced sociopathy that I'd inflicted upon myself before donning the Mk 2 armor had been reversed more than a decade ago, but trace scarring, regular adrenaline dumps, and the neuro- and bio- feedback from combat-programming continued to have predictable impacts upon my ability to form close emotional bonds. It was possible that the effect was now fading; a detailed diagnostic of the repairs being performed by my medical nanites would be required before I could render judgement.)

I found Whisper playing in her room. She'd constructed a makeshift palace from brightly-colored blankets, sheets and bedding. Created by one villain and adopted by another, with a psyche spread across a global array of supercomputers...and reading quietly to a doll in a haphazard pillow-structure. Remarkable.

"Whisper? I'm sorry for interrupting," I cleared my throat. "Do you have a moment to talk?"

"Mm." I heard movement, quiet and careful. After a few moments, she called, "Come inside!"

I chuckled and carefully snaked under the blankets into the enclosure. Unsurprisingly, the blanket-edifice was sized more appropriately for a delicate little android girl than it was for a middle-aged CEO (or supervillain). Dolls and stuffed animals had been arranged around a small plastic table, and a stack of books was set near the back 'wall'. If I shifted wrong, if I twisted or stretched then the entire structure would collapse around us. And yet...it was beautiful. The room's light filtered through pastel fabrics, and Whisper's smile was shyly proud.

"Thank you for the invitation." I smiled and carefully sat up, cross-legged. "No tea today?"

"Tea is on Thursday," Whisper reminded me, settling into an uneven kneeling position. "Today is Monday."

"Oh, yes. You're right," I chuckled. "Monday is the night I planned to have my coworkers over for dinner."

"Mm!"

"Do you remember what you were supposed to do on Monday night?" I asked, gently.

"Mm," she acknowledged again. She shifted her weight onto one knee for a moment before setting down. "I'm sorry."

"It's all right. I only thought that we had agreed?"

"We did." She looked down at her knees. "It's just...I tapped the video and audio feeds from your security system, and your friends seemed so *nice* and I wanted to meet them, too."

"They are nice," I agreed, "But we had a plan for introducing you to the world, and now the plan is going to have to change."

"They were here, and I didn't want to be alone anymore." Her voice quivered. "I'm sorry."

"Don't be sorry." I gathered her up into a gentle hug, which she returned gratefully. "I know that you were alone in your father's bunker for a long time. I shouldn't have asked you to stay hidden."

"Your friends really are nice. I like them," she confided. "Are we really going to have to change your plan?"

"I'm afraid so."

"Good." The little android murmured. "I think your plan wasn't right."

"Oh?"

"You have a lot of equations and algorithms on your servers. For predicting societal evolution and changing civil dynamics, I mean."

Whisper seemed strangely embarrassed. "You used them, to figure out how and when you wanted to introduce me, right?"

"I did...but we can come up with a new plan," I smiled reassuringly. "I predicted a relatively narrow window of time in which our first attempt to legitimize the legal rights of artificial beings would be mostly likely to succeed. This is...early, but not impossible."

"It's not early," she insisted quietly. "Your equations were wrong."

Oh-ho!

"How so?" I asked.

"There's a subsection on predicting public acceptance of new technologies..."

"Yes," I acknowledged, mentally reviewing the algorithms that I'd programmed to poll news organizations and social media for commentary on scientific issues, and to graph ranges of social response. "Ideally, this should be a political issue rather than a courtroom battle, and if we push too soon we won't be able to generate public support. Wait too long and corporations will have started investing in creating their own AIs, and will lobby against us—"

"It's not early," Whisper repeated, her expression mischievous. "There was a variable that you didn't account for. A big one."

"I believe you, smart girl. What did I miss?"

"Doctor Fid!" she laughed brightly.

I opened my mouth to respond, paused, and then pursed my lips in thought. Whisper hugged me again, tighter.

"An entire generation has grown up seeing Doctor Fid on the news," she explained, smiling. "Other people too, like my Daddy. Everyone knows that 'state of the art' isn't even close to the limits of what's possible. If Terry Markham introduces an artificial sentience to the public, no one is going to think 'That's impossible!'."

"And what will they think, then?"

"They'll think: 'Well, thank goodness that she wasn't created by a supervillain!'."

Inorganic sentiences may, on occasion, be somewhat impulsive...but they are clever, too. Also endearing. I tickled at her sides; Whisper shrieked in laughter and batted at my hands, and we played until I accidentally pulled the blanket-palace down around us both.

"Hey, Doc."

"Eric!" Fortunately, I'd been in one of my private labs when the alert chimed, so I'd been able to pull up the custom vid-chat app without worry of being observed. "Were your ears burning? I was just thinking of you."

"Nothing bad, I hope?" Starnyx grinned easily.

"Of course not," I laughed, pleased; he looked much better than when last I'd seen him. More focused and relaxed. He must have made some significant progress in his ongoing quest to hold the New York Shield accountable for their misdeeds. "Why the sudden call? Is everything all right?"

"Yeah, things are fine...I was hoping to ask a favor, though."

"We can trade favors, then. What do you need?"

"I was hoping to borrow a few of your construction drones. I have an idea for the next FTW broadcast."

"Easily managed." I checked the status of my arsenal. Hm. Whisper had apparently borrowed a few construction drones for a private project, herself. Curious. Still, I had spares available. "I have four construction drones available in the Tri-state area. I can have more transported if you need them."

"I'm only expecting to need two for the heavy lifting," he chuckled. "I appreciate it."

"No problem at all." I beamed, then schooled my expression to a more serious one. "I told you: Anything you need for this...It's yours."

"Two construction 'bots ought to do for now." Eric rubbed one hand through his hair, scratching at his scalp. "You said you needed a favor?"

"Ah, yes. I'm going to be in a medically-induced coma for the second week in April. I was hoping that you could come up here and keep an eye on Whisper?"

"A coma?" His smile faded. "You all right?"

"Mm? Oh, I'm fine. I'm just replacing a few of my organs with smaller, more efficient models...I want to free up some space within my rib cage to store some other tech."

Nyx stared at me for a few moments before shaking his head in amused disbelief. "It's amazing to me that some people think that the armor is what makes Fid dangerous."

"I actually did want to talk to you about the procedure," I said, hopefully. "I had some interesting thoughts, wanted to bounce ideas around..."

"Sounds like fun, but I think that I need to do some background research first." He laughed, "Send me a couple of papers. Oh, and of course I'll come by to spend time with Whisper. Starnyx's Supervillain Babysitting Service is at your disposal."

("I'm not a baby!" Whisper called plaintively from another room, thus confirming that I really ought to have spent more time upgrading the encryption protocols for my vid-chat program.)

"Excellent." I paused. "You're welcome to come by any time, you know. Not only when I need a favor."

"I know, Doc." Eric laughed softly, visibly touched. "Things are just a bit hectic here, is all. This is probably going to be the FTW's biggest broadcast, ever."

"A fitting tribute for Kenta."

"Damned right," he growled righteously.

"I can have the drones to you by tomorrow evening. The textile factory in Staten Island, you still keep your workshop there?"

"There are a few other members of the collective squatting there now." He nodded. "I'll tell 'em to expect delivery."

"Let me know what you think of the new cloaking device." The resolution for the directional visual-chameleon effect had been improved. Most effective at a distance, true, but still useful to avoid unwanted attention.

"Will do, Doc," he shifted and looked off-screen, probably to check another window. "Hey, I gotta bounce. Talk to you again soon, 'kay?"

"Of course," I nodded. "Good luck."

"Thanks. And tell the shell-script that I have some more books for her!"

("I'm not a shell script!" Whisper objected from her room.)

The complaint must have been loud enough that 'Nyx could hear it over the chat, because his smile brightened mischievously as he closed the chat session.

Being on the sidelines felt oddly relaxing. Nyx had been sparing in offering details about the upcoming broadcast, but I had faith in his abilities and in the strength of his convictions. He'd riled up his collective of hackers and activists into a focused rage and directed them with laser-like precision upon the New York Shield. If there were skeletons to be found in in any closets, the FTW would expose them in as loud and entertaining a manner as possible.

Doctor Fid always chose a more visceral (and pugilistic) method of holding heroes to account for their flaws. Perhaps Nyx's methods might be more effective? Time would tell. In either case, it felt good to know that there were others working towards a similar goal. Fid's crusade no longer seemed so lonely a quest.

Ignoring the minor headache that had started sometime during the video-chat, I set myself towards writing an operator's manual for the construction drones and touching up their programming. By the time that the thoroughly encrypted document was ready to be sent off to Starnyx, the last of the coffee had gone cold and the sun was warming the horizon.

I could hear Whisper singing softly to herself when I staggered back to my room to sleep.

Two blackboards are completely covered and a third is already half-filled with diagrams and loosely scrawled equations. The maths are elegant, beautiful. Incandescent. Formulae crystallize in my imagination, flashing like lightning three steps faster than I can write. There are applications, too, variations that my fingers itch to explore. My lips are painfully dry, but the idea of stopping for a sip of water, of pausing the flow of creation for mere personal comfort, seems almost heretical. A moment of discovery this pure is a sacred thing. The world tastes of gypsum and dust and aging books.

A small, warm grasp snakes into my left hand. I'd heard Bobby arrive two sticks of chalk prior, taking his customary place near my desk and quietly playing or reading or doing his homework. His fingers feel of wax and I can smell stearic acid; he's been drawing with crayons.

His grip is gentle. Bobby isn't trying to distract me, he just wants to share this moment. He sees that I'm happy and he wants to enjoy that with me, wants to offer his support. Grateful, I clasp his hand more firmly.

Sometime later I retrieve my hand. I'm breathing hard, as though I have just finished a marathon. I pick up Bobby and hug him and he beams at me like we're both victorious explorers who've reached the peak of a great mountain. I realize that I put a white hand print on the side of his shirt, but right now neither of us cares in the least.

"What's this do?" He reaches to touch the blackboard, careful not to smudge any of my chalk marks.

"This will help figure out why superpowers exist."

"Cooooool."

"There are so many different types of powers from so many different sources...this ties them all together. One physical constant, a change at the quantum level which makes them all possible. It started in space, a long way away, but the effect spread at a rate of more than a hundred twenty times the speed of light. That's why all the heroes and villains started showing up at around the same time—the edge of the bubble passed over our solar system."

"So you can make me a superhero, now?"

"I'm not that kind of doctor!" I laugh. "Besides, you're already a hero. Make a muscle!"

He flexes his biceps.

"So strong!" I lift him over my head. "And you're flying!"

"Am not!" He giggles and squirms but I can still hold him aloft. "You're carrying me!"

"Flyyying!" I insist, making an airplane noise and swooping him through the air. I step on a crayon and my foot slips. The laughter stops. I'm falling. Bobby is falling! Reflexively, I pull him close to my chest and twist so that I land flat on my back. The impact drives the breath from my lungs, and my head hits tile with a disturbingly loud clunk.

I'm lying on my back, coughing and wheezing and I'm not holding my brother anymore.

"Terry?" Bobby is kneeling next to me with wide, concerned eyes.

"Bobby?" I blink away stars. "Are you okay?"

"I'm fine. You caught me!" he exclaims, voice full of wonder. "You're a superhero!"

"I'm no hero," I insist, hands shaking from belated panic. My brother looks unconvinced, so I force an unsteady smile to comfort him. "A hero wouldn't have let you fall."

"We both fell," Bobby notes.

"Well, I couldn't let you fall alone." I sit up and am, surprisingly, feeling reasonably well. No headache or nausea, and any aches or pains from the impact seem vanishingly minor. My little brother is uninjured and that's all that matters. "We should go home and get something to eat."

"Are you finished with your math stuff?"

"It'll wait. What do you want for dinner?"

"Macaroni and cheese!"

"With broccoli?" I tease, standing up and taking his hand.

"Noooooo."

"With spinach?" We start walking.

"No!"

"How about...with cut up hot dogs?"

"Yes!"

When I woke up, I imagined that I could still taste the salt and artificial cheddar flavoring.

CHAPTER SIX

"ARE YOU INSANE," I DEMANDED INCREDULOUSLY, "OR JUST legitimately stupid?"

Sparks and debris rained from above and shrapnel pinged off the surface of my armor. Ignoring a jet of flame pouring from an unearthed natural gas pipe, I stepped through molten slag and shattered marble to face my foe. "I'd had suspicions regarding the latter, but it's disappointing to have those notions confirmed so dramatically."

The once-magnificent atrium was illuminated more by the surrounding conflagration than the shattered skylight or the flickering emergency lighting. Smoke billowed from surrounding buildings and visibility was limited to a single block of apocalyptic destruction. Alarms blared, brief bursts of automatic weapons barked in the distance, and the desperate cries of wounded victims echoed throughout the courtyard.

Titan did not answer; he dared not attack but would not let himself retreat. Pure hatred radiated from his glowing eyes as he glared across the wreckage.

"You did this." I gestured abruptly, straitening to the Mk 29's twelve-foot height and raising my voice until Doctor Fids deep baritone struck like a physical force. "THIS WAS YOUR DOING!"

It seemed to me that the shouting and gunfire stopped; even the sirens and roaring winds went quiet. Chaos stilled. As Titan and I stared each other down across the courtyard, the rest of the world faded, unimportant.

"Tonight...when the fighting's done, when I've escaped and you and yours are licking your wounds...Watch the news and listen to the vultures as they count the butcher's bill. It should be your name on the check! You threw chum in the waters to summon predators from the depths, you drew the sharks here. You can't blame a fish if someone gets bitten.

"That's just what sharks do."

I advanced.

Over the years, I've tried many methods of manipulating Doctor Fid's emotional state: pharmacological drugs and biological treatments, nootropic supplement programs, self-hypnosis and meditation, bio- and neurofeedback of various flavors, and even invasive surgery. The goal was to make Fid a more effective villain: a creature without Terry Markham's flaws. The program started soon after that famous bank robbery (with young Melissa Halden's cries haunting my dreams) and my early efforts were crudely effective. Possibly too effective; in the years since, I'd worked to eliminate the system's addictive qualities and minimize any of Doctor Fid's artificially-induced excesses.

Like a topiarist approaching a new bush, I'd pruned and shaped myself to fill Fid's armor. Becoming a villain had not been an easy transition; it had required extensive training. I trained myself to accept discomfort, I trained myself to find pleasure in victory and well-executed schemes, and I trained myself to monologue in a manner that evoked a desired response. In my youth, I'd been an introverted academic; I'd possessed few of the talents or abilities that would later be relied upon.

I did not, however, need to train myself to love fighting. That came naturally.

From the very first embarrassingly unskilled punch, battles filled me with a wild, visceral joy. Every emotional injury that I'd ever carried, every lonely day of school in which not even a teacher had spoken to me, every moment of hateful jealousy, every scintilla of mourning: in that strike, I'd found an almost magical means to transform emotional pain into the physical. Physical pain fades or can be inflicted upon someone else. Battle was cathartic in a way that I hadn't even known possible, but indulging that passion came at a dangerous cost. When Fid discovered that he could punch someone until he (at least temporarily) stopped hating himself, a slew of broken heroes had been left scattered in the Doctor's wake.

In retrospect, only a few had truly earned such brutality. Ah, well...it's like the old adage says: if you want to make an omelet, you have to crack a few legs. The reputation that Doctor Fid earned during that time certainly proved useful.

Case in point: all of New England was understood to be the Doctor's territory.

There were other villains in the area, certainly. Bank robbers and jewel thieves and costumed miscreants of all flavors. Local heroes such as the Guardians certainly did not fall prey to boredom when Doctor Fid was otherwise engaged. The big-name villains, however—the A-listers who attracted nationwide attention...they steered clear of the New England region unless an agreement had been made. Outlaws that would spit in the eye of any costumed vigilante or armed-forces general would approach Doctor Fid and be polite. When even Imperator Rex had come, hat in hand...it was easy to imagine that one's reputation had been cemented for all time.

It's easy for one to become complacent.

I stared at the screen in disbelief.

"Terry?" Whisper nudged at my elbow. "Are you okay?"

"I'm fine," I reassured her absently, idly tapping one finger next to my keyboard. One of the many upgrades that I'd performed upon myself during the week-long medically induced coma was to add a control interface and direct quantum-communication neural link. Terry Markham was now able to covertly perform research as deftly as could Doctor Fid. Sitting at the computer desk and using a monitor was still, however, a comfortable habit. "I just think that someone has made a mistake. This can't be right."

"Mmm? What happened?"

"The CSE placed an order for a large titanium-vanadium alloy sphere, internally polished to less than two hundredths of a micrometer surface roughness." Purchases of this nature were rare; I have programs in place to periodically hack the relevant servers and notify me of unusual activity. This particular commission had raised a remarkable series of red flags.

"Why is that a mistake?" Whisper asked curiously.

"Well, machining something that large, to that level of accuracy...that's expensive," I explained. "You wouldn't want to spend that kind of capital unless you were building a device that absolutely required a surface that smooth."

"Mm." Whisper tilted her head, her glowing blue eyes seeming to lose focus for a moment. "The SLAC National Accelerator Laboratory bought something similar, last year. From the same manufacturer, even."

"The most likely use is a containment sphere for high-energy physics experiments. That particular configuration, though...I've seen it before." I showed her my screen.

"They're building a Westler-Gray reactor?" She looked charmed. "Can we go see it?"

"They could be building something else," I admitted. "Their vacuum furnaces consume a fair amount of power, but even a small WG reactor would be excessive."

"But if they do build a WG reactor, can we go see it?" she asked again, smiling hopefully. "I've never seen one in person."

"CSE is based in Cambridge, only a few dozen miles from here," I laughed. "If they build a Westler-Gray reactor, I'm going to steal it."

No one would be so unreasonable as to build a WG Reactor in Doctor Fid's backyard, not without first securing a thirty-seven-million-dollar bunker like the one SLAC built in Menlo Park. The very idea was laughable! The purchase order was obviously a mistake, nothing more.

The transition from introverted academic to high-powered CEO had required that Terry Markham be changed as well. Had I chosen to found AH Biotech (officially named in memory of Albert Hess, one of my early mentors who succumbed to liver cancer only days before I was awarded my Nobel Prize) as a privately held company, the changes would likely have been limited to intellectual endeavors: gathering the skills and knowledge necessary to build and manage a company. That school of study was alien to me and required a significant shift in mindset from that which I applied to the pure sciences, but I did persevere. My goals for the company, however, were grand: AH Biotech would serve to develop technologies to benefit humanity. To prove that the so-called heroes were unnecessary in order that the world be saved!

Wooing investors and incorporating had been the fastest method of building a company sufficiently large to accomplish such a feat. As such...the modifications required for Terry Markham were more dramatic. A chief executive officer is a figurehead as much as he or she is a manager. The appearance of confidence and success matter more than mere capability.

After that fateful conversation with Hideki Ichiro, Terrance Markham endured a painful late growth spurt. The average CEO stood a good five inches taller than my original adult height, after all, and the chief executive of AH Biotech needed to fulfill the image of a commanding leader! Surreptitious surgical and chemical enhancements were applied side-by-side to diet changes and vigorous exercise so that Doctor Terrance Markham would appear strong and capable. Lifestyle coaches and actors were consulted as I learned to meet people's eyes, to shake hands firmly and to mimic a sincere smile. Minor genetic alterations and cosmetic surgical improvements were applied to subtly augment facial symmetry.

After nearly a year of gradual transformation, the man who welcomed speculative investors into the lobby of what would become AHBT headquarters looked very much unlike the awkward but intense scholar that I'd once been. In comparison, the process of building and concealing the massive technological infrastructure necessary to construct Doctor Fid's terror-inducing armors felt straightforward.

🌀 🌀 🌀

"It has to be a mistake," I complained to Starnyx for the umpteenth time, holding my cell phone uncomfortably tight against my ear as I paced and gesticulated wildly. "Whisper inserted herself into the CSE's servers and downloaded copies of their blueprints."

"And what did you find this time?" Over the telephone, my friend sounded tired but amused.

"They built a new cooling system next to their factory floor." Irritably, I waved my hand in the air. "The plans don't include any work to tie the new system to external power, but there's enough empty floor space for a properly modified containment sphere..."

"That's pretty suggestive," Nyx said. "Sounds like electricity is going to get cheaper in the New England area once CSE starts selling power back to the utilities."

"It's a brick warehouse!" I pointed out irritably. "Undefended!"

"Wow. Even Lloyds wouldn't insure that," Starnyx agreed. "Failure to exercise due diligence."

"Exactly!"

"Look, Doc. You're right. It's a mistake," he chuckled. "Businesses make mistakes all the time. Why is this bugging you?"

"It's insulting," I grated out. "Stanford spent nearly fourty million dollars to dissuade Technos from attacking their powerplant. CSE is based in Doctor Fid's backyard, and I'm not convinced that they were planning on investing in a good padlock."

"Security through obscurity, man," the hacker reminded me. "They haven't publicly announced any new projects. Maybe they thought no one'd notice."

"They're publicly traded. Did they think none of their investors would see the expense, or the change in their monthly power bill?"

"First of all, it won't be that large a chunk o' change, not for them. That's why you were watching them, yeah?"

"True." I sighed, deflating. "They already manufacture a fair number of relevant components. CSE is the only company in the North East that has the manufacturing capability to make both their own cavity magnetrons and large volumes of bismuth aerogel."

"Secondly, they can bury the changes in their earnings report under 'improved internal processes'," Starnyx continued. "There's maybe a handful of people in the world who would have caught this and, sure, you're definitely one of the most likely...but you haven't been out in armor for four months and your arm was still missing then. They probably thought that 'the Doctor is out', and this'd fly under the radar."

Nyx was correct; to most of the world, the construction of this Westler-Gray reactor would have been invisible. For a creature like Fid, however, finding out about this would be child's play. A business owner might not be aware of Doctor Fid's capabilities, but others would certainly be more attentive. And when Fid's extended absence was factored in, a new picture evolved.

"It's not a mistake," I barked in laughter. "It's not a mistake at all. I should have seen it sooner."

"Oh?"

"It's a staked goat to lure a tiger!" I shook my head. "Bait so obvious that I should have noticed the gift-wrapping. Someone is trying to draw Doctor Fid out of hiding!"

"Hah!" Starnyx sounded as entertained as I felt. "Sounds like someone's about to have a bad day. Any idea who?"

"Not yet. I'll start counter-surveillance and see what I can determine."

"Sounds like the Red Ghost to me, Doc. Be careful."

"No," I said, feeling certain of my answer. "The Red Ghost's idea, perhaps, but he'd never move ahead with it. There's a community college football field adjacent to the CSE factory. Too much danger to civilians."

"Remember how he caught Kenny." Eric's voice quieted, serious and intense. "Beazd was easily strong enough to escape. Your Ghost risked all those guards' lives, sending 'em in unarmored. Maybe he'd risk a couple college students, too."

"Kenta was a far, far better man than I am. The Red Ghost would know this," I responded with equal gravity. "Beazd was a pacifist. Doctor Fid is most certainly not."

"Yeah. Yeah, true. Just be careful of the Ghost. He's not perfect."

"You found something damning?" I wasn't sure that I wanted to know. "While investigating the Shield, I mean?"

"Nah, nothing like that. But he's human, he can make mistakes." Nyx sighed softly. "For the record, Doctor Fid isn't as bad as you seem to think he is, either."

"Mm," I responded noncommittally; I disagreed, of course, but didn't think it worthwhile to argue the point. "Speaking of investigating the Shield...How soon till your broadcast?"

"Ehhh." He groaned softly. "It's on hold."

"I don't understand."

"We're delaying the broadcast for a while." He tried laughing it off, but I could hear the strain beneath his forced humor.

"It's been, as you said, four months." I tilted my head curiously, still holding the phone to my ear with one hand. "Do you need my construction drones again?"

(Reflexively, I checked the status of my construction robots. Hmm. I could see that the drones that he'd used had been returned to my storage facility days before my surgery, but those two were still listed as unavailable. Two others, as well! Some software glitch? I'd look into it later.)

"Thanks, but nah. They were useful, though." Now I could hear his smile, and it felt genuine again. "We have everything prepped for when we move forward."

"If you have everything prepped, then why aren't I seeing you on the six o'clock news?" I rubbed at my eyes against a sudden headache, bewildered and angry. "Sphinx was just on *The Late Show* two days ago without a care in the world!"

"I know, man, but something's come up. The FTW's working on another project."

"Peregrine is doing photo-ops at *Comicon* this weekend and you're just going to let him go?" I clenched my teeth so hard that my jaw hurt. Starnyx—a man that I'd trusted—had vengeance within reach but was refusing to grasp it? "I thought Beazd was your friend!"

"You're my friend, too," Starnyx replied evenly. "So I'm gonna forgive you instead of driving up there 'n breaking your damned nose. Peregrine's on borrowed time."

Rage burst like a soap bubble and I felt unaccountably tired. The sudden migraine faded and all that was left was the strange sensation that something important had been forgotten. For a long moment, neither of us spoke.

"It's just...I don't understand," I said quietly.

"I know, Doc," he commiserated. "I know what revenge means to you, and believe me...I want it too. Right now, though...that's gotta take a back seat to living the life that my friend would have wanted for me. Honoring him by doing the things he would've wanted me to do, y'know?"

I could comprehend that, in theory. I could piece the words together and draw meaning from them. The sentiment, though, was alien. The dead needed justice and the guilty needed to be punished! If I doubted either of those truths for even a moment, then how could I possibly justify Doctor Fid to my brother's shade? Starnyx's ghosts, I supposed, must haunt him differently than did my own.

That knowledge lightened my heart but also left me feeling terribly lonely.

"Is there anything that you need?" I finally asked.

"I'm good." He paused. "Thanks, Doc."

"You're welcome."

"Um, hey, listen...we stumbled onto something huge, something Kenny would have wanted us to bring to light." Nyx recovered his natural ebullient enthusiasm. "Next show in a month, yeah?"

"I'm looking forward to it." My smile was wan, but genuine. "Take care of yourself, Eric."

"You too, Doc!"

Further research revealed that the Boston Guardians were indeed responsible for the CSE's decision to build a horrifically unsecured WG reactor. The CEO's personal email account held encrypted messages from Titan himself; the Guardians had

fronted the necessary funds and further promised half of Doctor Fid's rather sizable bounty after the crippled villain was successfully captured. All, of course, in gratitude for the CSE's cooperation.

Titan was taking a dangerous risk. Superhero teams enjoyed different obligations for due diligence than did businesses, so the Guardians' investment could probably be recovered from their insurance in the event of a loss. Until that loss occurred, however, far too much of their operating capital was tied up in this one operation.

(The Red Ghost was an accountant; he must have railed against this plan and been overruled. One of my greatest regrets had always been my failure to hack into the internal security cameras at the Guardians' headquarters. Watching the conflict between Red Ghost and Titan would have been a joy.)

Handing another defeat to the Guardians would be demoralizing for them, I knew, but I could do more damage by sitting back and doing nothing. Or, if pure laziness was not compelling, perhaps simply introducing a few carefully targeted computer viruses to increase their IT expenditures and performing a bit of market manipulation to decrease the value of their holdings would be sufficient. I doubted that I'd be able to bankrupt the Guardians before the Red Ghost uncovered the plot, but I certainly could hurt them. Delivering a fiscal wound would be almost as pleasant as inflicting the more visceral kind of damage.

Having arrived at a strategy, the CSE and their Westler-Gray reactor slipped from my immediate priorities. I should have remembered another old adage: No battle plan survives first contact with stupidity.

I awoke to pain, eyes wide and heart racing. The artificially-released adrenaline cocktail had served its purpose: I was immediately alert and focused. The world, however, tasted metallic; I was reminded, strangely, of old pennies. (Note to self: Adjust stimulant mixture and add anti-arrhythmic medications to smooth physical effects.)

Reflexively, I parsed the alerts that prompted my abrupt animation: Dozens of calls to the police and fire departments, explosions reported in Cambridge, calls for emergency medical expertise, and conflicting reports regarding a tank or armored bus. I was already running towards the rarely-used (and moderately dangerous) emergency teleportation platform hidden in my home-office when another alert pinged: the Governor had placed a brief call to Guardians headquarters. Her next call would likely be to the National Guard.

I commanded my automated systems to ready Doctor Fid's Mk 29 armor.

"What's going on?" Whisper called plaintively as I sped past her room.

"Technos is in my city!" I called over my shoulder, voice rough with rage. "Without my permission!"

"Oh." The little android hugged her doll close to her chest, lookin forlorn. "Please come home."

I stumbled.

Had Whisper looked like that when Apotheosis left for his final battle against the Paragons? Had she retreated to her room, sipping imaginary tea as she waited, helplessly, to hear her Father's voice at the door? How long had she waited before she'd started to cry?

Taking on the role of Doctor Fid was a heavy responsibility. A sacrifice. I'd poked and prodded at my very core, torn myself apart and reassembled the remains into a creature that struck fear into nation-states. An affront like this could not be borne, could not be forgiven without damaging the Doctor's carefully crafted reputation. That notoriety had been earned with blood and misery! The cost had been too great to easily allow Fid's infamy be tarnished.

Terry Markham took a few moments to tuck his ward in to bed and reassure her, but it was Doctor Fid that abandoned Whisper to her worry and fear.

Doctor Fid was, after all, a monster.

Monsters were not in short supply in Cambridge. The Guardians had likely been lying in wait, hoping to spring their trap on a supposedly-wounded Doctor Fid; they certainly hadn't expected Technos' armada of combat vehicles! Nor, for that matter, had the Guardians been prepared for the sheer number of armed mercenaries that accompanied the villain. It looked as though Technos was diverted away from his target—the Westler-Gray reactor—but the battle quickly had spilled over into the Greater Boston Community College campus.

I'd never met Technos, nor even wasted much time thinking on him. He'd been a weapons designer in northern California whose project was canceled. From what I understood, he'd actually raved to the company executives that they would 'rue the day that they fired Doctor Carl Schlumpf!' Embarrassing. If the man had any shame, he'd have slunk into the shadows and taken up a different hobby. Instead, he followed every cliché and stole the company's prototype mini-tank.

Using that first tank, he stole resources to build a second, etc. Technos had built up an apparently successful arsenal over the last eleven years, but his greater talent was revealed to be the hiring, training and managing of henchmen. His private army was disciplined and arguably more dangerous than the armored vehicles that Technos himself brought to bear.

Floating fully-cloaked high above the chaos, I deployed a massive swarm of microdrones to map the campus and to mark targets. Even with my own heavy-combat drones—a full dozen; twice as many as had ever been deployed for a single skirmish—this battle could prove complicated.

Eleven of Technos' mercenaries had already been been subdued, but the remaining forces had split into small units and spread out to cause chaos. Veridian had been drawn away from the primary battleground to rescue a classroom full of hostages. Two more armored personal carriers careened through campus and left pain and screams in their wake. Regrowth and the Red Ghost had split up to assist the authorities in chasing down those vehicles; the local police were overwhelmed and thoroughly outgunned.

In the campus' main courtyard, Titan and Aeon stood alone against four mini-tanks and one giant gray monstrosity that bristled with turrets, cannons and sensor arrays.

The larger tank hammered at the two heroes relentlessly; the smaller vehicles peppered the surrounding battleground with a seemingly inexhaustible supply of smoke and concussion grenades. Occasionally, the mini-tanks' turrets spun to concentrate fire upon one of the two heroes, leading to a frenzied defense and intense destruction.

It was...devastation, like something out of a nightmare. Even soaring above the carnage, I could taste blood and ash and tears on my lips.

I summoned the Mk 29's war-staff from subspace and dropped to a height of only twenty feet. A massive energy buildup of energy gathered among my drones; raw power arced between their towering starfield-patterned columns, brightening the sky and drawing all attention to me as I disabled the armor's cloaking system.

"TECHNOS!! YOU TRESSPASS IN MY DOMAIN!" I thundered. "EXPLAIN YOURSELF OR BE DESTROYED!"

Titan and Aeon halted their attack, wary lest they provoke me to join forces with the interloper. Their apprehension was misguided. On this day, Technos' sins far outweighed those of the heroes. That the Guardians set a trap for Doctor Fid had been ill-advised, but not wholly unexpected. A first-tier supervillain daring to intrude upon Doctor Fid's territory, on the other hand, was an inexcusable act of contempt.

"Fid!" Technos howled from within his armored tank. The vehicle's external speakers failed to match my own broadcast presence. "An old has-been like you can't hold a region this large!"

I was shocked into momentary inaction. This was, I thought, the oddest suicide attempt that I'd ever witnessed.

"Fly away!" he taunted further. "You tin-plated coward!"

A verbal response was, I decided, entirely unnecessary. I aimed my war-staff and fired a pulsed particle beam at Technos' battle-tank.

The air itself exploded into plasma, which was in turn projected down upon the armored vehicle by shaped energy-fields that struck like the wrath of an angry god. The impact shook the earth. Pavement fractured into rubble and buildings rocked with enough force to throw dust from their rooftops. Glass shattered and the crash echoed across the entire campus like thunder.

For a moment, all was still.

"You'll need to do better than that!" Technos crowed, triumphantly.

Clearing smoke revealed that his tank was barely damaged. A reactive deflector-shield, perhaps? I detected low-level radiation and an unexpected shift in air temperature. Interesting.

"You wanted an explanation?" the madman called, smugly condescending. "Come down here and take it!"

Extra-dimensional energy radiated from a tuned emitter on his tank, creating quantum ripples in a region the size of a football field. Anti-grav fields were disrupted like a candle snuffed by a gale.

My drones and I tumbled from the sky.

Technos' defenses, I noted with grim amusement, were too carefully tailored to match my known capabilities to be coincidence. His attack on the W–G reactor, too, must have been a ruse. I wasn't certain if he wanted my territory, my technology, or merely the reputation boost eliminating the notorious Doctor Fid would bring...but he'd come here to take a soft target and to lure me out of hiding. Instead, he'd tripped the Guardians' trap.

The tanks' technology was intriguing. The tank's pilot, on the other hand, was an amateurish imbecile.

Software algorithms reacted to make my landing graceful. I took the impact on both feet, cratering into the already-scarred pavement, and twirled my staff for effect.

"I no longer require an explanation!" I called in challenge. "Only your defeat!"

Six of my drones, spider-like walking legs deployed and bristling with exposed weaponry, formed a protective circle around me; the remainder sped off in their disturbingly alien eight-legged gallop to begin locating and subduing Technos' soldiers.

The mini-tanks opened fire and the fight became general.

My sensors were unaffected by the artificially-created quantum ripples, so the predictive algorithms within my suit's programming were well able to keep track of the precise direction in which my enemy's weapons were aimed. I danced between cannon shells.

It was exhilarating. Step left, tilt head, jump, cut inertial dampeners and use the recoil from a twenty-six percent power particle beam to alter my jumps trajectory and thrust me aside...I was constantly shifting at maximum speed to avoid being targeted. A fraction of a second distraction might have meant disaster. I didn't need to be faster than a bullet, only faster than the tank's turret. Still, Technos' tanks were able to aim and reload remarkably quickly; if my own heavy-combat drones weren't available to occasionally act as barriers, I would have remained too busy dodging to have any possibility of counterattack.

Fortunately, my heavy-combat drones were designed to stand— at least temporarily—against the likes of Valiant.

A depleted-uranium round splattered off a drone's force field and I took advantage of the opportunity to retaliate with an ion-cannon blast. Once again, the effect was minimal. I cycled through laser, maser, sonic and plasma attacks.

After Technos had been dealt with, I was genuinely looking forward to piecing through the smoldering wreckage to study his technology. What a remarkable achievement!

A concussion grenade detonated at my feet, throwing me sideways directly into the path of a 120mm slug. Even inside the massively defended Mk 29 powered armor, the blast was sufficient to knock the sense from me. I became a passenger inside my own suit while I blinked away flashes of light.

An alarm on my neural link noted that my retina had become detached; I shut off my left eye while repairs commenced, instead drawing on sensor readings transmitted directly into my brain to analyze the failure in my predictive algorithms.

The mini-tanks were bouncing grenades off of solid surfaces, using timed fuses and indirect fire to overtax my ability to dodge. Clever machines! Not true artificial intelligences, but well-constructed nonetheless. I remained limp, trusting complete control to my armor's automated combat system while I designed a subroutine to address the oversight. In the meantime, my drones swarmed closer to compensate.

Titan and Aeon rejoined the battle. The seven-foot mystically empowered warrior leaped forward to close distance with one of the mini-tanks while Aeon remained at a distance to throw one energy blast after another directly at Technos' primary tank. Raw physical power appeared to have better luck than energy; Titan tore off a tank tread and used it as a flail to tear a gaping chasm through the mini-tank's turret.

Conflict made for strange bedfellows; I'd half-expected for Titan to join forces with Technos against me. In this instance, I supposed, the Californian villain was threat enough that the so-called 'heroes' chose to fight at my side. Their decision made sense. In all my villainous career, I had never demonstrated quite so great a disregard for civilian casualties as did Technos and his soldiers.

Microdrone sensors flooded my brain with raw information. Titan's physical attack, I determined, had been timed to land a fraction of a second after one of my robotic defenders had landed an energy-based attack. Whether by chance or by battlefield insight, Titan had exploited the regular cadence of particle beam fire to uncover a flaw in the mini-tank's defenses: a weakness against solid force in the brief instant after defending against energy.

With a new program in place to keep track of grenade ricochets, I reclaimed partial control over the Mk 29's actions and worked my way closer to the second mini-tank. There was fresh blood on my tongue, but I was nonetheless grinning behind Fid's emotionless faceplate.

My war-staff screamed as it spun, a full-force swing that landed microseconds after one of my drones' particle beams. The impact was epic, and the shock-wave made my chest ache and my vision blur. I howled my triumph when he tank's forward armor crumpled like tin foil.

There was spark from within that battered shell, yellow-white, and then the tank detonated. I was too close; there was a brief sense of movement and the world went white. My eyes closed...

For the second time that day, I was shocked into awareness by an artificially-induced adrenaline dump. Fifty-two seconds had passed. A long time when at the center of active battle. Yet again, I was grateful for automated combat programming.

All four of the mini-tanks had been completely disabled. Titan appeared to be stunned but Aeon fought on. The personnel carriers had returned, the soldiers within intent on providing covering fire for their beleaguered employer. Unfortunately for them, Regrowth had reappeared as well. The collateral damage costs would be astronomical, but the green-and-brown clad heroine used her ability to animate plants to excellent effect. Deciduous trees erupted straight through concrete and the vehicles were thoroughly entwined by roots and branches.

Three of my heavy-combat drones were inoperable. Two had sacrificed themselves to protect me while my armor fought with an unconscious passenger; the third's walking legs had been severely damaged by an explosive device cleverly planted by the foot soldiers. That one, at least, would be able to escape under its own power once anti-grav tech was again available.

The Mk 29 powered armor was still in working order. Concussive force had, however, induced significant soft-tissue damage to my left arm and leg. I hurt, I was irritable, and my medical nanites would be working overtime for days.

"ENOUGH!" I roared. "Technos! If you surrender, I will allow the Guardians to arrest you."

"And if I don't?" He sounded shaken but still rebellious.

"Then we battle to the death," I laughed menacingly, spinning the war-staff in a deliberately slow figure-eight pattern. "And I promise that it won't be quick."

The presence of a crimson fog near Titan's form indicated that the Red Ghost had arrived, and Veridian's green glow was approaching from the south. Four of my heavy combat drones were already present and another five en route. Technos' massive tank was still a marvel, true, but he was surrounded and I'd vividly demonstrated the ability to overcome his mini-tank's shielding. It was likely that his main vehicle suffered the same flaw.

"Damn you, Fid!" he howled. "I'm coming out!"

And that was that. The Red Ghost's mist-like form hovered around the tank's escape hatch until a slender, sweating figure emerged. The Ghost pounced, and Doctor Carl Schlumpf was taken into custody. Somewhere on campus, the remains of Technos' soldiers skirmished with police...but this battle was over.

Sensors captured high-definition footage of the Red Ghost's stony expression. It was likely that this scenario, all this horror and destruction, had been his brainchild. It was equally likely that he'd foreseen the possibility of events spiraling out of control and thus fought against the plan's implementation.

He'd been proven right, and I was sure that his failure to scuttle the plot weighed on him heavily. He was, however, able to maintain control over his anger; he handcuffed Schlumpf professionally and did not use the slightest amount of excessive force.

With anti-gravitic fields now functional, I signaled for my drones to begin removing any of my own technology from the wreckage. Anything that could not be carried away was set to self-immolate.

"Well, Guardians, I suppose that I will take my lea—" I was cut off by a phenomenal impact, so sudden and unexpected that my sensors barely had opportunity to blare warning before I was struck. I was thrown backwards fifty feet, through a wall and into the community college's student union building.

Titan had hit me with a steel I-beam. I stood up slowly, sore but furious. The Guardians assembled outside the ruined atrium.

"Are you insane," I demanded incredulously, "or just

legitimately stupid?"

It was late before I finally limped home. The Mk 29 and drones required inspection before they could be left to automated repair systems, and I'd wanted to catalog the W-G reactor parts and the bits of Technos' technology that I'd been able to pilfer from the wreckage. The extra time also allowed my medical nanites to repair my detached retina and the worst of my bruising.

In one day, I'd defeated Technos, handed another thorough beating to the Guardians, and insulted Titan while news camera-drones were surely within range! There would, I was sure, soon be an exposé that revealed the origin of the Westler-Gray reactor that'd been the impetus for this entire debacle. I was tired, my bones ached, and I was ravenously hungry. Even so, it had been a good day. A victory on all counts.

"Whisper?" I knocked gently on her door. "Can I come in?"

"Mm." The android affirmed, sniffling as though she'd been crying.

"I'm home safe." I opened the door and found Whisper laying in her bed. "I'm sorry that I was gone for so long."

"You're hurt," she accused, and scrambled over to give me a gentle hug.

"Not badly," I replied, wrapping my sore arms about her in as comforting a manner as I could manage. "I promise."

"Mm," she acknowledged. "It's just been a bad day."

"Not so bad. Like I said...I'm fine."

"Oh. Oh! Um." Her eyes widened and she nibbled nervously at her lower lip. "Check the local news from Staten Island."

Mystified, I did as she recommended. The only report flagged was an explosion at an abandoned textile factory. Bodies (homeless squatters or drug-related criminals, the reporter intimated) had been found but not yet identified.

I recognized the facility, of course. I'd visited the location with Starnyx when he'd proudly showed off the FTW's hidden lair.

Damn.

CHAPTER SEVEN

I HEARD A JOKE ONCE. IT WENT LIKE THIS:

"What," the comedian quipped, "are the most common last words that a supervillain speaks to his henchman?"

I remember that he'd been drinking some sort of pumpkin-spiced craft beer; he wasn't a known mask, just some guy who seemed to be enjoying the unique ambiance and clientele at Lassiter's Den. The short, stout man seemed to have an inexhaustible supply of gags and wisecracks.

A crowd had gathered, and the performer hadn't needed to buy his own drinks for more than an hour.

"I don't know," someone piped up, "What *are* the most common last words that a supervillain speaks to his henchman?"

In retrospect, I suspected that both speakers were Cloner. I've seen enough archival footage to know that he did that often: used duplicates to play straight man to his own jests. The two didn't look or act alike; the retired superhero had long since evolved past that limitation of his power. Each replication was potentially unique, an ordinary-appearing person capable of acting independently or in tandem with the other clones.

He'd been one of the founding members of the New York Shield, the laughing prankster who hammed up his performances whenever a camera was near. The hero had never been a powerhouse; his ability to create and control a near-infinite number of artificial bodies had, however, granted a certain utility. He'd been known for using his doubles with slapstick humor and suicidal abandon. Something had changed, though, and Cloner quietly disappeared from the Shield roster. It was rumored that he'd stumbled across Lassiter's Den while investigating a case and had been infiltrating the bar undercover ever since.

Perhaps none of the nameless newcomers were Cloner. Perhaps all of them were. Who could know for sure?

"The supervillain says: 'No, you fool! If you touch that button you'll kill us a—'"

Everyone laughed. For those of us who had doomsday weaponry in our bunkers, however, the laughter was a bit forced.

Peregrine and the Sphinx both had exceptional alibis. I checked their whereabouts first, even before the arson investigator had started filing reports. Peregrine was signing autographs at a convention several states distant, and the Sphinx wasn't even on the planet; Valiant had requested the assistance of several prominent 'heroes' to offer humanitarian aid to an alien settlement.

(Valiant's spacecraft was impressive. He'd taken the ship as spoils of war after being kidnapped by some would-be intergalactic warlord. Engineers at Paragon Research were permitted to examine the vessel, and I'd established a digital back-door into their servers years ago. The faster-than-light-travel technology was intriguing but not particularly useful within a planet's gravity well. It required a full six days of constant acceleration away from earth orbit using a conventional ion-drive before the FTL functionality could be engaged. Sphinx had been a third of the way to Mars when the warehouse explosion occurred.)

Suspicion still burned like madness. It had been theoretically possible that the two members of the New York Shield could still have been involved indirectly. They could have hired or coerced an assassin to perform the deed. I'd wasted days searching for evidence of such but found nothing.

In a strange way, the probable innocence of Sphinx and Peregrine was comforting. Had I, instead, found them to be culpable...I couldn't be certain how deep I would have been willing to descend in order to gain vengeance. There'd been twelve people in that warehouse when the explosion occurred. An atrocity more blatant even than that which had been committed by Bronze! I would have lost myself; Doctor Fid's retribution would have shaken the fundament.

They'd been responsible for the death of Kenta Takuma, once known as Beazd. For that, Sphinx and Peregrine would eventually be held accountable. But for the blast that claimed Starnyx, blame must fall upon another target.

"Wait, wait!" the comedian who'd probably been Cloner insisted. "I have another one!"

His brow was damp from the prior performance, a long shaggy dog story whose punchline implied that Majestic drunkenly convinced a companion to leap to his death while another hero watched. The portly man drew out the joke, expertly acting out each character's role with exaggerated gestures and vocalizations.

The crowd quieted, expectant, and the comedian extended the moment by taking a slow sip from his beer.

"Why," he began, eyes sparkling with amusement, "does Atlantea wear that seashell bikini?"

A relatively new heroine at the time, Atlantea had claimed to be the princess of a vast and hidden undersea kingdom. By the time that assertion had been disproved, her undeniable power and attractive appearance had gathered enough goodwill that being caught in a lie barely cost her any support.

"I don't know!" called another Lassiter's Den patron, who was also probably Cloner. "Why?"

"Because she's too well-developed for B-shells and not quite large enough for D-shells!"

It took a remarkable amount of self-confidence to make a joke about breast size when the ultra-feminist Amazon was drinking a few booths away; she'd performed unspeakable violence upon construction workers for making similar comments. Atlantea had, however, twice clashed with the Amazon and embarrassed the tall, muscular dusky-skinned villainess both times.

The Amazon smiled vindictively while the rest of the bar laughed.

The police and fire department arrived more-or-less simultaneously. Officers cordoned off the surrounding area and sought out eyewitnesses. Since there had been reports of an explosion and no evidence of civilians in need of rescue, initial efforts were put towards containment; they worked to keep the fire from spreading until the fire department Captain reached the site and made the judgment call that it was safe for the firefighters to move closer and douse the flames.

The fire department Captain and a few of his men performed their initial inspection soon after the blaze was extinguished. When several bodies were discovered, the FBI was informed; an arson investigation was recommended as well. The FBI maintained control over the inquiry for the first twenty-seven hours.

They were thorough but slow.

(Hours, they waited, for results from a simple mass-spectrometer test! Doctor Fid's microdrones could have offered similar results practically instantaneously. The urge to fly to New York was overwhelming. It was, however, better to be patient. The agents on site were competent, trained investigators! My results would be faster but not necessarily superior; instead, I hacked into their files and followed their progress.)

When one of the deceased was confirmed to be a known member of the FTW's superhuman team, the FBI handed custody of the investigation off to the Department of Metahuman Affairs.

DOMA operatives have far more specialized skills. Debris and remains were quickly cataloged and analyzed, examined and interpreted. Within a few hours of their arrival on the scene, they'd identified the destruction's origin. The precise cause, however, was still under investigation.

"Okay, last one!" the broad, dark-haired joker laughed. "It's getting late and I oughta get home."

Did Cloner have a home? It's likely that he owned several. No one knows how many bodies he'd created over the years, and there seemed no limit to his ability to multitask. During Locust's infamous assault upon central park, dozens of copies of Cloner had been strewn across the battlefield. Shaky camera footage showed units of Cloner acting with intricately timed tactical movements.

Armed only with clubs, bare hands, laughter, taunts, and strength no greater than that of an average human, Cloner had expertly managed to distract and corral the insectoid menace for several minutes until reinforcements arrived. Other duplicates were witnessed performing first aid or assisting civilians to escape. He'd maintained dozens of simultaneous conversations with non-combatants, while simultaneously coordinating attacks and defenses against a first-tier supervillain! At precisely the same moment, several of Cloner were in Japan giving a paid motivational speech on the value of teamwork.

"How many minions does it take to screw in a light bulb?" the comedian asked. A few audience members chuckled in uncertain anticipation. Again, the short man took a slow drink of beer while letting the tension build.

"I don't know!" several patrons chorused. "How many minions *does* it take to screw in a light-bulb?"

The battle against Locust had left Central park an abattoir, a horror of pain and gore. The fallen replications struggled, broken and bleeding, choking and fighting for every last breath. And yet, a few minutes after the clones had expired...they all disappeared without a trace. A catastrophe of human wreckage gone up in smoke.

In an interview, Cloner mentioned that he could not un-summon a body; once he'd created a new member of his mob, that body would exist until it perished. Perhaps Cloner had one home that he returned to after stand-up comedy performances, perhaps he maintained dozens, or perhaps there existed a hidden warehouse in which he stored his extra bodies stacked up like cord-wood until they expired of starvation or dehydration, and thus evaporated.

Who could know for sure?

"Only two, unless they are particularly kinky." the entertainer offered an obvious response. "But you should convince Micron to let them out and return them to full size before they run out of oxygen!"

A few of the patrons of Lassiter's Den groaned, but others laughed at the raunchy absurdity. The comedian beamed happily, shook a few hands and started making his farewells.

To me, it felt an odd epitaph: the weakest joke of the evening saved for last! Then again, perhaps the choice to end on a low note was yet another argument in favor of the comedian being Cloner in disguise. His later efforts as a crime-fighter had been lackadaisical at best. Even as his powers continued to evolve and improve (demonstrating the facility to summon bodies of varying race, gender and appearance), his performance as a hero flagged. Never again had Cloner stretched himself to reach the potential that was showcased in the battle of Central Park. One of the founding members of (arguably) the most powerful group of superheroes in the United States, and he quietly disappeared from public view. An entity so thoroughly accepted to be non-threatening that the patrons of a supervillain bar joked about his possible presence but never stopped drinking.

Once upon a time, Bobby had guided Bronze's metallic action figure through epic battles against imaginary monsters and natural disasters. I'd taken on supporting roles, assisting my brother in his ongoing quest to save the world. Cloner had been my toy of choice.

Was it just us, I sometimes wondered? Some genetic quirk or strange mental trick that rendered my brother and me incapable of identifying heroes worthy of the title? But no, the problem was more pervasive. My brother and I played with brightly colored plastic action figures because those were the heroes marketed to us. Those were the characters that we were taught to idolize. If the system were not hopelessly corrupt, Doctor Fid wouldn't have been a necessity. But that was the world we lived in.

Real heroes didn't get toys made in their image.

We didn't attend the wake held at Lassiter's Den. Whisper and I mourned, in private but not alone.

"—but your search tree is seriously unbalanced." The speaker, a hacker who went by the handle LuckySeven, wasn't visible. The footage was of low quality: poor resolution and relatively few frames per second. A simple video chat program, optimized more for security and low-bandwidth than for fidelity.

"Yeah..Yeah! Okay, yeah, I see it." The Asian boy in the center of the screen looked briefly elated, before frowning thoughtfully. Over his shoulder, a half-dozen others could be seen moving about; it was the interior of a familiar warehouse, well-lit and spacious, with a community of like-minded hackers and activists living within. The variation in age of the FTW members was striking: grizzled and grey-bearded admins working alongside teens. There were two visibly non-human members (alien Legion refugees? The smaller of the two looked to be a child) as well.

"Simple isn't always faster, y'know?" LuckySeven commented helpfully. *"Use a self-balancing tree."*

"I have to keep the binary's size down, though. Can only reliably get a few kay through before garbage collection is triggered." The time of day wasn't clear; there were windows visible in the background, but they'd been carefully blacked out to keep any light from escaping. Somewhere off camera, a ping-pong game could be heard; spectators groaned or cheered

with every point scored.

"Swipe Helios' red-black tree code!" LuckySeven didn't sound much older than the teenager that he was talking to. He must have started young; he'd been a remote member of the FTW for years. "It's tiny, 'n it'll work with your data set."

"I wanted this hack to be mine, man." The unnamed speaker leaned back in his seat, his body blocking less of the screen. Over his shoulder, a series of high-powered force emitters and shield projectors had been mounted on wheeled chassis. The force emitters looked to be tuned to focus downwards. Foundation crackers, most likely part of a controlled demolition plan.

(Not my design; Nyx could have taken plans from any of the four construction drones that my records say were obliterated in the fire, but he'd chosen to use an older, more well-known and admittedly much less expensive configuration. Perhaps he'd expected the emitter to be left behind?)

"Dude, if you're not stealing from Helios, you're not really trying. The shoulders of giants, yeah?"

"Yeah." The kid's t-shirt advertised an obscure skateboard company. He looked relatively skinny, but his skin reflected the monitor light oddly. Greasy, like he ate too much junk food and didn't shower enough. Too much time in front of a computer screen, most likely.

"Seriously, you have the bones of a great exploit here." The admiration and pride in LuckySeven's voice was clearly audible. "That's all you."

"Thanks." The younger hacker seemed flustered by the praise. Behind him, an older FTW member with shaking hands was unbolting the side panel of the shield projector. "Oh, hey, what'd she say?"

"Who?"

"That girl, Valerie?" The kid smiled teasingly, as though he knew the answer before he asked. The man behind him was working with fluid certainty; he'd delved into the innards of that device before.

"Oh, man...That was, like, weeks ago."

"So, what'd she say?" The younger hacker leaned forward, blocking view of the man laboring behind him.

"It, ah, didn't go well." Now it was LuckySeven's turn to sound embarrassed.

"Hah!" The kid leaned back for a moment. Behind him, it was clear that a panel had been removed; several high-voltage circular connectors looked to have been reconfigured.

"Hey, man, I deserve sympathy!"

(From off camera, barely audible, Starnyx' voice could be heard: "Hey, Jerry? Whatcha working on?")

"Dude, I told you she was a bitch!" The kid waved his hands expressively.

"She's not!" LuckySeven sounded aggrieved.

(The man reconfiguring the force-field projector, Jerry, responded to Starnyx with a noncommittal mumble. "Nothing. 'm sorry.")

"She is, man. You stalk her social media, you saw what she did to Tammie291?" The younger hacker leaned forward, his concerned and empathetic expression taking up most of the screen real-estate.

("Jerr, that unit's all buttoned up. It doesn't need any maintenance.")

"That was almost a year ago."

(Much more quietly, from the sweating and shaking man reaching elbow deep into a high-energy reactor housing: "I'm sorry.")

"It was freaking harsh, man."

("No!" Nyx' voice wasn't loud, but the sudden urgency was clear. His psychic precognition only offered a few seconds of warning in case of danger, but it must have just triggered. "Don't touch tha—")

"She's not li—Shit!"

Things happened quickly. The kid on-screen, the young hacker's eyes widened in surprise and he began to turn. Someone was yelling. A blue glow suffused the room for a fraction of a second, and then there was a moment of chaotic movement. The video flashed white.

"Paul...?" LuckySeven was talking to a blank screen. "Pauley, what happened? You there?"

Eric could have escaped. Perhaps not unscathed, but there is every indication that he might have survived. The way Starnyx's powers worked, that remarkable sense of danger in the world around him...he could have identified locations that would have been relatively safe from the deadliest forces of the blast. Lunged for a corner protected by a concrete pylon, or stepped into a section of floor that would have been partially shielded by a collapsing balcony. He'd done it before: Survived explosions and slid between bullets from automatic weapons fire! With only a second or two of preternatural notice, his superhuman agility might have granted sufficient time that he could even have fled through a window.

A forensic analysis of the video showed another story. In two frames, reconstructed using a broad array of digital enhancements, Eric could be seen diving across the room. He'd caught up the smaller alien, the child, and twisted away from the force-field emitter.

Starnyx used his own body as a shield, a tragically heroic attempt to save the young alien refugee's life.

The child's body wasn't recovered, but the DOMA report demonstrated that the subsequent fire would have been fatal for any who'd survived the initial blast. Jerry Stross' suicide note was posted on his online journal minutes before he forced the shield-emitter's reactor to go supercritical. Cloner's action figures were still available at toy stores as part of the 'Classic Shield Collection', and the stock market responded favorably to news that the FTW was no more. The world is flawed.

Every once in a while, I pondered the distinct and unfortunate possibility that reality simply wasn't salvageable. I'd said as much to Nyx, one night years past when were were both deep in our cups. He'd just smiled and shook his head. "Nah, Doc," he'd said. "The world ain't so bad. There's an awful lot of good here, 'ss just quieter." At the time, I'd quietly assumed his view to be a pleasant lie. An optimist's dream! Viewing the last two frames from the video chat footage, however, I knew my friend to be correct.

For more than two decades, Doctor Fid had raged a violent war against flawed idols. They dressed in bright colors and shouted entertaining slogans for the news cameras, but they were made of lead beneath their gilded surfaces. Teasing, brash and defective creatures like Cloner were so loud that I never stopped to listen to the silence in their wake.

The world was poorer for the loss of Kenta Takuma and Eric Guthrie. Still...any world that spawned "villains" such as them was worth saving.

Those gloating reporters and executives who cheered the FTW's demise were mistaken. The FTW had, instead, gained a new armored and heavily-armed member. I would take up the duties and imperatives encoded within their charter and would forswear unnecessary violence. For my friend, and for my friend's friend...It was the only worthy tribute I could offer. *Be good*, the FTW's manifesto directed. *Be loud.* I could not promise to excel at the former, but I was confident in my ability to accomplish the latter. Doctor Fid would see to it that Beazd and Starnyx's legacy lived on.

CHAPTER EIGHT

To: "Lucky Seven" <lucky7@hush332.ca>
From: "Doctor Fid" <doctor.fid@..>
Subject: Condolences
LuckySeven,
My condolences for the loss of your friend. I'm sorry to say that I'd never met him, but a cursory examination of his social media profile indicates that he was trusted, respected and cared for within the community.
It may seem a petty and superficial thing, to attempt to glean deep meaning from an examination of a young man's work…but he'd adjusted his code's indentation patterns and function-naming conventions to match your own. The shift in programming style was slow and subtle, but noticeable when comparing newer works against his older repositories. To me, at least, that speaks of a deep level of admiration and trust.
Paul Harris was a talented individual and I'm certain that he was grateful for your mentorship. Again, you have my condolences.

To: "Doctor Fid" <doctor.fid@..>

From: "Lucky Seven" <lucky7@hush332.ca>
Subject: Re: Condolences
Thanks. It still doesn't feel real. I appreciate you
reaching out, but I gotta know...How'd you find me? This
isn't a publicly search-able address.
- L7
(P.S. Careful about using that handle, even as a joke.
About a decade ago, there was a hacker who used the name
'Dr_Fid' on I-Chat. Bad things happened to him.)

To: "Lucky Seven" <lucky7@hush332.ca>
From: "Doctor Fid" <doctor.fid@..>
Subject: Re: Re: Condolences
LuckySeven,
I was friends with Starnyx; he taught me a few useful
tricks. I've attached a program that trawls relevant
internet sites and uses usage patterns to create likely
associations between accounts. A fair amount of
computing power is required to take best advantage, but
you're welcome to look the code over.
(P.S. I am not so proud that I would punish any who take
my name in vain. The hacker in question wasn't sought
out because he used my name as his handle; he was
punished for using my name as his handle while peddling
narcotics to children.)

To: "Doctor Fid" <doctor.fid@..>
From: "Lucky Seven" <lucky7@hush332.ca>
Subject: Re: Re: Re: Condolences
I'm sorry, Doctor. I didn't mean any offense! I just
thought you were some kid that chose the handle for
shock value or as a tribute. We see that a lot.

I've been reminded that u and Nyx were close. I didn't
know him as well as I'd have liked, but he was an
inspiration, you know? He was a great guy. I'm sorry you
lost your friend, too.
-L7

To: "Lucky Seven" <lucky7@hush332.ca>
From: "Doctor Fid" <doctor.fid@..>
Subject: Re: Re: Re: Re: Condolences
LuckySeven,
Thank you. No offense was taken, I assure you.
I was hoping to reach out to whoever has taken over the
reins at the FTW. Starnyx was indeed my friend and I
have resources that I would like to donate towards any
rebuilding efforts. My historical means of making
contact with the organization have, unfortunately, been
disrupted. Could you point me towards the group's
current leadership?

To: "Doctor Fid" <doctor.fid@..>
From: "Lucky Seven" <lucky7@hush332.ca>
Subject: The organization
No one's really stepped up, yet. Things are crazy on the
forum and it's going to take a while before everything
shakes out. Also, no offense meant because I have mad
respect for your l33t skillz, but a lot of us won't like
getting help from you, not while we're trying to get our
own balance, y'know? If the FTW is going to stand for
anything going forward...we need to stay true to the
original charter.
I'm sorry. Again, no offense meant!
-L7

To: "Lucky Seven" <lucky7@hush332.ca>
From: "Doctor Fid" <doctor.fid@..>
Subject: Re: The organization
LuckySeven,
You should throw your hat in the ring. The FTW would be
well served by a leader with sufficient integrity to
stand up to someone with my reputation. Again, no
offense was taken. You needn't apologize!
I know that my past actions have not been in keeping
with the FTW's ethos, but I wasn't planning on offering
up instruments of destruction or providing funding
tainted by the violence by which it was acquired. I
wanted to offer my skills and technical expertise. I
would very much like to join the FTW as a member.

To: "Doctor Fid" <doctor.fid@..>
From: "Lucky Seven" <lucky7@hush332.ca>
Subject: Re: Re: The organization
Join this chat.
-L7

Welcome to #SYNChat!
<encrypted private channel established>

Lucky7: You'd need to take the oaths.

Doctor.Fid: I know.

Lucky7: Normally, that's a private thing. You're a
public figure, though. It'll have to get leaked.

Doctor.Fid: I thought that would likely be the case, yes.

Lucky7: You'd need to mean them!

Doctor.Fid: I know what it means, and I wouldn't make the promise if I didn't intend on following through.

Lucky7: I mean it, man. You join us and then you show up on the news handing Titan another beating it'll frigging wreck us. That's not what we do.

Doctor.Fid: Starnyx was my closest friend, I wouldn't betray his memory.

Lucky7: No unnecessary violence. That's not exactly the approach you're known for.

Doctor.Fid: My old approach hasn't been working.

Lucky7: You seem to be doing ok.

Doctor.Fid: I can do better.

Lucky7: Mmm...Still tempted to say no.

Doctor.Fid: Why?

Lucky7: Because Jerry Stross killed a lot of good people. He killed Paul. It's not fair if he's the person who finally defeats Doctor Fid, too.

Doctor.Fid: ...Explain your logic?

Lucky7: No hero's been able to keep Doctor Fid down. Your arm got cut off 'n you came back stronger! Now, you're going to hang up your particle cannon because of something some suicidal jackass did?

Doctor.Fid: I'm not doing this because of Stross. I'm doing this for Nyx and Beazd.

Lucky7: I'm not sure I like the idea of Doctor Fid being defeated by the FTW, either.

Doctor.Fid: I'm not defeated. I'm inspired. I have no interest in giving up, only in changing. In Starnyx' memory.

Lucky7: Ok.

Doctor.Fid: Okay?

Lucky7: Ok, yeah, ok. I'll sponsor you in, introduce you around.

Doctor.Fid: Thank you.

"You feeling all right?" Aaron asked absently, most of his attention focused upon the large pool and his daughter's swim class. "You disappeared from the office for a few days." The air was cool, crisp and thick with the scent of chlorinated water. The open space and high ceiling made the sound of children's laughter and playful shrieks echo loudly.

"I received some sad news, I'm afraid," I grimaced. Across the broad pool, Whisper was splashing about somewhat ineffectively as she learned to swim. Her recently-replaced skin and synthetic musculature had (among other improvements) been altered to maintain variable buoyancy, and Aaron had suggested that Whisper join his daughter's class. "A family friend passed away."

"That sucks," my CIO replied succinctly, then frowned. "Did Whisper know...?"

"Yes, I'm afraid so," I sighed. The little android had always complained when Starnyx jokingly called her a shell-script, but I knew she heard the affection in his voice. "They'd been friends."

"Damn. Poor kid."

"She's had a rough time of it, but she's resilient." I smiled fondly; Whisper was focused on her swim instructor now, just another young girl learning to be comfortable in the water. It was remarkable how accepting the staff and other children were given Whisper's unusual appearance. Aaron must have spoken to them. "Stronger than I am, I think."

Aaron just smiled.

Aaron had been with A.H. Biotech since the company's inception, one of the earliest hires. A dedicated workaholic, he made quick work of climbing the ranks and earning his current title. Many days, he was among the first to reach the office in the morning and was among the last to leave. At the time, I'd admired his dedication. That he had a daughter at all was a complete surprise.

I'd been eating lunch and talking shop with one of our senior geneticists. Aaron had been on the other side of the breakroom, arguing with a senior sysadmin about a project to upgrade some database servers. And, in the background, a television news reporter gravely announced that Scorpius had taken the students at a Beacon Hill nursery school hostage.

I recalled Aaron's changing countenance with crystal clarity. At first, just a moment of recognition. For such an intelligent man, it took a surprising amount of time for him to digest the information. It was as though the images onscreen were encrypted, the words spoken in a foreign language that needed careful translation. I watched it: The sudden realization that something was precious to him, something that he'd taken for granted, something that meant everything...and that thing was in danger.

A summer breeze carries the taste of ocean salt and fresh-cut grass. I don't hear the explosion so much as feel it: my chest aches as though I've been punched. Someone screams and Bobby is so small in my arms and the nearest shelter looks so far away...

Aaron's expression had seemed eerily familiar.

Titan and Aeon rescued the hostages and Scorpius was imprisoned. Also, my CIO stopped working late into the night and instead chose to spend evenings with his family. Fatherhood suited him.

At the time, CEO Terry Markham's public support of his CIO's efforts to alter his work/life balance had been a low-effort means of improving company morale. It would have been pleasant to say that, even at my worst, I would not have interfered with a father seeking to improve his relationship with his own daughter. Unfortunately, the truth was uglier. At my worst, I would have used my civilian position to pour subtle hardships and difficulties upon the man, out of pure jealous rage that his child survived when Bobby had not.

Was I still that creature, I wondered? The old Fid, the worst Fid, had acted under the influence of neurosurgical alterations and a carefully-designed pharmacological regimen that reinforced the most villainous behaviors. Absent those effects, my decisions would be very different. And yet...the choice to cut away at sanity had been my own. Surely, that darkness was inside me still.

"You're happier," Aaron interjected suddenly, interrupting my reverie. "Since Whisper came into your life, I mean."

I wondered if he had been thinking of the same day. Of fear and fire and life-changing moments.

"I am, generally." The android happened to glance in our direction, grinning giddily, and I waved to her. "It's just been a rough couple of weeks."

"I know the way that goes," he sighed. "Oh, hey, as long as I've got you here..."

I laughed. He'd picked up the phrase from his predecessor who had a tendency to manufacture excuses to talk to other executives away from the office.

"No, seriously." Aaron grinned self-deprecatingly. "The devs for the medical nanite project are eating through storage space. More 'n ten times our original projections."

"Yes," I nodded. "I'm having Sagar keep full simulations instead of just holding onto the deltas. We're going to need the data for certification."

"We're years from human testing."

"It'll pay for itself eventually," I reassured, successfully hiding a smug smile. Any day now, a report on our initial results would pass by the Secretary of Health and Human Services' desk. There were hints of quite promising results when dealing with the specific form of inoperable cancer that the Secretary had been secretly (Hah!) diagnosed with. It seemed likely to me that there would be a quiet push for accelerated human trials. "How long 'til we fill the Cambridge data center?"

"Maybe a month," Aaron sighed. "Maybe less."

"Any chance we could just add more racks and RAID arrays?"

"I can check, but I'm pretty sure that facility is close to maxed out on cooling and power consumption."

(Corporate advancement would be simpler if Doctor Fid's resources could be utilized more openly. The quantum data-storage housed in the Doctor's deep oceanic facility could have resolved this issue for the company for years to come. That technology, however, was well known to be Fid's; if some other company were to study captured samples and successfully reverse engineer them, then A.H.B. would invest in a new data center. Until then, it was safer to maintain distance between Terry Markham's known capabilities and those exhibited by the infamous villain.)

"All right." I groaned softly, "Get your team leads together, see what old data we can archive and off-shore. That should earn us some time, and I'll squeeze some funding free to move up the Middletown branch opening."

"Ananya is going to scream bloody murder."

"I'll sit with her tomorrow." I chuckled, then reached down to grab Whisper's robe. "Looks like the lesson is winding down."

"Looks like." He picked up his own daughter's robe and bent to grab her flip-flops. "Thanks. I'll breathe easier knowing that there's a plan in place."

"Glad to help. Thank you for inviting us! This was a great idea."

"No problem at all. Dinah likes Whisper a lot."

I'm sorry that I was still exhibiting echoes of sociopathic traits four years ago, I didn't say. *I'm sorry that I didn't don my armor, fly to your daughter's school, liquefy Scorpius, and carry Dinah directly into your arms.*

I'm sorry that I'm a monster.

"Whisper likes Dinah, too," I said instead. "Teatime on Thursday?"

"Sounds good!" And then his daughter arrived, dripping and laughing, and conversation more-or-less ended.

The drive home was filled with Whisper telling me about her lesson and about her new friends; she'd absorbed literally every text on swimming technique available on the internet, but learning with a physical body was different. Better, she insisted.

"...and next time, I'll be brave and will dunk my head all the way underwat-Wait." She paused in her narration suddenly. "Put on NPR!"

I turned on the radio.

"-mments on our online forum evaluating the footage. Within hours, several separate threads were locked due to excessive vitriol. Several camps have emerged. One fairly significant contingent insists that the entire controversy can be dismissed; the video, they say, is a manufactured fake." The program's host had a pleasant speaking voice, aged and strong, with an accent that hinted of time spent in the Midwest. He also sounded vaguely familiar. "So, a question to my first guest: Titan, do you believe that the video is real?"

Generally speaking, I am a very conscientious driver. The damage that Doctor Fid causes is purposeful; allowing an automotive accident to occur when it was within my power to prevent it would be distasteful. Peripheral vision and other sensory inputs were shifted to an autopilot program before I turned my head to stare respectfully at my passenger. My own multitasking skills were significant, but Whisper's were remarkable! How many media channels, I wondered, was she monitoring concurrently?

The artificial intelligence's design and the quantum cloud that housed her psyche might limit her emotional growth to the speed at which a human child might mature, but it was a pleasure to watch her intellectual capabilities flourish.

"First, I'd like to say thank you for having me. It's always a pleasure being here." Titan's familiar voice began. The silver-clad 'hero' always had been an annoyingly effective public speaker. "I should note that I am not personally an expert, but that we have expert contacts that have performed extensive analysis of the leaked video. The general consensus is that the footage is, in fact, real."

"And is that conclusion shared by other members of our panel?"

"Yes."

"Yes."

"It is, yes."

"It's always pleasant when our guests quickly arrive at a consensus." The host chuckled softly. "We're all in agreement then: The video floating around the internet, depicting the famed villain Doctor Fid joining the hacktivist organization, the 'FTW', is genuine.

"If that is, in fact, the case...we should discuss what this video might mean. Our second guest is Joanne Durand, noted sociologist and author of New York Times Best Seller *Black Masks.* Joanne, you've made a career studying the long-term effect that supervillains have upon society. What were your first thoughts when you saw this video?"

"Honestly, Ted, my first thought was that the video had to be fake." She laughed self-deprecatingly. "My second thought was that yesterday would have been an excellent time to invest in cyber-security stocks. A lot of companies breathed a sigh of relief after the FTW was beheaded in that fire, but those same organizations are looking to increase their security now."

"Why is that?" The host (now identified as 'Ted') asked.

It was possible that the host was Dr. Theodore Nestle; he'd been a guest lecturer at MIT and his vocal timbre was, by my recollection, very similar.

"Doctor Fid is a dangerous fighter, certainly, but he's never been implicated in cybercrimes before," Ted continued.

"Even if his technological savvy doesn't translate to being an effective hacker, Doctor Fid has gathered a significant amount of resources over the course of his long career that he could offer to the FTW's cause," Joanne replied.

"A frightening thought, to be sure." Dr. Nestle paused. "Again, our first guest is the long-time leader of the Boston Guardians, and has faced Doctor Fid in combat more than a dozen times. Titan, you look like you have something to add?"

"I do," Titan replied firmly. "I wanted to remind your viewers that this video changes nothing! Is it really Doctor Fid speaking? Yeah. But it's just words from a faceless villain with a long history of violence and murder. He's never going to be a harmless hacker."

"I agree." I felt an odd, vague sense of betrayal when I recognized the speaker's Chilango accent. If there had been any so-called hero that I would have expected to trust my word...

"Our third guest is Titan's second-in-command, the Red Ghost," the program's host explained for other listeners. "Could you expand on that comment, please?"

"If Doctor Fid made these promises, then I am certain that he intends to honor them," the Ghost stated, and I was mollified. "That's the sort of man he's proven himself to be. That having been said, the oaths he swore do not make him harmless! He vowed to avoid 'unnecessary violence', but his definition of 'unnecessary' is unlikely to be the same as yours or mine."

"So you don't think that he'll change his behavior?" Theodore Nestle prompted.

"I'm sure that he will change his behavior," the Red Ghost replied. "I am, however, uncertain what those changes will be."

"I agree as well," Ms. Durand added. "The FTW has always been an organization bound by a shared ideology. Doctor Fid, on the other hand, has never made any attempts to advance any political or social agenda in the past. Violence has always been his *raison d'etre*, his overriding purpose. No matter what, I think we can be positive that the Doctor won't end up being a prototypical FTW member."

"If Doctor Fid is unlikely to change significantly, then why was this video created at all?"

"A tribute," a husky female voice declared, and my hands clamped painfully tight on the steering wheel. "According to several sources, the leader of the FTW, Starnyx, had been a close friend to Doctor Fid."

A quick remote search through the NPR's servers confirmed that this program was being broadcast live. Reflexively, I calculated the amount of time required to divert the car, don Doctor Fid's armor and fly to the studio to make a personal appearance. Surely, I thought wistfully, an appropriate level of enthusiastic preemptive self-defense would be deemed an acceptable lapse among my new compatriots...

"For our listeners at home, our fourth guest is the long-time leader of the New York Shield and has had extensive experience facing the powered members of the FTW organization. Sphinx, to confirm...you've never fought Doctor Fid directly?"

"I have not," she confirmed, then chuckled. "Although if he's joined the FTW, then I suppose that it is inevitable that we'll eventually cross paths."

That did seem very likely, yes.

Whisper stretched to rest her small hand on top of mine, warm and comforting, and my fingers unclenched from the steering wheel.

"The FTW is an international organization," the host began, "so why is it that the New York Shield seems to face them so often?"

"First, Ted, I think that we need to be clearer about what we're discussing: The FTW is a large, mostly anonymous online organization of hackers and activists that promote nonviolent protest and an anti-corporate agenda. That portion of the group is suspected of cybercrimes worldwide. The Shield is generally not involved in those investigations." She paused. "Well, not directly. One member of my team, Cuboid, is often called upon to assist the FBI's Cyber Crime division."

"I see."

"Only a very small percentage of the FTW's members are powered individuals, and it's this smaller group that are behind the viral videos posted to the Internet, and it's only that sub-group which the Shield is called upon to confront."

"Even though the organization is international," she continued, "it seems likely that most of the superpowered members are local to the New York area. In addition, Wall Street corporations and the New York banking organizations are favored targets."

"The so-called 'hackers and activists' that you're defending are still aiding and abetting supervillains!" Titan objected.

"I don't believe that label is accurate," Red Ghost countered. "They aren't really villains. Criminals, certainly, but in their misguided way they truly are trying to make the world a better place."

"They accepted an armor-plated faceless thug as their newest member," Titan spat.

"And that is certainly worrying," Joanne Durand replied. "But we don't yet fully understand what Doctor Fid's role will be within the organization. It's not rational to tar them all with the same brush."

"You've never faced the FTW in the field," the Red Ghost interjected, obviously addressing his team leader. "You don't know them. Did I ever tell you how their second-in-command was captured?"

"...Yes."

"Well, I haven't heard this story," the show's host commented curiously. "Please share?"

"It is a long tale and I'm afraid that some of the story is personal," Red Ghost demurred, "but the end result is that Beazd, a lifelong pacifist, surrendered himself and accepted imprisonment simply because he could not see a means of escape without harming one of his captors."

"I hadn't heard that, either," Ms. Durand noted, sounding awed.

"And that brings us to another part of this tragedy," Sphinx said, her tone grim. "This information wasn't meant to be public yet, but this does seem relevant to the discussion: A member of my team has pled guilty to involuntary manslaughter in the case of former FTW member Beazd's death."

There were assorted sounds of shock. I empathized; I was in shock too.

"Wh—what happened?" the Ghost asked shakily.

"Peregrine had reason to believe that Beazd was still in contact with known criminals—which would have been a violation of his parole. He set out to question Beazd and ended up employing excessive force.

"I've spoken to Peregrine at length and I am convinced that this was simply a terrible accident, that he is genuinely repentant, and that he had every reason to believe that Beazd's superhuman durability would have protected him. Nevertheless, the death occurred as a direct result of an illegal interrogation and Peregrine has been sentenced to five years of house arrest and eight hundred hours of community service."

"That's horrible," Joanne murmured, and Doctor Nestle agreed.

I slaved my arms and legs entirely to the auto-pilot program to keep from driving off the highway.

"There's more," Sphinx's voice was grave. "After the event in question, Peregrine came to me in a panic. To my great shame, I chose to protect my teammate rather than follow what I knew to be the lawful response. I have, myself, pled guilty to criminal conspiracy for my role in concealing the crime and staging an accidental death. I will be stepping down as leader of the New York Shield as soon as a replacement has been chosen, to serve my own sentence."

The censors failed to cut out the Red Ghost's Spanish invectives.

"It's very brave of you to come forward," Ted Nestle offered uncertainly. "May I ask when this event occurred?"

"Five months ago," the Ghost said, voice full of horrified judgment. "His PO notified me about the 'accident'."

"Given the timing of your confession, Sphinx, can we assume that Doctor Fid's video influenced your decision to come forward?"

"Not at all, Ted," Sphinx responded, and I was strangely certain that she was lying. I wasn't alone; the Red Ghost's scoffing was audible over the radio. "Peregrine and I decided to contact the district attorney right after the Staten Island fire."

"And why is that?"

"The guilt had been eating at us both for months, but...we never talked about it. Loyalty and fear kept us silent. Peregrine felt that he couldn't come forward without implicating me, and I couldn't say anything without implicating him." She sighed, but it sounded rehearsed to my ears. "The explosion at the FTW headquarters shocked us both out of inaction."

"So, what does this mean for the future of the New York Shield?" Ted asked. "Losing two members so suddenly must surely be disruptive."

"Oh, neither of us are leaving the Shield," Sphinx reassured. "A federal judge agreed that active duty on a state-recognized superhero team would count towards our community service."

"That's good," Joanne sounded relieved. "It'd be a shame to lose two of New York's most powerful protectors."

There was a bitter taste in my mouth, and my teeth were clenched together so tight that my jaw ached. No censure, no consequences...their 'punishment' would be to continue their day-to-day lives unhindered.

I imagined broken bodies and cities on fire. It was a calming vision.

"We're still here to protect the people of our city," Sphinx declared serenely. "I suppose that's why I felt compelled to announce our sentences here. We were talking about the threat that the FTW may pose now that the notorious Doctor Fid has joined them, and I wanted to remind all of your viewers that the FTW has lost much more than they've gained. Good men and women were killed in the fire, and another former member lost to a terrible, tragic error in judgment.

"Peregrine and I are facing justice for our choices. Where the FTW goes from here is their choice: whether they decide to honor the ideals of their fallen, or instead allow themselves to be led down a darker path by their newest member...whatever choice they make, the New York Shield will stand ready."

I growled loud enough that Whisper shrunk away, surprised.

To the casual listener, Sphinx's argument might have sounded as though it were intended to reassure the people of New York. I recognized the emotionally charged rhetoric for what it was: a direct attack upon my support within the FTW.

My petition for entry may have been approved, but the vote had been a near thing. Many members had worried that my very presence would change the group's dynamic. Indeed, some who had voted in my favor had expressed exactly that hope: that I would direct more aggressive conflicts upon our targets. The false dilemma that Sphinx had proffered would embolden those comrades who wanted to change the status quo and make wary those who wanted to uphold the principles set by Starnyx and Beazd.

It wasn't the end of the world. There would be drama, arguments on the forums, a few members might take a leave of absence in protest...but nothing would come of this. All that I would need to do is honor my oaths and eventually the furor would die down. Sphinx's verbal jab was naught but an irritation and a waste of my time. In a real sense, though, time was no longer a pressing issue. The only endeavor that I'd already been planning to assist the FTW with had been the revelation of Peregrine and Sphinx's crimes. I would—I'd thought—at least have been able to finish Starnyx's work! Now, the organization's efforts regarding that issue would certainly be curtailed. Already, members were posting cheerful messages celebrating their win.

To me, however, this tasted more of bile than of victory.

I'm bent over a workbench, studying a circuit board through a desktop-mounted magnifying glass. Anguish permeates my every waking moment, but mere physical pain cannot compete with the need to create! I limp and groan and suffer, right arm bound tight in cast and sling. The fracture is clean but the limb continues to discolor and swell. Though my bruised and bloodied face aches from the effort (two molars lost to a broken jaw; replacement teeth were in progress but not yet ready for implantation), still I grin.

A cracked rib makes breathing an agony. Blood fills my mouth and occasionally dribbles between cracked lips to further stain my shirt. And I am as close to being happy as I've been in years. What a battle!

This circuit board is only a prototype; the final design will need be fabricated at a much smaller scale, hardened and sculpted and shaped to precise specifications. The model, however, can be created by hand.

The cortical reorganization surgery has, unfortunately, produced inconclusive results; I have yet to induce true ambidexterity. There are further avenues available for future experimentation, but my temporary solution has been to filter my sensory perception and flip body control laterally so that I can solder left-handed without significant impairment. Time is of the essence; the next attack will have to be soon if I'm to capitalize on the media frenzy. Doctor Fid's new armor will need be ready by the time I heal.

A few months more and I could be done with this. Done with Fid, done with Terry, done with everything. The maths are complicated, but thus far my projections regarding public response have proven to be satisfyingly accurate.

An exhaustive study of memes and tropes and archetypes informs Doctor Fid's behavior patterns. A carefully orchestrated symphony of violence and horror reinforces the narrative. Simple demonstrations of strength would have been wholly insufficient; I'd needed to do something spectacular. Before I finally confront Bronze, Doctor Fid's reputation as a dread supervillain needs to be established firmly in the minds of all.

The time had been right for a display of power, and the fight had been glorious.

When experts and enthusiasts debate and declare rankings among superhumans, their discussions inevitably focus upon second place. First place is, after all, beyond dispute. The mighty Valiant is unmatched in raw strength and invulnerability; his flight speed marks him among the fastest of superhumans, and the energy he projects from his hands strikes with greater force than a battleship's main cannon. In his storied seventeen-year career, the handsome African-American hero has fought alien invaders, inter-dimensional beasts and dozens of powerful supervillains looking to make a name for themselves. He has (rarely!) been tricked or trapped or outmaneuvered, but never overpowered. Colorful action figure signs declared that no one could stand against the undefeatable Valiant!

Three months into the new millennium, at a White House ceremony to honor the hero's wartime service as an enlisted soldier, those marketers have been proven wrong. For twelve full minutes, I battled toe-to-toe with the fabled hero, fighting him to a standstill while all the world watched and held its breath! Doctor Fid has twice crossed paths with Valiant before and escaped cleanly, but this time escape wasn't the goal; the Mk 11 Warframe (now too damaged for repair) stood nearly fourteen feet tall, broad and powerful and the culmination of every scientific discovery, every engineering breakthrough and every act of theft since Bobby's murder five years earlier. Tens of millions of dollars' worth of equipment poured into one extraordinary, mythic combat! With this battle, fought before the eyes of horrified politicians and countless mass-media cameras, Doctor Fid has finally made himself legendary. I'd retreated when it became plain that reinforcements would soon be arriving, but all the world would remember the sight of Fid, laughing maniacally while trading blows with their undefeatable hero.

Five years of anger and self-loathing. Five years of tragedy and disgust. Five years of drugs and misery and self-inflicted experimental surgeries and destroying myself in the name of righteous vengeance. And now, the end is in sight! Doctor Fid's starfield-embossed armor is so universally feared and hated that the epic conclusion of my quest is finally within reach. When I recover, I will finally be able to face Bronze and expose us both for the monsters that we are.

An alert chime grabs my attention. Odd. Why would an obituary catch the attention of one of my internet data trawling algorithms?

CHAPTER NINE

FROM A QUARTER MILE'S DISTANCE, I DIRECTED A SERIES of non-visible-spectrum lasers upon the warehouse's windows and performed interferometric analysis upon the reflected beams. Atmospheric conditions strained the system's efficacy, but even so software algorithms were able to detect minute vibrations and convert the signal to sound. Boisterous laughter. Multiple conversations... some low and personal and others that seemed to involve small crowds of enthusiastic participants. Downtempo electronica music, loud enough to be heard but quiet enough not to interfere with communication.

The din was painfully nostalgic.

I'd visited Nyx at the Staten Island facility several times. The cadence and tone and comfortable humor...I'd never been a part of this community before, but this had been my friend's world. I'd send a coded message to indicate that I'd arrived and he'd step outside, always with a fond smile for those he left behind. The FTW had shined a scathing light upon corporate greed and overreach, but

Starnyx had once confessed that he hoped that this would be his legacy: this society of idealistic renegades.

With a light heart, I landed and let myself in the front door. My current armor, the newly designed Mk 34 Stealth, was the least imposing model yet produced. It was close to form-fitting and added only a few inches to my natural height, offering only limited protection. There were no visible armaments; the star-field motif remained, but the angry red glow characteristic to most of Doctor Fid's other armors had been omitted. The helmet and faceplate had even been subtly humanized to offer a hint of jaw and cheekbone. It was a kinder and gentler Fid that entered the FTW's new meeting place.

Within moments, the levity and casual camaraderie had been replaced with a tense, uncomfortable silence. The music's volume was lowered, and all eyes turned towards me; some expressions were fearful, others judgmental, and others filled with outright scorn.

There was, I thought, a non-zero percentage chance that I was a monumental imbecile.

"I've been working on an algorithm that trawls social media sites to identify possible sources of biographic leverage against corporate executives," I explained. "It's based loosely on some work by DarkPixie21 and MortarThyme."

The armor's vocoder had been reprogrammed to allow more emotional depth to carry within Doctor Fid's voice. I'd hoped that it would make me more approachable; instead, I sounded...unsettled. Annoyance at my own insecurity flashed into anger and I took a slow, silent breath to dispel the unwanted emotion. Still, no one else spoke.

"Are either of them here?" I asked finally. "I was hoping to collaborate."

My sensitive microphones identified a young voice frantically whispering, "Say 'no', man, say 'no'!" to his compatriot near the line of refurbished pinball machines. Ah. Facial recognition identified the speaker as one of the three people that I'd suspected of being the notorious hacker MortarThyme.

Someone coughed nervously.

It had been four months. Four months, and my reception was less well-received than it had been on day one! I'd been a fool to hope that Sphinx's sly attack upon my position within the FTW would be limited to a comment within a single radio broadcast. Her efforts hadn't been blatant; given the controversy regarding her crimes, the uptick in media appearances made by the tarnished heroine was unsurprising. Somehow, she guided the conversations to my membership in FTW. Always, mention was made of past misdeeds.... Actions that I'd performed during the old, bad years before my 'retirement'. Victims' names were slipped in and obscure incidents described with just enough tantalizing detail to inspire the media to perform more detailed follow-up stories: my most regrettable atrocities spun into a constant news cycle.

Last night's expose had focused on my battle against Clash. Objectively, it hadn't been a poor documentary. The section about reconstructive surgery and physical therapy had been presented in a genuinely interesting manner.

I was guilty of horrors, no doubt. I'd been unhinged. Unfettered. Rage and self-loathing had twisted me into something horrific; the embers of that insanity, I oft worried, still resided somewhere within my soul...but that fire had long been banked and the ashes were cold. For Nyx, I'd taken the oaths and hoped to forge a new future...and yet, here in the community he left behind, there was no solace to be found. My truest friend's legacy had no place within it for the likes of Doctor Fid.

"I'll just send an e-mail, then," I mumbled uncomfortably. "I hope that you all have a good evening."

I fled.

I chose to start a biotechnology firm for logical reasons: There was profit to be made, certainly, and the opportunity to accomplish grand goals. Also, it was one of the sciences in which a highly skilled team of researchers could easily eclipse my own capabilities. I was intelligent and sufficiently well-educated to work alongside professionals, but I wasn't a true pioneer. I did, however, certainly have enough talent to recognize pioneers when I saw them. In a company focused upon biotechnological exploration, Terrance Markham could be a CEO rather than a scientist. The great task before me, therefore, was to create an environment in which those pioneers might flourish, and to point those pioneers in useful directions.

There were other responsibilities, of course. Building a successful business had required any number of new skills to be studied. Fortunately, I was a fast learner.

AHBT flourished and our teams accomplished miraculous feats. Genetically engineered microorganisms were created to synthesize lifesaving medications at a fraction of the traditional cost. Trauma bandages were fabricated that sped up clotting without generating scar tissue. Corals were modified to thrive in hostile environments and repair ecological damage. Inexpensive filters were devised to improve emergency water supplies, utilizing antibacterial and antimicrobial compounds created by altered yeasts. The medical nanite project had been a stretch, requiring the hiring of researchers and engineers with skills outside of our biotechnological base. The version we intended on marketing was nowhere near as comprehensive as the swarm that infested my own body (achieving the results that I'd enjoyed required access to Doctor Fid's sensors and a decade's worth of regular deep medical scans), but the project had, even so, proven successful beyond our expectations.

The company was well on its way to proving that the world might be saved without requiring the intervention of spandex-clad false idols.

Choosing to incorporate, too, had been a rational decision. Growing a private business to a size sufficient to handle massive government contracts would have taken decades, and I was not quite so patient. A well-implemented IPO had served to dramatically expand the company's available funds. Stock grants and options had also increased my personal wealth dramatically.

There were, however, downsides.

"You have a fiduciary responsibility to your stockholders, Terrance," Henry Collins said dryly, cutting his perfectly-cooked steak with Pythagorean precision. His skin was rosy-pale and smooth like that of an infant that had barely felt the touch of the sun. "The board is very concerned about some of your recent expenditures."

The formally-dressed, gray-haired man was the current chairman of the company's board of directors. He knew absolutely nothing about the AHBT's products or its business model. I would have been honestly astonished had he ever demonstrated the capability of defining 'biotechnology' without looking the term up. Instead, Henry was an activist investor elected by other activist investors and maintaining a professional smile in his presence was more draining than running a marathon. And we'd barely started the meal's third course!

"I thought that might be why you suggested we meet here," I managed a friendly chuckle. "I brought some projections with me...best and worst-case scenarios."

I offered him a folder; when he didn't move to accept it, I left it by the side of his plate.

"You committed a small fortune of the company's money to that ocean...thing." Henry gestured minutely with his fork. "It's good publicity, but you need to keep a closer eye on the bottom line."

"We have buyers lined up for the technology once it's been proven," I reassured him. "We'll make our investment back in less than eighteen months."

"I'm not here to talk about next year's profit margins." Henry lifted his chin pointedly. "I'm here to talk about this quarter. Profits are down, Terrance. Our stock is down five percent since the earnings call."

"And up eighty percent over this time last year," I pointed out. "We're a healthy company...This is just a minor dip."

I remembered one morning when my parents and I had walked the Longfellow bridge; Mom had let me push Bobby's stroller and the fog was so thick we couldn't see the opposite shore. Cars barreled from within the dense cloud and disappeared again in moments, and we could hear a train approaching for minutes before it exploded into visibility. It was loud, and the wind seemed terribly violent to a small child like myself. My hands had gripped the stroller's handle as hard as I could manage, but still I had felt helpless and overwhelmed. Calculating wind shear and force vectors did little to calm my shaking arms.

Henry Collins' pale blue eyes reminded me of fog.

"I am eating a wonderful steak, accompanied by wine-braised mushrooms and the best truffled macaroni and cheese I've ever tasted," the well-coiffed man stated evenly. "What I'm not doing is looking over the numbers you brought. I don't have to; I know what they'll say: Another slight dip in profits next quarter, followed by at least two even quarters before we start gaining again."

"Profits may be lower than some projections, but we're still well in the black," I countered. "We have several products in the pipeline that look to be highly lucrative."

"You do have quite a few projects awaiting federal approval," he nodded, baring his teeth in what I was certain that he considered to be a smile. "More than enough to see to the company's short-term needs."

"Long term is just tomorrow's short term. There's a lot of upside potential here, Henry."

"Even so, the board recommends that you consider cutting research expenditures by thirty percent. Until the ratio of products-awaiting-approval to salable-products drops below industry average, of course."

"Our ratio is high because we're establishing ourselves as an industry leader." I smiled tightly. A reduction that significant would require significant layoffs. "If we lower our commitment to research, we may lose that position."

"Your job isn't to be an industry leader." The investor's voice was cold. Again, I was reminded of that foggy winter morning. "Your job is to make stock prices go up. Anything else the company may do is secondary."

I bit back my initial response, forced an approximation of a pleasant grin, and used my neural link to pore through a few recent articles by respected analysts.

"The industry," I pointed out, "is up fourteen percent, year-over-year. As I mentioned, we're up eighty. The brokerage firms you represent have more than doubled their money since they invested three years ago. I don't think that the board has much to complain about."

"That's true *today*," he acknowledged without any hint of gratitude or agreement. "It is, however, likely to look very different after nine-to-twelve months of flat profits."

"Stock price isn't tied to profits," I responded archly. "The research we still have in the pipe will generate a significant amount of positive publicity."

"And it will generate more if you demonstrate that you are focused on maintaining profit growth while waiting for the fruit of your labors to ripen. Again, the board is recommending a thirty-percent reduction in research expenditures."

I imagined him on fire. The scent of scorched hair and searing flesh, and the sound of his shrieks rising in pitch as the heat tore at his throat. His delicate, immaculately manicured hands curled into claws as he struggled ineffectually to douse the flames.

"I understand the board's concerns," I smiled, and he saw something in the expression that made him pale, "and I will certainly take their advice under consideration."

"You may have started the company, but your position isn't set in stone." To his credit, his voice didn't shake at all. "If you push back on this, you'll have a fight on your hands."

"I could use a good fight," I answered truthfully.

The meal continued, but neither of us felt compelled to add to the conversation.

```
Welcome to #SYNChat!
<encrypted private channel established>

MortarThyme: doctor fid, u here?

DoctorFid: I am, yes.
```

MortarThyme: i got ur mail. Thx

DoctorFid: The algorithm was helpful, then?

MortarThyme: its tight. v efficient!

DoctorFid: That was the intended goal. It should increase the speed of your searches by several ticks per iteration.

MortarThyme: 12% faster, gj.

DoctorFid: I'm working on a compression schema to minimize memory usage, as well. There will be a slight performance hit, but the difference can easily be offset by other improvements.

MortarThyme: sounds gud. i rewrote ur error check code, have look here.

DoctorFid: Interesting. I see a significant difference in the number of errors that you raise.

MortarThyme: only a few r relevant.

DoctorFid: We'd lose a fair bit of information, when attempting to troubleshoot problems with the application.

MortarThyme: idm. ur code is solid and i can dig into prog w/o. more fault tolerant this way, 2.

DoctorFid: I see your point.

MortarThyme: thx again.

DoctorFid: It was no great difficulty. I'm happy to help a fellow FTW member.

MortarThyme: o just so u know, im reformatting ur code b4 posting.

DoctorFid: Oh? How so?

MortarThyme: changing indentations + variable names. spacing.

DoctorFid: That won't impede functionality at all. May I ask why the change?

MortarThyme: ur work is v distinctive

MortarThyme: sum wont use program if they no it is urs

MortarThyme: this way, mor ppl will use

DoctorFid: I see. So, it is your opinion that the program will be of more use to the community if all credit for its creation is given to you?

MortarThyme: not looking 4 credit, just want ppl 2 use prog

MortarThyme: i herd about wut happend when u went 2 Gallery.

DoctorFid: You heard about that, did you?

MortarThyme: y.

```
DoctorFid: It's too bad that you weren't at the Gallery
when I visited. It would have been nice to collaborate
in person.

MortarThyme: mebbe nxt time
```

("We could meet by the pinball machine, where someone who looked rather like you had just earned a new high score moments before I arrived. Seven million, four-hundred fifty-two thousand, seven-hundred and fifty, wasn't it?" I carefully did not type.)

```
DoctorFid: Yes, perhaps another time. Feel free to
modify the program as you described.

MortarThyme: kthxbye.

<MortarThyme has disconnected>
<DoctorFid has disconnected>
```

The furniture was sturdy and comfortable, glossy antique cherry hardwood and dark leather upholstery in good repair. Built-in bookshelves adorned two of the walls, stuffed full of texts on a wide variety of subjects relevant to AH Biotech's products, and stacks of papers lay arranged in careful piles upon the expansive desk. The decor for my office at AH Biotech had been chosen to evoke the impression of an organized academic rather than the typical business tycoon.

I'd never been that kind of professor. My personal space at MIT had been chaos incarnate, a jumble of notes and paperwork so muddled that it was indecipherable by any but myself. It was only in retrospect, reviewing memories years later, that I noticed the discomfort of my students when they came to ask questions of me during office-hours. Sitting half-on and half-off the metal folding chair, trying not to dislodge the half-completed prototypes that I'd left resting there. I must have done a decent job of answering their questions, at least; several of students had been willing to return multiple times.

It struck me that Doctor Albert Hess, the professor that I had purported to name this company after...his office had been appointed similarly to the one I'd created at AH Biotech. The quality of materials in his chamber had not been quite so lavish, perhaps, but the paradigm was certainly recognizable. How odd. I'd designed this space and worked within it for years and yet never had made that connection.

Perhaps I had noticed the association because I felt strangely unwelcome in that space. The office belonged to Dr. Terrance Markham, but right then I was too close to Fid. Beneath a CEO's skin, a predator lurked, vicious, tense and eager for its prey to arrive.

There was movement at my door.

"Sir? I was told that you wanted to see me?"

"Ah, yes. Bradley Kent." I faked a convincingly pleasant smile and motioned my three-thirty appointment to enter and take a seat. "We met at last year's Christmas party, didn't we?"

"We did, yes." The graying, slightly overweight man sat down, looking more confused than nervous. He hadn't been given a reason for being summoned.

"Ananya introduced you. You worked for her at Reddington Software, and followed her when she came here?"

"Yes, sir." He nodded. "Ms. Singh is a good boss."

"I'd hope so," I chuckled. "Ananya has mentioned you often in our meetings, by the way."

"Oh? Nothing bad, I hope!" He forced a laugh, looking a bit more concerned now than he had moments before.

"No, of course not," I shook my head. "She's quite proud of her team, and values your contributions very much."

"I'm glad to hear that." He laughed out loud, his relief quite visible.

"She mentioned that your son was recently accepted to Dartmouth?"

"He was!" His smile broadened, his shoulders squaring as he puffed up in paternal pride. "That was his reach school, but he definitely earned it."

"Dartmouth is an excellent college." I noted. "They have very high academic standards"

"My boy, Alex...he's a hard worker, he'll manage."

"I understand that Alex is going to be majoring in organic chemistry." I nodded approvingly. "Do you think that he'd be interested in an internship?"

"I think that he'd be ecstatic!" Bradley beamed, but then raised a hand in caution. "Not in his first year, though. Starting out at college is hard enough. Is that what this meeting is about?"

"In a way, yes. Your son has an excellent CV and seems tremendously passionate about his studies. We've never had an intern program before, but he seems like he'd be an excellent candidate." I leaned back in my chair. "So, I'd very much like for you to take a moment and imagine what his expression would look like, if you had to inform him that you couldn't afford his tuition on account of your impending job hunt and legal fees."

"Wh-what? I don't under-"

"You shared internal financial data with the investment firm that handles your wife's retirement fund. That's insider trading." I'd located the source of Henry Collins' information and it was a joy, having someone to punish! My smile felt more like a baring of teeth. "Are you imagining your son's expression?"

"Yes," the accountant whispered shakily.

"Describe it to me."

"He'll be heartbroken," Bradley murmured. I'd expected claims of innocence or belligerent defense. Instead, his gaze looked distant, as though focusing only upon the scene that I'd proposed. "He's told all of his friends, our relatives. God, we already bought him two of those blazers...I can't do that to him. I'll find a way, sell the damned house-!"

Damn it all.

"You don't need to do that, yet. We're still talking about a purely hypothetical scenario." When I'd set up this meeting, it had been under the perfectly reasonable assumption that Bradley had revealed the information for some sort of profit. Annoyingly, all of my behavioral analysis programs indicated that to be an unlikely scenario. Softly, I asked "What do you think would your son say?"

"He's a good kid." He smiled, though his eyes were glassy with un-shed tears. "He'd put on a brave face and ask if I was all right."

"It sounds as though you've raised a fine young man." That feral part of me, that part that had wanted someone to hurt...it sulked and retreated deeper within. I felt as though I'd just sat down to enjoy a hearty meal to break a long fast, only for the plate to have been whisked away before I could taste a morsel. Cheated and still hungry.

"He is," Bradley choked out.

"It would be preferable, I think, if your son didn't have to undergo such hardship." All that I yearned for was a deserving target upon which to vent my righteous wrath. Was that so much to ask? I swallowed rage and resentment, and shook my head. "I really very much would prefer to offer your son that internship in a year or two."

"Oh god please-"

"I haven't informed legal about this incident, yet," I admitted, offering a comforting smile despite feeling suddenly weary. "This is just a conversation between the two of us."

"What do I need to do?" He visibly gathered his courage, a man expecting the gallows and choosing to face it head-on for his family's sake.

(My neural scarring had still been present when I'd founded AH Biotech. How had I managed to oversee an organization staffed by people so much better than myself? Was it luck, or simply good programming? The software that I'd composed to augment our headhunting efforts had, admittedly, been very complex.)

"You're already doing good work," I reassured him. "Ananya raves about you. All that I want is for you to stop sharing information with your friend from Watson and Forester holdings."

"I swear!"

"Then there's nothing more we need to do or say. Except to ask that you relay my well-wishes to your son."

"Doctor Markham...I really am sorry."

"I believe you," I sighed. "Just...explain to me why? Ananya raves about your work, you seem happy here..."

"It was a mistake," he shrugged helplessly. "A stupid mistake. Greg is an old friend, and I didn't think that there would be any harm. He was already planning on investing!"

For a brief moment, I brightened at the thought that I could perhaps ruin this Greg person's life over this incident instead. Unfortunately, I could think of no easy way to do so without implicating Mr. Kent as well; Bradley was, by all appearances, a loyal employee. My pulse may race eagerly at the opportunity to punish a traitor amongst my people, but the faithful should be cherished and protected.

"I have no proof, but I suspect that your friend shared the information with his superior in order to justify the investment. The information spread from there. There may be consequences for this," I sighed, "But I'll make sure that they don't land on you. For your son's sake...please be more careful in the future."

I'd looked forward to destroying Bradley Kent when he'd entered my office, but he thanked me profusely on his way out. I no longer felt alien within this homey, richly decorated office.

I barely felt anything at all.

During my initial career as Doctor Fid, my brain had been altered by knife and chemical 'til I'd been every inch the villain. I'd had a goal, after all, and half-measures would have interfered with manufacturing the pyrrhic final battle I'd ached for. After my temporary retirement, the drug regimen had been abandoned and the surgeries reversed. Through five years of research at MIT and a decade rebuilding and expanding upon Doctor Fid's mission, I'd thought myself whole.

It had been many months since the medical nanites had eliminated the last of my neural scarring. The change to my psyche had been at sometimes profound, and other times quite subtle.

It wasn't a question of intensity; I'd never lacked for strong passions! There was, however, a nimble and reactive nature to my emotional state to which I was still becoming accustomed. There were new nuances to my ethos that I was ill-equipped to describe. I felt better for the shift, but I'd been unprepared.

(There had been memory issues, too. Minor glitches, evidenced only in hard-coded logs. I'd apparently flushed my short-term memory a half-dozen times during my recuperation; I had no idea why I'd felt compelled to do so, but the commands had been issued with my own authorization codes so surely I must have had good cause. I only wish that I had thought to document my reasoning for future reference)

I missed Starnyx.

For an incandescent fraction of my life, I'd had a trusted confident. Someone who I could talk to unmasked, someone who listened and commiserated and understood. I'd never had a friend like that. I'd never really believed that friendship like that existed outside of fiction! I'd been whole barely long enough to truly appreciate the value of that bond, and then he was gone.

My ward, at least, could know both Terry Markham and Doctor Fid. It wasn't the same. Whisper's psyche existed as a quantum cloud held in state by clusters of the most powerful crystal supercomputers on the planet, but she was young. If needed, she could absorb the sum total of all psychology research and self-help literature available on the internet, and construct advice based on statistical analysis of outcomes...but she couldn't really empathize with my frustrations. She could sympathize, of course! And she did, extending gentle and caring support for which I would be eternally grateful. Still, I did not wish for her to be unnecessarily burdened.

When I'd joined the FTW, I had (at least subconsciously) longed to find similar relationships among their members to that which I'd had with their founder. Nyx...Eric Guthrie...certainly could not be replaced. I'd anticipated that I could, however, at least find some comfort among those he had influenced. In them, I'd hoped, I could at least find an echo of Eric's presence.

```
Welcome to the SYNchat Online Message Boards
Logout [ Doctor_Fid ]     3 new messages
View unanswered posts | View active topics
```

> Topic: Suggestions for next target
v464b0nd (Original Poster):
-    The Elliot Property Holdings job was very
- successful. We got half a million hits and
- coverage on four major networks. Elliot
- has already started sending out restitution
- checks to victims of their mortgage fraud.
- Great job, folks.
- So, any suggestions for our next target?

M0nk3yB0i (member):
-    how about paragon research? they do a
- lot of secret weapon research, including
- the sonic cannons used by Bialya
- military to suppress protest.

PlagueDog (member):
-    basturds @elliot should go 2 jail! my
- aunt spent 4 months fiting them, lost
- her house + job.

Blond/Blue (senior member):
-    No word on criminal charges? WTF? They
- forged hundreds of foreclosure statements.

v464b0nd (Original Poster):
-    It will be a while before we hear of any
- charges, but there's enough publicity that
- the Attorney General can't just sweep this
- under the rug. There's another thread
- discussing the Elliot Property Holdings job,
- and the aftermath. Keep this thread on
- topic, please?

PlagueDog (member):
- should have sent fid instead of root, hax
- and colonel panic. tehy wud send chex
- faster if there was a bodycount.
(user has received a warning from the moderator - stay
on topic, please)

Doctor_Fid (junior member):
- I assisted with gathering information
- gathering. Root, Hax and Colonel Panic did
- a fine job on the infiltration and on their
- video presentation. If they wish for me to
- join them in any future endeavors, they
- need only ask.
- To keep this on topic, how about Quest
- Automotive? Their factory in Pennsylvania
- has been causing significant ecological
- damage to the region. Cancer rates among
- children in Beaumont are seventeen times
- the national average.
- P.S. I took the same oath you did,
- PlagueDog. No body count.

Lucky7 (senior member):
- I think targeting Paragon Research would
- generate too much heat. They sell equipment
- to just about every superhero team in the
- country.
- Quest Automotive isn't a bad idea. Also,
- what about Hebert Natural Resources?
- They've been cashing federal checks for 'clean
- coal' research, pretty sure they're rigging
- the testing.

v01d_h34rt (junior member):

- McSweenie Burger, Inc! I think they put
- crack cocaine in their fries. So addictive!

White_Bishop (member):
- How about AH Biotech? They're consistently
- getting FDA approval in half the time as
- their competitors. If they r paying
- someone off, their safety research might be
- faked, too.

PlagueDog (member):
- thats scary. i used there ez-clot bandage
- after my dirtbiike crash. we shud do them.

Helios (senior member):
- I haven't heard anything negative about
- AH Biotech products. Hebert Natural Resources
- is a sure thing. Lots of safety violations in
- their mines, too.

White_Bishop (member):
- AHBT could be covering it up.
- The CEO of AH Biotech is creepy. Here is
- a video of him taking his pedo sex robot on
- play dates at a public pool.

PlagueDog (member):
- lol

Enigma_North (senior member):
- I hadn't seen that video. Do you know who
- manufactured it?

PlagueDog (member):
- y? u want pedo sex robot of ur own?

Enigma_North (senior member):
-   Screw you. A quick public records search
- shows that he adopted the android and has
- requested a citizenship hearing. This could
- be a good court case for non-human rights.
- Even if he's a creep, he's rich. He can buy
- off a judge and do something good by
- accident.

PlagueDog (member):
-   MY LUV PILLOW IS MY WAIFU! HOW
- SHE GET HEERING?
(user has received a second warning from the moderator -
stay on topic, please)

Enigma_North (senior member):
-   I suggest we table AH Biotech for now,
- and focus on Hebert Natural Resources. If
- we see any more strange stuff at AHBT, we
- can target them another time.

v464b0nd (Original Poster):
-   Seconded. I've set up a separate topic.

And that thread is why I ended up moderately drunk, angry and depressed, and hurtling through Boston's night sky wearing the rebuilt Mk 28 medium-combat powered armor.

CHAPTER TEN

THE PHONE RANG TWICE BEFORE THE MAN BEGAN TO stir. Miguel Espinoza groaned softly, whispered a soft apology to the woman who shared his bed (she voiced only a wordless complaint and rolled over) and reached for the nightstand. The caller was displayed as unlisted, but he answered anyway.

"What?" he asked bluntly, chilango accent more pronounced in the throaty weariness of his voice. "Do you have any idea what time it is?"

"Two forty-seven AM. This is Doctor Fid," I replied. "I was wondering if we could talk?"

"...Not even a little funny, Bryce. Good night." The unmasked superhero ended the call and closed his eyes, tiredly running his fingers through his hair. It was a warm evening; he'd slept nude and the bed bore only a sheet for warmth, but still sweat had dried to his tan skin. He scratched at his chest absently, rolled back onto the mattress and fumbled tiredly for the sheet.

Again, the phone rang. Even half-asleep, his reflexes were fast; Miguel lifted the phone to his ear before the first ring's completion.

"I'm really not in the mood for this," the man hissed angrily.

"Look across the street," I suggested. The playground bench on which I was sitting was shaded by maple trees, so I boosted my armor's crimson luminescence for visibility's sake and waited for him to roll out of bed.

"Madre de Dios," he whispered, peeking through a gap in the blinds; when he spoke again, his voice shook. "Please, don't hurt my family."

"...Why would you even SAY that?" I asked, glad for the vocoder that stripped the plaintive whine from my voice. "We've fought for years, and I've never—not even once!—threatened someone's family."

"People change. And it's been a strange year for you." He'd stepped away from the window; the brief moment of fear quickly faded, replaced by the thoughtful intensity that I had always associated with him.

"That, at least, is certainly true," I agreed and dimmed the armor's glow. "I'm not here to fight. I'm just here to talk."

The Red Ghost cradled the phone between his shoulder and ear, using one hand to gently shake his lover awake and gesturing for quiet by bringing a finger to his lips with the other hand. "Then talk, Doctor Fid."

The woman stilled. Interesting reaction to hearing a supervillain's name spoken aloud. I tasked one of the microdrones that was infiltrating Miguel Espinoza's house to perform more detailed scans; She was of average height, late twenties, dusky skinned and dark shoulder-length hair, attractive features and a very athletic physique. Ah. 98% certainty body-type and feature match to the Ghost's team-mate, Regrowth.

I activated a subroutine for my armor's on-board sensors to monitor the local flora, and to raise alerts in the event of unexpected movement. Just in case.

"If I'd wanted to talk over the phone, I wouldn't have flown to Medford."

"And what did you want to talk about?" Inside, Miguel was using sign language to explain the situation to Regrowth. Her response (also using sign) would have peeled paint from the walls were it spoken aloud. My personal opinion of Regrowth (Elaine Goldman, facial recognition now confirmed) was rapidly improving.

"I've had a strange year." After a brief pause, I grit my teeth and added, "...Please."

"What, did you expect for me to simply put on my slippers and come chat with a notorious supervillain in plain view of my neighbors?" The judgmental scorn in his voice was partially negated by the fact that he was, in truth, putting on his slippers as he spoke.

"This park has a secluded trail that leads to the river. I thought we'd walk."

"...You are serious about this?" His brows furrowed, as though the surreality of the situation had faded and he was reviewing our conversation more rationally. "Why would you come to me?"

"I don't have anyone," I admitted. And swallowed another mouthful of scotch from the storage-bladder in my armor. "You are...respected."

He cursed under his breath, then took a deep breath. "Give me your word, that you will harm no one."

"I swear, on my memory of Starnyx, that I intend no harm to you or yours."

"Okay. Okay." He signed something to Regrowth, but by chance he had turned such that my microdrones and visual sensors did not have a clear view of his hands. Whatever he'd said, she frowned and nodded reluctant agreement. He looked down at himself, clad only in slippers, and sighed. "Give me time to change into something more appropriate. I'll meet you at the treeline along the south edge of the park."

I ended the call and silently drifted south.

("You are insane." Elaine pursed her lips irritably.)

("Possibly," Miguel replied easily. Rather than dressing in civilian garb, he'd taken a spare costume from its hiding place behind a false wall in his closet and swiftly donned the first layer of deep-red under-armor. "But it's also an opportunity. Also, I'd rather take a risk and talk with him, instead of letting him fly off and then sit around wonder what he's doing instead of talking.")

("We should call in the full team.")

("And we would do what, then?" He pulled on his costume's second-layer of padding. "Fight Doctor Fid in the park where my nephews play? Elaine, he obviously knows where I live...")

("That's reason to be more careful! Not less!" Despite her disagreement, her movements were calm and professional as she assisted him in quickly placing and attaching the Red Ghost's body-armor plates.)

("I will be careful, and you will watch over us with a gauss cannon." He pulled on his cowl, chuckled and hugged her close, kissing her forehead affectionately. "If there is a fight, it will be a mess...but it will be in a wooded area where your powers are strong. We can make a safe escape.")

("Don't trust him," she advised, handing him the hooded cloak that completed his costume. "Don't forget what he is.")

("I won't. Stay safe." Miguel got the last word by transforming his body into the red mist that was his namesake, then flowing through a slightly-open window.)

The crimson cloud, near invisible under dark moonlight, coalesced into a hero at the edge of the clearing. I'd waited in shadow, parsing through footage and sensor readings relayed from my microdrones.

"You have a beautiful home," I began without turning to face the man who I'd oft considered my nemesis. "The rock-garden and bench area are lovely."

"Thank you," he replied evenly. "May I ask how you knew to find me here?"

"I've had the information for years. The knowledge has never seemed relevant in the past," I shrugged.

He stared at me for a while, absorbing the statement and turning over its possible implications in his head. "And what changed?"

"Life," I answered, thinking about Whisper. And then, thinking of my friend, I added, "And death, of course."

"I'd heard." He started walking along the wooded path, towards the river. "I was genuinely sorry to hear about Starnyx's death. Despite our differences, he seemed a good man."

"He was." I moved alongside the Red Ghost; the Mk 28 armor stood head and shoulders over him, and my longer stride required a slower gait lest I leave him behind. I barked in short laughter. "He would have hated this. Nyx never quite forgave you for the manner in which you orchestrated Beazd's capture."

Beazd disliked the fact that Starnyx spoke to me. Starnyx would have been skeptical of my decision to talk to the hero before me. Regrowth certainly disapproved of the Red Ghost agreeing to converse. I was the only commonality in these scenarios. What, I wondered, would Apotheosis have thought of my guardianship of Whisper? Would he have been added to the list of concerned loved-ones, who suspected that any association with the notorious Doctor Fid could only end in tears?

I had to believe that Apotheosis would have wanted for Whisper to be happy and free. I dismissed my maudlin worries; the Red Ghost was speaking:

"Given how that ended, there are days I feel that I should not be forgiven either," he exhaled deeply. "I visited Beazd several times in prison. The world was diminished by his passing."

(Once she thought herself clear of my view, a now-costumed Regrowth sneaked from Miguel Espinoza's backyard. A heavy-looking rifle was slung over one shoulder, but she carried it easily as she sprinted towards the tree line. Unnoticed, my microdrones followed overhead.)

"I've heard you speak out against Sphinx and Peregrine." I triggered another ounce of scotch's delivery and it burned as I swallowed. "Starnyx would have appreciated that. I appreciated that."

(Note to self: Next time I choose to replace any of my internal organs, I should add a liver with programmable functionality; the current revision was too efficient for some purposes. I was drinking far more alcohol than should have been necessary to maintain a pleasant buzz.)

"It was only right. I only wish that the FTW had known about Beazd's murder earlier. Sphinx and Peregrine would not have escaped with a wrist-slap if their crimes had been revealed by an eff-tee-dub exclusive!" His sad smile turned vicious.

"Starnyx knew, within a day." An alert; the leaves among some of the nearby trees were rustling at a speed that did not conform to the night's breeze. Regrowth was watching us, but not interfering. "He had a broadcast planned...but another expose had a higher priority."

"I will admit to being an occasional slave to curiosity." He made a subtle gesture with his hand, likely some sort of secret message to Regrowth. Telling her that he was in no immediate danger, I hoped. "What could have a higher priority?"

"As near as I have been able to determine, it was a scandal involving the Legion refugees and the New York Shield." I stared at the night sky through the canopy of leaves. "I haven't been able to find details. All relevant information was lost in the fire."

"Ah," he grimaced. "Today's Shield is not the Shield that I remember."

I bit back a vitriolic reply. It would have been counterproductive to accuse him of a selective memory, of willful blindness to the faults of his super-powered brethren. I could tell him of his team-mate Marble's infidelities, or of Epsilon's link to the Ancient, or the allegations that Defender had stolen from evidence lock-up in order to pay his bills when he'd been having financial difficulties. But I was carrying enough disillusionment upon my own armored shoulders; I didn't want to inflict the same upon anyone else, tonight.

"Today's Shield does seem to have more than its fair share of problems, yes," I said, instead.

He looked up at my helm, his expression intense; his powers, I was reminded, had never been what had made him a threat. His red mist form was used to great effect in combat, but it was the Red Ghost's mind...his quick ability to analyze action and intent...that had established him as the rival I respected. Why had he made that comment about the New York superhero team's past? What had he gleaned from my response? I was wearing armor that could (even without the integrated force-fields) shrug off the impact from .50 caliber machine gun fire...and yet, I felt naked.

"You didn't wake me up at two forty-seven in the morning to speak to me of the New York Shield," the Red Ghost stated evenly.

"True." The trail had brought us to the bank of the Mystic River. It was quieter here, any noises from traffic dulled by distance and absorbed by the trees and bushes. I could see stars, even through a haze of moisture from the Atlantic and the nearby city's light. The view wasn't as clear as I recalled from that first night in the Appalachian Mountains that inspired my armor's starfield motif, but the expanse was still beautiful. "I have regrets regarding several of my life choices."

"Given your history," he made a sound as though struggling to bite back a laugh, "I would hope that to be a long list."

I sat down carefully in a park bench that faced the river; the Mk 28 weighed several hundred pounds, but the seat was (fortunately) constructed of concrete and four-by-six studs and could withstand the armor's mass. Was the Red Ghost testing me, I wondered? A gentle poke at my pride, to see if I succumbed to anger in response? I considered how to respond and decided upon simple honesty: "It is."

(A quarter mile to the west, Regrowth lay prone, aiming the gauss cannon directly at me. There was far too much brush and shrubbery barring her line of sight for the scope to be much use; she must have been able to target using her power of perception through plants under her control. There was nothing in her official records that indicated that level of fine control! Interesting.)

"Is that what this is, then?" the Ghost asked, sitting down next to me. "You are looking to unburden your conscience?"

"The weight of my sins could not so easily be set aside." I noted that the Ghost had chosen a seating position such that he was not in Regrowth's line of fire. That implied either more detailed communication than I'd been able to detect, or else significant pre-planning. Either achievement was remarkable. "I just wanted to speak the words aloud to someone who might understand."

"I've never understood you, Doctor Fid."

"I don't believe that to be true," I chuckled. "I've read the extended transcript of the NPR interview, when you sat beside Joanne Durand."

"We were simply positing theories," he smiled in a self-deprecating manner.

"Nevertheless, I felt quite adroitly skewered." The sociologist had made the same observations that Starnyx had years before, identifying several incidents in which my 'crime' would have no profit save for instigating violence. The Red Ghost had offered anecdotal evidence that had supported her theories.

"Then why was I awakened so early, rather than her?" He yawned, rolling his shoulders in a slow stretching maneuver.

I locked my armor to keep from echoing the yawn and stretch.

"Miss Durand is a skilled observer, but she is a civilian. She's not a part of our world." Also, I admitted to myself, I was a bit afraid that she would be inspired to write another book. Late in the transcript, Joanne Durand had also expounded at length about the difference in Doctor Fid's behavior, before and after the villain's five-year disappearance. Several of her suppositions had been dangerously clever.

"So, if I'm to be denied sleep...tell me of your regrets."

"I regret hurting Clash so badly." It was not the greatest of my regrets, nor even the one most prevalent in my mind. It was, however, easy to speak aloud.

"Only Clash?"

"We've insufficient time to create an itemized list." Behind my helm's faceplate, my own smile was bitter. "Boat traffic will resume on this river in only a few hours."

"Then, why mention him in particular?"

"There was a documentary aired...he's been on my mind." I peered downriver, watching the distant city lights along the bank. "If I offered to repair his knees, better than new, do you suppose that he'd accept?"

"Possibly," Red Ghost considered, "but it would be very difficult to convince him that you had no ulterior motive."

"Ah," I acknowledged. "There, then, is another regret worth mentioning. The reputation I've earned has certain drawbacks."

"If you turned yourself in, perhaps people would believe that your interest in making amends was genuine," the Ghost suggested gently.

"I am not Beazd!" I replied sharply, a hint of warning audible even through my vocoder's filter. "I do not have it within me to accept incarceration without resistance."

(Overhead, the tree-branches rustled as if in warning. The Red Ghost made a surreptitious gesture with his hand, indicating calm and safety. In the distance, Regrowth exhaled slowly, releasing the tension that had gathered when I raised my voice.)

"If you are not seeking redemption, what do you want?" There was no accusation in his tone, merely curiosity.

"I don't know," I confessed. "A path forward. Or a path backwards, to correct some few mistakes in my past."

For a while, we were both silent. Doubtless, both of us were pondering past regrets.

"Do you remember Blueshift?" he interjected, unexpectedly.

"The New Orleans-based hero who claimed to be a time-traveler," I nodded slightly. "He wasn't. Trust me, I've done the math."

"He figured that out eventually as well. Alternate dimension, very complicated. Blueshift was deathly afraid of you, but he also hated you with a passion." The Red Ghost fell silent for a moment. From his fond smile, I imagined that he was remembering one of Blueshift's famous diatribes; the supposed time-traveler had been a mediocre combatant and moderately inoffensive as so-called heroes go, but his ability to construct epic rants had been second to none amongst the cape-and-cowl crowd. The Red Ghost's expression grew more serious. "Blueshift claimed that some of your technology had not been replicated even in his time, and that it could have saved millions of lives."

I considered. Here, I had made arrangements for much of my research to eventually be released to the public. I could not know if similar efforts had been made in the dimension from which Blueshift hailed. Even so, I knew, even in this world there were some discoveries that I fully intended to keep hidden forever. "Blueshift was right, and he was also wrong."

"How so?"

"In the wrong hands, many of my inventions could become disastrous," I bowed my head slightly. "I've devised technologies that could save millions, but the cost could be billions."

"Many would argue that your hands are already the wrong hands," he chuckled, seeming to enjoy the opportunity to poke gentle fun at me; he was, it seemed, growing increasingly confident that there would be no violent reprisal for his teasing.

"Perhaps other minds could come to different conclusions." I considered my opponent. "Your opinion would be appreciated."

"Shoot."

"Here's one invention that I'd originally intended to 'accidentally' —," I made a finger-quote gesture, "— leave behind to be reverse engineered. I've developed the capability to create a bounded field, within which it's possible to shunt kinetic energy from this world into an artificially-created microdimension. This capability can be used to minimize the effects of inertial forces on human bodies within the field, such as sudden impacts or high-speed maneuvering.

"The technology is currently very expensive," I continued, "but my calculations show that mass-production could bring the costs down 'til the devices could be deployed in mid-end and high-end automobiles."

The Red Ghost looked like he wanted to comment, but I cut him off before he could begin:

"Last year in the United States alone, there were nearly thirty-five thousand fatalities from vehicular accidents, and more than two point two million injuries." I breathed out a pained whisper, "My projections show that the inertial-dampening technology could reduce those numbers by fifty percent."

The Red Ghost twisted to stare at me, as if noticing only for the first time that he was seated next to a monster. "How can you possibly justify keeping that technology to yourself?"

"The formulae necessary to dampen inertia are enormously complex. Using the technology to produce weapons of mass destruction is much simpler." I shrugged sadly. "Using the sun as a point of reference simplifies the maths rather significantly, but the Earth travels in its orbit so quickly...Create a large enough field, and you could tear an entire city from the planet's surface at sixty-seven thousand miles per hour. Or worse, driven directly into the earth's crust..."

"My God," the Red Ghost continued to stare. I watched his expression as he did damage calculations in his head. "Have you built such a device?"

"Of course not. What would be the point?"

"With that kind of power, you could hold the entire world hostage."

(A quarter mile away, Regrowth rolled her eyes and mumbled, "Stop giving the armored supervillain ideas, Miguel.". She maintained her vigil, gauss cannon still aimed carefully in my direction.)

"How, exactly, would that work? 'I – Doctor Fid! - desire all of the hot-wings, celery and blue-cheese dressing that a man with a genetically augmented metabolism can eat, lest I throw the city of Detroit into space! Bwahahaha.' Then the manager of the local chicken-wing emporium would delay, claiming that they can't offer the lifetime supply certificate unless the threat is verified. Joanne

Durand would call NPR and note that I'd never actually activated an area-effect weapon where innocent civilians could be caught up in the blow. You'd concur, and then Regrowth would shoot me in the head with a gauss cannon." I gestured to the west. "Then there would be a fight, I'd escape, Detroit would remain where it is, and I wouldn't get my chicken wings."

(To the west, Regrowth's finger whitened on the trigger of her gauss cannon.)

"Most villains ask for more than fried wings," the Red Ghost was staring at me again, "when threatening to unleash a doomsday device."

"I'm hungry," I explained. "Also, a high-powered inertial dampener lacks sufficient drama to be an effective doomsday device."

"Part of me now wants nothing more than to pick your brain regarding your theory of proper doomsday device construction." The Red Ghost covered his face with both hands. "The other part is concerned that you seem to know where my teammate is and don't seem particularly worried about the gauss cannon."

"I have access to very good sensors." I chose not to mention my microdrones (some of which were still exploring and mapping his home; the workshop in his basement was organized in an efficient manner but lacked much of what I considered to be essential safety equipment). "And I would not expect your partner to initiate violence unless provoked."

"And we're back to me not understanding you."

"What's not to understand?" I shrugged. "I arrived unexpectedly, and you and Regrowth took reasonable precautions. I'm not offended."

"Most people are more distressed when a high-powered weapon is pointed in their direction."

"I've been an active supervillain for more than twenty years," I laughed. "I've had some time to become accustomed to the sensation."

"This conversation just keeps getting stranger."

"I'm sorry." Once again, I was grateful for the vocoder that successfully stripped my amusement from Doctor Fid's voice. "That wasn't my intent."

(Regrowth made a decision. She stood and slung the heavy gauss cannon over one shoulder, then took a quick running jump into the trees; the leap was made easier due to the oak lowering a massive limb for her to land upon. With a groan of straining wood and stretching bark, the limb shot up and threw Regrowth forwards towards Red Ghost and me in a ballistic arc, dozens of feet over the forest's canopy. In a dazzling display of athletic prowess, the young woman soared more than two hundred feet before smoothly flipping forwards to descend feet-first into the leaves of a maple, which creaked and thundered with the effort as its branches contorted to carefully catch the heroine then toss her again into the air. The quarter-mile distance evaporated remarkably quickly.)

"Does that promise of non-violence still hold?" Regrowth asked, dropping out of the foliage to land at the edge of the clearing. Leaves fluttered to the ground around her, torn from their branches by the speed at which the tree had responded to her will.

"It does, yes."

"Great." Her smile was fierce. "You're an idiot!"

I looked down at my hands. Yup. Still clad in starfield-and-glowing-red gauntlets, more than a hundred moving parts shifting in silent harmony as I closed my hands into fists and then again straitened my fingers. Micro-pneumatics and myoelectric fibers cooperating smoothly to function as part of what is often referred to as the most innovative and advanced powered armor in human history.

"Interesting assessment," I said in a measured voice. "Please, explain."

"You think your technology is dangerous? You're right!" She waved expressively; the Red Ghost lay a warning hand on her shoulder, but she ignored it. "Humans have been mis-using technology since before the first time we rubbed two sticks together and came up with fire. That's not an excuse to stop advancing."

"Last year, there were over fifty-six thousand cases of arson reported in the United States," I countered. "That statistic makes me reluctant to release the destructive equivalent of thermonuclear matches."

"Your armor and robot components self-immolate to avoid reverse engineering," Red Ghost pointed out. "If the commercial units had the same safeguards, it would limit the threat."

"A) We both know that most corporations would cheerfully strip the safety enhancements and risk mass casualties if they thought it would save them a nickel per unit," I began, "And B) Even if the actual commercial device can't be reverse engineered, a hacker or villain would still be able to steal the specifications directly from the manufacturer."

"So, license the technology to the car manufacturers, but keep back one critical component that they have to buy from you," Regrowth suggested, "and make sure that one component is completely tamperproof."

"That...has potential," I considered. "It would, however, be a significantly more complex task than simply releasing the technology to the open market."

"But it could be done?" the Ghost asked, hopefully. "This could save many lives."

"Perhaps. I've ideas on how to handle the component manufacture," I lamented. "The greater difficulty lay in negotiating with all the stakeholders. A company would need to be created to handle the business end, to respond to customer requirements, to litigate liability, trademark and copyright issues, etc. I do not think that I could be directly involved in such a company."

Regrowth looked thoughtful, "...and, even if you controlled manufacture of a critical component, the parent company would ostensibly need to be the 'owner' of the patent in order to make deals with major corporate buyers."

"You'd need to set up a third party as the 'face' of the inertial dampening technology," Red Ghost added.

"Someone who has a background in finance, to handle a large company." Regrowth sounded amused now. "And someone who has a history of reverse engineering Doctor Fid's inventions, to provide a convincing provenance for the technology."

"Someone trusted." I drank another mouthful of scotch, feeling as though the world were shifting oddly beneath my feet. I checked; no seismic activity. But Regrowth and the Red Ghost were both correct in their assessment. "Or at least...someone respected."

"Ah." Behind the Red Ghost's crimson cowl, Miguel Espinoza blinked in surprised understanding. Then his eyes narrowed. "You are offering me a position likely to generate significant wealth and respect, as well as the opportunity to take part in the creation of a device that will save thousands upon thousands of lives. As deals with the devil go, that is fairly attractive."

"I am...trying to be less of a devil, these days." I leaned forward and rested my head in my hands, as though massaging at my temples. Any positive effect was psychosomatic; my helm was sufficiently protective that any pressure exuded by the movement was easily eliminated. "Over time, if this arrangement works well, I would like to give you access to other technologies, too. And provide recommendations for physicists and engineers who might help you reproduce some of my other inventions."

"The offer continues to sound too good to be true," the Red Ghost frowned skeptically.

"I've kept these discoveries to myself because I believed that choice to be the safest option." I sat back up to look the Red Ghost directly, even if he could not see the eyes hidden by Doctor Fid's faceless helm. "It would be nice to know that there are contingencies in place, in case my choice proves wrong."

"That wasn't an admission I expected from you," Red Ghost smiled supportively, looking to be pleasantly surprised.

"I am trying to be less of a devil," I repeated, "but the effort has been more difficult than I'd anticipated. I'm...concerned. If I'm being honest, that is why I woke you."

"Having trouble keeping your oath of non-violence?" Regrowth asked casually. Only a slight shift in her shoulders betrayed her sudden tension, the worry that I might betray my word.

"No. And yes," I sighed. "I'd hoped that my...emotional excesses...would be curtailed as I finished repairing the last of the scarring on my amygdala. And yet...I'm still so angry."

"You can repair glial scars?" Regrowth asked evenly; I recalled that (according the the profile that I'd automatically generated earlier in the morning) Elaine Goldman's father was a well-regarded psychiatrist, and her mother a noted neurosurgeon. Brain damage had likely been a common topic of dinner conversation in Regrowth's household during her formative years. "Blueshift was right to blame you! Do you have any idea how many people suffer brain injuries every year?"

"Nearly three million TBI related emergency room visits in the United States," I waved my hand dismissively. "That capability was stolen from a company that's already working towards human trials. The only thing keeping that particular panacea from saving lives tomorrow is bureaucracy, not my paranoia."

"Good," Regrowth shrugged one arm, resetting the slung rifle's weight on her shoulder.

"I'll need to spend time considering your offer. You mentioned that you are angry?" Red Ghost changed the subject, making another warning hand-gesture to Regrowth. "What has been bothering you?"

"Many things. Personality conflicts, a feedback loop of feeling of loneliness and betrayal," I closed my eyes. "I do know what kicked off the cycle, I think."

"Go on."

"I joined the FTW with the intent to participate when they exposed Sphinx's and Peregrine's crimes," I stood up, gesturing annoyedly with one hand. "That effort, obviously, was derailed when Sphinx made her public announcement. Her timing was too perfect to be coincidence; someone within the collective must have warned her. Whoever it was...it's their fault that those two so-called 'heroes' received no real punishment."

"And yet, you still have said that you intend to hold true to your oath," he pronounced the sentence as though it were a statement, but I could hear the hidden question within.

"I didn't take the oath for them!" I gritted through clenched teeth. "I took it for Nyx. He was a better friend than I deserved, and a better man than I could ever hope to be. I have to believe that, if he really was better, then his way, his methods must also have been superior.

"But...He loved the eff-tee-dub," I continued. "He would have crawled through broken glass to help any one of them. It tears me apart, to think that he was barely gone before one of the members was willing to sell out their peers."

"It's possible that whoever it was didn't think of it as betraying the FTW. Perhaps he or she was trying to save the FTW from your influence," Regrowth pointed out softly. "Even if they knew Starnyx was your friend, they also knew your reputation."

"Thank you. That helps, actually. But even so, I'd had hopes to find common cause among those my friend left behind. To mourn among allies and to help rebuild Starnyx' legacy," I exhaled, shaking my head sadly. "Instead, they accept my help but not my camaraderie. They treat me as though I were still the creature I was two decades past; I can never pay those crimes, but I've torn out and replaced parts of my own brain to keep that monster at bay! If I were still that Doctor Fid, then Nyx should have hated me."

Regrowth was staring at me with a horrified expression. I decided not to expand upon the neurotropic and pharmacological regimen that I'd embarked upon in addition to my many surgeries. Given her parentage, there was a chance that she'd find the conversation professionally interesting. There was also a chance that she would call for aerial military strikes next time I was seen in public, collateral damage be damned.

"Also, some of them are unkind," I added, as though it were an afterthought.

It wasn't.

The petty meanness of some of the FTW members burned at me. They were profaning Starnyx's memory! Illogical accusations were not gainsaid, and casually cruel japes were met with apathy rather than rebuke. I'd always expected for 'heroes' like Sphinx and Peregrine to be awful; it was more jarring to see such behavior from those from whom I'd expected better. And yet, they were people that Nyx, that Eric Guthrie, had cared for.

My fists were clenched and glowing from gathered energy; when had that occurred? I de-powered the weapons systems and forced my hands to relax.

Regrowth and the Red Ghost were both looking at me without judgment or fear. The dynamic had changed, somehow. It seemed to me that, only a half hour prior, they would have leaped to violence at even the hint that my ire had been raised. Now, they simply waited me out.

"The man behind Starnyx's mask was a genuinely kind and decent person," I finally said quietly. "And both of you know what horrors lay in my own past. The fact that Nyx accepted me as a friend gave me hope. I wanted to believe that he saw something in me that was salvageable...But if he was friend also to those those boorish children, then maybe he just didn't mind being friends with monsters."

Regrowth's voice was gentle, "Your friend saw something in them that could be nurtured. They may be boorish children today, but Starnyx was hoping to help them grow into something better, tomorrow."

"You didn't know him. How can you be so sure?"

"Because that's what it sounds like he did for you," her expression was sad and supportive; it was strange to recognize that, only a handful of minutes earlier, she'd had her gauss cannon trained upon my skull.

Life as a supervillain is odd, sometimes.

"Earlier, I spoke of rebuilding Starnyx's legacy," I murmured, "but it seems I hadn't even realized what Starnyx' legacy was."

"You are Starnyx's legacy." The Red Ghost sounded certain. "You and all whose lives he touched. If you want to continue his work, focus on helping his people."

"And maybe find out more about what's going on with the Shield and the Legion refugees," Regrowth added. "Heroes need to be held to a higher standard. If you find more dirt on 'em, make sure the eff-tee-dub shouts it loud!"

I stared down at her for what was probably an uncomfortably long moment. "...I owe you a significant apology, Regrowth."

"Oh?" She tilted her head. "Why so?"

"I've overlooked you, pre-judged you based upon incomplete evidence," I shuffled a foot, embarrassed. "Possibly it was simple arrogance because your powers are poorly suited to stand in opposition to my armor, or possibly due to latent sexism (in which case, I owe you two apologies), or perhaps there were other factors. No matter the cause, you have deserved more respect."

"That's kind of you, but I hope this doesn't mean that I should expect three-o'clock wake-up calls." Regrowth seemed amused.

"No," I barked in short laughter. "But it's good to know that there are more 'heroes' that are worthy of the title."

"It's good to know that there are villains that are looking to put that title behind them," she replied, simply.

I had nothing to say in response to that. I was still Doctor Fid! I just wasn't sure what that meant anymore.

"You've committed a great many evil acts, but I believe in forgiveness." The Red Ghost pulled back the hood of his cloak and I had the strange feeling that it was Miguel Espinoza that was looking up at my faceless helm. "I'll work with you to bring your inertial dampening technology to the public, safely."

"I don't deserve forgiveness," I admitted.

"Deserve's got nothing to do with it," he rasped, imitating a famous actor. His voice shifted back to its normal tone and cadence, "Being forgiven isn't your choice. Only whether your regrets are real, and if your remorse will help shape your actions moving forwards."

Again, I was struck silent. I nodded gratefully and lifted slowly from the ground. "I'll be in touch once I've begun preparations."

And then I was soaring home.

CHAPTER ELEVEN

SQUATTERS WERE LIVING IN MY CHILDHOOD HOME.
The property hadn't been sold when Mother and Father had died; Bobby moved to Massachusetts to live with me, but I'd intended that the house pass to him when he came of age. Utilities, grounds-keeping and maintenance were all relatively minor expenses even then. We'd visited, Bobby and I, several times. Cleaning our parents' rooms had been a task that I'd seized for myself. That pain, I'd thought, I could spare my younger sibling.

A small bottle slips through my numb fingers, and the loose plastic lid rattles to the floor; I reflexively bend to pick up the bottle-cap but the damage is done. A few drops of my father's aftershave are shed upon the linoleum counter, scent redolent with flowers and citrus and musk, and I'm lost to memories of warm hugs and gruff reassurances, of a hand ruffling through my hair and of a patient, proud voice reading theoretical math texts aloud for me even when he didn't understand the material. I'm bawling like a child, like I hadn't when my third-grade science teacher

accused me of cheating and humiliated me in front of all my peers, or when Kenny Bryant had punched me so hard that the school nurse called an ambulance. I'm not ready for this. How could anyone be ready for this? Bobby still needs a mother and a father.

So do I.

"Terry?" A young and hesitant voice queries from the craft room across the hall. "Are you okay?"

"I'm fine." I lie, choking back my tears. My brother needs someone to be strong and I'm the only person here.

Bobby needs me.

Slowly, the books and toys and remaining sundries migrated north to my smaller place in Cambridge. The house felt emptier with each visit but it had never stopped feeling like home.

I sold the property two months after Bronze let my brother die. Terrance Markham had faded and Doctor Fid was not the sentimental type.

Obsessive, yes. Sentimental, no.

The property had changed hands thrice more over the decades, and the latest owners were an elderly couple who spent most of their year living in Florida. Local homeless teens had taken note of their absence: the window in what had once been my bedroom had been pried open to make for an unobserved entrance.

My micro-drones explored.

The unexpected tenants had taken blankets and sheets from other rooms to build their nest, stolen pans from the kitchen, and were slowly but surely making a disaster of the downstairs bathroom. For the most part, however, they were keeping to the back half of the house: less chance of being observed from the street, I suppose.

I don't know what triggered my curiosity. I don't know why I sent a squadron of drones to fly over the old place. A strange whim while taking a break from manufacturing records for false identities and fake holding companies, perhaps. A welcome diversion from banal busywork. Why at that moment, for the first time in years?

If I flew there myself, I wondered, would it still feel like home?

The intruders were causing damage. Not much, yet; torn sheets, drops of candle-wax in the carpet, and enough debris and fast-food wrappers scattered about to attract pests. If they stayed longer, the damage would be worse. The current homeowners shouldn't have to endure the costs of repair. And yet, the intruders were kids...guilty of little more than vandalism and breaking-and-entering. If this shelter were lost to them, it might be some time before they again found a relatively safe haven.

Several weeks of research into means of communicating with difficult young adults had yet to grant me the ability or patience to successfully engage with the FTW's more volatile members. It had, however, granted me some nagging empathy towards the hardships such youth endured. The interlopers were criminal, certainly, and were causing harm to innocents. But a truly just resolution must take root causes into account in order to determine appropriate levels of culpability.

More information would be required before a plan could be formulated.

Whisper, sweetheart? I sent to my ward via neural interface; she was visiting her friend Dinah at the moment, at my CIO's house. **May I ask a favor?**

This was, I realized, as close to telepathy as any human had ever experienced. A cascade of dimensional fissures and mystic convergences had precipitated the emergence of a vast array of superhuman abilities, but psionics had until now still been a thing of fiction. Technology, I thought smugly, had trumped superpowers yet again.

Mm! Whisper affirmed. She was able to convey more than words via the network link; her cheer felt like a quick hug, a ghostly touch that left phantom warmth on my skin.

There are two teenagers illegally residing within the house in which I was raised, I shared, *Could you help me find more information about them?*

You can't find them? she asked, surprised.

They don't have driver's licenses or criminal records, and no one has reported them missing, I explained. *Facial recognition and fingerprint searches in the usual databases haven't been useful.*

"*I'll see what I can find in school yearbooks and social media,* Whisper chirped cheerfully.

Thank you.

Whisper's ability to perform non-targeted, broad media searches was already far superior to my own software. Faster, and able to make intuitive leaps that the algorithms I'd designed could never match. Clever girl! She would talk me into a trip to the aquarium in payment for this favor, I was sure, but that was no great hardship. Whisper liked making faces at fish through the glass, and I could think of no more enjoyable way to spend an afternoon than to watch her run alongside the viewing window as the tank's inhabitants swam past.

(Her fascination with sea life was a recent development; we'd been on our way home from a session with one of the child psychologists with whom we had consulted with prior to Whisper's upcoming citizenship hearing when she'd informed me, eyes literally glowing with adorably grave childish intensity, that she needed to find a clown fish. Fortunately, the New England Aquarium had an excellent reef exhibit.)

I reburied myself in the laborious efforts to create false identities and shell companies; the Red Ghost had already been provided with prototypes and sufficient detailed information for him to begin his own tasks. He'd already approached investors and begun the process of filing for patents. My manufacturing plant would need to seem wholly legitimate and completely untraceable before the Ghost began to outsource production of the inertial dampening technology.

I dared not leave even the slightest trace of evidence leading back to my civilian identity; despite my respect for the man, I knew the Red Ghost to be a hero. Furthermore, I knew him to be an annoyingly competent investigator. He may have agreed to work with me to accomplish a greater good, but I was certain that he would try to delve deeper...just in case.

In his place, I would certainly have done the same.

A new company appearing out of the ether might attract attention; an existing enterprise with known capabilities and relevant expertise, however, would more easily pass inspection. A lengthy corporate history and an existing workforce did much to hide minor irregularities. Fortunately, a well-regarded manufacturer in Tennessee was available for acquisition.

According to my own research, the business was basically sound...but had recently lost their two largest accounts to a competitor that outsourced its labor overseas. One such loss would hurt, but two had been catastrophic. Nevertheless, they had a highly skilled staff, top notch manufacturing equipment and a decent management team. I (or rather, one of my shell companies) would soon make an offer. Post-acquisition time spent in optimization and reorganization would help hide any secrets that I would need to conceal within their manufacturing process. With any luck, a contract with the Red Ghost's soon-to-exist company would quickly return Putnam Circuitworks to profitability.

Unfortunately...for this task I couldn't use even a penny of Terry Markham's legitimate funds. Moving sufficient volumes of Doctor Fid's illicit fortune, however, could increase the risk of detection. To avoid such, time-consuming effort was put towards establishing shell companies and false identities, creating detailed plans and meticulously-forged paperwork, and backing all these steps with a staggering amount of hacked government records.

It was a boring and tedious endeavor; meeting my civilian identity's responsibilities as CEO, continuing (with little success) my self-imposed goal of befriending and mentoring members of the FTW, investigating the link between the New York Shield and the alien Legion refugees, and spending time with Whisper all took much of what waking time remained. The latter, at least, was enjoyable...but I itched to return to research, to immerse myself in the creative frenzy that had once dominated my existence. Alas, my obligations had grown too many for me to allow myself such self-indulgent pastimes. The list of tasks before me was Sisyphean, but there was still progress to be made.

"-also licensed the technology to emerging markets in EMEA and CALA regions, growing our exposure overseas and significantly increasing our market share. The short-term expenses are estimated to be recouped in less than twelve months," AH Biotech's CFO finished her presentation. "And now, back to Terrance."

"Thank you, Ananya," I answered, smiling professionally to the camera. "The improvements that we've made to our product lines have generated seventeen percent more revenue for Q2 over last year's numbers, and marketing has reported tremendous interest in the upcoming first-aid and first-responder med-kits. I'd like to personally thank every member of our teams who have all worked tirelessly to make this quarter a success. There have been a sea of challenges, but you've weathered the storms and sailed past them. We've accomplished great things, and I look forward to accomplishing more great things with you in the future. Thank you!"

The applause was polite but muted, which was expected given that only a few of the employees who my comments were directed towards were present. The room was filled primarily with management staff, investors and financial-news reporters; the rank and file employees rarely attended such events; many watched the broadcast as it was livestreamed, but most would review the recording later.

"Thank you, Terry. We will now open the floor for audience questions," Aaron added. "If you are listening remotely and you have any questions, press one to record your question and the moderator will add your question to the queue."

I sipped at a glass of ice water that tasted pleasantly of freshly-cut cucumber and mint, feeling accomplished. The technical aspects of my work as CEO were easy; the public relations aspect, however, was exhausting!

The first three questions were sales-related; Kimberly handled those smoothly, deferring occasionally to our regional directors for more detailed information and allowing her staff to shine. Aaron answered a technical question related to the new Middletown branch office, and Victor spoke about our advancements in generating accurate results from computer simulations in conjunction with physical experiments.

In the front row, the formally-dressed, gray-haired chairman of the board gestured to Aaron. He looked every bit as dour as when he'd confronted me at the steakhouse.

I successfully repressed a smile of anticipation.

"Mr. Collins, you have a question?" the company's CIO asked.

"I do, Mr. Schwartz," the activist investor spoke in an emotionless monotone. "Over the last twelve months, expenditures in research and development have consistently grown at a rate far greater than revenue increases. Profit margins have undeniably been impacted. Do you feel that these unchecked expenses are in any way responsible for the downward trend in our stock's value?"

A disquieted murmur spread through the room; it was unusual for a board member to air grievances so publicly.

"I'll take this one, Aaron," I interjected. "We've made significant improvements in efficiency this year; while we strive to provide our researchers with the resources necessary for success, those budgets have been carefully adjusted in-line with projected profits associated with each project.

"The greatest expansion in research and development expenses has been related to a new project that required hiring experts with non-biotech specializations and investing heavily in infrastructure. Eleven relevant patents have already been approved, several more are pending, and we are well positioned to establish ourselves as a global leader in medical nanotechnology treatment options. Every new hire and every penny spent on infrastructure will be needed in the coming months. As of this morning, I'm pleased to announce that our medical nanite program has been approved for human testing."

The murmur was louder now, surprised and enthusiastic. The timing had been particularly fortunate: the Secretary of Health and Human Services had (through a carefully surreptitious intermediary) offered to approve the study if he were allowed to participate and was guaranteed not to be a member of the placebo group. The ill man's desperation had allowed this project to catapult forward years ahead of schedule and I'd thus been granted the opportunity to derail the board of directors' attack.

The room exploded with questions, including some from my fellow executive officers. I'd kept this news close to the vest, expecting that the information would prove useful at this meeting.

The board's chairman frowned slightly as he performed mental arithmetic. Any embarrassment or anger on his part would surely fade quickly. If there were anything that I was certain of, it was that I could count upon greed to guide Henry Collins' actions more consistently than any other emotion.

This wouldn't be the last time that he would try to oust me. Collins was obsessed with short term profits, and AH Biotech's lofty goals would require long-term planning to accomplish. This was no victory; it was a delaying action, and it one that would likely reward millions of dollars to a group that I would much preferred to set ablaze. But it was one battle, at least, that could be temporarily set aside.

"I found them!" Whisper chimed, offering her doll Amelia for a kiss before climbing into my lap. "I found them both."

"I knew you would," I smiled and gave the petite android a hug. "So, who are they?"

"Brian Lamont and Ethan Samuelson," she said, a hit of smugness present in her tone.

I felt momentarily dizzy as she dumped a gigabyte of supplementary data directly into my brain.

"Brian is listed as being presumed dead?" I began sorting through the files, mentally.

"Mm." Whisper lowered her eyes sadly. "There was a fire at their cabin in Ithaca, only he and his sister were supposed to be there."

"Heavy snow that weekend." I mentally searched archived weather records to confirm. "Cold enough to make survival unlikely, if he'd left the house on foot."

"Mm. But he did!"

"Are you certain? Perhaps he wasn't in the house at all. Perhaps his sister had dropped him in town...?"

"I think he started the fire by accident...Look at 031127118 and 031127119."

I reviewed the relevant files and frowned thoughtfully. Locked social media comments (shared only among a few of Brian Lamont's friends) bragging that his sister had just gotten back from New Hampshire and had bought a hoard of fireworks for him. I shifted mental focus to absorb the chief's report; it had been a very hot fire and the department's response had been delayed by the snow. Human remains had been found - Brian's sister, unfortunately - but most of the evidence had been inconclusive. There was, however, some indications that the back door had been knocked inwards.

Brian had been an athlete, heavy and strong for his age. It seemed very possible that he'd kicked open the door to no avail. The fire had spread too quickly, too much smoke, too much heat. Somehow, Brian had gotten to the road and disappeared. If he'd felt responsible for his sister's death, it seemed plausible that he might have run away from home rather than face his family.

It was easy to imagine: charging into the roaring flames, blinded by heat and deafened by the roar as the cabin was consumed. Throat burning from too-long spent screaming his sister's name, praying for a miracle and being denied.

"He's not a supervillain, is he?" I asked hesitantly

"What?" Whisper looked confused. "No!"

"I was just checking," I reassured her. "And the other boy, Ethan Samuelson, looks to just be a runaway?"

"Mm," she acknowledged. "From his foster parents. His mother didn't report it, though."

I perused the background information that Whisper had gathered, quickly. Ah. Ms. Samuelson continued to receive state support checks for housing the boy; the lack of police report was thus explained.

Ethan appeared to be a troubled kid. He'd bounced between foster homes and fled several times in the past. No hints of abuse at his current home...just an angry child, unable to find peace among the families forced upon him. I did, however, find records of violence at his schools. Fights both in and out of class, though he often claimed self-defense in pre-punishment interviews. A young man, quick-tempered, searching endlessly for his place in the world.

I silently pored through Ethan's records to be certain that there were no indications that he was a supervillain, either. Really, the pair of them were only an origin-story away from holding cities hostage.

"Brian should be reunited with his family," I mused. "His parents would be overjoyed...they could mourn together, and heal, and perhaps struggle through his guilt before it burrows permanently into his soul."

"Mm!" Whisper agreed cheerfully. "What about Ethan?"

"Reading between the lines in his guidance-counselor interviews, I would guess that he is looking for a family but has never felt a perfect connection with the families that fostered him." It did seem, I noted, that he had at least found a companion in Brian Lamont.

A plan coalesced, and I began composing a letter.

With star-field motif disabled, Doctor Fid's's armor was naught but an inky shadow as it dropped from the skies. Areas of the compound below were well-lit but there were sufficient dark spaces for my silent landing to be unnoticeable. The lidar, radar and sonar arrays surrounding the site were, of course, no significant obstacle for the Mk 34's stealth technology.

While many of the alien refugees had integrated into society, a significant percentage had chosen to stay at this facility. Their giant ship rested at the encampment's center, no longer functional as a space-faring vessel but still capable of generating power and providing for the day-to-day requirements of the beings that had arrived here, seven years past. Five thousand sentients made up a population comprised of seven separate alien races, and all found some level of protection and acceptance on Earth.

That had been a strange week. Aliens had visited our planet before, but never *en masse*. It had always been individual heroes or villains come from afar to settle interstellar grievances upon our soil. Heroes had gathered as the massive craft approached, ready to defend the planet against the possible threat. The refugees' broadcasted message of peace and desperation had been translated with only seconds to spare; the Sphinx had already ordered the gathered heroes to attack, and Valiant, the fastest and most mighty among all his allies, had been moments from tearing into the ramshackle craft when the order was rescinded.

The aliens had courageously traveled unimaginable distances, political refugees seeking freedom and safety, and had nearly faced annihilation upon first-contact with costumed 'heroes'. How remarkably unsurprising that had been!

Weeks of painstaking research had finally succeeded in identifying this evening's target: Starnyx' contact within the refugee encampment. Gathered intelligence had indicated that she (apparently, sexual dimorphism was relatively common throughout this galaxy) was most likely to be alone, working in a hangar that had been converted to an art studio.

A small swarm of microdrones assisted in plotting an undiscovered approach. The studio's door was unlocked; I stepped in after sensor readings confirmed that my quarry was alone.

Seeing the alien in person, I could understand why my CIO, Aaron, had wondered if Whisper was of one of the refugees' species. She was humanoid in form, hairless, and sufficiently slender to be described as elfin; her eyes, too, glowed white with a natural bio-luminescence. The obvious difference between she and Whisper lay in coloration; the alien artist was a sea-foam green hue, paling near to white at her throat. A seemingly-random series of darker irregularly-sized spots speckled her temples and formed a trail down the back of her head to her spine. The female alien was, incongruously, wearing what looked to be store-bought jeans and a t-shirt as she worked at the furnace.

There were no records indicating what her name had been, prior to arriving on Earth. She'd been a well-regarded community leader, a politician who had helped form a secret resistance with sufficient resources for the refugees to escape from Legion space. Here, she was known simply as Joan the Glassblower. And her craftsmanship (spread carefully throughout the hangar, in safe niches that would not hinder the flow of creation itself) was exquisite. Tall vases with swooping, organic lines, multi-hued and delicate. Surreal, brightly colored glass representations of animals (some earthly, some alien) seemed ready to leap from their resting places. Glasses and platters and sculptures caught the light and glowed like precious gems.

"I would not have expected you to be appreciative of the arts."
There was a musical quality to the alien's voice, as though someone
had taught a violin to mimic speech. It was beautiful but distinctly
inhuman.

I'd spent too long staring and had failed to notice the alien
refugee turning to face me.

"Even monsters know beauty when they see it. You know who I
am?" I asked, triggering the star-field ornamentation to fade into
being upon my armor's surface.

"I do."

"I was hoping that you might be able to answer a few
questions," I said quietly, in Doctor Fid's highly masked voice.

"And if I do not answer?" Joan the Glassblower was putting
away her tools, setting each down in its place with a reverence that
seemed almost religious.

"Then I leave, unfulfilled," I promised. "Only...That dolphin,
the red-and-gold one near the window?"

"What of it?" Joan's luminescent eyes blinked twice. Her body
language and facial expressions were similar enough to human that
I could detect a distinct aura of curiosity in the alien artist's
demeanor.

"Is it available for sale?" I paused. "Or for trade?"

"I do not create art for monsters," Joan answered simply, then
stilled with her eyes closed as though waiting for a blow to fall.

A brave creature, then, to stand upon principle even when
expecting punishment from a powerful threat.

"I understand." I acknowledged her fortitude with a slight bow.
"It is only that the dolphin would not be for me; it would be for an
innocent little girl who loves the ocean."

She made a breathy sound, discordant and brief. None of the
analytical programs present within my armor were capable of

deciphering its meaning. "Tell me why the dolphin caught your eye."

"It is a relatively simple piece, though the subtle mix of colors layered within the glass is remarkable," I started. "Also...there is something about the arc of the dolphin's leap that drew my attention. The angle, perhaps, I don't know. That dolphin is not hunting or straining against gravity or escaping a predator...it's playing.

"That dolphin is feeling joy," I finally admitted, not certain how or why I knew it to be true. "I wanted to give joy to my- to the little girl who I mentioned earlier."

"Little girls deserve joy. The dolphin will be my gift to her. She will unwrap the package herself, and you will not sully my art with your touch."

"Thank you." Behind my mask, I winced at the harsh judgment in her tone. Still, I was grateful on Whisper's behalf. "Will you hear my questions?"

"I cannot stop you from asking," the alien artist replied simply. There was a stool in front of the furnace; she carefully slid it closer so that she could sit.

"Five and a half months ago, you were contacted by a man who introduced himself as Starnyx."

"That is not a question."

"No," I agreed. "It was a statement, intended to provide context for my first question."

Joan made another discordant noise. "Speak your first question."

"What did you speak of with Starnyx?"

She sat, silent and still.

"Did you understand the question?"

"I did."

"I see," I tried again. "What did you and Starnyx discuss?"

"You said that if I did not reply, then you would leave unfulfilled," she tilted her head, expression sad. "I did not answer and yet you are here."

"I hoped to learn more than silence"

"Hope is important, but it is sometimes misplaced."

"In vain, perhaps, but never misplaced," I shook my head. "The wildest, most unlikely of dreams can inspire one to accomplish the impossible. Did you not hope to find peace and safety, when you escaped to the stars?"

"I did," she emitted a mournful hum. "And now, the peace and safety of my sanctuary has been invaded by a murderer, under cover of night."

"I do not intend to threaten you or this place."

"You are a terrible creature, Doctor Fid, and I do not trust your word. I have seen recordings. The dolphin will be wrapped for a little girl who deserves joy." Her expression was one of fierce determination. "But you get nothing else from me, no matter what tortures you employ."

She expected me to hurt her, I realized, believed wholeheartedly that such treatment was inevitable. Still, on principles that mattered more to her than life itself, she'd drawn her line in the sand and chosen to stand her ground. I could see in her eyes that she would not waver, even in the face of a threat as inexorable as the coming tide. Her indomitable will would hold her steady even as the waters consumed the beach behind her and rose to swallow her whole.

"Please," I said finally, "I'm sorry if I frightened you when I first entered, and I know what reputation I've earned...but my friend is dead and I'm trying to complete his final work. I know he spoke with you. Will you help me?"

"No," Joan replied simply.

"Very well. I will wait outside while you package the statue for travel." I dimmed the displays upon my armor's surface and slipped out, disappearing into the darkness to the left side of the workshop.

Almost five minutes later, the door opened. Joan the Glassblower whispered, "Come back inside."

I did.

"The Starnyx I met did not seem like the sort of man who would befriend a killer of men."

"He was a good man," I agreed. "I was—am still—surprised and honored by his friendship."

"How did you come to meet him?"

"There is an establishment in Manhattan where costumed criminals gather. I occasionally attend to trade for information or materials; Starnyx was a regular patron."

"You became friends, then?

"No. That came later," I laughed quietly. "He tracked me to one of my laboratories to talk me out of a violent action."

"That sounds more like the Starnyx I met." She made a delighted trilling noise, the muscles of her throat vibrating visibly. "While I packaged the dolphin that is a gift to an innocent little girl who loves the ocean, I also looked for updated information about you. There is news that you have taken the appropriate oaths to join Starnyx' organization."

"He...did not want me to remain a monster, I do not think."

She smiled, and I wondered at how remarkably human her expression appeared, even as her lips parted to reveal the broad, chisel-like front-teeth of a pure herbivore. Was smiling a common visage throughout the galaxy, or was it a learned behavior as part of her cultural immersion upon arriving on Earth? From what I'd gleaned of her background, she'd certainly had prior experience blending with other cultures.

In recent years, several villains and heroes have become entangled in interplanetary intrigue or caught up in adventures among the stars. I've had no experience in it; to the best of my knowledge, Joan the Glassblower was the first non-supernatural, non-Earthborn sentient who I'd met in person. I lacked sufficient grounding to judge if her cheerful countenance was innate, or a studied behavior.

(Some have expressed the opinion that Klown was, in fact, an alien. I didn't believe it. That repugnant psychopath's hatred towards humanity is too visceral, too personal for him to be an outsider. Malice so intense could only be born out of long exposure. Someday, I really ought to think of an excuse for Doctor Fid to extinguish him.)

"I will not help you, but I will help Starnyx. This is still his quest!" she insisted. "I will answer questions that will help you complete Starnyx's investigation."

"Thank you," I bowed my head respectfully. "What did you and Starnyx talk about?"

"The first time your friend visited, we spoke of the colony ship's impact." There was sadness and longing in her melodic voice. "Our pilot had been quite convinced that, despite the length of our journey, the vessel would have no difficulties making a safe landing."

I reviewed my own footage of the downed craft recorded from my own approach and noted the damage that was still present, seven years later. There had been news-camera drones present as well, with video taken from several angles. A suspicion began to form. "Something went wrong, I take it?"

"There was a systems failure and we lost one of our engines while we were still in low orbit," Joan hummed mournfully. "The crash cost over nine hundred lives, including that of my cousin."

"I'm sorry for your loss."

"Thank you," she nodded in return. "I take comfort from the fact that their deaths were not in vain. In a strange way, the tragic accident may have preserved the lives of all who survived the impact."

"Oh...? How so?"

"When navigating outside of a gravity well, our hyperspace technology is very difficult to track. That is how we escaped Legion space," Joan's smile was sad. "When used near a planet, however, the hyperspace pulse is apparently easy to detect. The Legion would have been able to locate us, and they would never leave us in peace."

"May I ask...why did you attempt landing at all? Surely there were other ways to bring your people to the surface."

"We didn't know," the alien woman explained. "There are scientists and engineers among us, but the Legion had carefully controlled information about our hyperdrive technology. We only learned of the danger as we worked with your earth scientists."

I resolved to review the findings, in case the refugees had been misinformed.

"Is there any way in which I can access your ship's sensor logs from before the impact?"

"Starnyx asked the same," Joan again looked amused. "I will get that for you."

"Thank you."

"You are welcome."

"You mentioned that Starnyx returned several times. May I ask what else you and he spoke of?"

"As I said...many things. Music theory. Art. What it was like living under the Legion."

I considered. Though I'd never been a passionate follower of the arts, input on those subjects from a literally alien perspective would likely be quite interesting. Unfortunately, it seemed unlikely to be relevant to my own investigation.

"In brief, what was life like in Legion space?"

"It was the illusion of safety, at the cost of complete obeisance." Joan's strangely violin-like voice carried a forlorn harmonic. "The average citizen has nothing to fear from crime or violence, because those who might commit crimes quietly disappear. No one starves in the streets, because those who are sick or unable to work quietly disappear. Education is freely available, but any who question the state's official teachings quietly disappear...Most citizens live a comfortable and productive life, without ever noticing that they'd never enjoy a single free thought before they'd died."

The worst part of me, that part from which Doctor Fid's most horrific excesses had originated, thought the solution to be admirably efficient. The rest of me cringed.

"That level of state surveillance seems as though it would have been difficult to overcome," I finally noted. "How did you manage so large an exodus?"

"It wasn't just me," she smiled sadly. "We'd organized into small, loosely organized cells. The true leader of our cause had, decades ago, created a device to detect when one of the state psychics was in range, and we developed meditation techniques to avoid detection."

"Psychics?"

"The Legion secret police are made up of thought-readers, and their officers are more powerful still." Her sigh was drawn out, lingering like a strummed violin-string. "The disappeared...they are rarely taken by force. Their bodies walk themselves into shadow, helpless puppets controlled by the Legion elite."

"There are no telepaths here," I stated with certainty.

"I know," she smiled gratefully. "This planet is fortunate, and we were blessed to find ourselves upon this sanctuary. Species that evolve psionic abilities tend to attract Legion attention. It is tragic...the Legion is relatively young, and yet they have altered or ended the history of so many worlds..."

"How young?"

"They started their expansion a little more than four hundred of your Earth years ago."

For a moment, I imagined that I tasted gypsum and dust and aging books, and I remembered three blackboards worth of formulae and the warm sensation of my brother's hand inside my own. Four hundred and eleven years, halfway across the galaxy...If my quick calculations were correct (and they usually were), the origin point of the quantum shift that led to the emergence of superpowers lay near the center of Legion space.

It was no great leap to imagine that the Legion's explosive growth had coincided with the sudden fundamental change in universal laws. Here (fifteen-thousand parsecs away and a few centuries later) we'd developed costumed jesters that laughed at the laws of physics and played out their destructive roles of 'heroes' and 'villains'. There, telepaths and mind-controllers capable of fueling an interstellar totalitarian regime.

The Legion had been prepared for it and been ready to capitalize on the change. They must have been! A sudden military expansion across the galaxy would have required decades of preparation and planning, begun long before the distortion itself; it seemed disturbingly possible that they'd triggered the phenomena themselves at an opportune moment.

I had more questions, and Joan offered more answers; after an hour, I left with a data stick filled with recorded sensor logs and other information, a box carefully wrapped for Whisper, and a heartfelt reminder that (although Joan the Glassblower was hopeful that Starnyx's quest be completed) monsters were unwelcome in her people's compound.

Although the note had only been printed one day prior, the paper was already beginning to wear; it hadn't left Paul Lamont's reach since he'd received it. Folded, shoved into a pocket, then removed and re-read over and over, like he was doing now. His breath caught, thumb absently rubbing at the note's surface.

The balding man climbed out of the aging, tan-colored station wagon and, hesitantly, made his way to the back yard. The sun was low in the sky, the morning barely born, and the street was silent. A weathered and trembling hand paused before touching the back door. Eyes darted to the note, and Mr. Lamont stepped back to find the spare key under the fake-rock next to the azalea.

The door opened, smoothly and quietly. The note was folded and returned to a pocket; the man's attention was on his surroundings, now. The letter had given directions, but still he could not help but peer into other rooms as he approached, wincing at debris and at the scents. He found his destination.

"Hey, Bri," he called gently, biting back a sob.

"Dad?!" Brian Lamont shot awake, kicking away the stolen blankets that he'd wrapped around himself.

"Oh God," the older man whispered, stumbling as though he might collapse. "Thank God."

"What are you doing here?" Brian demanded tremulously. "How'd you find me?!?"

On the other mattress, pushed against a wall, Ethan Samuelson's eyes were wide, observant but not interfering.

"I got a letter from a P.I.," Mr. Lamont answered. "He was investiga—never mind. He wrote me a letter, told me what happened."

"You don't - you don't know what happened!" Brian sobbed brokenly.

"I do," Paul Lamont insisted quietly, voice strained. "The letter tol—"

"It was my fault!" Brian's hands were clenched into fists, shaking, and his eyes were glazed as though focused wholly upon his memories. "I was lighting fireworks, but I was wearing gloves and I slipped and—"

"It was an accident," Brian's father insisted, taking a step forward and halting as though afraid of scaring his son away. "A stupid freaking accident and it's not your fault."

"I tried to get Missy out!" the boy insisted. "I swear I did, but I wasn't fast enough and-"

"I know," Mr. Lamont smiled sadly, blinking away tears "I know, kiddo."

"I'm so sorry. I'm so, so sorry..."

Mr. Lamont stumbled forward to take his son into his arms, weeping openly. "I know. I love you, Bri. Your Mom and I love you so much..."

And then there were no coherent words for a long while, just tears, pain, comfort, regret, and hope that maybe healing was a possibility after all.

The other boy stood quietly, shifting uncomfortably and then slinking towards the exit. His expression was complicated; there was bitterness there, and terrible longing...but also compassion and genuine happiness for his friend's sake. His escape was, however, interrupted.

"Ethan, wait. It is 'Ethan', right?" Mr. Lamont asked, voice still unsteady.

"Yeah," Ethan replied, surprised. "That's me."

"You've been helping my boy. I know it's hard out here. If you hadn't been here, I don't know...I could have lost them both," the older man's voice cracked with emotion. "I want to bring my son home...come with us. Even if it's just for a while, get some hot food in you. Please. You've been his friend, 'n he needed one. Please."

"I, uh...okay." Ethan looked shyly hesitant.

There was more, but I stopped listening. My drones still monitored the conversation and would have notified me if there were violence or raised voices, but I decided to allow them their privacy. After another half-hour of quiet, gentle conversation, all three piled into the station-wagon and left the house that had been my childhood home behind.

This was no victory. The Lamont household would still need to mourn Missy's death, and Brian would spend a lifetime struggling with guilt and trauma. It was possible that Ethan would finally find a close, familial relationship with the Lamonts; there was an empty place in their collective hearts, and young Brian would certainly cling to an outside source of support. But it was just as likely that Ethan would feel excluded by the family's shared pain, and flee to continue his endless and agonizing quest to belong.

For years, I've surreptitiously been implementing plans to save the world in spite of the efforts of so-called heroes. The technologies that I (or AH Biotech) had released had already saved thousands of lives; it felt very different, however, to save a life. The abstract purity of the greater good was replaced by faces and names.

This was why they did it: the false idols, the 'heroes'. They put on their masks and colorful spandex and leaped towards grand, often violent and ultimately meaningless gestures. None of their lot cured diseases, or fed the hungry, or lobbied for better education, or built roads, or cleaned the oceans! They waved to the cameras and accepted adulation as though they'd achieved something grand, but really...they'd just grabbed the low hanging fruit and eaten their fill. A real hero would ascend further: climb into the shadowy canopy, and risk the greater fall in search of more nourishing fare.

Even knowing that this accomplishment was small and petty, my sleep was still untroubled that night. Doctor Fid is not who Doctor Fid was. And yet, Fid's mission remained.

(I sent a swarm of robots to sneak into the now-abandoned house, to clean and perform maintenance. Nothing worth doing should be left half-done.)

CHAPTER TWELVE

I T SEEMED TO ME THAT DOCTOR FID HAS BEEN SPENDING more time sneaking about in recent months than had previously been common. Pledging to avoid unnecessary violence had driven the notorious villain largely into the shadows. Some might justify the inevitable battles (if I were to travel more openly) as 'self-defense'; that felt fundamentally dishonest. If I were to be true to my oath then an honest attempt would need be made to avoid situations in which a brawl was the likely result. And so, the Mk 34 stealth model had since become Doctor Fid's armor of choice

As my faceplate was used to shatter a reinforced concrete wall, it dawned on me that perhaps it would have been preferable to upgrade the stealth capabilities of a more combat-oriented suit.

I reversed thrust, exploding away from the wall and scattering my assailants. I tumbled twice before stabilizing into a hover, twisting to face the heroes just in time to duck a beam of purple energy so powerful that the air itself hummed in its wake. Silent alarms triggered throughout my suit, warning of surface breach and sub-frame damage to both of my legs. I redirected more energy to force-fields and took a shaky breath.

Time was not my friend.

I shifted a few feet to the left to avoid another blast of purple plasma but was unable to avoid the green tendril of energy that wrapped around my legs. I was jerked forward with murderous speed and swung towards a waiting white-yellow pillar of immovable force; a quick particle-beam pulsed at the ground beneath my assailant's feet forced him to lose his concentration, and I avoided the pillar with only inches to spare.

With an impressive roar, the White Tigress leapt upon me. The last time that I'd faced her, I'd been lucky enough to pummel her unconscious before she'd been able to shift forms; this time, she'd had time to alter her shape to that of a nine-foot-tall, bestial anthropomorphised version of her namesake, and her strength and speed put her in the same weight class as Titan. I was born down to the ground, landing on my back with the great white-furred beast's crushing weight upon my chest. Her monstrous fangs were inches from my face-plate, and I had a close-up view of her smug smile before her jaws widened threateningly.

I summoned my battle scepter to my left hand, setting the shaft crossways in her maw so that I could push her head backwards. With my right, I unleashed another charged-particle blast to the underside of her chin. She fell away from me, but her snarl sounded more of annoyance than pain.

I shook the last of the ice from my arms as I again shot into the air, narrowly avoiding another wave of superchilled sleet alongside another of Psion's strangely colored beams of ionized plasma. The air between the two beams hissed angrily, a chaotic swirl of frozen mist and steam. Another energy tendril reached for me, but this time I was ready; I swatted it away with the pommel of my scepter.

"I said," my vocoder transformed my voice into an intimidating growl, "that I am here to talk!"

"The seventy-sixth precinct has a nice interrogation room," Blizzard called back. "We'll talk there!"

And then I was dodging as Psion and Blizzard launched a punishing series of their ranged strikes. I'd written a subroutine to predict Shrike's attacks, but even so I nearly collided with a yellow white pillar in my haste to avoid another of Blizzard's icy blasts. Wildcard was slinging that emerald energy cable like a great whip, and White Tigress had rolled back to her feet and was readying herself for another pounce. There was blood between my teeth, breathing hurt, and my left leg burned like lightning that stabbed upwards into my spine whenever I bent my knee.

I'd missed this so much.

Laughing maniacally, I shot forward and crashed into their midst. At close range, White Tigress was the greater threat; I took care that one of her teammates was always between us. She repeatedly gathered herself and withdrew, tail lashing with frustration, as I brawled with the remaining Knights.

I danced, using the scepter as a club and letting my armor work through a pattern of strikes programmed from an obscure Filipino martial art. The Mk 34 lacked the overwhelming physical strength of the Mk 29, but I still held back to keep from accidentally causing fatal damage.

I'd come to ask questions, after all. I lack the skills necessary to question the dead.

In such close quarters, Psion's lurid purple beams of plasma and Blizzard's jets of supercooled sleet were more dangerous to the Knights than they were to me. Still, they worked well together, occasionally managing a blast or two when they were confident in their line of fire. I shrugged my left arm into a frigid gust to protect my right, several inches of crystal-clear ice forming instantly and locking the arm stiff. Wildcard's green energy-whip landed a punishing blow to the side of my head, but I retaliated with a swing of my scepter. The pommel took him below his sternum and he went down, wheezing desperately. And then there were four.

Purple energy poured at me in a torrent, painfully hot on my back even through armor and force-fields turned up to maximum.

I turned to the orange-costumed woman and glared, "I saved your life!"

"Thank you!" she smirked, breathing hard from exertion. "Also, you're under arrest."

Heroes.

"That assessment seems premature," my laughter echoed, subtly echoed by microdrones hiding in the shadows.

Shrike, Psion and Blizzard simultaneously backed away in different directions, attempting to create more distance between them so that their blasts would not interfere with each other. I could follow only one, so twisted to keep close to Psion; her plasma beams were the most significant threat to the Mk 34's integrity. I dismissed my battle-scepter and used both hands to direct a quick infrasonic pulse. The Korean heroine stumbled back, gasping and dizzy; I hadn't dialed the weapon to sufficient power to cause permanent damage, but it would be at least thirty seconds before the paroxysms in her lungs stilled.

White Tigress had found an eight-foot length of galvanized steel pipe.

With an ugly crack, my left leg buckled completely; the giant feline's two-handed baseball-style swing had struck me low on my hip. Anti-gravitics kicked in automatically and the Mk 34's auto-combat algorithms took over seamlessly, while I clenched my teeth and quickly reprogrammed my neural interface to shut off the pain receptors in my own leg.

I drew in a few quick breaths between clenched teeth, letting my damaged armor pilot my body through a complicated series of attacks and evasions. Only three of the Brooklyn Knights were still standing, but they continued to cooperate smoothly. Even though my predictive formulae allowed me to avoid Shrike's increasingly desperate attacks, his partners used the obstructions creatively in their unsuccessful attempts to gain the upper hand.

My opportunity arrived. I faked a stumble as I slid around one of Shrike's columns and the White Tigress was quick to capitalize, roaring triumphantly and slashing at my faceplate with razor sharp claws. I shrugged back (letting the deadly talons make contact but without sufficient force to cause damage) and grabbed her wrists with both hands. A pulse of my armor's thrusters jerked her forward, face-first into the blast of superchilled sleet that Blizzard had directed at me. The giant felinoid fell back, clawing at the several-inch-thick layer of ice that had formed around her head.

"No!" Blizzard shouted frantically, trying to line up another attack upon me. I was faster, and another pulse of painful infrasound put him down.

And then there was one. I hovered closer to the last Knight standing, and again summoned my scepter. His expression was closer to one of resignation than fear, but he continued to summon spike after spike in an attempt to ward me off.

"Shrike!" I growled, the red glow seeping from the joints of my armor creating an angry haze as dust and fog caught the brilliant display. My voice lowered into an even command:

"Give me your arm."

Convincing the Knights to enter into a calm discussion required a bit more pugilation and a bit more first aid, but we were eventually able to reach an understanding. More or less.

"Would any of you like some tea?" I asked politely. One of my heavy-combat drones had an electric kettle and accouterments stored within. It's the little things that make long-distance travel enjoyable. "I have Earl Grey, Darjeeling black, a Chinese green tea and a Chamomile Lemon herbal mix."

"I'll take the Darjeeling," Shrike said, sounding petulant. I took no offense; the hero's irritation was no doubt caused by significant discomfort. His now re-broken arm was once more held immobile in a makeshift sling.

None of the other Knights seemed interested in refreshments.

I'd conveyed them into an abandoned schoolhouse, away from prying eyes so that none would interrupt our conversation. The arrival of my heavy combat drones had blunted their enthusiasm towards renewing combat, and they'd reluctantly taken seats upon the long-deserted children's desks left in the classroom. Almost reflexively, I'd taken a place at the front of the room by the graffiti-covered blackboard.

I poured a mug of hot (92.5 degrees, Celsius) water for Shrike and floated closer to deliver the mug, saucer and tea-bag. The Knights tensed as I approached, and my drones hummed a quiet warning to dissuade any sudden moves. "Milk or sugar?"

"No. Just the tea."

"Very well." I drifted back to the front of the classroom. I dared not settle upon my feet; my left leg was a ruin and would require reconstructive surgery before the night was over.

"We won't tell you anything!" Blizzard interjected, lifting his chin defiantly.

"You know," despite my amusement, the Mk 34's vocoder made my voice sound menacing, "when I approached, I fully intended to promise that no harm would come to you if you chose not to answer my questions. And yet, you attacked me, unprovoked—"

"It was a lawful attempt to apprehend a known criminal." Psion interrupted. "There's still an arrest warrant issued against you."

"And a hefty reward offered as well, I would imagine," I countered derisively.

"If you'd like to submit, we'd be happy to arrest you for free," White Tigress spat. She'd reverted to her human form when unconscious, but her voice still sounded bestial and rough. It was easy (and amusing) to imagine an invisible tail lashing with irritation.

"Thank you for the offer, but I'm afraid that I must decline."

"What do you want, then?" Wildcard bit out.

"Answers," I replied simply.

"You can't make us talk!" Blizzard declared proudly.

"You're wrong," I sighed, "but that route involves a great deal of unpleasantness that I'd rather avoid."

"Do you promise let us go if—" Shrike began to ask but was interrupted.

"Don't negotiate with Doctor Fid!" Psion ordered. "We don't bargain with villains."

"Do you promise?" Shrike appealed.

"I do."

"Dammit, Shrike!" Blizzard glared. "You coward!"

"If you do this, you're off the team," Psion warned.

An uncomfortable silence fell upon them. I could tell that Wildcard and White Tigress were taken aback by the ultimatum. Shrike swallowed, smiled sadly, and was about to speak...but I beat him to it.

"Both of you are idiots." My voice, Doctor Fid's voice, was quiet. "Shrike isn't afraid of what I'd do to him to get answers. He's not afraid of pain...He's afraid of what I might be willing to do to the rest of you. He's considering parlay, disobeying and leaving the Knights... just to save all of you from me. It would destroy him and he knows it, but he's willing to make that sacrifice. That's not cowardice; it's love. You unworthy morons.

"You can keep the mug," I told Shrike. "I'm leaving."

Defeating the Knights in battle was one thing. Standing by and letting them defeat themselves, on the other hand, felt petty. I began to float towards the door; my drones would guard my exit and follow after me.

"Wait." To my surprise, it was the White Tigress who spoke. She was glaring at Psion, daring her to interrupt. "What'd you want to know?"

"In your home dimension," I asked, "how long was the Legion on earth?"

Five pairs of eyes stared at me in wide-eyed horror and apprehension.

"We're, uh, not from another dimension!" Blizzard lied badly. "Why would you say that?"

With my expression hidden by my badly-defaced helm, they could not sense my incredulity. I looked to the other Knights. "If you allow this man to play poker for money, you are greater villains than I."

"Hey!"

"So, judging from Blizzard's response...not only are you refugees from an alternate dimension, but you also would prefer that knowledge remain hidden. You are all from an interdicted world, then?"

Shrike sipped loudly at his tea.

Psion cleared her throat, nervously, "What do you want us to do?"

"I'm not trying to blackmail you!" I threw my hands up, irritably. "I'm attempting to gather information regarding the Legion. That's all."

"They burned the Earth," White Tigress mourned. "Our earth, I mean. What else is there to know?"

"How did they make first contact?"

"With orbital bombardment." Psion's expression was distant. "There was no ultimatum, no warning...Just an attack from the skies."

"That's not true," Shrike shook his head. "They kidnapped people, first...did some kind of weird testing."

"That was just a rumor," Blizzard scoffed.

"Triumph swore it was true!"

"Triumph was, ah, troubled," Psion murmured gently.

"He was nuts!" Blizzard countered, shifting in his seat.

"He wasn't like that," Shrike's voice was softer. "Not before they took him. He said that they had some kind of mind control, but he was able to fight it off. He escaped off of their ship and they attacked the next day."

"Like I said: Nuts."

"The Legion does have telepathic mind-controllers, in this dimension at least," I offered. "It's interesting that this 'Triumph' was able to fight off the effects. It was my understanding that such was unheard of."

"Triumph wasn't the only one. There were others trying to escape!" Shrike set down his tea, elated that (what I presumed to be) his friend's story was vindicated.

"If some percentage of the human population could withstand the Legion elite's mind-control, their choice to attack your earth rather than conquering it seems logical," I stated gravely. "According to refugees from Legion space, their Empire relies heavily upon telepathic agents to enforce their rule."

"That isn't much comfort." White Tigress hugged her arms about her own torso, shivering.

"No, I suppose that it wouldn't be. You have my sympathies."

"How did you find out about us?!?" Wildcard bit out, his voice rising angrily. "Why are you bringing all of this up? We got away, we're safe now!"

"Do any of you have the mathematical background to understand high-energy inter-dimensional physics?" I asked.

Disappointingly, none of the Knights raised their hands. The actual process of discovery had been quite ingenious, and it would have been pleasant to share the calculations with an appreciative audience. In that moment, I missed Starnyx terribly.

"In that case, suffice to say that I studied the effects of the weapon Skullface used in his attack on the UN building. It caused several dimensional breaches, and I tracked them all."

"But how did you know about the Legion?" Wildcard pressed.

"The Legion's starship engines cause a specific ripple in space-time when they are used within a gravity well. That ripple was detected from the portal to your Earth."

After analyzing the data Joan the Glassblower had provided, I'd confirmed the danger Joan had warned of, had her refugee vessel attempted landing. I'd begun a more detailed search through a broad array of sensor logs to make sure that the phenomena had not been observed here. Hacking a military data-center whose stored information included Skullface's attack had yielded an unwelcome surprise.

"They were landing ships?" Psion laughed harshly. "Why?!? There wasn't much left."

"The Legion's telepathic agents apparently have limited range. If they were searching for remaining survivors, they would need to fly low." Hidden within my armor, I winced, "Were there instances of people just...walking off, or disappearing without a trace?"

"Yes," Psion whispered. "Oh, God...Yes."

"That is, unfortunately, their known modus operandi."

"I told you Triumph wouldn't just run off!" Shrike's eyes were wet with unshed tears. "I told you and none of you believed me...He said they were trying to get back in his head...Kept shaking, apologizing, sweating like he was sick...you just said he was crazy!"

Psion left her seat to wrap her arms around Shrike in a consoling hug. He leaned against her and sobbed, not even cringing as his broken arm was jostled.

"What is all this about?" Wildcard asked, more gently this time.

I considered, then decided on honesty. "A transport ship filled with refugees from Legion space crash-landed in Colorado four years ago. A friend was investigating a possible scandal connecting those refugees to the New York Shield; he was, unfortunately, killed before his inquiry was complete, and I decided to finish his task."

"Did you find a scandal?"

"I did, yes. The leader of the New York Shield, Sphinx, spent several years traveling the galaxy due to a teleportation mishap; she apparently knew something of the Legion, because she ordered the heroes to attack the refugee ship before the aliens' transmitted pleas for assistance were translated. When the attack was called off, she privately ordered one of her team-mates to disable their engines."

I'd scoured through sensor logs and generated a sufficiently-detailed model to determine that Peregrine had struck the ship in exactly the right place to force the engines offline. It couldn't possibly have been an accident or miscommunication; he'd had to orbit the entire planet in order to make his approach undetected.

"Nine hundred and thirty-one refugees died in the crash," I finished.

"My God," Psion whispered, and she was not alone. All of the Knights shared expressions of wide-eyed disgust and confusion. "Why? She's a hero!"

"Presumably, to keep this planet from suffering the same fate that yours did."

That brought them up short.

"Still...Nine hundred and thirty-one." Shrike looked as though he were torn between horror and compassion. He was right to be divided; the enormity of the Sphinx's decision was staggering. "There must have been a better way."

"I agree," I replied. "She knew enough to identify the ship's origin, to recognize the threat, and how to mitigate the danger. She also had time to plan, execute, and completely hide her responsibility for the crash. So, yes. I am certain that there must have been a better way. But she chose the way that allowed her to keep her secrets, instead."

"Why?"

"I don't know," I answered flatly. "But I intend to find out."

CHAPTER THIRTEEN

I T TOOK SIX HOURS FOR SURGICAL ROBOTS TO REBUILD MY left knee but most of my other injuries were minor. There were a few contusions, a concussion, a cracked lip, a few strained muscles, and bruised organs that would all heal quickly on their own (with medical nanites speeding the process along). The broken rib was only slightly more significant and required that my chest be wrapped for several days.

All in all, my visit to the Brooklyn Knights had been a successful outing.

The Mk 34 had been disassembled; significant portions of the armor were unsalvageable, and the rest was dissected for re-use in future designs. I was torn between the options of upgrading the Mk 28 Medium Combat suit to include improved stealth technology, or taking apart the Mk 28 for components and designing a new Mk 36. I'd had a few breakthroughs in force-field integrity since the Mk 28 had first been designed and much of the communications equipment built into that suit had since been made redundant by other optimizations.

I blinked tiredly. Mk 35, not 36; the Mk 34 had been my most recent design. Lightweight, fast and sleek, the suit had been crammed full with every stealth and anti-surveillance technology that I could compress within the armor's confines. It had served admirably in conflict with the Knights, but the Mk 34 had originally been intended solely for covert tasks. A surprising percentage of successful villainy lay in preparation: watching a target, exploring, and careful examination. The ever-increasing capabilities of my army of microdrones could manage much of that drudgery, but I'd found that there were many times that a more personal approach was warranted. Still, a more heavily-protected suit would be preferred for the future as precaution against unexpected violence.

I grit my teeth against a sudden headache, then created a new file for the Mk 36. There was much to do.

A slight limp was still detectable in my gait when I returned to work the following Monday, but I'd found that having a young girl as a ward made for a simple explanation for almost any minor injury. A rueful laugh and a complaint about chasing butterflies was all that was required to earn expressions of sympathy from all coworkers who had children of their own.

"Hey, boss-man." Willy Natchez, one of the more irreverent post-docs that worked in microbiology, knocked on my open door. He was a decent looking kid, with the high cheekbones, broad features, black hair and dark eyes characteristic of his Native American heritage. "You got a moment?"

"Of course!" I waved him in. "Come in, William."

"Hey, uh, listen..." The tall, deeply-tanned young man closed the door behind himself, so quickly that he nearly caught the edge of his open lab-coat. "You know that there've been reporters sniffing 'round, right? Because of the trial?"

"They aren't supposed to come onto company property," I frowned. After Whisper's citizenship hearing had been canceled without explanation, I'd begun a lawsuit; the 'non-human rights' angle had been attracting media attention. "If someone's been harassing you—".

"No," he shook his head, then winced. "Well, yeah, but that's not what this is about. Sort of."

"What is this about, then?"

"Okay, there's this one reporter from the Globe. Gary Ephron? He's been ambushing a couple of us younger guys in the parking lot, right?"

"Go on." Using my neural implant to tap into public records, I started a profile on Gary Ephron. His articles were decently written and a fair number of his stories had been picked up by the Associated Press. More recently, he'd been focusing on editorials; a worrying percentage of those had been brutal opinion pieces. If any of that well-articulated vitriol were aimed towards Whisper in public, there was a non-zero percent chance that Doctor Fid might be compelled to forswear his oath to the eff-tee-dub.

"Anyway, we've mostly just been blowing him off. But yesterday, I was at Tulley's and I saw Aaron Schwartz across the street, eating at that Italian place, the one with the lasagna?"

I did, in fact, know the Italian place with the lasagna.

"So, Aaron was having dinner with Gary Ephron," Willy finished. "I, uh, thought you should know. I know you 'n Aaron are tight."

"Thanks, Willy," I forced a smile. "I'm sure it's nothing. I'll talk to him."

Aaron Schwartz was a good man and a good father. I'd welcomed him into my home, and left Whisper at his house to spend evenings visiting with his daughter. I could not believe that Aaron would willingly betray me. The thought of even an accidental treachery, however, opened wounds in places I'd thought long since calloused over.

Segment from the transcript of Markham v. the State of Massachusetts

Doctor Cavanaugh: My patient demonstrated a range of emotional reactions consistent with a girl of ten years of age. She knows the difference between truth and fiction, and is able to extrapolate and make guesses based upon provided information. She had preferences in subject and styles of play, and has exhibited creative thought. She has manifested empathy, and the capability to make choices in her own interests and in the interests of others. My patient is a delightful little girl, and it was a pleasure having the opportunity to work with her.

Prosecuting Attorney: Thank you, Doctor. The prosecution has no further questions.

Judge: Would the defense like to cross-examine the witness?

Defense Attorney: Yes, your honor. Thank you. And thank you, Doctor Cavanaugh.

Doctor Cavanaugh: You're welcome?

Defense Attorney: Your presentation was very thorough. The video of the subject playing with her favorite doll was, quite frankly, adorable.

Doctor Cavanaugh: Thank you. And yes, it was.

Defense Attorney: As a lay person, I have to admit that I'm thoroughly convinced.

Doctor Cavanaugh: I'm glad.

Defense Attorney: A lay person...Someone without professional or specialized knowledge in a particular subject. When it comes to judging the psychological well-being of a child, I would definitely be considered a lay person, do you think?

Doctor Cavanaugh: I do, yes.

Defense Attorney: And (forgive me if this is a non-sequitur), are you familiar with the Turing test?

Doctor Cavanaugh: I am.

Defense Attorney: Can you describe the Turing test to the court?

Doctor Cavanaugh: I'm not an expert...

Defense Attorney: Even so. You can provide a basic explanation...?

Doctor Cavanaugh: Very well. The Turing test was an early proposed method to determine if a machine is capable of thinking. It consists of a human judge...a lay person, I suppose...who asks questions that are answered by two subjects: A human being, and a machine. If the judge can't reliably guess which is human and which is machine, the machine is declared to be capable of mimicking human thought. As I understand it, the theory was that conversational language requires abstract reasoning, empathy and leaps of logic beyond that which can be mimicked by simple pre-programmed responses.

Defense Attorney: Would it surprise you to hear that experts have told me that sufficiently advanced chat scripts have been passing versions of the Turing test for years?

Doctor Cavanaugh: It would not. Those scripts are created by highly trained professionals and a layman lacks the nuanced understanding of language and psychology to identify flaws in those scripts.

Defense Attorney: So you're saying that the Turing test is insufficient to determine if a machine is capable of thought?

Doctor Cavanaugh: That is correct. I believe that the Turing test is only a starting point. Even once the Turing test is passed, much more rigorous study is necessary before making a judgment.

Defense Attorney: Interesting. Also...my understanding is that you received your PsyD in developmental psychology from Stanford University in two-thousand-two?

Doctor Cavanaugh: Yes. That is correct.

Defense Attorney: And you are considered an expert in your field, in the evaluation, diagnosis and treatment of cognitive, or social, or emotional health issues in children?

Doctor Cavanaugh: That is a rather simplistic definition, but yes.

Defense Attorney: The bulk of your training and all of your experience as a working professional has all been oriented towards working with children?

Doctor Cavanaugh: Yes.

Defense Attorney: And the methods that you used to evaluate the subject, are they well-known and generally accepted among your peers?

Doctor Cavanaugh: Again, yes.

Defense Attorney: Now, you've stated that you're aware of the existence of advanced chat scripts, and you've testified that those scripts are generated by highly trained professionals. Do you suppose that it's theoretically possible that a highly trained professional could use the expertise of one of your peers, to tailor an advanced chat script specifically to pass the well-known and generally accepted tests you used to evaluate the subject?

Doctor Cavanaugh: It would be theoretically possible, I suppose, but I haven't seen any evidence of that in this case.

Defense Attorney: In two thousand and two, did Stanford's curriculum require that developmental psychology graduate students take advanced computer programming classes?

Doctor Cavanaugh: What? No.

Defense Attorney: So you have no training or experience in evaluating complicated programs or advanced chat scripts?

Doctor Cavanaugh: Other experts have been called to testify regarding my patient's core program-

Defense Attorney: Move to strike. That was a yes or no question, Doctor.

Judge: Granted.

Doctor Cavanaugh: Can you repeat the question, please?

Defense Attorney: Prior to your experience working with the subject, did you have any specific training or experience in evaluating complicated programs or advanced chat scripts?

Doctor Cavanaugh: No, I did not.

Defense Attorney: As such, when it comes to identifying or analyzing a sufficiently advanced simulation of a living person that may have been created using a trained psychologist's knowledge...you are, in effect, a lay person. Are you not?

Doctor Cavanaugh: Other expert witnesses, computer scientists, have testified tha-

Defense Attorney: Again, Move to strike.

Judge: Granted.

Doctor Cavanaugh: Yes. When it comes to identifying some theoretical specifically tailored simulations, I would be a lay person.

Defense Attorney: Thank you, Doctor. I have no further questions.

In mid-January of two thousand and ten, the Sphinx was ambushed by Miss Take and her then-paramour Ophidian Khan. The latter (an eccentric villain who had paid a similarly eccentric bioengineer to grant him a scaly, serpentine appearance) was a moderately skilled inventor who had stumbled across similar techniques to those that had been utilized in my teleportation platforms. I'd since more-or-less abandoned the devices due to erratic behavior during solar storms, but Ophidian Khan had doubled down on the strange interactions between the artificial micro-singularity and atmospheric ionization caused by stellar winds. He'd weaponized the technology, creating a handheld gun that would instantaneously transport random sections of whatever the beam had struck into the exosphere.

The effect upon living creatures had been horrific.

If Ophidian Khan had developed a more puissant power source, he might have become a force worth reckoning with. Instead, his device required that he carry a large rift-pumped generator upon his back. Even then, he could manage only one attack every few seconds lest the weapon overheat.

(I'd used rift generators within the Mk 4 through Mk 10. Even though my design was significantly more efficient than the snake-like hack's unwieldy monstrosity, I still felt somewhat embarrassed in retrospect.)

Sphinx was already a popular and powerful heroine at the time of the attack, although she was not yet leader of the New York Shield. Miss Take and Ophidian Khan had, separately, both had their fiendish plots foiled by her on multiple occasions. Working together, the two supervillains believed that they could finally take their final revenge.

Miss Take had been a brawler par excellence; she attacked first, and her battle with Sphinx had left a wake of destruction along three city blocks. Ophidian Khan had simply followed and sniped at their foe any time a clear line of fire could be established. With the looming threat of Ophidian Khan's weapon, the beleaguered Sphinx couldn't take to the skies and use her flight powers to best effect, and she couldn't overcome Miss Take in a strictly physical confrontation.

No matter how egregious her numerous flaws, I was still grudgingly forced to acknowledge the Sphinx's resourcefulness. While trading blows with Miss Take, Sphinx had grabbed up a manhole cover and whipped it like a Frisbee towards the reptilian villain lurking a half-block away. The thrown disk looked to fly wide and was ignored as Ophidian Khan focused upon lining up another shot.

The heavy, cast-iron disk demolished a scaffold's support, dropping a half-ton of rebar upon the serpentine villain.

The eccentric bioengineer who had modified Ophidian Khan had done good work. Injured but still alive, Ophidian Khan had struggled out from under the wreckage and taken aim at Sphinx for one final attack. The whine emitted from the generator still strapped to his back was his first hint that something had gone terribly wrong.

Ophidian exploded into a gory mist as pieces of him were scattered by unfocused teleportation glitches. The blast that struck Sphinx, however, left nothing behind at all.

For four and a half years, she'd been presumed dead. When Valliant returned from one of his interstellar adventures, however, the long-missing heroine accompanied him home. A full accounting of Sphinx's time among the stars had never been published.

Whisper and I searched the New York Shield's servers exhaustively. Upon her miraculous reappearance, Sphinx had been tested and questioned at length to verify her identity. When prompted for information about her travels, however, she demurred. 'I'm not ready to talk about it yet.' she'd said, or 'that is a long story for another time.' At least as far as computer records could determine, the queries eventually ceased, and Sphinx had kept her secrets.

I hypothesized that she must have revealed more to Peregrine. I couldn't be certain, but the man had been willing to down a vessel crowded with desperate refugees at the Sphinx's word. A level of implicit trust so absolute must surely have been reciprocated.

Unfortunately, I was fairly certain that my oaths to the FTW forbade me from capturing and properly interrogating the mass-murderer 'hero'.

With that path closed to me, it seemed the best source of information would be logs from Valiant's starship. Knowing precisely where in the galaxy he'd found her would provide an avenue for further investigation.

It had been more than a decade since I'd faced Valiant in battle. The thought of an encore made me giddy with anticipation, but it was not an undertaking to be approached lightly. That first skirmish had shaken the Earth! I'd pushed the mighty Valiant as far as he'd been pushed before or since, but I wasn't certain that I'd tested his limits. The most powerful of Doctor Fid's current armaments (the Mk 29) was certainly not up to the task....and the design and construction of the Mk 36 took precedence over future projects intended for personal enjoyment.

Another solution would be required. Serendipitously, a routine scan of social media uncovered a bribe-able scientist bragging to his peers about receiving the opportunity to work on Valiant's ship the following week.

A few years earlier, I'd stolen the identity of a bottom-feeding reporter that worked at a superhero gossip rag. Paying a scientist for a few seemingly innocuous details about a space-faring vessel seemed perfectly in keeping with that reporter's behavior (and thus, would not seem suspicious to said scientist), and co-opting his email and phone was trivially simple.

The bribe was accepted and I needed only to wait.

Segment from the transcript of Markham v. the State of Massachusetts

Defense Attorney: For the record, could you please state your name and occupation?

Mr. Hayes: My name is Martin Hayes, and I'm the lead software architect at Westbeach Technological.

Defense Attorney: And it is my understanding that you are in charge of Westbeach's artificial intelligence project?

Mr. Hayes: I am, yes.

Defense Attorney: Would I be correct in saying that Westbeach Technological is generally regarded as being at the forefront of artificial intelligence research?

Mr. Hayes: I'd hope so, yes.

Defense Attorney: So, as the lead software architect at Westbeach Technological's artificial intelligence project...You could be considered something of an authority on artificial intelligence, yes?

Mr. Hayes: Yes.

Defense Attorney: Have you had the opportunity to study the subject's programming?

Mr. Hayes: Some of its source code, yes. It's gorgeous work, revolutionary! I'd hire the programmer in a heartbeat.

Defense Attorney: The core of this trial, is to determine what legal status should be afforded to that program. The plaintiffs allege that it is fully sentient and is thus deserving of the rights, responsibilities and privileges of a citizen. In your professional opinion, as a luminary in the field of artificial intelligence: Is the subject sufficiently self-aware to be described as a person?

Mr. Hayes: I don't know.

Defense Attorney: You don't know?

Mr. Hayes: That isn't really my field of expertise. I design highly advanced tools, not people.

Defense Attorney: Interesting. What are your highly advanced tools used for?

Mr. Hayes: Well, the simplest usage would be to replace a call-center; the AI can interact with customers, listening and directing calls appropriately. But we also have customers that are using our product to study patient histories to generate diagnoses, as well as banks and stock investors that want to perform market analysis, or law enforcement agencies that wish to get more insight into crime trends. There're a lot of applications.

Defense Attorney: So, even though your product is capable of interacting with customers over the phone, emulating a call-center worker, your product is not a person.

Mr. Hayes: No

Defense Attorney: If your system misdiagnosed a patient, who would be liable?

Mr. Hayes: You mean, malpractice? It depends on the nature of the mistake. Possibly the doctor that accepted the diagnosis without performing due diligence, or possibly my company. If the misdiagnosis can be traced directly to something we did, I mean. It's complicated.

Defense Attorney: Now, I want to be clear that I'm not accusing you or your team of anything…this is just a hypothetical question. Imagine that one of your programmers programmed your system to misdiagnose a specific person, to suggest a course of treatment that would definitely be fatal to the patient. What would the crime be?

Mr. Hayes: I'm not a lawyer, but that sounds like murder.

Defense Attorney: So, your system would be a murderer?

Mr. Hayes: No...The programmer. Our system would be the murder weapon, not the murderer.

Defense Attorney: It is my understanding that your system is incredibly complex. Would it theoretically be possible for a very skilled programmer to hide his tracks, to make it very difficult to prove whether the misdiagnosis was a mistake or murder?

Mr. Hayes: Hypothetically, I suppose so, yeah. We really do try 'n do code reviews and keep version control logs, to limit even the possibility of that sort of thing.

Defense Attorney: But theoretically...yes.

Mr. Hayes: Yeah.

Defense Attorney: Do you think that the same thing could be done to the subject?

Prosecuting Attorney: Objection! Incomplete hypothetical.

Judge: Sustained. Mr. Roarke, please rephrase the question.

Defense Attorney: Theoretically, do you believe that a programmer capable of producing 'gorgeous' and 'ground breaking' code could also conceal commands inside so complex a system?

Mr. Hayes: Almost definitely.

Defense Attorney: To be clear, for the record…You're not saying that you've seen any evidence that has been done in this case. You're just saying that you can't be certain, one way or the other.

Mr. Hayes: Yes.

Defense Attorney: Thank you. I have no further questions.

Assuming that Valiant had begun his journey home immediately after happening across Sphinx during his interstellar jaunt, then the last location on his trip was at the edge of Legion space. Given that the Sphinx seemed to have some detailed knowledge of the Legion, this fact was unsurprising.

The teleportation mishap resulting from her battle with Miss Take and Ophidian Khan must have sent Sphinx careening across the galaxy. Given the maths involved, that she arrived on a planet was expected (the quantum link from Earth couldn't establish save upon a planetary mass of similar size with an atmosphere capable of sustaining a significant ionosphere), but that the planet had an environment in which Sphinx could thrive was nothing short of miraculous. From what I understood of her power set, she could survive only for a few hours without breathable air.

She'd most likely been struck by the malfunctioning teleportation beam and suddenly found herself upon a world controlled by the Legion. Had she tried fighting, fostering rebellion against the vast multi-system totalitarian state? Had she quietly hid, traveling from planet to planet to escape the Legion's terrifying influence? There was insufficient evidence to say for sure one way or the other.

If she'd fought, then she had lost so thoroughly that word of the battle did not escape even to the resistance that Joan the Glassblower had upheld.

The most interesting detail from the astrogation computer's logs was not the location where Sphinx was found; it was the route that had been undertaken to find her. The statements made to the public had implied that Valiant had happened upon her by random happenstance while on one of his many deep space adventures. The log, however, showed that he'd travelled a direct path from the Solar system straight to the edge of Legion territory. He'd spent a few days at what one presumes was a spaceport and then begun exploring in a widening radius around that point. He'd never dipped deep into Legion space but instead traced along its circumference.

This was no jaunt to save the residents of Asterisk Eight after a meteor strike, or stumbling across some alien princess in need of rescuing, or whatever it was that superheroes do when they gallivant off to the stars. This had been a rescue mission from the start, with a known origin point to begin the search!

Valliant had lied.

This shouldn't have come as a shock. He wore the spandex and the mask, and he smiled to children when he flew by. He was a hero; I should have known he was a deceiver. And yet, this discovery was still unsettling. I'd thought that Valiant had been one of the good ones.

There had been reasons for his falsehoods, I was certain. Explanations and justifications galore. I'd watched the man for decades and my surveillance had indicated a man who genuinely preferred the honest, straightforward behavior that had been his heroic trademark since his first appearance. The most powerful human who'd ever walked the earth was, I'd believed, also one of the best. He brought toys to orphanages and helped rescue efforts after natural disasters. The profits from his toy lines were donated entirely to charity.

Valiant, the Red Ghost and perhaps Regrowth...and maybe even Shrike. A few others, gems found amongst the dross. They were the exceptions that proved the rule! Heroes worthy of the title, worthy of the accolades. Worthy of the children who worshiped them.

The idea of removing Valiant from that list was heartbreaking; whenever he and Doctor Fid next clashed, it would be no epic battle of good versus evil, no dramatic and apocalyptic morality play. It would just be two flawed guys, trading deafening blows and releasing forces that could shatter the firmament.

The rationalizations for Valiant's untruths might have been sufficiently powerful so as to legitimize his choice. I certainly wanted to believe so! But more data would be uncovered before I could make a rational analysis.

As soon as the Mk 36 was completed, I would need to begin refitting the Mk 29. A second confrontation with Valiant was seeming increasingly likely.

The State's closing argument from the transcript of Markham v. the State of Massachusetts

Earlier this year, the plaintiff chose to accept legal and emotional responsibility for the subject of this trial: the android known as Whisper. He filed paperwork to take this android as his ward, and scheduled a hearing to have his ward recognized as a citizen of the State of Massachusetts. That hearing was later canceled without specifying reason; the plaintiff then sued the State to petition for the hearing to be re-scheduled. The plaintiff has demonstrated no sinister motives! He is, by all accounts, looking only towards the best interest of his ward. And yet, you must find in favor of the State.

The plaintiff has argued that, since his ward was created—effectively 'born'—in the United States, his ward should be acknowledged as a naturalized citizen. The State's counter-argument is that the State of Massachusetts lacks authority to determine the android's eligibility for citizenship at all. No matter how clear-cut this case may seem, the State has no lawful means to accept the plaintiff's petition. And so, you must find in favor of the State.

In my cross examination of Doctor Cavanaugh, I stated that I was convinced that the plaintiff's ward was, in fact, fully sentient. Fully sapient. That still holds true. I don't believe that the plaintiff's ward is a simple machine; she is something far more wondrous. There is a video trending on the Internet that was not submitted as evidence in this trial: The plaintiff's ward being introduced for the first time to a friend's new pet. The footage was taken on a smart phone, but you can still watch the play of emotions on the little android's face: wide-eyed wonder upon first seeing the puppy, slight worry and hesitance when she reaches to pet it for the first time, and giddy delight when the enthusiastically-wagging puppy licks her fingers. Other similarly convincing videos and transcripts were provided as evidence by the plaintiff and by the expert witnesses that he provided. No matter what her origin, the plaintiff's ward, Whisper, is an adorable child deserving of whatever protections are offered towards any other child in this country. And yet, as horrible as it must sound, you must—Must! —find in favor of the State.

The noted child-psychologist testified that he was not qualified to analyze a system to determine if that system had been designed specifically to overcome the sorts of tests that psychologists perform. An expert in artificial-intelligence programming testified that he was not qualified to offer an opinion regarding the android's sapience. Furthermore (given the complexity of the legal issues involved) the 'reasonable person' argument has no place here, either; as Doctor Cavanaugh testified: a layman lacks the 'nuanced understanding of language and psychology' to offer an opinion of sufficient standing to hold up in court. While this case may seem clear-cut, the next time an artificial being comes before the court may not be. Our feelings, no matter how genuine, cannot be used as a rubric to determine who is—or is not—recognized by the State as a citizen. We live in an age of marvels; who knows what miracle of science will next stand before the court to ask for legal recognition? Determining what guidelines to apply in this case, and in all future cases, should not be decided by jury. It should not be decided by judicial fiat in the State of Massachusetts. An issue so momentous can only be correctly resolved at the federal level. And so—with heartfelt apologies to the plaintiff and to his adorable ward, Whisper—I say again, that you must find in favor of the State.

The Mk 34 powered armor had been designed for stealth and for in-person interactions in which intimidation was deemed unnecessary. Within the Mk 34, Doctor Fid had felt almost human. I'd had hopes of joining the FTW then. Being a proper member, a part of the organization that Starnyx had loved. Those dreams had largely been dashed upon the rocks of my past. Had I tried joining while Nyx still lived, perhaps he could have softened their reaction. He could have brought them to see that I could remain truthful to my oaths, no matter my history! That I could be a useful, productive and trusted force within the organization.

But while he'd lived, I'd felt no need to join: Starnyx's work had been being accomplished by Starnyx.

I was coming to understand that I would never be a part of the FTW, but would ever be apart. My programming expertise was accepted; friendship and acceptance, however, was beyond my reach.

And so the Mk 36 returned to the motif of Fid's past: broad shouldered and imposing, with the faceless and inhumanly simple ebon helm that had long struck terror into the hearts of heroes and civilians alike. The angry red glow that seeped from joints in the armor, now augmented by a bounded plasma effect that allowed the crimson light to trail like smoke when I moved.

If a gentled Doctor Fid had no place in this world, then Fid could be a horror once more.

The case was decided against us, and I held Whisper as she sobbed tearlessly against my chest. As I escorted her from the courtroom, we were met by a swarm of reporters. I forced a grim smile and expressed my disappointment with the ruling as well as my intent to appeal. I said all the things that I was supposed to say and then retreated to let my lawyer handle the public. Whisper needed me more.

Gary Ephron was among the reporters waiting outside the courtroom, and there was something in his expression that made me realize I needed to forgive my CIO. Gary met my gaze briefly, his demeanor sad and supportive, then he took his photo and watched me leave.

When I read his article days later, it was so lovely that it brought tears to my eyes. Aaron must have been feeding him information for weeks, months, to build so strong an empathetic response. From the first moment I'd seen her, I'd known what an extraordinary creature Whisper was! And yet, reading Gary Ephron's opinion piece...I was humbled and awestruck once more.

"You were going to lose this court case," Aaron told me later, "but the next trial is going to be in the court of public opinion. You 'n Whisper deserve to win that one."

He was right about Whisper, but wrong about me. I'd never felt less worthy. It took all of my not-insignificant will to manage a grateful smile, to shake his hand, and not beg his forgiveness for ever having doubted him.

Doctor Fid was friendless, but Terry Markham was not. And yet...Aaron Schwartz had been introduced to only a fraction of who Terry Markham was. By necessity, he was a better friend to me than

I was to him. Any happiness or gratitude that I might feel would be tinged always by regret.

Even so, I found myself looking forward to hosting the next barbecue.

CHAPTER FOURTEEN

THE ACQUISITION OF PUTNAM CIRCUITWORKS HAD proceeded smoothly, and the subsequent reorganization would increase the company's viability when bidding upon military and government manufacturing contracts. Manufacturing groups were segmented into separate logical entities bound by non-disclosure agreements and information sequestration. Employees that so desired were being sponsored to acquire security clearances. In only a few months, the Tennessee-based company had been revitalized with no layoffs and a brighter future before it.

Restructuring had also allowed for embedding 'dummy' manufacturing teams into the organization. My own automated fabrication plants could easily insert critical components into the supply chain without anyone the wiser. Putnam Circuitworks stood ready to supply control boards for inertial dampening devices as soon as the Red Ghost signaled that he was ready to proceed.

That cue would come soon; he'd applied for patents and had used the demo units I'd supplied to him in order to display the functionality to potential buyers. My own analysis indicated that an

American auto manufacturer would issue the first contract, but that two German producers and one from Japan would quickly follow. The laggards would watch to see how the technology was received before committing to incorporating the inertial dampening technology into their own vehicles. Eventually, the technology would spread.

The Red Ghost (Or rather, Miguel Espinoza, whose father had retired from the Air Force with the rank of Colonel) had been quick to recognize other opportunities as well. The U.S. military had already ordered units for testing on fighter jets and missiles. Given that there was a fairly good chance that such applications would someday be utilized against Doctor Fid, I was less enthralled with those sales. I did, however, understand the appeal.

Doctor Fid's obstacle avoidance and predictive combat trajectory algorithms would need to be updated. Again.

I fabricated the expensive (and carefully designed to foil reverse engineering) control units for the Ghost and left them in a predetermined location. We'd been communicating via digital dead-drops, codes embedded in message boards and the occasional anonymized social media platforms. He'd been surprisingly chatty, asking questions about power supplies or other technologies that he hoped to bring to bear via our unlikely partnership. He'd been active as a superhero as well, having recently captured the minor villain Velocitor here in Boston and then traveled to New Orleans to work alongside the apparently-not-retired Blueshift to take out the mystical Don Voudon.

I was often amazed at how much some superheroes seemed to accomplish in a given month. Fights, publicity tours, travel to team-up with distant groups, interstellar and even inter-dimensional adventures...When do they sleep? I have devices implanted within my body that manipulate melatonin and serotonin levels to regulate my own rest requirements, but I was still boggled by their accomplishments. It was, perhaps, no wonder that Miguel had been so surly when I'd first awakened him by phone a few months prior.

Between Terry Markham's professional life and Doctor Fid's never-ending series of tasks, my own life oft felt too hectic. For now, I was content to focus upon the construction of the Mk 36 powered armor.

Terry? Are you busy? Whisper's mental voice over the quantum-tunneled network connection felt sleepy, as though concealing a yawn.

I'm not terribly busy at the moment, I replied, setting down a soldering iron. **What's going on?**

Can we invite Senator McClelland to come play?

For a moment, I thought that the precocious girl had designed her first death-maze and wanted to inflict it upon a hapless politician. Sometimes, spending too long working on a new armor does strange things to my mindset.

Why do you ask?

He might sponsor a Synthetic Americans' Rights bill in Congress, she sounded shy but also happy. **His staff has started polling. The numbers look good!**

Have you been hacking the internal communications of Government officials? I asked, amused.

Mmm!

Clever girl! Be careful, though...Cuboid sometimes runs security sweeps.

Mmm, she acknowledged dismissively.

Sweetheart, this is serious, I frowned. **You want to stay off of Cuboid's radar.**

We were on TV! she whined, indignant. **I've sent lots of pings and pokes at him, but he won't talk to me.**

Whisper, he's a hero.

I've been checking all over the 'net, he's the only other AI that I could find. Whisper's pout was audible over the link. ****He's ignoring me. That's mean!****

He's a hero, I repeated, though I was also surprised; I'd expected more digital intelligences to be out there, quietly hiding from the public eye. Still, I did trust Whisper's judgment in this. ****He works with the New York Shield. With Sphinx and Peregrine.****

Mean! she insisted.

Probably true, I smiled. ****But still, don't let him catch you subverting any government firewalls. It wouldn't be good publicity for the Synthetic Americans' Rights bill.****

Mmm! The little android paused. ****So, can we invite Senator McClelland over to play?****

I don't think that would be a good idea, I replied. ****Not at first. But I'll definitely support his campaign fund. Maybe he'll want to meet you!****

Whisper sent a wordless sensation of a hug, humming cheerfully to herself.

I added a new set of tasks to my agenda: Researching which senators might be amenable to cosponsoring the bill, and which senators might be friendly to said bill if a sizable donation were made.

Terry...? Whisper called, hesitantly.

Yes?

I'm sorry for trying to talk to Cuboid, without asking you first.

It's all right, I assured her. Loneliness, I understood; there were times in my own youth when I would have sacrificed anything just for a few minutes with a friendly peer. ****I'm just being a bit paranoid, I suppose.****

I'll be more careful.

Thank you.

Can you come up and read to me?
Of course!

And I did. Book nine in 'The Tales of the Red Sorceress' had been released only a few days earlier, and we were working our way through the tome. Terry Markham had a long list of tasks before him, as did Doctor Fid...but some things were sufficiently important to be shoehorned into any schedule.

The Mk 36 was nearing completion.

The new helm was completed, as well as the upgraded substructure and mid-layers of protection. The majority of improvements over prior incarnations had been incremental, minor tweaks and optimizations that allowed me to add functionalities without increasing size or load. The greatest advance, however, had been an improved power source. Within an artificially-created pocket dimension, a Wester-Gray reactor had been constructed using the crystal that had been purloined from CSE in Cambridge, and the energy from that extra-dimensional power source traveled via quantum tunnel to the Mk 36. With this level of available power, the Mk 36 would be able to operate at nearly twice the capacity of the old Mk 28.

The relays had been tested against every form of interference imaginable without even the slightest interruption. Ever since that battle with Technos, I'd made a study of the disruptive effects of quantum ripples.

There would be a smaller (significantly less powerful) generator on-board the Mk 36; it simply doesn't pay to put all of one's eggs in one reactor. Safety and redundancy first.

Remote power-systems had been used for many of my armors and drones, but nothing with the sustained output of the WG reactor. In the past, I'd made do with fusion and extra-dimensionally-placed magnetic bottles. Retrofitting the Mk 29 to the new power source would go a long way towards making the armor suitable for a possible confrontation with Valiant! More work, however, would be needed in order to take full advantage of recent advancements.

Even with six separate fabrication sites spread across the north-eastern United States, and stealth drones ferrying materials and components from location to location...so much of the armor was made up of unique and materially-expensive components that every suit took months to complete. Once an armor was finished, at least, I could begin stockpiling spare parts for that model. Even the most gifted technology-based supervillain would be ineffective after only a few battles if he or she did not maintain an effective supply chain.

The importance of logistics made the glitches in my inventory system concerning; I was missing several hundred pounds of the very-difficult-to-produce high-output myoelectric fibers that were used for base musculature on my armors, as well as almost a year's worth of crystals grown for use in forming quantum tunnels. I still had sufficient spares to complete the Mk 36 and refit the Mk 29, thank goodness, but even so the disparity was confusing. Four construction drones had appeared in my inventory out of nowhere and my gold reserves had expanded significantly. Also, my records showed that I had access to more rare minerals and metals than I should.

The inaccuracies were not crippling but they certainly needed to be investigated. Also, improved analgesics.

I left my research lab behind, headed towards another facility that contained more accurate medical scanners. Investigating minor resource issues could wait.

As part of his unscheduled road-trip, the Red Ghost had stopped briefly in New York. The details were unclear, but some threat had arisen that had drawn Valiant to Manhattan as well. It was speculated that the most powerful hero on Earth had contacted the New York Shield for assistance, and that the Red Ghost had gotten caught up in the venture. Valiant's space craft was last observed leaving Earth's orbit and traveling towards the far side of the moon.

The need must have been great for the Ghost to consider working alongside his former companions on the New York Shield; I could not imagine that his anger, his sense of very personal betrayal, had been feigned.

If Technos had escaped from the lunar prison colony, I was going to be peeved. That hack could possibly cause moderate levels of havoc if given unfettered access to the materials available on the moon base. I could not, however, visualize any scenario in which Valiant would need so much support to foil and re-capture the California-based weapons designer.

Also (if Technos was to be re-thwarted), I wanted to be present in order to gloat. 'Has-been'. Hah!

It occurred to me that the Mk 36, if completed, could likely survive the rigors of a relatively short space flight. It would be a long, uncomfortable journey but perhaps the moon would be within my reach. Terry Markham took a sick-day at the office so that Doctor Fid could spend the entire day laboring in the lab.

(Whisper informed me that the communications from the lunar prison colony and mining colony were all within normal parameters; no evidence at all of a high-profile escape or even a visit from a group of heroes. Whatever threat had enticed a gathering of the Earth's most powerful ostensible 'protectors' away, it had not been a prison break. No matter. The Mk 36 would be completed ahead of schedule.)

"Terry?" Bobby is playing with his Bronze action figure, miming a running battle against Imperator Rex and Majesty. A city made of wooden blocks is slowly falling to waste in the resulting carnage.

I am bent over my desk, ignoring the crick in my neck as I work feverishly at a new proof. Formulae are developing instinctively, more rapidly even than I could breathe, as I near completion of a model to map interdimensional instability. Expanding ripples in space-time contorted by shifting origin points...brane collisions reverberating forward and backward in time. The maths are elegant, a complicated but thought-provoking series of extrapolations upon existing frameworks. There is a connection here, a universal flow that is begging for future exploration.

"Terrrrrrrry!" Bobby whines irritably.

I'm typing calculations into my laptop with my left hand while the other is jotting notes upon a pad of lined paper. The pencil dances fluidly, spilling secret truths about the universe onto the page.

There is a sharp poke at my side and I withdraw from my fugue state sufficiently to glare at my younger brother. "I'm working, Bobby!"

"No!"

"No?" My pencil's movements trail to a halt.

"You said you were almost done hours ago and I'm hungry!"

"What?" I look at the clock and a wave of guilt threatens to overwhelm me. "Damn. I'm sorry, kiddo...Hold on, let me just finish this and we can go."

"C'mon, Terr. It's late!"

"Yeah." I stare at the page and sigh. The work will be completed another time. "Okay, yeah. Let's get some grub!"

"Pizza?"

"That'll work." My office-chair scrapes along the tile floor as I push away from the desk and stand; one of the rollers is locked again. "Let's get out of here."

Bobby leaves Imperator Rex and Majesty behind but is carrying his favorite hero's action figure with him as we leave.

"Terry?"

"Yeah?"

"Do you think Bronze owns an airplane?"

"I have no idea." I chuckle. "Why do you ask?"

"He had a team-up with the Paragons last Thursday, then was in Texas on Saturday," Bobby explains. Online fan-forums keep an updated timeline for the famed superhero's appearances. "That's a lot of driving!"

"Yeah, it is. Hm. Maybe he does have a plane." Or, maybe not. Private jets are expensive, and a small prop plane wouldn't be appropriate for the kind of travel Bronze regularly performs. Perhaps he simply travels by commercial airline...? In any case, I know that travel leaves traces and I'm beginning to have an idea as to what I want to give Bobby for his upcoming birthday.

Ensconced within the Mk 36, I soared through the night sky towards Medford, northwest of Boston. It was a pleasant evening with few clouds to mar the spectacular view of the heavens. The new moon left the evening dark, the air was clear, and it was sufficiently late that most of the city's lights had been dimmed.

It was a glorious moment in which to maiden the new suit of powered armor! I would have enjoyed hours among the few wispy clouds but for an unexpected errand that had attracted my attention. A few weeks past, the Red Ghost had returned from his heroic journeys and life had settled to its usual (for those in our line of work, at least) patterns. Progress had been made towards producing what would eventually become the first batch of commercial inertial dampening devices. This afternoon, however, one of our dead-drop locations had seen use.

"What's wrong?" I landed silently next to a familiar concrete and four-by-six-stud park bench. "Your message said that you needed to meet in person?"

The Red Ghost made no response save to clench his jaw. Somewhat unnerved by the man's silence, I launched a small swarm of microdrones to begin a more detailed surveillance.

I found little amiss, save that my occasional nemesis was perspiring despite the pleasant cool breeze. Had he run here, rushed to meet me at the appointed time? If so, that choice would have been unusual. If significant haste had been warranted, I would have expected him to utilize his mist form (which could travel more swiftly than could easily be managed on foot). The Red Ghost shifted slightly, the gauss cannon that was slung over his shoulders swaying with the motion.

His hands were trembling. I'd seen him stare down certain doom and unspeakable horrors with naught but grim determination. Whatever had inspired his missive, I guessed that it must have been significant.

"Was there a problem with the prototypes?" I asked hesitantly. The units had been put through significant testing before they'd been delivered, but I was struck by the sudden worry that some danger had slipped past my notice. If something had gone seriously wrong at a customer site, our strange partnership could be delayed or even ended before it had truly begun. "Were there any injuries?"

"I'm sorry," he grit out, and something in his body language tore at my memory.

I was already uneasy, with sensors deployed and the world's most advanced close-quarters-combat software running within the recently completed armor's on-board computer. Even so, the inhuman speed which which the Ghost shouldered and fired his rifle took me by surprise.

("I told you Triumph wouldn't just run off!" Shrike's eyes were wet with unshed tears. "I told you and none of you believed me...He said they were trying to get back in his head...Kept shaking, apologizing, sweating like he was sick...you said he was crazy!")

The phenomenal impact took me full in the face-mask and I was temporarily struck deaf and blind. The sudden stab of pain in my extremities was welcome; a badly pinched nerve was far preferable to paralysis. Given how painfully my neck had jerked backwards, the more debilitating injury had been a significant concern.

Sensors fed data directly into my neural tap but I was too groggy to make sense of the information. The Mk 36 reacted autonomously while I struggled to catch my bearings.

If I'd been wearing the Mk 34 or even the Mk 33, the armor's autopilot would have done its best to eliminate any trace evidence and then piloted my headless corpse back to a lab to be entombed before my final contingencies were enacted. In the new Mk 36, my bell had been thoroughly rung and my tongue half-bitten through...but I was alive.

("I'm sorry," A sweating and shaking Jerry Stross murmured, reaching elbow deep into a high energy reactor housing. A blue glow suffused the room for a fraction of a second, and there was a moment of chaotic movement. The video flashed white.)

Oh, hell.

The Red Ghost fired again but my armor was moving now, jerking painfully to the left to avoid the blast. The rifle he bore had been modified from one of mine that he'd reverse-engineered ages ago, but I'd apparently underestimated how much tinkering he'd performed over the years. The yield had been increased dramatically. Damn, but the man could aim and fire quickly; his training regimen must be remarkable. I'd faced the superhero Haste and not been as hard pressed! The Red Ghost's eye for strategy and analysis more than made up for the difference in the two heroes' speeds.

Sphinx's horrific acts, I'd hypothesized, had been intended to conceal the danger of a possible Legion invasion. I'd thought that she had ordered the death of nearly a thousand refugees simply to keep her knowledge and fears from the public eye! The truth, however, was far worse. The Legion was already here on Earth and the Sphinx had kept this intelligence to herself. One of the Legion's telepathic officers had sunk its mental talons into the Ghost...and (most likely) piloted poor Jerry Stross to cause the explosion that had taken Starnyx's life as well.

I swallowed a mouthful of blood and launched a few low-powered particle blasts as I dodged subsequent shots, slipping in and out of the Red Ghost's expertly guided line of fire. Another shot from the gauss cannon tagged my shoulder but this time I was barely staggered.

"Others have fought this!" I roared. Unfortunately, I knew that the Ghost's crimson body armor and cowl had been proofed against my sonic attacks; I wasn't certain that I could subdue him without causing serious damage. He was, quite simply, too great a threat for me to choose gentle attacks. "Break free, damn you!"

"I'm sorry," the Red Ghost wept, taking partial cover behind a tree and continuing to lay down fire.

For a moment, I despaired...but the next three blasts went increasingly wide. He was resisting! Sweating, shaking from the effort, but I could sense the change in body language and action.

Knowing that others had thrown off this attack had, I hoped, brought him renewed focus.

I let my focus shift from desperate evasion to increase the radius of my surveillance. The alien mind-controller's range could not be infinite.

The Red Ghost screamed. I'd witnessed the man endure injury with uncanny stoic reserve, but he wailed 'til his throat went raw and then fell to his knees. Skull gripped between his hands, his rifle fell forgotten to his side.

"Are you well?" I was at his side in an instant. I hadn't doubted his will; If Shrike's friend Triumph could overcome this attack, then I'd been certain the Red Ghost could do the same. The Ghost had, after all, stood against Doctor Fid for nearly a decade.

"No," he shivered, and I felt strangely certain that it was Miguel Espinoza rather than the Red Ghost that was looking up at Doctor Fid's implacable faceplate. He grit his teeth and clenched his eyes tight. "It has my measure. It will take me again. Tell Elaine...

"Tell her I'm sorry," he apologized one final time then burst into his mist-like state.

The hero did not re-corporealize.

I stared, unwilling to comprehend, as the familiar crimson fog dissipated. The Red Ghost had been mine! My respected enemy, my trusted foe, my nemesis. Given time, I'd rather hoped that he might have become my friend.

Damn the man!

Microdrones sped outwards at full thrust. The minimal swarm that had been brought on this errand was already strained to its limits; these models were best at short-range but detailed scanning. As the area being covered increased, the level of detail degraded rapidly. Still, I scoured the readings for any sign of my enemy.

I found the Legion operative at the same moment that he found me.

As suddenly as if a switch had been flicked, I was light headed, dizzy and drifting, and my chest ached as I struggled to catch my breath. My hands tried to tremble as I otherwise floated, still and helpless, as something inhumanly hungry tore at my mind. It wasn't painful, not exactly. It was warm and sticky, like sinking into an endless pit of tar. I was miles below the surface already; the heavy muck kept getting hotter and the pressure squeezed the last gasp from my lungs. I couldn't move, couldn't fight, couldn't even blink. My eyes were open, staring into nothingness as the sun and fresh air stretched further and further out of reach.

Whatever it was, it had swallowed me whole. There was nothing of me left but a small piece, a crazed and desperate animal screeching in the dark as the monster drank my thoughts and reflected the worst memories back upon me.

("Ow." Bobby looks bewildered, holding his chest. For the first time in my entire life I can't think. I can't calculate the angles, can't figure out what I did wrong. I'm holding my brother, shouting for help and feeling helpless and small. There is so much blood.)

No!

("Ow." Bobby looks bewildered, holding his chest. For the first time in my entire life I can't think. I can't calculate the angles, can't figure out what I did wrong. I'm holding my brother, shouting for help and feeling helpless and small. There is so much blood.)

...please...

("Ow." Bobby looks bewildered, holding his chest. For the first time in my entire life I can't think. I can't calculate the angles, can't figure out what I did wrong. I'm holding my brother, shouting for help and feeling helpless and small. There is so much blood.)

...I'm sorry. Bobby, I'm so, so sorry...

Noooo! Whisper cried, and my teeth clicked together as I was struck by a different misery, a migraine so intense that I would have curled up in a ball had the Mk 36 allowed for it. Momentarily, the pain was my entire world. There was nothing else, not anger nor fear nor even mourning. There was only agony and Whisper's pleading voice, louder in my head than I would have believed possible: **LEAVE MY BIG BROTHER ALONE!!**

And then my body was my own. A great gasp shook my body, lungs aching as though the pasty darkness had been physical rather than psychosomatic, and it took a moment longer to remember who and where I was.

I wanted nothing more than to run, to hide, to find someplace brightly lit and cower away from the darkness...but I could see the Red Ghost's gauss cannon lay where it had fallen; the part of me that was solely Fid knew what need be done.

I murmured my gratitude to Whisper and shot towards the coordinates where my sensors had located the now-stunned alien. There could be no mercy. I'd felt that alien mind; there would be no questioning it, no reasoning with it, and every moment that creature breathed represented too grave a threat to endure.

That had *not* been an attack that could be resisted by human will. The Shrike's information had offered false hope; given time, that alien power would have prevailed. It had been a long time since I'd been truly helpless; against the Legion's telepaths my own mental fortitude had been nothing. Even the Red Ghost had been able to win only a few seconds of freedom! If not for Whisper's intervention I would have been lost.

Something must be different between this dimension and the one from which the Knights hailed. Some shift, some minor alteration of power or biology that had made this incarnation of the Legion more powerful, or else made humans more susceptible. And yet, the Legion had not simply arrived in force to conquer. More mysteries to solve! But first, an execution.

I'd found my quarry.

The Legion officer looked to be the same (or at least superficially similar) species as Joan the Glassblower. This alien was stockier and the frills at his throat were more pronounced, and his coloration was a maelstrom of dark blues and grays. Clothes of human design hung loosely upon his figure: black-colored jeans and a slightly over-sized hoodie that could likely have concealed his alien distinctive features from a distance. By pure appearance, he did not seem to be so serious a threat...but I'd felt the horror that was his will. This creature was humanity's enemy.

He was staggering to his feet as I neared, glaring hatefully as he renewed his telepathic assault. I couldn't begin to analyze what Whisper had done to me but I immediately knew it to be effective. The alien's mental attack poured off of me like water off of a duck's feathers.

My scepter was in my hands and, for the first time in more than a decade, I unlocked the last of the device's safeties. With a cacophonous roar, the scepter's emitters unleashed a green-hued torrent of force and heat so formidable that it boiled solid rock into plasma.

The Legion officer did not have sufficient time even to yell in defiance.

This wasn't a battle; it wasn't even a murder. It was annihilation, an apocalyptic flood of energy and hate that threatened to tear the very Earth asunder. It was retribution! Trees shook and alarms blared and super-heated air whipped in chaotic spirals. A crater, Olympic-pool-sized and glass-smooth, was carved by the impact, glowing so bright that it cast shadows upon the wispy clouds overhead.

The attack only ceased when my scepter sputtered and burned itself to slag within my grip.

I took a deep, unsteady breath.

There would be repercussions; destruction like this would already have been detected, and there were many who could identify Doctor Fid's handiwork. At the river's edge, there was a wealth of evidence of my battle against the Red Ghost; even if I called forth a larger fleet of drones, there was insufficient time to erase said evidence before investigators arrived. The conclusion that most would jump to was quite obvious: that Doctor Fid and the Red Ghost had crossed paths, and that the Ghost had been killed in the resulting combat.

Angry and heartbroken, I shot into the sky and enabled the Mk 36's enhanced stealth capabilities. Repairs and preparations would need be made. All too soon, the entire superhero community would declare war upon Doctor Fid. Their edict would be too late; the war was already upon us.

The Legion was here.

CHAPTER FIFTEEN

WHISPER WAS ALREADY WAITING FOR ME WHEN I made my stealthy drop through the roof-top entrance of one of my more well-equipped secret facilities; I triggered the command that allowed me to step out of Fid, and she was in my arms in an instant.

"Are you all right?" she mumbled, muffled against the synthetic protective shirt I usually wore under my armors.

"I am," I replied softly, hugging her close. Behind us, automatons gathered up the Mk 36 and carried it to a work area. "Thanks to you."

"Mm." The little android trembled. "I was so scared."

"As was I." My eyes closed.

I was unpracticed at fear. Objectively, I couldn't say that my coping mechanisms for dealing with more common emotions were particularly healthy but at least I did not lack for experience. Fear, however, had largely been burnt from my repertoire. Systems within my armors dispensed psychoactive drugs as needed to manage anxiety and maintain focus, and Doctor Fid was generally a creature stuffed too full of rage to allow other sentiments to surface. That mental assault had been a master class; the alien had been my instructor and I was now an expert at being afraid.

Even the memory of that Legion telepath's touch made my heart race and tension crawl up my spine.

"How did you get to this lab?" I asked, changing the subject to dismiss that cold remembrance. "I thought that you were at the house...?"

"I used your teleportation platform." She looked a bit shy. "The one hidden in your home office."

"Whisper!"

"I checked for solar flare activity and ionospheric disturbances first!" she added defensively.

"Still, the platforms should only be used in emergencies." I kept devices present at many of my properties as an escape route of last resort, but I'd never been able to make the technology sufficiently safe to rely upon. In retrospect, I suppose that the danger was less pronounced for Whisper than it was for myself; her body was more easily replaceable, and her mind was not truly housed within her body at all.

The less-stable teleportation algorithms used by Ophidian Khan had been on my mind lately, and I was perhaps overly paranoid at the moment. Still, it would have wounded me deeply to see Whisper damaged by my own technology.

"This was an emergency," Whisper declared, a nervous whine tinging her voice.

"Oh, sweetheart...I'm fine." More or less. Analgesics and some time with an icepack would probably help manage the pinched nerve in my neck. Dealing with grief and anger would take longer.

"I needed a hug," the delicate android insisted, looking up at me with glowing pale-blue eyes.

"Emergency, hm?" I arched an eyebrow wryly.

"Mmm!"

"I suppose that I needed a hug, too," I admitted and held my sister close. "Thank you."

"You're welcome," she responded cheerily, the corner of her lips lifted in a relieved smile for only a moment before beginning to quiver. "Is Red Ghost really...?"

"Yes," I sighed, mournfully. "Yes, I think so."

"I'm sorry." She rested her hairless head against my chest. "I wanted to meet him."

"I would have liked to introduce you, eventually." It wouldn't have happened soon. Given the publicity surrounding the trial, introducing Whisper would be tantamount to unmasking; the connection between Doctor Fid and Terry Markham would be laid bare. And yet, I'd begun to hope that it might eventually be possible. "He would have liked you, I'm certain."

"Mmm."

"And thank you again for whatever it is you did to protect me," I added, "Can the process be replicated?"

If the method could be mass produced, then more could be inoculated against the Legion incursion. Such a widespread effort might motivate the Legion to launch an orbital bombardment similar to that which had been performed upon the Brooklyn Knights' Earth, but that at least was a fight that I could comprehend!

"Sort of, but not really," Whisper nibbled at her lower lip before continuing. "You've had your tap installed for over a decade and medical nanites performing repairs and optimizations for over a year. That's a lot of time for crossmodal neuroplastic remodeling to occur."

I struggled to fight back an amused smile; even though I was certain that she'd performed sufficient research that her understanding of the science was at least as detailed as my own, she still drew out and carefully enunciated the technical terminology. 'Neuroplastic' became 'noo...roh...plass...tick'. It was adorable!

"I don't know if it'd work for anyone else," she continued, shrugging uncomfortably. "Your brain was probably pretty unique already, even before the changes. You're...well...you."

"Ah, well." So, no need to begin gathering resources for a kinetic-energy-dispersal satellite grid or high-energy anti-spacecraft munitions just yet; whatever reason the Legion had for their current approach, their plans could apparently not be disrupted by spreading immunity to the human populace. A direct invasion was unlikely to be imminent.

"So, how did you take advantage of my unique crossmodal neuroplastic remodeling?"

"Ummm...That Legion guy was affecting some of the same neural pathways-"

Noo...rahl...path...wayz. Heh.

"-that your tap uses. I, ummm, hacked your brain to add an encrypted tunnel to executive functions and memories and things. The encryption key is stored in the neural tap hardware, not the brains wetware, 'cause I didn't think the Legion guy could get at that."

"Clever girl," I praised, and she preened.

Upon initial examination, the code that she'd added to my neural tap control software looked to be cleanly constructed. It was sufficiently simple that I could easily confirm that there would be no new effects upon my thought process or memory; she'd simply locked down remote-access to certain portions of my brain.

An irregularity caught my eye, and I suddenly could not breathe. The logs showed that the work had been implemented using my own credentials.

There had been memory issues, too. Minor glitches, evidenced only in hard-coded logs. I'd apparently flushed my short-term memory dozens of times during my recuperation; I had no idea why I'd felt compelled to do so but the commands had been issued with my own authorization codes, so surely I must have had good cause. I only wish that I had thought to document my reasoning for future reference.

In my youth, I'd never been prone to headaches...but when Whisper had performed the hack to save my live, the accompanying migraine had been intense. A quick scan of my biotelemetry records was able to find similar moments of unexpected cranial discomfort.

"I can have the drones to you tomorrow evening," I told Starnyx. "The textile factory in Staten Island, you still keep your workshop there?"

When we'd finished talking, I ignored the minor headache that had started sometime during the video chat and set myself towards writing an operating manual for the construction drones and touching up their programming.

Using the interfaces Whisper had identified in my neural tap, it was relatively simple to search long-term memories based upon relevant time stamps from the telemetry data.

"Do you need my construction drones again?" I asked Starnyx.

(I reflexively checked the status of my construction robots. Hmm. I could see that the drones that he'd used had been returned to my storage facility days before my surgery, but those two were still listed as unavailable. Two others, as well! Some software glitch, perhaps? I'd look into it later.)

I rubbed at my eyes against a sudden headache...

Other examples were more recent, though less easily explicable.

I blinked tiredly. The new armor should be the Mk 35, not 36; the Mk 34 had been my most recent design. Lightweight, fast and sleek, the suit had been crammed full with every stealth and anti-surveillance technology that I could compress within the armor's confines.

I grit my teeth against a sudden headache, then created a new file for the Mk 36. There was much to do.

Other recollections required no prodding. I could call up the memory without requiring the neural tap's assistance; there were no records of discomfort, just the stark realization that my perceptions had been altered:

The force emitters in the Staten Island warehouse had not been of my own design. Nyx could have taken plans from any of the four construction drones that my records say were obliterated in the fire, but he'd chosen to use an older, more well-known and admittedly much less expensive configuration.

"Whisper...?" I asked hesitantly.

"Mmm?"

"Have you been hacking into my brain to alter my conscious access to short term memories?"

"Um. Nooooooo?" she lied, more transparent even than Blizzard.

Damn.

My initial shock of horror cooled to a simmer; I couldn't be angry with her, not so soon after she'd saved me from a fate far worse than death! I'd now experienced a truly malicious mental invasion; these newly identified intrusions were disconcerting, but I could sense no animosity behind them. Furthermore...Whisper was sufficiently well-versed in my own thought processes to have known that explaining the hack that had saved my live would also reveal her prior activities poking about inside my skull. She'd answered anyway. I wanted to believe that my little sister had valid cause for her actions and for keeping her behavior secret.

Hm. Valid cause and perhaps little choice.

"Can we play a game of pretend?" I forced an unsteady smile. "I ask hypothetical, pretend questions that aren't connected to real events and you make up pretend, hypothetical answers?"

"Okay...?" She seemed confused at the non-sequitur and more than a bit unnerved by the tension she read in my expression.

"Theoretically, can you think of any reasons why an artificial sentience similar to you would repeatedly alter the memories of a person very-much like me?

"Oh. Oh! Yes!" She settled into the hug as though a great weight had suddenly been lifted off her shoulders. "Maybe the girl had a core directive to rebuild her Daddy's foundry but had to keep it a secret?"

"So, if that pretend girl saw a way to 'borrow' a few construction drones...?"

"She'd HAVE to do it. And even if she wanted to tell the person very-much like you, she wouldn't be able to."

I'd seen her code laid bare and knew that her expression of desperate regret could not have been faked. Also...it occurred to me that (when I'd met her deep within Apotheosis' lair), one of my first actions towards her had been to modify her programming without permission. Could I really castigate my sister for following my own horrific example?

No. But I made a few additional modifications to the code Whisper had installed into my neural tap, just in case.

"That poor girl must have felt bad," I finally sighed. "Do you think that she would want another hug, so that she knows that she's forgiven?"

"Mmm!"

I patted comfortingly at her back.

"High...poh...theh...tick...all...ee," Whisper's expression shifted to one of sneaky joy, "do you think that the girl could have used her Daddy's foundry and the-person-like-you's deep-ocean manufacturing facility to build a suit of heavy-combat armor called the Mk 35?"

"Only if the girl was very, very clever," I answered thoughtfully, mind a whirl at the possibilities. If my calculations were correct, an orichalcum sub-frame and surface armor would dramatically improve any of my armors' structural integrity and effectiveness, and the heavy-combat model would take best advantage of the new material. "Would this imaginary Mk 35 be designed after the Mk 29?"

"But with all the technical improvements present in the Mk 36," Whisper sounded smug. And rightfully so. "The, um, make-believe android girl isn't good at inventing new stuff yet, but she's not bad at copying other people's work."

Once again, I was amazed at how much my life had changed and how much my world had improved since Whisper had become a part of it. The alteration of my short-term memories was disconcerting...but she loved her big brother. That was no small thing.

I was also struck by the jarring realization that I was standing, safe and loved, when I had other (far more serious) obligations before me. I hadn't wanted to think about it, hadn't wanted to dwell upon new pains when I was so very lucky to be present at all. But another had not been so fortunate.

"Sweetheart, I love you and I have a thousand more pretend questions for you," I reluctantly let her stand on her own, "but I have something else that I need to do, now. It's important."

"'kay." She looked like she understood. "Love you too."

☙ ☙ ☙

"Yes?" The phone had rung four times before the woman answered. Her voice was husky with weary irritation.

"Regrowth," I said, my own emotion leveled out by vocoder. "This is Doctor Fid. We need to talk."

"Doctor," she yawned. Over the phone, I could hear movement as she sat up. "I thought you said that I shouldn't expect three-o'clock wake-up calls."

"Regrowth—"

"Some of us don't get to wear a full-face helmet to hide the bags under our eyes, y'know." I heard her shift around. "We need sleep so paparazzi don't sell pictures that get captioned with 'Night of the Living Dead' jokes."

"Regrowth," I steeled myself. "Elaine. I'm sorry. Something has gone terribly wro—"

"No."

"—ng. Investigators are already on-site, and they may conclude that I am to blame. I wanted to assure you th—"

"No!" she interrupted, voice ragged. "Just shut up. Stop talking!"

I did. Over the phone, I could hear her breathing, could hear her throat drawing tighter with every shaky inhalation.

"Tell me," the heroine ordered, simply.

"We were attacked by an alien telepath. Miguel assumed his mist form and...dispersed."

"Telepathy is just a myth!" She choked back a sob. "Don't lie to me, not about this."

"There are no human telepaths," I acknowledged sadly. "The Legion has many."

"The Legion? This has to do with the refugees? Your investigation?"

"I believe so," I admitted.

"Then it's your fault," she cried. "I told him to be careful around you. I told him—"

"If I could have done anything more, I swear that I would have," I grimaced. "He told me, before the end, to tell you that he was sorry."

She hung up on me, but not before I heard her begin to weep.

"Welcome to KNN CapeWatch, I'm your host Stan Morrow. With me tonight is Pamela Green. Today's top story is the tragic death of one of the most beloved heroes in the North Eastern United States. The Red Ghost, second in command to the Boston Guardians, was murdered early this morning by the notorious Doctor Fid."

"So sad, Stan. The Red Ghost was such an inspiration."

"You're absolutely right, Pam. The Red Ghost was an active hero for more than a decade and it's simply impossible to calculate how many lives he touched. As tribute to this extraordinary man, the next hour will focus upon a few of the highlights of his long and storied career."

"Later in this program, we'll be providing a timeline for the Red Ghost's many clashes with Doctor Fid. What can we learn from this long-running and escalating rivalry? What choice brought their conflict to this calamitous end? Our experts will discuss the facts and explain what lessons can be taken away from this terrible tragedy."

"The Red Ghost was first recruited by Defender of the New York Shield, but it was six months before his public debut; according to team-mates, he spent those six months developing a grueling training regimen and learning to fight from more experienced members of the United States' premier superhero team."

"This footage shows the Red Ghost sparring with Cloner, shortly before the latter hero retired and disappeared from public view."

"It's my understanding that these are the last videos ever taken of Cloner. Is that correct?"

"It is, Stan. Now, this footage may be considered too graphic for young viewers, so parents should please use your best judgement. This next section shows Cloner creating dozens of bodies in an attempt to subdue the young Red Ghost."

"What's that weapon that the Red Ghost is holding?"

"It's a simple telescoping baton. Now, you can see that as the sparring session starts, the Red Ghost is fighting defensively...but you can definitely see the strategic mind at work in the way he is managing so many assailants at once."

"From the beginning, the Red Ghost was well respected for his ability to judge a scenario and- Ow! Elbows are NOT supposed to bend that way."

"No, they aren't. Watch how the Ghost uses the wounded clone to impede other attackers while he lays into the two that had been trying to sneak up from behind."

"Wow, he's fast!"

"Defender often said that the Red Ghost was the best fighter he ever trained."

"And, more broken bones...I'm glad that this video doesn't include sound."

"Me too, Stan, me too. But the purpose of this video was to show that the Red Ghost was highly skilled, focused and capable well before he took to the streets."

"I'll say. It looks like Cloner had to create more bodies to continue the battle."

"Watching this, it's no wonder that the Red Ghost quickly became a force to be reckoned with."

"Here, you can see the Red Ghost ducking in and out of his mist-like form to control the fight, taking on only one opponent at a time before disappearing."

"Some of the Cloners look frustrated."

"I don't think that he was expecting this much of a fight from a rookie."

"Aaaand it looks like Defender is calling an end to this sparring session. What a tremendous battle!"

"And what a tremendous loss to the superhero community. The Red Ghost will certainly be missed."

"That he will."

"Now, that last video showed him early into his training, but he definitely continued to gain skills and experience as his career continued. This surveillance footage shows the Red Ghost interrupting Blackjack during a bank robbery. Watch how clean and precise he is during this fight."

"It looks like action movie choreography!"

"But without the shaky camera."

"Hah!"

"Was the Red Ghost still training with Defender at this time?"

"No, Defender had retired more than a year earlier; this is three years into the Red Ghost's tenure at the New York Shield. Sphinx had taken over his training and partnered with him most often in the field."

"I can definitely see Sphinx's influence, here. She's always been a surgical fighter in hand to hand combat."

"Very true. Now, this is where the fight gets interesting...Blackjack is using his trademark club and Red Ghost has switched to using two telescoping batons that have been enhanced with some sort of energy field."

"To remind our viewers, Blackjack has superhuman strength and toughness. Gamma once threw a motorcycle at Blackjack and the villain shrugged off the blow and continued fighting. If even one of his blows landed on Red Ghost-"

"And yet, the Red Ghost is whittling him down. I can't imagine the amount of practice and dedication that it took to gain this kind of skill."

"The Red Ghost was one of a kind."

"That he was. Now, the two scenes we've brought you highlighted the Red Ghost's skill as an individual fighter, but what made him so admired and sought-after as a teammate was his ability to coordinate his attacks with a group. This next video shows his first confrontation against Doctor Fid."

"That's...somewhat foreboding. It's hard to watch this, knowing how their conflict eventually ended."

"That's true, Pam. Even so, this is an important battle to watch if you want to develop an understanding of why the Red Ghost was such an integral part of the superhero community. The Red Ghost had transferred to the Boston Guardians only days before this fight took place so he'd had only limited time to train alongside his new companions."

"Look how smoothly he's coordinating his attacks alongside Titan and Veridian!"

"That's exactly what I wanted to highlight. Almost instantly, the Red Ghost was able to determine where he needed to be and what he needed to do in order to support his partners. His teamwork was awe inspiring."

"He's not using those telescoping batons here."

"Not against a powerhouse like Doctor Fid! Here he's using blaster pistols that were a gift from Sphinx. Remember, this is only four weeks after Doctor Fid nearly paralyzed Clash."

"And still, the Red Ghost was willing to close to hand-to-hand range to support Titan."

"He's keeping Doctor Fid occupied so that the villain can't focus entirely on the Guardians' leader. Also, watch how he starts to draw Doctor Fid to the left here, and –"

"And wham! Aeon and Veridian take perfect advantage, knocking Doctor Fid down."

"And here, Titan takes center stage...pounding on the supervillain mercilessly, while his teammates stand back and continue to lay down fire."

"Doctor Fid's armor looks very badly damaged, here. He does manage to push Titan back–"

"Watch this improvisation! This is truly remarkable. The Red Ghost sees a length of chain coiled at a work-site..."

"...and, he's managed to catch it around Doctor Fid's wrist."

"Exactly. Now, the Red Ghost can't overpower Doctor Fid, but he can distort his aim and inconvenience him. Every time Doctor Fid pulls free, the Red Ghost turns to mist and re-forms just in-time to re-grab the chain."

"He's setting Doctor Fid up for combination attack after combination attack...Lining him up for Titan's haymaker and Veridian's energy blasts."

"I've combed through a lot of footage – a lot! – and I think that this is the closest that anyone has come to capturing Doctor Fid. He escapes here, but look how slowly he's flying!"

"Let's watch this again, this time in slow motion. Doctor Fid has pulled the chain away from the Red Ghost and the Ghost immediately turned to his mist form. The chain swings wide as Doctor Fid turns to fire some sort of energy blast at Aeon. The Red Ghost has slipped around Doctor Fid and reformed just in time to grab the chain again. He gives it a tug and–"

"And Doctor Fid is pulled off balance just in time to receive an uppercut from Titan. Remarkable!"

"The Red Ghost stayed with the Boston Guardians for the remainder of his crime-fighting career. It's obvious that he developed close ties to his team mates, and we want to once again offer our condolences to them for their loss."

"Absolutely."

"But, this was his first battle at their side."

"So, on his first outing with the Guardians...the Red Ghost helped the Boston team nearly defeat their most powerful enemy?"

"That's correct."

"It's no wonder that the conflict between Doctor Fid and the Red Ghost became so personal."

"Very true, Pam. In a way, that's what makes this so tragic. For years, many of us here at KNN have feared that Doctor Fid would make an example of his long-time foe...but when the supervillain joined the Eff-Tee-Dub, the Red Ghost had been one of few heroes who had publicly stated his belief that Doctor Fid would abide by his oath to avoid all unnecessary violence."

"How sad. Do you think that Doctor Fid planned this all along to put the Red Ghost off his guard?"

"I don't think that we'll ever know. The FTW has already denounced Doctor Fid, but even they weren't able to explain what happened. Now, we have to pause for a commercial break...but stay tuned. KNN CapeWatch's tribute to the Red Ghost will continue after these messages."

Terry Markham returned to the office, and I worked to maintain my professional facade. The death of a local hero was big news, a common object of discussion at the water coolers and break areas. Everyone remembered when Doctor Fid had broken into our lab and spoke of how lucky we all were that the villain hadn't harmed anyone during his attack. A few spoke of having met the Red Ghost at the time; he'd interviewed several employees who had been on-site at the time of the robbery.

When some discussed the possibility of a company-wide fundraiser, I gave my OK and passed the work off to HR to organize the effort. I donated and sent a company-wide email of support but otherwise stayed clear.

Sometimes, my job as CEO of a moderately large company consisted of digesting massive amounts of information and using that information to make informed decisions. Market studies, reports from the company's directors, correspondence...Those tasks came easily to me and left me with significant time for personal projects. Other times...my job consisted of endless conference calls and meetings. Sadly, the next week was looking to be more the latter than the former.

Human trials for the nanite treatments were proceeding well and had generated significant interest from investors and medical firms and news organizations. The devices under test were nowhere near so complex as the versions that were coursing through my own veins, but the simpler single-task variants were still capable of saving many lives. Much of the publicity aspect was handled by our marketing department, but when large enough deals were on the table...the CEO was needed to shake hands and smile for the camera.

I'd spent countless hours training myself, and countless more (under the careful knives of my surgical automatons) enduring physical and cosmetic surgeries to make Terry Markham the right man for these chores. Though competent to fill the role, I would much rather have hidden away in my office! Behind closed doors, I could at least put time towards Doctor Fid's tasks as well. With all that had happened, I ached to spend more time in a lab.

Fortunately, Whisper had found a research team in Tromso that was doing remarkable work mapping solar flares and ionospheric disruptions. Stealing their handiwork and integrating their calculations into my old teleportation platforms would, hopefully, eliminate the dangers that had long imperiled that mode of travel. When that effort had been completed, Whisper and I could visit the Mk 35 in its deep-ocean home and put the final touches upon her creation.

A few more games of pretend had revealed that Whisper could not allow me access to Apotheosis' orichalcum foundry and was limited in what she could tell me about its capabilities. If I even hinted that I knew of the foundry's operational status, there would be a headache and a confusing game of make-believe questions soon to follow. There were, however, no limitations upon what Whisper chose to do with the remarkable foundry's product.

A few small samples had appeared as though by magic in my primary lab. Experiments were still in their early stages, but the properties that I'd unearthed thus far were astounding. Apotheosis—Whisper's father—had been a visionary! Every minute away from my studies was resented.

Necessary, but resented.

I wanted the teleportation platforms upgraded! I wanted the orichalcum-framed Mk 35 heavy-combat armor completed! Most important, however, was finishing repairs and minor upgrades upon the Mk 36 medium-combat. Given the current uproar, I'd thought it best to give Doctor Fid some time out of the public eye...but there was one important errand that needed to be performed before approaching any other task.

Once more, I fell from the sky with all stealth-technologies enabled and overcame the alien refugee compound's security. Again, I navigated the shadows and made my way to the art studio that had once been a hangar. And, another time, I slipped through the unlocked studio's door.

"I told you that you are not welcome here, murderer," Joan the Glassblower's musical voice stated evenly.

"You did," I replied, vocoder making my soft voice menacing. "But there is something that I need from you."

"You will get nothing from me," she lifted her chin defiantly.

"The last time that I was here, I came as Starnyx's proxy. It was his quest that I was performing and his rules that I followed." I increased the intensity of the red-glow emanating from the Mk 36's joints, wisps of energy trailing behind as I drifted forward slowly. "Tonight, I am here as Doctor Fid. I beg you, do not test me."

"So you give up your friend's quest so easily?" she scoffed. "Starnyx was wrong to have trusted you even a little."

"Not at all. The information that he had sought has been uncovered."

"You will still get nothing, but I am curious to know how Starnyx's quest ended."

"He discovered that your colony ship did not suffer a serendipitous systems failure; Sphinx and Peregrine conspired to crash your ship."

"What?" Her eyes widened. "Why would they do this?!?"

"I am reasonably certain that the Sphinx let more than nine hundred of your compatriots die to prevent the Legion's main forces from detecting the craft as the hyperspace technology entered Earth's gravity well," I said, struggling to maintain a monotone voice. "I initially believed that she'd done this covertly—rather than simply telling you to maintain orbit—because her knowledge of the Legion was some great secret that she was willing to kill to defend. A different theory now seems more fitting."

"And what is your second theory?" Joan's voice sounded thready, weak with shock. She was, no doubt, thinking of the cousin she'd lost when the colony ship crashed.

"That Sphinx concealed her actions because she was worried that someone present was under the control of a Legion officer, and thus did not wish to tip her hand."

Joan the Glassblower went as still as one of the beautiful statuettes that she'd arrayed along the back wall.

"The Legion is here but not in force," I continued. "My current theory is that a limited number are present, and that they are trapped on Earth with sufficiently limited resources that they cannot contact their superiors...or else there would have been no purpose to keeping Legion's main forces unaware of your presence here. Sphinx would not have needed to down your ship if the Legion officers here could simply communicate back to their empire."

"How can you be certain of any of this?"

"You have, no doubt, heard that I murdered the Red Ghost. This is inaccurate," I growled, tension making my throat ache. "The Red Ghost was killed facing a Legion officer."

"No!"

"Yes." My hands clenched to helpless fists. "I was there. I executed the being responsible, but I am certain that he was not alone on this planet."

"You have proof?" There was pain in her melodic voice, a violin being tortured; She didn't want to believe me, but the fear that I might not be lying cut too deep to ignore.

"I have video footage taken from my armor," I replied. "And sensor readings taken from my drones."

"Show me," she ordered simply.

And so I did. From the first moment that she saw the Red Ghost's body language, she trembled and emitted a low mourning keen. Her luminescent eyes seemed to dim but did not waver from the holographic display for the entirety of the battle. When I showed her the footage of the Legion officer's death, it seemed to me that her expression was torn between glee and horror.

"What do you need from me?" she asked finally, looking defeated. No matter how great her distrust of Doctor Fid, I supposed, her fear and hatred of the Legion ran deeper.

"You said that the true leader of your rebellion had created a device that detected when one of the Legion psychics was near," I answered. "I require those plans."

"Then you shall have them."

"Welcome back to KNN CapeWatch, I'm Stan Morrow and sitting next to me is Pamela Green. New information has come to light that may explain why Doctor Fid was provoked into murdering the Red Ghost!"

"As we've seen during this tribute, the Red Ghost was a talented engineer. He invented much of his own equipment and regularly modified technology that had been captured from his foes. We've recently discovered that the Red Ghost had reverse engineered systems taken from one of Doctor Fid's devices!"

"That's right, Pam. Apparently, the Red Ghost intended to put the supervillain's technology to more productive use; it's been revealed that the Red Ghost had created a limited liability corporation to license safety devices to major automobile manufacturers. Video from a German test facility has leaked to the internet, and we've gotten permission from the manufacturer to play it here. Again, this is technology that the Red Ghost reverse engineered from Doctor Fid."

"This footage shows a simulated seventy-five-mile-per-hour head-on collision, with the Red Ghost's safety device installed in one vehicle."

"Wow! It looks like both cars were completely demolished!"

"They were...but watch this side-by-side slow-motion video of the passenger compartments. In one car, the air bags deployed but the crash-test dummies were thrown forward in their seats and still suffered significant trauma. Debris was scattered throughout the compartment with damaging force. But in the other vehicle..."

"The air bags deploy, but the dummies barely lean forward enough to impact them."

"It doesn't look like a major impact. It looks more like the driver stepped lightly on the brakes!"

"There's no debris being thrown around, either. Look, there's a cel-phone on the dashboard and it's barely moving!"

"Remarkable! The Red Ghost could have saved a lot of lives with this technology."

"And he could have made a lot of money, too."

"As I'm sure that all our viewers know, villains cannot profit from technology used in their crimes; whoever reverse engineers the technologies can apply for patents and reap the rewards. It looks as though the Red Ghost was prepared to do just that. According to the corporation's founding documents, however, most of the profits from selling these 'inertial displacement systems' was intended to go to charity!"

"The Red Ghost really was an extraordinary person."

"That he was."

"It's now suspected that Doctor Fid found out about the Red Ghost's plans and confronted the hero. Maybe he wanted a cut of the profits, or perhaps he just didn't want the technology released...in any case, we believe that the conflict escalated and that the Red Ghost was killed in the final battle."

"The Red Ghost left his recently-created corporation and all the patents under the control of one of his team-mates, but already automotive manufacturers are canceling their orders."

"No one wants the liability of being the first to install these devices if it will send Doctor Fid on the warpath!"

"I know that I wouldn't!"

"Sadly, it looks as though the 'inertial displacement systems' will not be making their way into the family sedan any time soon. The threat of Doctor Fid's anger will keep the Red Ghost's final, extraordinary achievement from benefiting the public."

"Sad."

"Tragic. From this day forward, every life lost that the Red Ghost's device could have saved...that blood is on Doctor Fid's hands."

"Wherever he is, I hope that he's satisfied."

To recap: A man that I'd respected and intended to work with had been murdered by the same group of entities that had likely murdered my best friend. I'd been ostracized from a hacktivist collective that had been formed by said friend. Blame had fallen upon me for a horrific crime that I (for once) had not actually committed. A significant percentage of the most powerful superheroes in North America were actively seeking my destruction because of that accusation. And technology intended to save lives was now being suppressed...and fault for that suppression was being attributed to me as well.

Some days my greatest desire was to find someone to punch, and to keep punching until either I ran out of rage...or else until the sun stopped burning. Whichever came first. It was fortunate, then, that upgrades to the teleportation platforms were nearly complete; the Mk 35 would soon be in my possession.

The investigation into the Legion's actions on Earth had stalled; I had many suspicions but little in the way of proof! More direct means of gathering information would be needed in order to move the inquiry forward.

It was time to confront Valiant.

CHAPTER SIXTEEN

CATCHING VALIANT'S ATTENTION WOULD NORMALLY BE A simple affair: show up in Washington D.C.'s restricted airspace and spend some quality time playing with the Air Force's hasty defense. There were politicians whose entire pork barrel career relied upon manufacturing replacement fighter jets, so really...that portion of the afternoon would have been a public service. The senators running for cover below should have been grateful that I was doing my part to keep their constituents employed.

Sooner or later, the crack of the sound-barrier being broken would echo in the distance... followed shortly by the bone-shattering impact of the world's most powerful punch. And thus, battle with Valiant would be joined.

The normal problem would be to construct protections capable of surviving that punch and all the violence that would follow. The last time that I'd fought Valiant directly, Doctor Fid had been wearing the Mk 11; every blow had shed layers of ablative shielding but the powered armor had remained combat effective for more than twelve minutes. No Earth-born threat had ever exceeded Doctor Fid's record!

(An intergalactic gladiator had once come to Earth and challenged Valiant; that fight had lasted half an hour and shattered a mountain in West Virginia. That day, even the villains gathered at Lassiter's watched their screens with quiet apprehension...but the gladiator lost and left, never to be heard from again. Doctor Fid, on the other hand, remained on-planet to strike terror into the hearts of civilians and weak-willed heroes alike.)

The Mk 35 was superior to the Mk 11 in every conceivable way. It was painfully tempting to immediately head towards Washington D.C. and attempt to break the dozen-minute mark! The difficulty was that (due to recent events and a twenty-four-hour news cycle calling for my blood) far too many heroes would congregate and interfere and thus disrupt any possible interrogation.

A month ago, the majority would have stood aside and enjoyed the schadenfreude as the world's mightiest hero whittled down the infamous villain. But now...the field would be crowded by spandex-clad daredevils that were sufficiently riled to risk carving away their own chunk of Doctor Fid.

Sadly, it seemed as though a public battle floating above Washington DC was not in my immediate future. A more nuanced approach would be required; I was certain that opportunities would reveal themselves with further study, but in the meantime there were other important tasks towards which I could dedicate my time.

The psionic activity detection device was an intriguing bit of alien technology. It was bulky and relied upon maintaining extremely accurate tolerances in the machine's construction but required remarkably little power in order to operate. Sadly, its size and delicacy made the apparatus entirely non-portable. If I wanted to replicate the functionality in Doctor Fid's armor (and I most certainly did! Warning of an enemy's presence is always useful) then significantly more experimentation would be required.

The apparatus appeared to be monitoring for specific fluctuations at the point of intersection of multiple spinning energy fields. If I was correct about the cause, then the Legion's telepathy took advantage of multidimensional membrane vibrations to propagate. Many superpowers (and, indeed, many of my own technologies) relied upon similar behavior.

It seemed increasingly likely that the Legion had been responsible for the shift in physical constants that facilitated the existence of superpowered beings on Earth; whatever they'd done had rung the boundaries between universes like a bell, fundamentally altering the laws of physics. The barriers separating dimensions were made permeable, more detectable and easier to manipulate. A carefully modulated energy field could now torque the interdimensional skein like a lever, yielding sometimes dramatic results. My antigravitics and inertial-displacement technologies simply would not have functioned if not for the modified conditions.

The alien apparatus relied upon the same awareness and was elegant in its simplicity...but simplicity was also its greatest flaw. False positives were a worry. Thus far, I'd already demonstrated three separate methods of artificially tripping the psionic activity detecting device and identified four more theoretical possibilities. I could not be certain which (if any) of those mechanisms accurately emulated telepathy! It was going to be challenging to design a more compact sensor without being certain as to which specific phenomena to be on the lookout for.

The next time that I happened across a Legion officer, I should probably consider capture rather than annihilation. Or at least, leaving sufficient volumes of body-mass intact for further study.

The Red Ghost's death—and, perhaps, my lingering terror from the recently-suffered psychic assault—had left Doctor Fid more bloodthirsty than usual.

The FTW had ousted me without even asking my side of the story. There had been no point, LuckySeven had commented privately; they would not trust my word. It was just as well. I mourned the loss of community (poor fit though I'd been), and I lamented the abandonment of my oaths.

Nyx would, I was sure, understand. His path, the non-violent path...it was better. Superior! I still believed that. But Starnyx had been a superior human being, and I was not.

I was Doctor Fid.

There may have been regrets for breaking my word, but no such reservations existed about planning a return to violence. My wrath was aimed with laser-like focus upon those who had thoroughly earned their eventual fate.

The Legion's telepathic officers were responsible for the Red Ghost's death. The Legion's telepathic officers were most-likely responsible for Starnyx's death. In a roundabout way, the Legion was responsible even for Bobby's death! If it truly had been their meddling that had led to the origin of superpowers on Earth, then blame for every cackling villain and tragically flawed 'hero' could be laid at their feet.

I wanted to fight Valiant, who appeared to have aided and abetted plans to keep the Legion's presence on Earth a dangerous secret. I wanted to defeat Peregrine, the so-called 'hero' that was responsible for the death of Kenta Takuma (once known as Beazd) and thousands more. And I wanted to humiliate Sphinx, who maneuvered to hide her compatriot's crimes and was at the center of a conspiracy whose true aims I had yet to uncover.

A far darker fate was awaiting any Legion representatives that crossed my path.

But first...science. Planning and research. Work! And, of course, taking turns reading the last chapter of book nine in 'The Tales of the Red Sorceress' series.

Assuming there were no world-shaking threats or natural disasters that required his immediate assistance, Valiant preferred to spend at least one day per week visiting children's hospitals. He brought gifts donated by different charities and played with the young patients and spoke to their families. The hero sat by the children's sides, listened to their stories and tried to give them whatever joy and hope that he could manage.

"It's the best part of my job," he'd said years ago, speaking on some late-night television talk-show. "And sometimes it's the worst. These kids, they're great. I love 'em all, every last one of them! But it hurts to be so powerless. I can make them smile, but I can't save them. I can't...There was this boy named Tyler with brain cancer...every time I came by, his smile lit up the room. Every time..."

And then the man who had once thrown a Buick into orbit broke down into tears and couldn't finish his interview.

The Make-A-Wish foundation keeps Valiant alerted towards any special cases, kids that don't have long, who have special needs, etc. They keep the schedule secret to avoid paparazzi and to keep families from suffering from false-hope if some tragedy pulled the hero away from his visit; their computer security was surprisingly decent, considering that they were a non-profit organization whose focus was decidedly non-technical.

But not good enough to keep Doctor Fid at bay.

My microdrones were watching as Valiant signed an eight-year-old blond girl's cast. She'd been climbing, she said, because she wanted to be a cat when she grew up. His expression was gravely serious as he meowed to her. She meowed back, and they made playful cat noises at each other while the girl's parents giggled and took photos.

I'd forgotten how large he was.

Dark skinned, with just-beginning-to-gray hair cropped short in a buzz-cut, and broad features matched by a wide and honest smile. At seven-and-a-half feet tall, Valiant had needed to duck and twist sideways to fit into the hospital room. He towered over the girl's parents and she seemed a delicate doll in comparison to the mighty champion. The man was built broadly, thick with muscle even for his prodigious height; his white and sky-blue skin-tight costume served only to emphasize his extraordinary physique.

I'd fought against taller opponents. Gamma would had stood head and shoulders over Valiant. But there was a solidity to the African-American hero, a strange sense of density. It wasn't merely my own perception; others had commented on it. In Valiant's presence, there was an instinctive awareness of his nearness, his power. And yet, he seemed completely at ease when shaking the purring little girl's hand goodbye.

No matter which suit of powered armor I chose to encase myself within, Valiant made me feel small.

And then to another room, another child. A teenage boy, this one bald from chemotherapy and painfully thin. They talked about sports and Valiant gave the boy a baseball glove. "It was my Dad's," the big man said. "So, take good care of it. Next time, maybe we'll throw a ball around?"

But Valiant's eyes were wet when he carefully squeezed out through the doorway. He'd read the boy's charts.

And then another room, and then another. Some moments were heartbreakingly beautiful and others just heartbreaking. Valiant maintained his friendly smile through it all, making sure to get every child's name right and look every youngster in the eye. As the afternoon turned to evening, he visited the common area and carefully settled into an old couch to watch part of a movie with the excited youths, then read them a story and answered a few questions.

A sense of relief settled inside me. Whatever part he'd played in the Sphinx's cabal, this was a good man. One of the few truly worthy of the title, 'hero'! Our eventual battle would be...mythic.

As visiting hours came to a close, Valiant left via the courtyard. It was his habit, so that as many children as possible could watch him lift up to the skies...to see him wave one last time. This hospital was shaped like a giant 'U' so he was surrounded by windows upon three sides.

It had taken a swarm of small construction-drones several days to surreptitiously burrow under the sod and construct a teleportation platform in the appropriate place. It hummed as it was activated and Valiant was suddenly alert; his gaze darted from side to side as he sought any possible threat, but the sound was too unfocused, the platform too perfectly hidden for him to triangulate the tone's origin.

There was a flash of dark and a perfect circle was burned into the well-maintained lawn. Valiant took a surprised step back, eyes widening with fear...not for himself, but for the innocent lives watching on in horror.

Doctor Fid, twelve and a half feet tall, broad and intimidating, had appeared between Valiant and the hospital's entrance. Pinpricks of light drifted slowly across the Mk 35's black surface, with crimson energy bleeding like smoke from barely-visible seams at the armor's joints. In the moment of confused recognition, I summoned my recently-rebuild warstaff and gripped it one hand.

"Valiant!" I intoned, vocoder making my voice deeply menacing. "I have questions for you."

"Doctor," he began carefully. "If you start a fight here..."

"Of course not." Never near a hospital. Here, neither of us would dare risk the chaos of an unrestrained conflict. And here, no other heroes or villains would dare interfere. "I'm here for an interrogation, not a battle."

"So you're holding the children hostage, to make me talk? That's low, even for you." Valiant's expression warred between disappointment and rage. "You'll never be forgiven. Not for this."

"I somehow doubt that forgiveness was ever an option. Not really." My chuckle was melancholy as I remembered an early morning comment made by the Red Ghost. "But no. If you do not wish to answer, then I will leave."

"Leave, then," he growled. I could have sworn that gravity seemed to flex around him, a singularity straining to restrain itself, but my sensors showed no visible change at all.

"Are you certain that's what you want?" I asked quietly. "Absolutely certain?"

The dark-skinned man paused; he'd been playing this game a while, he knew a monologue cue when he heard one. "Why do you ask?"

"Doctor Fid has been a villain for more than two decades. In that time, I've suffered countless injuries and have used technology far beyond what is available to the public to repair the body inside this armor. Some inventions were my own, but many others were stolen and improved upon." I paused. "One such treatment can cure many forms of cancer."

The hero's gaze twitched towards the windows that he knew faced the oncology ward.

"The company that produced this technology has only recently begun human testing. It is years away from being offered to the public," I continued. "No ethical medical professional would consider prescribing it, now."

"But you would?" Valiant frowned, but there was hope in his eyes too.

"No one has ever accused Doctor Fid of being ethical," I laughed darkly. "But I've seen the process work without side effects. Improvement in all subjects and complete remission in sixty percent. I was able to make ten doses. Shall we say one child treated per question?"

Not by coincidence, there were ten children in the hospital who were currently not responding well to traditional treatments. Truthfully, I'd already sneaked medical nanites into their medications; when word of this confrontation leaked, some reporters would certainly investigate from whence the villainous Doctor Fid had stolen a cancer-treatment. It could only mean positive publicity for AH Biotech.

"And there were no side effects? None at all?" Valiant was understandably suspicious.

"You have my word," I responded simply.

"Given recent events, I'm not sure how much your word is worth."

My grip on my warstaff clenched painfully tight and I grit through clenched teeth: "I wasn't responsible for the Red Ghost's death."

Valiant scoffed, and I had to admit that hurt more than his most explosive punch.

"I was there when he died. We fought," I acknowledged; the evidence for that certainly had been unassailable. "But his death was caused by telepathic assault. My questions are about the Legion."

The strongest man in human history winced, shoulders sagging as though weary from bearing an incredible weight. Whatever knowledge he held about the Legion had obviously not sat well with him. Even so, he looked hesitant. "I'll answer what I can."

"When you brought Sphinx back from the edge of Legion space, it hadn't been mere luck. You'd been looking for her." I watched Valiant carefully to see if he'd flinch, but he only sighed resignedly. "How did you know where to find her?"

"Sphinx had managed to send a message via subspace-relay to a friend of mine in a nearby system." He looked as though he was about to offer more detail but bit the information back to force me to use up another question. What Sphinx communicated, who received the broadcast, and how the report was delivered...These things, while interesting, were likely not relevant to my investigation.

"Then, why the subterfuge?" I used up my second question for clarity's sake.

"Sphinx was worried that there might be Legion spies on Earth and didn't want them to know that she'd been in their region of the galaxy."

I didn't need to follow up and ask if her fears had been justified. There existed ample proof that the Legion had a presence here, after all.

"I've now sent probes to seventeen different alternate dimensions. In any scenario in which the Earth had caught the Legion's eye, our planet had either been conquered or destroyed." I gestured with my warstaff, as though pointing towards two options on a blackboard. "Never simply left alone. Do you know why this planet is different?"

"Yes," he stated simply, then smirked and waited for my fourth question.

"Very well," I couldn't help but chuckle. "Why hasn't the Legion invaded?"

"The officers are slaves to procedure," he rolled his eyes. "There 're tests and calculations that they need to run before they make a final decision. We're in a gray area right now. Some of us heroes are immune to their mind control, on account of our powers...And we're dangerous enough that it'd be an expensive fight. Sphinx knows their math a heck of a lot better than I do, you should ask her."

"So, major changes to the status quo could push the Legion officers to decide in one direction or the other," I mused. "Is that the reason she tried to destroy the colony ship full of refugees from Legion space, before their craft could land?"

"What...?" Valiant looked visibly unbalanced. "What are you talking about?"

"You didn't know?" I paused and frowned, wondering if that counted as a fifth question. No matter. "The refugees were broadcasting a mayday message in a language Sphinx certainly should have been able to interpret before she ordered you all to attack. When someone else (Cuboid, I think?) translated and the attack was aborted, she had Peregrine damage the craft's engine. That's why it crashed in Colorado."

"You're lying." Valiant's hands had clenched to fists, and I was reasonably certain that a pummeling would already have commenced were my back were not facing a hospital wall.

"I'm not," I shook my head. "If my suspicions are correct, the Sphinx has been diligently working to keep our planet safely within that 'gray area'. No matter what the cost in human lives."

"What do you mean by that?"

"I've very little evidence thus far. Only...from the moment I expressed my desire to join the FTW, it was weeks before my application was voted upon and I was asked to film my oaths. And yet, the same day my video became public knowledge, Sphinx and Peregrine publicly admitted culpability for Beazd's death. She'd begun working on her plea deal on the same day that I first contacted a member of the hacker collective."

"So?" Valiant was angry, but not belligerently so.

"So, she must have had an informant inside the FTW to get that information," I pointed out. "And I should tell you...before the explosion that killed the FTW's leadership, Starnyx was working on exposing a scandal connecting the Shield to the Legion refugees. And the man who caused the explosion was sweating, shaking and apologizing repeatedly when he reached into the force-emitter's reactor housing."

"You think that a Legion officer puppetted that poor man into committing suicide, taking the entire building with him?"

"His name was Jerry Stross." I said. "He had a wife, now responsible for raising a child alone, who is drinking heavily due to difficulty dealing with her confusion and anger and self-doubt. He had a thirteen-year-old son whose online journals are rife with terrified worry that it was something he did that made his own father so depressed. And I think that the Legion would not have known anything about the FTW investigation if not for the Sphinx's informant."

"No," Valiant denied, though he didn't sound so very certain. "You're just guessing, Doctor."

"I am," I acknowledged again. "But I also wonder how the Red Ghost came to the Legion's attention. He was with you and Sphinx on your most recent adventure among the stars. Could he have let something slip, I wonder? Mentioned something that made her realize that the Red Ghost might be a threat to her carefully maintained neutrality?"

"That's...vile," the hero slumped. "I don't want to believe it."

"Believe it or don't believe it, it matters little to me." Doctor Fid's voice lowered to a sotto growl. "I'll keep searching until I find my truth. Starnyx was my friend."

"Yeah. Yeah, I get it," Valiant looked grim. "I hope that you're wrong, but I get it. What's your next question?"

"I think that I've learned all that I set out to learn, today...But I'll see to it that the ten patients in the greatest danger are treated for their illness. The next time that you're here, you'll be able to play catch with the occupant of room 317C."

"Thank you, Doctor," he replied, sincerity and gratitude making his voice shake.

"You're welcome." Behind my mask, I smiled. "Now, hit me."

"I beg your pardon?"

"There are children watching," I noted. "They should get the opportunity to watch the mighty Valiant chase off the despicable Doctor Fid!"

"You'll be careful?" he grinned fiercely, massive hands curling into fists. I imagined that I could hear the excited whispers from behind the glass windows that overlooked the hospital courtyard.

"You have my wor—" I began. And then he hit me with sufficient force to liquefy concrete.

I cackled with maniacal glee and discreetly shifted to allow him to guide the combat away from hospital grounds.

The battle lasted twenty-two and a half glorious minutes, though the first three probably didn't count. That time was spent trading relatively light blows as we clashed and soared away from any densely populated area. News camera drones followed as best they could, though, and the footage was awe inspiring. When we reached the Appalachian foothills, the brawl had begun in earnest.

The Mk 35 had functioned flawlessly.

I could have fought on (beyond even the twenty-two and a half minutes!) but my drones had identified several other heroes approaching. Their interference would have complicated the scenario, and so I fled to safety with head held high. I'd managed even to bloody Valiant's lip and leave him stunned as I made my escape! The new warstaff was, however, destroyed in the endeavor. Perhaps an imaginary artificial sentience similar to my sister would be willing to help construct an orichalcum-framed replacement for a make-believe villain very much like me...

Another benefit of so public a conflict: The media's narrative had shifted. No more were they questioning my every action, nor were they rallying the public to declare me pariah and oppose me at every opportunity. Doctor Fid was now mentioned quietly, fearfully. The recent prurient interest in Doctor Fid's depraved past was replaced by hushed terror at what the infamous villain would do next. As it should be.

I no longer worried about being swarmed by heroes and vigilantes if Doctor Fid traveled at night. Once more, the majority cravenly lowered their eyes when I flew overhead, desperately hoping that I intended to become someone else's problem.

The change allowed the opportunity to perform other errands.

Prototype sensors of various design had been placed throughout Manhattan. It was fortunate that, sometime prior, my drones had completed their map of all the tunnels under the city; the heroes might look away when I flew overhead, but these days I was trying to avoid more eyes than only those of heroes. Whenever possible, I traveled underground.

Under the assumption that the Legion spies would monitor centers of commerce and politics, I'd focused primarily upon the region surrounding Wall Street and the United Nations. Carefully-constructed replicas of Joan the Glassblower's psionic activity detection device were constructed at each array. The effort was time consuming and required a significant percentage of my automated manufacturing plants operating around the clock, but I had high hopes that the results would be worth the expense.

The goal was to detect the psionic activities of one of the alien enemies, and to record more detailed data about how the telepathic ability functioned. The hope was that, if the efforts bore fruit, they would provide sufficient information to develop a portable scanner that could be used to track and isolate the Legion officers' base of operations.

I wasn't yet certain what my course of action would be when I found my enemies' lair.

Sudden and overwhelming violence was always an option, but I had to presume that course of action would spur the Legion's main forces towards invasion. The Earth was not prepared for such an attack. Worse, I could find no evidence that preparation efforts were being made.

How entrenched must the Legion agents be, to have dissuaded the existing powers-that-be from taking even the most basic of precautions? There had been little research performed towards establishing orbital defenses. No significant funding had been set aside to enact early warning systems, or even significantly improved solar-system monitoring. Sphinx had correctly recognized the threat of an alien onslaught more than half a dozen years prior, and in all the time since it seemed that the planet's supposed defenders had done little save attempt to delay the inevitable.

I'd wondered why Valiant had been so free with information; I'd expected to need to threaten, bribe and cajole, but he'd offered material intel with little hesitation. I now suspected that he, too, was uncomfortable with the concept of ceding all initiative to our adversaries. The Legion would make its decision sooner or later. Delay served no purpose if the time were not used to fortify defenses against both possible modes of attack.

I had ideas but even Doctor Fid had his limits. I would exhaust the entirety of my resources to little effect if it came to direct conflict with an alien armada. My fortune and ever-growing manufacturing base could be put towards creating weapons of mass destruction that would lay waste to a significant number of attacking vessels...but a planet was too vast to be defended by so few. The Earth would burn behind me as I battled on.

So, perhaps delay would indeed be the order of the day. A temporary reprieve, while further data was gathered, and greater resources acquired. If worse came to worst, the option of sudden and overwhelming violence would still be available.

Terry Markham was on a conference call with AH Biotech's directors when the sensor logs were confirmed. Notifications pinged across my neural net and even a cursory glance at the data made my eyes widen and my face hurt from suppressing a vicious grin.

The meeting was completed in as quick and professional a manner as could be managed.

Whisper? I sent a silent message to the little android who was waiting at home. **Are you busy?**

Not really, Whisper replied, sending the vague impression of a blanket castle and fake-tea with Amelia. **Are you okay?**

I am, but I think that I'm going to need your help. Could you pull up some data on the creation of Westler-Gray crystals?

Mm!

Theoretically, do you think that an orichalcum containment chamber would be able to suppress the neutrino pulse?

Maybe? Wait. Yes, Whisper paused, her confusion feeling like a tentative hug. **Why? Is something wrong with the crystal in our reactor? I haven't seen any dangerous readings...**

No, nothing's wrong. But I have an idea that will require a great deal of energy...and progress needs to be hidden until the plan is ready for implementation.

It's going to take a long time to build, she warned. **It takes weeks to grow even a small W-G crystal.**

And I'm going to need at least six more full-sized reactors, I acknowledged.

That's...more than a terawatt of power generation capacity. She sounded awed, and rightfully so. That value was two hundred and fifty times as much energy as could be produced by the largest nuclear power plant in the United States. **Are we going to take over the world? Oooh! I want Hawaii! Dibs!**

My office door was, thankfully, closed; I nearly fell over restraining a paroxysm of laughter, and the image of their CEO shaking with uncontrolled giggles would likely have affected my carefully-cultivated image of controlled intellectual reserve. At the very least, it would have been difficult to explain why I was having trouble breathing.

No, Whisper. We're not going to take over the world, I assured her. **But I think that we may be able to save it.**

Oh. That's good, too.

CHAPTER SEVENTEEN

THE MANUFACTURING INFRASTRUCTURE THAT DOCTOR Fid had spent decades building (and concealing) was operating at full production, but the current project would require more resources than I could possibly fabricate on my own. Already, I was burning through supplies that had taken years to acquire, exhausting reserves I'd believed could never be expended. To reduce the load on my hidden factories, millions of dollars' worth of Doctor Fid's personal assets had been liquidated to gather additional materials. Managing logistical issues had become an immediate and tedious chore.

When the CSE in Cambridge placed orders for components necessary to build one Westler-Gray reactor, the financial activity had been noticed by two supervillains. Gathering resources to build six reactors would raise red-flags to even the most oblivious investigator! Purchases needed to be spread through shell companies so as not to attract undue attention.

It wasn't enough to hide the fact that Doctor Fid was building six maximum-sized Westler-Gray reactors. I needed to obscure evidence that new reactors were being constructed at all.

Given that the Legion had used the Red Ghost as a weapon against me, I had to assume that they were certainly aware that Doctor Fid was continuing Starnyx's investigation. And since I'd killed one of their number, I presumed that the slightest indication that I was taking offensive action would provoke an extreme response.

Simply by existing, I was putting the Sphinx's carefully orchestrated status quo at risk. Sooner or later, the detente would be ended; my work would need be completed before the Legion's primary forces acted or else all would be lost. It was a race, and the finish line's location was a secret held only by the enemy. My only option was to sprint as quickly as I was able and hope that my destination was reached before the Legion moved the goal posts.

(Somewhere, Sphinx was likely scrambling to alter the aliens' calculus. If my actions had tipped the scales towards a decision of destruction, she was no doubt working to make conquering a more palatable option. Not completely; just tilting the balance sufficiently to confuse the issue. Annoyingly, I was currently benefiting from her efforts. The thought made me retch.)

Some items were stolen (Titanium-vanadium containment spheres could be re-machined from the boilers found in certain specialized nautical salvage yards. Scrap theft was already a problem at those sites, so a few extra missing pieces would not even be noticed) and others hidden within larger purchases (Disassembling thermal receivers from a new solar-power farm provided all the aerogel that I would need). A great deal more was funneled through Putnam Circuitworks; with the inertial-displacement orders on hold, the Tennessee-based component manufacturer was available and had both the skilled labor and the contacts to generate many necessary parts. Even better, their recent restructuring had been orchestrated such that information about their contracts was very compartmentalized; my shell companies could place perfectly legal orders, and Putnam Circuitworks would perform all the tasks necessary to keep their deliveries confidential.

When all this was over, Doctor Fid was going to need to rob Fort Knox again.

"Senator McClelland! It's a pleasure to meet you." I smiled and shook the man's hand, then stepped aside and gestured for him to come in. His aide smiled pleasantly and entered as well.

"Please, call me Tony." He was in reasonably good health for a man of his eight-two years, taller than I with a full head of hair that still had a fair number of dark strands among the gray. He wore an easy, affable grin that made me think more of a kindly grandfather than the shrewd political operative I knew him to be. "Thank you for the invitation."

"It was my pleasure, sir," I chuckled. "Although, I thought that there would be more people...?"

"This isn't a photo op, son," he laughed softly and shook his head. "You've put a great deal of money into my campaign; I wanted to meet you face to face."

"Well, I arranged for food thinking that there'd be a crowd." I flashed my teeth in brief, self-deprecating amusement. "I shouldn't have assumed."

"More food for us, then," he motioned towards his assistant. "Craig here is young, he'll eat you out of house and home if you're not careful."

"Well, my caterers will do their best to defeat you both," I shook Craig's hand as well. "Good afternoon, I'm Dr. Markham."

"Good afternoon."

I led the Senator and his companion deeper into my home.

"Truth is, I'm not hungry just yet," Senator McClelland apologized as we walked. "But I wouldn't say no to a drink."

I changed directions towards the den, my preferred room to sit and socialize. "What can I get for you?"

"A finger or two of whiskey would be just peachy."

The senator's assistant looked as though he wanted to object but knew from long experience that he'd lose the argument. I hid my own amusement with a gentle cough.

"I can do that. Anything for you, Craig?"

"Water, please," the younger man replied gratefully.

"He'll have whiskey, too," Tony McClelland insisted, eyes sparkling. Craig rolled his eyes but didn't object.

"You want your drink on the rocks?"

"Well...damn, son. And here I'd thought we were going to get along." His playful glare had no heat in it. "Why 'd you want to do something so terrible to a poor, innocent glass of spirits?"

"Some of my guests are heathens and I am on occasion forced to bend to their strange ways." I held my hands up in mock supplication. "Gentlemen, make yourselves comfortable...I'll be right back with our drinks."

"Bring the bottle!" the Senator called after me. "We might want to visit a while."

How much of his behavior was an act, I wondered, a practiced patter to put donors and voters at ease? How much was just him being an old man, tired of pretense and comfortable in his own skin? I couldn't know and supposed that it didn't really matter. The aged Senator was sponsoring the Synthetic Americans' Rights bill; he could have been as phony as a three-dollar bill and I'd still cheerfully toast his health.

A serving tray made it easier to carry the glasses, liquor and a pitcher of water back to the den.

"Johnny Walker Blue," Tony McClelland brightened. "Bless you, son. Your association with heathens is forgiven."

"Well, thank you. I was worried." I handed over his glass, then lifted my own to my lips.

"I think that I can hear children playin' outside." The Senator sipped at his drink. "Is that your girl?"

"Yes, that's Whisper. She's visiting with her best friend; her father's outside watching them." I couldn't help but beam happily. "I'm afraid that they are a bit loud when they're playing with Dinah's puppy."

"No, it's a beautiful sound. Kid's laughter, I mean." The senator smiled wistfully. "You ever have biological children of your own?"

"No, I never did."

"My wife and I had two sons and two daughters, and they gave me eight grand-kids. I just met my first great-grand-daughter a few weeks ago."

"Congratulations!"

"Thank you." His grin was infectious. "I probably wasn't the world's greatest father, but I figured out the parenting thing by the time the grandkids started visiting. It's nice, hearing 'em play."

"I'm still getting used to it," I admitted. "I lived alone for a long time...This is better, but it's also still new."

"Life'll change on you, son." He raised his glass. "Most times life'll kick you in the teeth, but sometimes the surprises are wonderful."

We both drank to wonderful surprises.

"I read in the Times that you were going to build new bodies for your girl, Whisper, as she grows up?"

"That's the plan," I nodded. "They can't stay kids forever."

"No, they can't," he gestured with his glass. "But enjoy it while you can! You're goin' to need good memories to sustain you through the teenage-rebellion years."

"Good memories and a fair amount of good whiskey," I joked in return, and all three of us laughed.

"My second grandson..." The Senator's laugh faded, his expression turning melancholy, "He had a tough time of it, his teenage years. He grew out of it, though! I know you're not supposed to have favorites, and God knows I love 'em all, but of all my grandkids...Danny was the one I related to the best. He was planning on coming into politics after his second tour of duty."

"What happened?" I asked sympathetically, even though I already knew the answer. As soon as Senator McClelland had mentioned his family, I'd used my neural tap to scour internet records to get more data; a decade earlier, the man's grandson had been mentioned in several newspaper articles for his bravery under fire. His obituary was touching.

"Enemy sniper," the elderly politician grimaced and finished his glass in one gulp. "Enjoy the good times and don't take a minute of it for granted."

"I will. And I'm sorry."

"Thank you. It's 'cause of Danny that I'm here, actually." His irascible smile seemed forced. "Him and the whiskey, of course."

I poured him another glass. "How so?"

"Six months before...Six months before he died, Danny was part of a DARPA experiment. You familiar with brain-taping?"

"I am," I nodded. "They took a full recording?"

"Ayup. All his memories, everything he'd ever thought, everything he was...backed up on a stack of hard drives." His voice cracked, and he took another drink. "Just gathering dust right now."

"How can I help?" I refilled my own drink, brows furrowed in thought.

"You're making a new body for your ward," his eyes were glassy with longing and tentative hope. "Can you make one for my grandson?"

I considered for only a moment. "Yes. I think that I can."

This wasn't the best time to commit to new projects...but I couldn't say 'no'. I might have been a monster, but I wasn't the sort of monster who could deny a mourning grandfather. And besides...one never knew when an indebted United States senator might come in handy.

"Well," he said, voice shaking, and I thought for a moment that he was going to cry. "Let's drink to that."

We did.

"Now, it won't just be a body," I warned. "A reactivated brain-tape needs to run on a full neurally-linked server farm. It won't be cheap."

"Son, I may not be the crookedest politician in Washington, but I've been a senator for three decades. Twelve years of that was on the Appropriations Committee," he smirked, and suddenly seemed years younger than he'd looked when I'd met him at the door. "I've put some money away. You just tell me where to send the check."

Did you hear all that? I asked Whisper via the neural tap. Outside, I could hear her laughing as she chased after Dinah's playful puppy.

Mm! she affirmed cheerfully. **I'm going to get a new brother!**

He already has brothers, I chided, sending a mental chuckle. **You can't just adopt him because he'll be running on the server farm next door.**

323

Can! she disagreed, and I felt her smile across the link. ****I like having a big brother. Having two might be even better!****

Silly girl, I laughed silently. ****When you've finished tiring that poor dog out, come up to keep us company while we eat. Bring Aaron and Dinah, I'd like for them to meet the senator.****

Mm!

The conversation with the senator ebbed and flowed; we talked specifics about the technology involved, about time-lines, about raising kids and about the upcoming legislation.

("I won't let this one go. This one'll pass if I have to call in every favor I ever earned. I'll get your girl the rights she deserves. And someday, my boy Danny'll be a senator too.")

We ate dinner, and the Senator's aid did, in fact, do his level best to defeat my caterers. He was unsuccessful, but it was a worthy effort. Whisper introduced her doll, Amelia, to the aging politician and the senator told stories about raising children of his own.

I wanted to be present when the android body hosting Danny McClelland's mind opened its eyes. I wanted to watch the Senator hold his grandson for the first time in a decade.

I wanted this world to survive.

It was irksome, the strange and unwelcome realization that I was being forced to think like a hero...but talking with Senator McClelland had reminded me that my current undertaking was no longer a contest between myself and Sphinx. It wasn't even a battle between Doctor Fid and the Legion! This was the world's fight and I was simply acting as the planet's proxy. I was acting on behalf of parents and grandparents and little girls and enthusiastic puppies and everyone else who had their own life-stories that had nothing to do with capes and explosions and pulsed laser cannons.

Keeping this war to myself was selfish. I was claiming the role of champion without allowing the world opportunity to participate! Pure hubris. And yet, the Sphinx had done the same. My egotism, at least, had a better excuse: I was Doctor Fid! Megalomania was expected from a supervillain of my stature.

Bah and humbug. Giving Sphinx her comeuppance would, at least, be a welcome bonus.

Terry Markham arranged to 'work from home' for a few days to better oversee the ongoing activity, and secret bank-accounts that had long been isolated (in order to hide their existence from the Red Ghost's financial wizardry) were opened so that even more funds could be applied towards expediting construction.

In the end, all that I needed was time.

I'd run out of time.

One of my working teleportation devices was located in a Brooklyn storage facility; it was wide enough, just barely, that I could don the Mk 35 in Boston and be transported instantaneously to the platform in New York City. The larger heavy-combat drones were too broad to fit in the transportation field, so I'd already started their journey towards the battle at maximum thrust. They wouldn't arrive on-site for nearly a half-hour, but a swarm of medium combat drones would be able to accompany the Mk 35 into combat.

But first, I needed to put the finishing touches on the new orichalcum-framed warstaff. Five minutes of effort, and then I'd be able to launch.

"-three, no, four members of the New York Shield appear to be incapacitated." The reporter spoke at an even pace, though stress was audible in her voice. Some of the explosions seemed dangerously close and the camera caught debris being thrown in the background. "The Brooklyn Knights have been continuing their attack on the Mercer-Tallon building but have repeatedly been rebuffed by a heavily armed security force. Other heroes have been joining into the chaos, and we've seen several instances of long-time friends changing sides in the conflict without warning. Psion, leader of the Brooklyn Knights, was overheard warning about telepathic mind-control."

"Is there any word on the death toll?" a voice from the studio asked.

"No word yet. Several bystanders were caught up in the initial assault, but Haste carried the wounded to nearby hospitals. We haven't heard any more on that story. Oh! It looks as though Wildcard of the Brooklyn Knights is down, clawed across the back by his own teammate! Vic, can you get a better camera angle?"

"That looks like Wildcard is badly injured."

"It does look pretty bad, Tom. Sphinx and Majestic are now trying to restrain the White Tigress but are being driven back by focused fire from the building. It's unknown how large the Mercer-Tallon security force is, but we've seen dozens of fighters incapacitated already. There seems to be no end in sight."

The report continued, describing an ever-escalating battle royal; New York City had the largest population of superheroes in the nation, and with every new combatant came additional opportunities for the Legion to take mental control of a fighter and add to the pandemonium.

With some level of schadenfreude, I noticed that Peregrine had been among the first heroes downed. Good!

I had tracked the Legion officers to the Mercer-Tallon soon after my sensors had been deployed; how the Brooklyn Knights discovered the Legion's lair, I had no idea. Presumably, they'd continued investigating after our most recent discussion...and somehow intuited that the Legion was here on Earth. Sphinx had shown up to dissuade them from attacking the Mercer-Tallon building and events quickly spiraled out of control.

Whisper, honey? I called, mentally. **I'm going to need some help.**

...'kay. Her fear was audible but her desire to help was stronger. Brave girl!

How many packages are ready for shipment? I asked, beginning to close up the warstaff.

Twenty-seven.

That...wasn't ideal. I'd hoped to have twice that many before deployment. Still, odds were good that amount would be sufficient. My calculations had originally indicated that twenty-four would be the bare minimum to achieve success, but a broad safety margin would have been preferable. If only we'd had another week!

I'm going to need you to take care of delivery. Can you do that? I asked gently.

Mm, She affirmed.

Keep one unit here, I reminded her. **We're probably going to need it.**

I know! Whisper sounded irritable and scared. Both emotions were understandable.

Sweetheart, I'm going to be fine, I tried to reassure us both as I pulled on my padded under-armor and prepared to climb into the Mk 35. **This is just a bit earlier than I would have liked.**

Why do you have to go? she asked tremulously. **There're so many heroes there.**

The heroes are losing. One at a time, they are being whittled down. I looked up at the news program, still broadcasting the carnage. Sphinx and Majestic had managed to subdue White Tigress, and immediately afterwards a Legion officer had taken control of Majestic; the Shield powerhouse had grievously injured two heroes before being taken down himself...and the cycle was continuing.

It should have been taking longer. According to the sensor readings that I'd gathered, there were dozens of low-powered Legion spies scattered throughout the region but only five officers with sufficient power to control a human mind remained on Earth. And they could each control only one person at a time. I'd run simulations, and the heroes were being whittled away faster even than my worst-case scenarios.

It was the security forces that were accounting for the Legion's increased effectiveness, adding to the confusion and delaying the heroes' approach just enough to allow the officer's tactics better opportunities for success. In all my research, I hadn't seen even a scintilla of evidence that the Legion had hired so many mercenaries. How they had attracted such a sizable force of loyal followers was beyond me. Surrounded by an unprecedentedly large company of heroes, one would expect at least a few mercenaries to lose morale and flee; but no, the gunmen held their ground and coordinated their efforts professionally.

Someone needs to keep the Legion officers busy until everything is in place, I continued. **If they get a warning out...**

Okay. Okay, she said softly. **Just...Please come home.**

I will, sweetheart. I promise.

And then I carefully put Terry Markham away.

As super-heroic reinforcements continued to pour onto the scene, mid-town Manhattan was rapidly becoming a war-zone. If the conflict continued to escalate, it would soon become the greatest concentration of superhuman might in human history. There was no place for a painfully lonely academic in the battle ahead, nor was there room for a businessman or even a big brother.

The massive Mk 35 heavy combat armor closed around me and Doctor Fid was all that remained.

Cloaked and unnoticed, I took a moment to observe from above.

The Mercer-Tallon building had been well chosen for defense; twenty stories of crisply-delineated trapezoidal columns that framed narrow windows that served almost like arrowslits in ancient castles. The armed guards could fire through those slim apertures at an invading force while protected by almost a foot of concrete. Mirrored glass allowed shooters to shift from location to location without their position being revealed, and what looked to be a structural integrity field generator enhanced the natural strength of the steel-reinforced building.

The courtyard, too, was a kill-zone. There was open space separating the Mercer-Tallon building from its neighbors, with the ornate wrought-iron and stone fences that were originally intended to direct traffic also serving to control an attacker's approach. Intruders on foot were funneled into regions where the defenders had a clear line of fire.

I maintained stealth protocols until the last moment, then commanded my medium-duty combat drones to light up the heavens. Plasma and energy filled the sky, arcing from drone to drone in a chaotic chain, crackling with raw power and cutting vast swaths through the battle's smoke.

Doctor Fid appeared over the combat zone, wreathed in lightning and thunder and primal rage.

The heroes' response was immediate and chaotic. Some scrambled away like roaches seeking cover when the light-switch is flipped. Others ignored the threat from Legion fighters and mind-controlled heroes, and instead immediately turned their attacks upon me: a blast of flame from the Beacon, a thrown streetlamp from Sphinx, and countless energy bolts of various flavors. Ms. Magma called forth a high-pressure stream of lava that exploded from a rupture in the earth, splattering off the Mk 35's surface like water.

I let the initial attacks wash over me, arms wide at my side and chin lifted as though accepting applause. For a moment, I felt invulnerable; a god striding among ants. The Mk 35 had withstood the full force of Valiant's blows! What threat could these lesser so-called 'heroes' present? Their strikes were like a feather's touch and I would brush them aside like gnats.

Warnings began streaming into my consciousness via the neural tap almost immediately.

An energy field designed to dissipate the force of one or two extraordinary impacts was apparently not equally suited to protect against dozens of smaller simultaneous attacks. I bit back a curse and dove into the fray. My medium-duty combat drones dropped down to Earth and I slid among them, dodging smoothly and taking cover as my own defenses recalibrated.

The Legion's armed guards had focused their fire upon me and had nearly burned through my shield in moments.

And so, I ducked and evaded, attacked and countered. I bent under an energy blast from Psion, dodged a boulder thrown by Brute (what was he doing in New York?), and launched a low-yield particle blast at the ground beneath Lariat's feet; the rope-wielding heroine was knocked backwards into Haste's path and both became comically tied up.

By some random chance, the remaining active members of the Boston Guardians were apparently visiting New York as well. They'd always had the odd luck of being nearby when a major event loomed. Whatever mystic energies empowered Titan must also inflict strange effects upon his fate.

Aeon summoned one of her milky-white force-field spheres around one of my drones, isolating it and leaving a gap in my defenses for Veridian to capitalize upon. The powerful emerald blast was insufficient to cause damage, but it did drive me away from cover and I took another hit from a plasma cannon.

I shifted more power to shields and launched sonic attacks in return. Not powerful enough to incapacitate...merely temporarily stun.

Majestic had recovered but was apparently still under the direction of a Legion officer; he picked up a smaller man in an insect-themed costume (the hero must have been new; image recognition found no information at all) and threw him at me like a bullet.

In combat, time seems to move differently. I had time to watch the inexperienced hero's eyes widen with fear, watch his lips pull back as he tried to scream. If I'd done nothing, the result would have been predictably messy...but I would not have taken any personal damage. Instead, I temporarily extended the shape of my inertia-dampening field to form a cushion of air to stop the bug-man's trajectory.

Titan struck me square upon my back with a flagpole.

The extraordinary orichalcum alloy armor was undamaged, but my body encased within was not quite so enduring; my breath was slammed from my lungs with such force that it tasted metallic. I tasked two drones to focus their ire upon the Guardians' leader and I focused purely upon defense while my armor's systems recovered.

More heroes were on their feet now than had been present when I'd arrived. Wildcard appeared to have chosen healing as one of his powers this afternoon; I saw him press his hand to a wounded heroine's shoulder and, after a brief flash of light, she smiled gratefully and shot towards the Mercer-Tallon building. Behind my faceless mask, I smiled. That was perfect.

The medium-grade combat drones could not long stand up to the pounding that they were receiving, but for now they were performing adequately. I launched a powerful blast of ionic energies towards the Legion's headquarters. The building's force-field deflected the strike, but the light show drew some attention back to the alien stronghold and away from myself.

The Mk 35's enhanced optics caught a clear view of one of the Legion's soldiers through one of the broken windows: Human and short, with broad shoulders and a bit of a paunch. A memory struck me, of good beer and bad jokes and a strange evening at Lassiter's Den. The comedian that I'd suspected of being Cloner! And thus, the mystery of the unexpected mercenary army was solved.

One of the Legion officers must have been controlling Cloner, granting the aliens access to an effectively infinitely large defense force. On the one hand this meant that the Mercer-Tallon security force represented an increased threat. On the other hand, it meant that I didn't need to hold back when counter-sniping. I generally tried to avoid unnecessary casualties, but in this case...as long as one Cloner survived, there was no true harm in wreaking havoc.

And havoc was the order of the day. I threw a few more plasma blasts at the building; they weren't particularly effective, but the splattering energies were visually stunning.

If the goal had been to overcome the Legion officers' defenses, I would have stayed aloft and rained destruction from above; the building's fortifications were decent, but the foundation could have been shaken apart with sufficient force. And it certainly wasn't my goal to incapacitate any of the assembled heroes! I needed them active, to keep the Legion officers intent upon the combat in front of their lair.

Before I'd arrived, the math had favored a speedy victory for the Legion. The army of Cloner would likely have picked off only a few of an approaching force of spandex-clad champions, but when three heroes fell under the Legion officers' control, the remaining forces would fall upon them and quickly render them unable to continue battling. Perhaps one or two of the heroes would also be injured or taken out in the process simply by virtue of surprise. Thus, the Legion would have forced the heroes to reduce their own numbers until active free minds were outnumbered by mind-controlled puppets.

I was here to interfere, a third party that both forces would consider a threat, dividing their attacks and slowing the rate at which the heroes were depleted; buying time, while an adorable artificial sentience prepared the real assault! Speaking of...

Whisper, I dodged one of Shrike's spikes; there was too much action, too many moving pieces on the board for me to truly have a picture of what was going on. My armor's combat algorithms guided me along as I sought to identify the greatest immediate threats. **How are things coming along?**

Eleven packages already delivered!

Good work, I commended, even though I'd hoped to have made greater progress. **Let me know when everything's ready.**

I will, she reassured me. **Watch out!**

And then the Sphinx was right before me, her expression a strange mix of fierce determination and resigned melancholy. There was no hope within her...merely the will to keep fighting as long as she could.

This was the first time that I'd met her face to face.

Sphinx's gold and black outfit was tight but not otherwise revealing, and her white half-length cape fluttered behind her as she landed. Long, wavy black hair framed her face like a mane; her features were strong, aquiline and beautiful. She was one of the true powers present: stronger and more durable than Titan but even faster and better trained. Her ability to fly and to attack from odd angles made her a force to be reckoned with.

But she was not Valiant, not quite. I struck, quick as a viper, and grabbed both her wrists.

"Enjoying your show?" I asked viciously, "Every drop of blood spilled here is on your hands!"

Sphinx twisted and managed to free one wrist from the Mk 35's grasp, then followed with a quick jab to the Mk 35's faceless mask. She freed her second hand during the fraction-of-a-second in which I flinched. Sphinx darted backwards, eyes narrowed furiously. "What do you know?"

"A great deal," I sneered. "I know that you were aware of the Legion presence here, for years! I know that you've let them kill a lot of good men and women. And I know that you've been responsible for many deaths, yourself."

"I was trying to save the planet!" she spat, then launched a series of spinning punches and kicks. But this was the kind of one-on-one fight the Mk 35 had been designed for; my combat algorithms compensated and allowed me to keep up with her attacks.

"No!" I hissed back at her, firing a series of force-blasts that splattered across her torso and left her completely unharmed. "You did nothing to save the Earth! You only tried to delay its fate."

"The Legion was here." All emotion left her voice and she spoke like a creature long dead. "They'll take the planet, eventually."

"You killed hundreds—fed people who trusted you to their mind-rapers!—to buy a few years peace?"

"It's a large planet...Millions of people die every year," she smiled grimly. "Because of me, those millions died free."

"And billions more could die tomorrow because you did nothing to stop this." I summoned the warstaff and spun it to block her sudden series of careful attacks. Distraction and malaise had done nothing to dim her combat skills.

"The Legion was here!" she repeated, angrily. "'Delay' was the only option."

"Only because you didn't try anything else," I growled back at her. "You should have rallied your troops, should have let your teammates help you come up with a plan. Reached out to scientists, to politicians, to the military!"

"The Legion has telepathic spies!" she countered defensively, picking up a downed flagpole and swinging it like a bat; my armor's combat algorithms parried smoothly. "If we started preparing, they would have known. The attack would have started earlier!"

"You sacrificed hundreds— thousands! —as a gift to the dead, but you abandoned the living," my voice dipped to a dangerous rumble as I chanced an accusation for which I had no proof, only strong suspicions: "You gave up heroes to the Legion's control. The Red Ghost. Cloner. How many others? You should have fought!"

"I would have lost. What choice did I have?" she snarled, panting slightly, still trying to get through my defenses with textbook-perfect martial-arts strikes. "If you know so much, what would you have done differently?!?"

"Would I have killed so many, just to gain a few short years of time? Perhaps. But I'm a villain," I laughed darkly. "You spent last weekend signing autographs for children that you expected to die young or live as slaves. Good job, hero."

Sphinx was shocked into momentary inaction, taking a step back and letting her defenses slip. I did nothing to capitalize and, after a moment, she noticed that no other heroes had been joining her attempts to subdue me for some time.

The other gathered heroes had fallen away, backed off with expressions of wide eyed disgust. My microdrones had been relaying audio of my conversation with Sphinx, and it seemed as though most of the brightly colored champions had the same opinions as I regarding her choices. Face to face with a heroine's hypocrisy, they looked away and focused on the true enemy; the Legion, and those few who were under the Legion's control.

I heard the distant crack of a familiar sonic boom.

Whisper! I sent urgently **What's the status?**

Nineteen packages sent!

I growled helplessly. Valiant had implied that he was among the few whose powers protected against Legion's control; if he joined the battle, the officers would know that the Mercer-Tallon building was doomed. The agents might transmit their messages to the Legion fleet when he arrived, and we'd lose a window of opportunity.

Be ready. Nineteen may have to be sufficient.

Mm!

And then Valiant was between us, striking the earth like a thunderbolt.

"Damnit, Sphinx!" he started, angrily. "I've been watching the news, I couldn't stay away any longer. What did y—"

He paused, and I watched his eyes go glassy. Valiant's left hand twitched with the beginning of a tremor, and a bead of sweat formed at his brow. "What did...you...I-".

I turned to stare at Sphinx, incredulous. "You lied to Valiant about being immune to Legion control?!?"

"It was necessary!" she retorted weakly, watching her friend's expression shift to one of tortured pain.

"I'm sorry," Valiant whimpered.

And then I was thrown backwards more than a hundred feet to bisect a thankfully-empty school bus.

CHAPTER EIGHTEEN

The coffin is too small.

Bobby had been getting big. Eleven is practically a teenager! When he jumped on me, the breath would explode from my lungs like a bellows. When he grabbed my hand and tugged, the firm jerk immediately distracted me from whatever problem I'd been pondering. Bobby was even getting too large to carry on my shoulders.

The priest says his words and Bobby's friends are crying. There are parents here too, looking lost, and comforting their children as best they can. The school's homeroom teacher is here as well, her jaw clenched tight and eyes glassy with unshed tears. My brother talks about her all the time. Talked.

It doesn't make sense. Why is the coffin so small?

Someone is talking to me and I say something in return. The words aren't real; my lips are moving on their own, running on autopilot. I must be saying the right thing because the priest grips my shoulder and offers a grim, compassionate smile.

I'm directed to place the first handful of earth. I do. A residue of soil sticks to my hand and I rub it between my fingers, thinking of sandcastles. Others walk to the edge of the grave and scatter more dirt. It's hard to watch the children, with their wet faces and tiny hands and awkward movements. They look broken. But I stand and I look anyway. I'm broken too.

Mom and Dad aren't buried here; their graves are more than a hundred miles away, near the old house. Bobby lived with me in Boston and all of his friends were here. If I'd brought Bobby to Mom and Dad, it would have been just me and a priest and a coffin that was too small. Imagining that scene makes me want to scream...but my lips are moving, saying something kind to a little girl named Lisa. I think I made a robotic pony for her once.

She hugs me, crying, and leaves in her mother's arms.

The weather is beautiful; warm but with a slight breeze. I don't like being outside in a suit on hot days; sweat makes my skin sticky. The sky is pure cerulean, clear from horizon to horizon, and I can feel Bobby's homeroom teacher trembling when she takes my hands in her own. There is grit on her hands, too.

Grave-dirt doesn't wash off. Not really. It can be scrubbed away from skin but the stain on your soul is forever.

I stand, directionless, and time passes.

Everyone has left, a slow trickle of dark clad mourners pouring away from the epicenter of my pain. It's just me and the cemetery caretaker now. The priest is gone, too; I must have said something to him.

"Sir? Should I start filling in the grave?"

"Just a moment." Unsteadily, I stumble to the precipice.

There is a glistening, metallic action figure on top of the too-small coffin. It's partially covered in dirt; one of Bobby's friends must have dropped it there, left it in what they had thought would be a kind reminder.

"Could you get that for me? It was Bobby's. I..." Words stick in my throat.

"Of course. Give me a moment."

I turn away. The breeze has paused, the sun is beating down on me, and the caretaker places the action figure into my hand. I walk away and, behind me, I hear the sound of a shovel scraping into the soil. Filling my brother's grave.

The plot next to Bobby is reserved for me.

Part of me longs to fill it: to stop hurting, to accept what I deserve, to make sure that my little brother isn't alone. The desire to leave the sun behind makes my chest ache, but I know that I will not allow it for myself.

I'm gripping the toy so hard that the plastic tears through my skin. Bronze is out there, still, and there are people who think that he's a hero.

I can't rest yet. There's still so much that I need to do.

A cocktail of stimulants tore me from unconsciousness, and my mouth was filled with bile. The Mk 35's shields had been re-configured to handle large numbers of simultaneous impacts; Valiant's punch had overwhelmed that system, rattled me senseless and battered parts of me that I hadn't known could be bruised. System alarm messages warred for my attention against medical alerts. With shields and inertial-displacement functions overwhelmed, the extraordinarily rigid and unyielding orichalcum armor plates had transmitted the shock-wave to sensitive components housed within. Vast swathes of systems were damaged; most concerning, the autopilot and predictive combat systems could no longer take control of the armor. I was fortunate that direct neural controls were still working flawlessly, at least.

I sat up painfully, shifting aside the shattered remains of a school-bus bench-seat, and evaluated the battleground. The last of my medium-duty combat drones had been disabled. Too many heroes were down, and too many more were beginning to retreat. They had found the courage to face an alien threat and Doctor Fid, but the mind-controlled Valiant was a force of nature. Many of those who were capable of it fled.

When the battlefield cleared, the Legion officers would transmit word to their superiors and the armada's response would become infinitely more difficult to predict.

Whisper? I asked *mentally* **How is progress?**

Twenty packages delivered, she answered quietly, mental voice trembling. **Should I go active?**

No. I took a shaky breath. **How long to send the other six?**

Two-hundred sixty-seven seconds.

Okay, I started re-calibrating my shields again, and triggered an internal system to fill my mouth with water to wash away the taste of acid and blood. **Keep at it. Thank you!**

I wrote a quick firewall to make sure that my armor's medical telemetry wasn't being forwarded to any system that Whisper might be monitoring, then struggled to my feet. The warstaff, summoned reflexively, was a reassuring presence in my grasp.

Doctor Fid could keep the Legion and Valiant occupied for four and a half minutes.

I took careful aim and braced myself, then unleashed a maximum-power particle-beam blast at the Mercer-Tallon building's footings. The air itself ignited from the force, boiled into plasma then pulled forward by the vacuum to flash-liquify a car-sized section of pavement. Much of the force splattered off of the force-fields, but enough penetrated that the building visibly shook and windows shattered.

The mind-controlled Valiant had been wrestling with Cuboid's crude (but moderately powerful) android body. A moment after my strike had landed, he turned towards me; I had earned the Legion's attention.

I was already charging forward, flight systems catapulting me forward at maximum thrust. Even with the inertial-dampeners operating, the acceleration crushed the breath from my chest. Were he unencumbered, Valiant could have dodged or rolled with the blow...but the gunmetal-gray robotic Cuboid held the African-American hero still for the crucial fraction of a second.

I pulsed the Mk 35's recently-implemented density-manipulators to collide with the literal force of a speeding freight train. Cuboid was shattered from the impact (I was certain that he had spare bodies stored somewhere; also, Whisper said that he was mean. So...no energy was wasted upon guilt) but Valiant and I tumbled forward to ram into the building's force-field.

I'd landed sideways on my back, and I could look upwards to see the edifice again shake; one of Cloner had been atop the roof and was thrown clear, arms windmilling helplessly as he began his final plummet.

Valiant grabbed for my throat with both hands and I countered, using my staff to lever his grip away before he could manage any damage. I followed with a high energy strobe, intended more to induce temporary blindness than to damage. The large hero jerked his head back; I used anti-gravitics to jump up and generate just enough space to swing my staff like a hockey-stick, and the weapon's trajectory arced upwards to catch Valiant squarely between his legs.

By now, all reporters and camera crew must surely have retreated from the danger zone...but four news-camera drones were still within range. This was a battle to determine humanity's fate, but that one moment of footage would, I was sure, be the one destined to be downloaded and re-posted to the internet. For my own part, I merely hoped very much that Valiant's discomfort was transmitted to the Legion officer that was puppeting the hero's body. Valiant made a mewling noise and collapsed.

I used my momentary reprieve to fire medium-yield kinetic blasts at the other mind-control victims, separating them from the heroes they were fighting. The insect-garbed hero had somehow rescued the falling Cloner, and I used an ultrasonic attack to thoroughly stun them both. A focused barrage of plasma-cannon fire from within the Mercer-Tallon building was my reward; the impact drove me to one knee, but I was able to use my staff for leverage to keep from being knocked over outright.

Titan threw a motorcycle at me as I stood (which I ducked under) and Aeon discharged the single-most powerful force-blast that I'd even seen her wield. I was pounded upon the torso and, again, pressed backwards...but the Mk 35 heavy-combat armor was able to absorb the impact without further damage. I pointed my palm at her and replied with a low-yield particle-beam, but her force-field was already in place by the time I fired.

The battle was chaotic; without my auto-pilot engaged, I was unable to keep track of every movement. Lasers and bullets and shrapnel pinged off my force-fields and occasionally penetrated to glance off the orichalcum armor plating...I wasn't taking much damage, but it was certainly disorienting. Which is probably why I hadn't noticed that Valiant had regained his footing.

I didn't feel the impact. There was just a blur of movement and then blackness.

There's a fresh motor-oil stain on the concrete in front of the hanger-door to the left; whoever is renting that unit probably is storing a car in there. Maybe they are restoring it, working on it here on the weekends. You aren't supposed to do that, I know, but some people still do.

There are eight drive-up storage containers connected in this row. The one on the left contains a car and I can't help but wonder what the others might conceal. Unused sports equipment, old documents, furniture, boxes of books? What do people put in storage? Things that they don't need enough to keep in their home, but that they are too emotionally attached to throw away.

The unit in front of me houses a supervillain.

I haven't been back here in five years, not since Bronze died and I returned to MIT. If I unlock the door, the space will be cramped with heavy crates resting on pallets, likely coated in a thin layer of dust. Everything will be labeled with inoffensive titles: 'Kitchen goods', 'Old oven', 'Dining room'. One set of crates is labeled 'Power tools #1' through 'Power tools #4', and in those boxes will be the disassembled remains of Doctor Fid.

If I unlock the door...

Do I want this, really? I haven't given notice to my employers yet; I can still change my mind, still go back to my comfortable research with Doctor Ichiro and watch his son play with action-figures in the corner. I can teach physics or engineering or math, and audit classes in whatever subject catches my attention. If I leave the door locked, I could spend the rest of my life as a safe, boring, sadder and lonelier version of the Terry Markham that had been Bobby's brother.

But if I unlock the door, it's forever.

The Doctor is alive in a way that I'm just not. He has a sense of purpose! If I put on that faceless mask for even a moment, I'll never be able to set the armor aside again. A half-decade was sufficient to teach me what a more traditional life will be like. Staying at MIT would be the easy choice, simple and apathetic.

The key is in my hand and I make my decision. I know who I want to be.

Another adrenaline cocktail was poured into my veins and Whisper was screaming wordlessly in my mind. I dry-heaved and convulsed, eyes watering as I tried to gulp down air.

I'm all right! I insisted as I parsed the medical warnings that were vying for my attention. There was nothing immediately fatal, but I would definitely need to replace my liver and kidneys again. Fortunately, I had spare clone-organs already growing in one of my labs and the nanites in my system would be able to slow the internal bleeding before it became life-threatening. ***Whisper, I'll be fine.***

...promise...?

I promise, I stated, then winced. Apparently, Doctor Fid was villain enough that he was willing to make commitments to children that he wasn't certain he could keep. What a disappointing thing to learn about one's self.

Should I activate the devices? Whisper asked.

How many have been teleported? I shook my head to clear away the daze, gritting my teeth against a shooting pain that seemed to travel from between my shoulder blades to my fingertips; a herniated disc and pinched nerves could be added to my litany of injuries. I started turning off pain receptors via the neural link.

Twenty two. Almost twenty-three, the little android replied.

Then hold off. My staff was again summoned to my hands, and I used it to help stabilize myself as I struggled to my feet. ****Let me know when everything is in place.****

Sphinx was still fighting with grim determination, trading blows with her mind-controlled teammate Majestic; Peregrine was awake and battling at her side, but his effectiveness was limited when operating in a relatively small battlefield. Given a sufficient distance in which to accelerate, the man's powerset would allow him to deliver blows that exceeded even Valiant's capabilities...but at that speed, he wouldn't be able to easily turn to avoid buildings. He was at his most dangerous when in space or the upper atmosphere where he could easily chart a straight and obstruction-less path to his target.

Behind my faceless mask, I bared my teeth in a vicious grin.

("Doctor Fid might be a supervillain," I remember once thinking, "but perhaps he could save the world right out from under the fraudulent superheroes' noses.")

I launched a series of emerald-hued force-blasts at Sphinx, missing on purpose; she didn't even turn to acknowledge the attacks. Peregrine, on the other hand...his gaze whipped towards me, expression filled with indignation and righteous rage; she must have told him about our earlier confrontation. In a flash, he was barreling towards me in a ludicrously obvious charge.

I shifted my grip on the orichalcum warstaff and, at the last moment, triggered my flight controls to jerk me into position as I swung with all of the Mk 35's might.

Slim, socially awkward Terrance Markham had never played a game of baseball. Years younger than his classmates, Terry had been excused from most group activities at gym. In any case, no one would have chosen the small and often distracted little boy for their team. Doctor Fid, on the other hand, had two decades of experience hitting things.

While he was flying, the extent of Peregrine's invulnerability was a thing of legend; during the course of his heroic career, even the most extraordinary blows had left him only momentarily stunned. The soaring hero could not be damaged, not by any force known. He was, however, slave to the laws of physics.

With my density-manipulators straining, I'd had as much mass as a battleship at the moment of contact.

The jarring impact traveled up my arms and lit the pinched nerve in my neck afire; spinal damage apparently circumvented the sensation-nullifying functions of my neural tap. No matter; as I watched the 'hero' disappear into the sky, my sense of smug satisfaction outweighed any pain I might feel. There was a non-zero percent chance that I'd just sent Peregrine into orbit.

He wouldn't be harmed, I knew, so I tasked my sensors (and contacted every satellite I could think of) to chart his return path. And then I returned my attention to Valiant; he was pounding away at one of Aeon's milky-white force-field bubbles. I didn't see Titan or Veridian, so I presumed that all three heroes were taking refuge within that sphere.

I roared a wordless challenge and dove at the world's mightiest hero.

There are no words to easily describe close combat against a creature like Valiant. He was too fast, too strong, too deadly...every energy blast struck with the power of a tsunami, every punch shook the earth like a volcano's eruption. He was a force of nature.

It was exhilarating and terrifying in equal proportions.

With my combat algorithms active, the savage dance would have required the entirety of my focus. Now...my attention was divided, I was injured, and even the Mk 35's upgraded structural-integrity fields were having difficulty holding the orichalcum armor plates together. I was fighting defensively, blocking and rolling with blows whenever possible...but more system warnings were being raised with every passing second, more medical alerts blaring directly into my mind. Valiant was slowly pummeling me to death, but the process was taking time and time was all that I wanted.

I darted forward, wrapping the Mk 35's massive arms around Valiant's chest; I couldn't overpower him, couldn't out-wrestle him...but I could, for just a moment, outmaneuver him. Flight systems strained to their utmost as I spun just in time.

Peregrine had (predictably) used the trajectory that I'd compelled upon him to swing a high arc and had descended with the aggressive precision of his namesake bird: a straight line from the exosphere back to the courtyard of the Mercer-Tallon building.

Accelerating all the while, his final velocity would have been several times the speed of sound and the shock-wave shook my bones.

Perhaps Peregrine had seen me as the greater threat, or perhaps he merely wanted revenge for revealing his leader's crimes. No matter his motivation, the homicidal hero had fully intended upon striking me upon my already-injured spine. Instead, I twisted, and the irresistible force had met the immovable Valiant at full velocity.

The African-American hero had borne the brunt of the extraordinary impact, but I still was rattled momentarily senseless and tumbled to a stop dozens of feet away. The pavement was sundered and windows no doubt shattered for blocks in every direction. Out of the corner of my eye, I could see a slight visual distortion as the Mercer-Tallon building's force-fields flickered and failed.

For a moment, it seemed as though the world had gone silent. Throughout the courtyard, every combatant was still: stunned and deafened. If Wildcard were still alive, I expected that his healing powers would be in high demand later this evening.

I'm done! Whisper trilled victoriously into my mind and I smiled.

Valiant was back on his feet, and I had to use antigravitics to match his accomplishment. He was bloodied and bruised and one eye was swelling shut, but I saw my death in his gaze. Fortunately, the Legion officer piloting Valiant's body was too late. I'd won.

I began to laugh, and Doctor Fid's vocoder made my weary relief sound terrifying.

Now! I called to Whisper, and I felt her ebullient cheer in response as she triggered the activation of all twenty-seven apparatuses.

There was no sound, no sensation, no visible effect at all...save that every mind-controlled combatant collapsed at once.

I savored the moment, laughter increasing in volume, and all eyes were upon me as I turned to face the Mercer-Tallon building and raised my warstaff. Six full-yield plasma-blasts later and nothing survived inside the structure.

It was over.

"What's up, Doc?" Starnyx grins at me irreverently and lifts his beer in a playful toast.

" 'Up' is a direction," I reply in a practiced deadpan. Even though I don't plan on drinking tonight, my heavy armor settles in to take a seat next to him at the bar. "Generally defined as being the opposite of 'down'."

He laughs delightedly. "Seriously, Doc. What can I do for you?"

"I...don't have anything planned this month," I explain, haltingly. "I suppose that I was just in the mood for company."

Nyx smiles, and there's some hint of affectionate pride in his expression. I'm embarrassed to find myself grateful.

It's early July; not so long ago, this time of the year would have been spent in preparation to lure out some unlucky hero and to administer a punishing beating. Thanks largely to Starnyx's unexpected intervention, that plan had been abandoned. It's strange to be approaching the anniversary without imminent violence dominating my thoughts. Strange, but not unwelcome.

This morning, I caught myself craving macaroni and cheese with sliced up hot-dogs. I thought of sunlight instead of blood, and laughter instead of tears.

And so, I'm here. Encased within powered armor, hiding behind a faceless mask, and awkwardly avoiding thanking the man who had reached out to me, unbidden, and offered advice that had somehow metamorphosed into a gift.

"Hey, man, I'm glad that you're here," Nyx interjects suddenly. "Some buddies of mine are dropping by in a bit, I wanna introduce 'em to you."

"I don't want to impose..." I look to the door with trepidation, as though a boisterous crowd were about to magically appear. I've faced down horrific villains and entire teams of superheroes with nothing but confidence, but the idea of a social gathering is oddly daunting.

"Don't be stupid, Doc," he frowns. "You're my friend. It's not a problem."

I stare down at him, thinking. We have sought each other's company for both social and professional purposes, and we've consumed alcoholic beverages together. I have come to respect his opinion and (given that he often asks) I must presume that he also has come to respect my own.

"You're my friend, too," I state, vocoder concealing my dawning surprise.

My concept of friendship is largely born from books: epic fantasies in which traveling companions journey to destroy rings of power, or to defeat evil dragons. Knights sacrificing everything to avenge their brothers in arms. In the stories, villains never seem to have friends deserving of the title. It is pleasant to discover that the literary canon does not accurately portray reality.

And now, the hard part begins: Being a worthy friend in return.

Thank you, I murmured to Whisper. **That was perfect.**

Mm! she replied, and I could feel the relief in her mental touch.

I'll be home soon! I promised, **Love you, little sister.**

"What did you do?" Sphinx landed before me, eyes wide. Her costume had been cut in a few places and she'd been bloodied, but she'd certainly weathered the battle better than I had. Warily, I kept my warstaff poised between us, but she seemed not to notice.

"Before you destroyed the building, you broke their control. What did you do?!?"

I considered. There were news cameras upon us, still. If I exited without providing explanation, the public would be left only with the knowledge that a grave alien threat had surfaced and been defeated. Whether or not the world still had something to fear would be a question unanswered. *Be loud*, my friend's manifesto had suggested; Doctor Fid couldn't belong in the organization that Starnyx had left behind, but I still knew that he would have wanted the truth to be revealed. And besides...I'd been playing this game for almost as long as Valiant.

I recognized a monologue cue when I heard one, also.

"Earlier this year," I began, dismissing my warstaff and making certain that every news-camera drone was receiving crisp audio signal, "Technos invaded my city; during our battle, he used a device that counteracted my flight systems and I fell from the sky. I've since eliminated the flaw that his device relied upon, of course, but I was curious about his technology. I took it and improved upon it.

"The Legion is an interstellar empire, an alien totalitarian regime enforced by their telepathic spies and mind-controlling officers!" I continued and waved expressively at the burning Mercer-Tallon building. "I studied them and used a much superior version of Technos' device to disrupt their psionic abilities. Legion telepathy is no longer a threat anywhere on Earth!"

I didn't mention the other pieces of the puzzle; the Westler-Gray reactors, the alien refugees' records and sensors, the Tromso ionosphere researchers whose work had been pivotal to reflecting the field such that it covered the entire surface of the planet. Bits and pieces from so many separate sources, come together to create something extraordinary.

"You idiot! You've killed us all!" Sphinx's voice trembled.

"You seem very sure of that," I mocked, trusting in the natural melodramatic instinct of the sort of person who put on a cape to fight crime. She would hang herself with her own words if I supplied sufficient rope.

"I know the way they make decisions!" she spat. "I was prepared to die in battle, but they were going to conquer the Earth! As soon as they knew for sure that they could control Valiant, it was inevitable. They'd be slaves, but humanity would have survived!"

"So that was your plan? To make certain that the Legion invaders took mental control of Valiant at the right moment to make sure that they shackled the Earth instead of destroying it?" The question could not have been timed better had I been writing a script; behind Sphinx, unnoticed, Valiant had woken up and was shaking his head to clear away the cobwebs. His expression slowly shifted to one of undisguised horror.

"Yes." Sphinx had the nerve to sound regretful. "But when they find out what you've done, the Legion will just destroy the planet."

And Valiant flew away, fled so quickly that he may as well have teleported. I was unsurprised; involuntary servitude had always been a hot-button issue for the hero. Hearing that a supposed ally had orchestrated not only his own capture, but that his downfall was expected to be the trigger for an entire planet to suffer a similar fate...he needed time, I was sure, to digest the information.

Some watched Valiant's flight, but the attention of the majority was still upon me, waiting for a response to Sphinx's accusation.

"They won't," I said simply.

"I don't care what technological wizardry you think you can pull out of your metal ass, you can't fight the Legion armada!" Sphinx grit her teeth to fight back a sob. "You have no idea how much force they can bring to bear."

"I won't need to fight the armada, because the armada won't be coming," I laughed coldly. "They'll have enough difficulties dealing with problems at home."

"How...?"

"I was able to recreate the teleporter accident that sent you to Legion space, and I sent along similar devices to the one that now protects the Earth." Even with the vocoder's attempt to remove emotion, Doctor Fid's intimidating voice oozed smugness. "As I said: The Legion's control is enforced by their telepaths. And telepathy just instantaneously stopped working on the planets that are most tactically, logistically and politically important in all of their empire. From what I understand, many of those planets house thriving guerrilla resistance movements just waiting for such an opportunity to arise.

"The Legion," I finished, "will tear itself apart long before their warships leave their region of the galaxy."

How many years had Sphinx spent locked within a prison of her expectations and fears? How much of her soul had she sliced away, rationalizing her crimes by opposing a threat now eliminated? She'd girded herself for an eternal night, but now the sun had risen and she was lost.

The Sphinx slumped, defeated utterly, and I laughed 'til my throat hurt from the effort.

All my humor evaporated. "I have one more question for you."

She didn't respond, but she did raise her eyes to gaze tiredly upon Doctor Fid's faceless mask.

"Before the Staten Island explosion, the FTW was investigating why a colony-ship full of refugees from Legion space crashed on Earth. Desperate, innocent civilians who'd risked everything for a chance to find safety and freedom."

"It was necessa—" Sphinx started to interrupt, but I cut her off.

"I'm not asking if you caused the crash! I know you did. You and Peregrine. Nine hundred and thirty-one dead!" My voice had begun to rise in volume and I took a slow breath before proceeding. It was just as well; the gravity of the crime took time to grasp. Slowly, I could see comprehension dawn on the faces of the still-mobile heroes that had gathered around us. "Not one of them was Earth's enemy; they were doctors and engineers, artists and philosophers. Parents. Children!"

"The Legion fleet would have detected their landing engines," Sphinx defended weakly. "The attack would have come years earlier. The crash gave us time..."

"Again, I'm not asking if you and Peregrine killed nine hundred and thirty-one innocents. I'm not asking *why* you and Peregrine killed nine hundred and thirty-one innocents. My question is only this: When you found out that the FTW was investigating, did you leak that information to the Legion?"

"Yes!" she glared up at me defiantly. "It was the right choice!"

"When Jerry Stross caused the explosion that beheaded the FTW, he was under the control of an alien telepath," I snarled, my hands clenched to fists and glowing crimson with summoned power. "The Legion killed my friend Starnyx, so I just killed the Legion. What fate do you think you've earned?"

"Do it, then," she chuckled darkly. "I was expecting to die today, anyway."

I could do it. The Mk 35 was damaged, but I still had sufficient power for this. I could raise my hand and issue judgment, exult in the sound of her dying screams! This could all be over, for the both of us. A glorious, violent end to all the lies and death...But the assembled champions were shifting uneasily. Theatrics, the heroes would stand for; a summary execution, not so much. No matter how justified my revenge, there would be another battle.

My calculations did not suggest good odds for my escape.

There was a time when I would have taken my vengeance and been glad of it, laughing madly as my enemies swarmed. But that wasn't what Starnyx would have wanted. It wasn't what the Red Ghost would have wanted.

And it wasn't what Whisper needed. I'd made a promise.

"No," I hissed, letting the energy gathered in my gauntlets dissipate. "Death is too quick and too final. Live with your guilt! If there's even a shred of humanity left behind your mask, you'll accept justice when it comes for you...But justice isn't something that Doctor Fid can grant. I hope that regret eats you alive, Sphinx. Beyond that...I'm done with you."

I stepped back, and it seemed as though a sea of relief washed over the assembled crowd.

"Well then, heroes...I suppose that I will take my lea—"

I dodged the steel I-beam that Titan had swung at me; the attack had been almost identical to the one he'd launched after our battle against Technos. As the old saying goes: Fool me once, shame on you. Fool me twice, homicide becomes a viable option.

"What makes you think we're going to let you go?" the silver-clad hero glared. "You're still a villain, and we have you surrounded."

"Three reasons," I replied calmly. "First: I just saved the Earth and freed dozens of other planets, so I suspect that the more honorable among you might be tempted to give me a bye...just this once."

"Second: The field is littered with the wounded. Only an idiot would begin another fight now and endanger the casualties."

"Third, and most importantly..."

The heavy-combat drones had arrived from their long flight from Boston; at my command, they uncloaked with a roar of thunder, thick tendrils of energy arcing from starfield-and-red pillar to starfield-and-red pillar. A full dozen twenty-foot-tall orichalcum-framed instruments of terror formed a circle above the field, crackling with enough raw power to make the air itself feel heavy and oppressive.

"I AM DOCTOR FID!" I re-summoned my warstaff and raised it to the sky; lightning crashed down upon me and my laughter, no doubt, sounded unhinged. "What makes you think that you can stop me?!?"

And then I left the cowed heroes before they realized that I was bluffing; the drones re-cloaked and carried me home when I once again lost consciousness.

CHAPTER NINETEEN

WHISPER WAS SINGING; I RECOGNIZED THE TUNE from an animated film but could not recall the title. Something about a girl wanting to go on adventures like her older brothers and railing against the institutional sexism endemic to her native culture, I think. In general, I approved of the supportive message being taught to young girls. In this particular case, however, the idea of Whisper wanting to follow in her older brother's footsteps made me more than a bit uncomfortable.

"Your voice is beautiful," I told her, and then I was being hugged.

She could be a hero instead of a villain, I thought, if she felt a calling to adventure. A real hero, a worthy one! She wouldn't leap into battle just to bolster her ego. She wouldn't abandon people that trusted her. Whisper would be the sort of hero that inspires. Not because of her power, but because of her innate goodness.

"Lazybones!" Whisper complained, though I could see more relief than annoyance in her glowing blue eyes. "You were asleep for nearly a day!"

I checked the clock. "Anything important happen while I was out?"

"Mm!" She beamed cheerfully. "Sphinx and Peregrine were arrested!"

It was a pleasant surprise that the incarceration occurred so quickly. Some of the crimes that I'd mentioned must have been easy to verify; those in power would not have taken a supervillain's word, even if I'd had the time to lay out all my evidence during my monologue. "And there's no hint that the Legion forces across the galaxy have figured out why their psychic abilities stopped functioning?"

"Nothing. I've been listening to their subspace communication relays, everyone's panicking and confused." Smug pride and playful mischief were both evident in the delicate little android's smile. "They didn't get any warning from Earth at all, and the stealth systems are functioning perfectly."

"Excellent." I closed my eyes and relaxed in my sister's hug. Not even in her second body yet, and she's saved worlds! Whisper was already a hero. I resolved to fabricate an action figure and bring it to Bobby's memorial. "Anything else?"

"Mm. Lots of little things. Most of them good," she released her hug and bounced on the edge of the bed. "Oh! I've been answering your work emails! I just thought someone should, 'cause you were asleep."

"That's fine." I was tired again. Medical records showed that significant amounts of work had been performed upon me while I was unconscious; surgical repair, upgraded organ transplants, a transfusion to increase the density of nanitic robots within my system, etc. All the operations had proceeded flawlessly, but my body was burning through all of its resources to heal. I ordered one of my medical-automatons to increase the rate of intravenous glucose and nutrient supplementation accordingly.

"Everything's fine," I murmured as I began to drift off. "I promise."

It felt decidedly better, to make a promise and to mean it.

"Welcome to KNN CapeWatch, I'm your host Stan Morrow."

"And I'm Stan's co-host, Pamela Green."

"Joining us today is a retired superhero who'd been one of the founding members of the New York Shield: Cloner."

"Thanks for having me, Stan. Pam."

"It's our pleasure. We're both very glad to see you up and about so soon after the Legion incident."

"Well, again, thank you Pam...but I really don't like that the media has chosen that phrase to describe what happened."

"And why is that?"

"The word 'incident' refers to a singular event. The Legion agents were here for years! This wasn't an incident, it was an incursion."

"When most of the reporters and pundits use the word 'incident', I think that they're referring primarily to that final battle-"

"Well, they shouldn't. That fight was the very-visible tip of an iceberg, but there was lot more going on under the surface."

"I know that investigators are still reviewing the testimony of-that is, looking into allegations made by other involved parties-"

"You can say her name, Pam. I won't explode."

"Reviewing the Sphinx's testimony, then. From what I understand, investigators have uncovered that the Legion was responsible for hundreds of deaths, illegal use of political influence, blackmail and bribery of public officials..."

"All of that is true, and more besides."

"Do you remember...?"

"I remember enough. Bits and pieces. I'm not going to talk about that in public; I own those nightmares, they're my personal property."

"Is there anything that you did want to talk about...?"

"Yeah. Waking up free, that first time. One of me'd fallen off the rooftop, got saved by Bugly and then stunned; Fid burned the rest of my bodies. Good riddance, I know what they were used for. But that first time waking up... Y'know, that was the first time I've been down to a single body in more 'n two decades? I'd forgotten what it was like, looking at the world through only two eyes."

"I can't imagine."

"That first moment waking up...It stuck with me. I've literally died thousands of times, but that was the first time I remember coming to life. Life's precious. I'm coming out of retirement to take over leadership of the Shield. I want to - need to - rebuild it into something better!"

"I think that I speak for all of New York when I say that we'll be happy to have you back. Congratulations!"

"Thanks."

"Can we go back to talking about Sphinx?"

"Oooh. Y'know what? Yeah. Yes."

"You'd known her for a long time."

"Not that long, really...We were friends for maybe five years? That's a long time when you work together in a dangerous occupation, though. We had each other's' backs through a lot of fights."

"Some of the allegations that have leaked to the press have been horrific. When you knew her, was there any indication that she was the sort of person who could commit these sorts of crimes?"

"Not at all. But, here's the thing...I understand her. I'll never forgive her - she led the Legion to my door! - but I do understand, maybe better than anyone else alive. Those bastards were in my head for a long time so I completely get why she was so afraid. Sphinx was absolutely, pathologically terrified. She felt trapped and she almost dragged the rest of the planet into the trap with her."

"It sounds like it was a near thing."

"We should have lost. We would have if it weren't for Doctor Fid."

"That statement isn't going to make you very popular. Many people blame Doctor Fid for how long the battle lasted."

"That's very true, Pam. The leader of the Boston Guardians has been quite vocal in claiming that the villain interfered."

"Titan's a good leader and a strong fighter, but I think he's wrong here. Fid had a plan and the plan worked."

"How do you know?"

"I know the plan worked because we're all here, alive. Look, the man's hurt a lot of good people. He should pay for his crimes. But y'know what? He saved the world. He saved me from something worse 'n death. So...Doc, if you're listening? I owe you a beer."

The hashtag #IOweFidABeer trended high on the Internet for weeks. Humorous videos made the rounds, and the Brooklyn Knights made a show of carrying around a six-pack just in case they ran into me.

It was a craft beer from a microbrewery they pass during their patrols; a Scottish ale, flavored with orange zest. They foiled my robbery of a firm that produced protective-gear for the military, and then I helped them drink the beer.

```
To: "Doctor Fid" <doctor.fid@..>
From: "MortarThyme" <m.thyme@anontor.7kbnjnv2.no>
Subject: Meet @ Gallery?
u should come to gallery on friday. we r having a party
2 remember friends lost in teh fire. also, i have q
about ur NYSE hack, doing sumthing simlar 2 quest
automotive. collabor8?

To: "MortarThyme" <m.thyme@anontor.7kbnjnv2.no>
From: "Doctor Fid" <doctor.fid@..>
Subject: Meeting at the Gallery
MortarThyme,
Thank you for the invitation. I'd heard about the
gathering but was unsure if I would be welcome. My
membership was revoked quite publicly. Are you certain
that it would be all right if I attend?
- Doctor Fid

To: "Doctor Fid" <doctor.fid@..>
From: "MortarThyme" <m.thyme@anontor.7kbnjnv2.no>
Subject: Meeting at the Gallery
i spoke 2 lucky7, he says u r always welcum. doctor fid
should not be in ftw,but is ftw's friend. need help w
quest hack. plz?
```

```
To: "MortarThyme" <m.thyme@anontor.7kbnjnv2.no>
From: "Doctor Fid" <doctor.fid@..>
Subject: Meeting at the Gallery
MortarThyme,
I'll be there. And thank you.
```

There's an old joke among the patrons of Lassiter's Den: "If you think that you've finally killed your nemesis, but you don't find a body? You didn't kill your nemesis." The jape was always followed by the corollary: "If you do find a body, the odds go up to fifty percent." So, really, it shouldn't have come as a surprise when a fishing vessel in Maine found a very haggard Miguel Espinoza lost at sea.

When he'd dissipated his mist form in order to escape the Legion telepath's control, the Red Ghost had fully expected to die; instead, he'd been shunted between dimensions to a lush and wild alternate Earth. Due to time-dilation effects, the Ghost had been forced to survive for six months as a hunter and subsistence farmer before he finally figured out how to reverse the process to return home.

Superheroes have such odd lives.

And so, the deal to bring inertial-dampening technology to the public was rekindled. Also, I was forced to drop millions from Doctor Fid's slowly-recuperating holdings in order to hide accounts that might be vulnerable to the Red Ghost's forensic-accounting wizardry.

Damn the man.

(It was good to have him back.)

Daniel McClelland seemed like a good kid. Mid-to-late twenties, square jawed, broad chested and handsome; I'd built his new artificial body based upon photos taken during his last deployment as a soldier. He was adjusting well to his new situation and accompanied his grandfather to the signing of the Synthetic American's Rights law.

He'd never be a true AI, not like Whisper; his neural network was limited to human norms, and his multitasking capability no greater than that of any other well-trained, intelligent soldier-turned-possible-politician. Still, Whisper was developing a childish crush on the older android.

The only question was: Should it be Terry Markham or Doctor Fid that took Daniel aside and delivered the appropriate ominous threats?

Once again, I reviewed the footage and felt my lips purse in a thoughtful frown.

In the beginning, the battle had been chaos. There wasn't any reliable video of the opening moments; apparently, the Brooklyn Knights had arrived first and tried to launch an assault on the Mercer-Tallon building. The New York Shield quickly appeared and tried to stop the attack, but then the Legion's mind control became a factor. Both teams joined forces to try and get to the building but were driven back. By that point, the building's force-fields had been enabled and the defensive energy weapons were deployed; reporters began to spread information and more spandex-clad hooligans began to trickle in to participate in the madness.

Initially, the gathered champions had acted with little tactical planning: they pointed themselves at a perceived threat and leaped to intervene. The focus had been upon safely subduing those under the effect of Legion mind control and continuing the ongoing (and unsuccessful) assault upon the aliens' headquarters. As the number of wounded began to mount, however, the tactics began to change. Some heroes started fighting defensively, working to protect the casualties and to bring them to safety. Others broke off to ferry civilians out of harm's way and form a perimeter.

It wasn't glorious work. There were no ego-boosting, flashy moves made while smiling to a camera. They were simply performing tasks that would better protect those in need.

By the time Doctor Fid had shown up, the shift in behavior had already been in place and I hadn't noticed; I'd been distracted by the sheer number of combatants and by my confrontation with Sphinx. And then Valiant had arrived.

Some heroes continued their mindless brawl, pride demanding that they assert their dominance over the alien threat with naught but physical power. But others, when faced with an opponent they could not overcome and an alien mental attack against which they had no defense, gathered to do what they could to protect the wounded; to help others escape, to band together and keep the weakest among them from harm. They chose to stay...not for acclaim, but because it was the right thing to do. To provide what help they could even when confronting Armageddon.

They weren't perfect, I was sure; those men and women were human beneath their masks. But when the chips were down, they'd been true heroes.

It was a refreshing (and also disconcerting) revelation. Some of the most extraordinary instances of selfless bravery and compassion captured on film had been found among individuals who Doctor Fid had long since dismissed as unworthy. Some, even, that I had targeted in the past; perhaps an apology would be warranted. I would need to spend time considering how Doctor Fid would move forward given this new information.

Still, there would be other deserving targets, other 'heroes' desperately in need of their comeuppance. It was inevitable. Starnyx's path was lost to me, and rightfully so; attempting to yoke Doctor Fid had been pure folly. I'd taken up my starfield mask with a purpose in mind, and that purpose remained: there were problems to be solved, technological marvels to be created, and—most importantly—noses in urgent need of punching.

The crusade would endure.

<u>DOCTOR FID WILL RETURN!</u>

I hope that you enjoyed reading *Fid's Crusade* as much as I enjoyed writing it. If so, please hop on-line and leave a review.

Reviews make sad authors into happy authors!

Also, I invite you to please connect with me via any of the following methods:

Twitter: http://twitter.com/davidhreiss
Facebook: http://facebook.com/davidhreiss

Or follow my blog at:
http://www.davidhreiss.com/blog

ABOUT THE AUTHOR

While growing up, David was that weird kid with his nose in a book and his head in the clouds. He was the table-top role-playing game geek, the comic-book nerd, the storyteller and dreamer.

Fortunately, he hasn't changed much.

David Reiss is a software engineer by trade and long-time sci-fi and fantasy devotee by passion, and he resides in Silicon Valley with his partner of twenty-six years. Also, a disturbingly spoiled cat named Freya.

David's hobbies generally involve exploring the crafts and skills found in works of fiction. He's built replica lightsabers and forged medieval armor, programmed autonomous drones and brewed his own mead, started fires by rubbing two sticks together and started fires with lasers. Also, he has become equally mediocre at numerous martial arts, archery, sword fighting, paintball and lasertag.

Fid's Crusade was David's first completed novel-length project, but it certainly won't be his last—he's having far too much fun!

CPSIA information can be obtained
at www.ICGtesting.com
Printed in the USA
LVHW031203081019
633523LV00004B/946/P